Necessary Madness

Jenn Crowell

CORONET BOOKS
Hodder and Stoughton

First published in Great Britain in 1997 by Hodder and Stoughton
First published in paperback in 1998 by Hodder and Stoughton
A division of Hodder Headline PLC
First published in the United States of America in 1997 by
G P Putnam's Sons

A Coronet Paperback

10 9 8 7 6 5 4

A CIP catalogue record for this title is available from the
British Library

ISBN 0 340 68495 X

Typeset by Palimpsest Book Production Limited,
Polmont, Stirlingshire
Printed and bound in Great Britain by
Mackays of Chatham PLC, Chatham, Kent

Hodder and Stoughton
A division of Hodder Headline PLC
338 Euston Road
London NW1 3BH

acknowledgements

Thanks first and foremost to Madison Smartt Bell for his avuncular advice and tremendous generosity; to Jane Gelfman and Liza Dawson for their sensitivity and support; to Carolyn Mays and Carole Blake for the Pimms and the marvellous hospitality in London; to all those at the Pennsylvania Governor's School for the Arts, especially Deb Burnham, Melissa Bender and Corinna Burns, for helping me hit fictive blood and bone; to Susan Dziengeleski, Nancy Springer and countless others for their encouragement and endless critiques of those early first chapters; and of course to S. Jane Beck-Dettinger, Barry and Bryant Dettinger, Robert, Braden and Kathy Crowell, Heather Cornell, and the rest of my friends and family for their continuing trust and love.

TO *my parents*,
for understanding the need,
for nurturing the words
which can only arise from ample space
and honest silence

No-one ever told me
that grief felt so like
fear.

– C. S. LEWIS

In struggling against
anguish one never
produces serenity;
the struggle against
anguish only produces
new forms of anguish.

– SIMONE WEIL

chapter one

My husband, Bill, was buried nine years to the day that my father died. During his funeral, I tried not to think about that fact or about the direction my life would now take. I simply stood on the raw ground of the Lamberhurst cemetery with my arm around my son, Curran, and my gaze on the young, shocked faces of the pallbearers as they lowered the coffin into the earth.

Across from us, Bill's mother dabbed her eyes with a tissue and made hysterical gasping sounds. I drew Curran closer and pressed my cheek to his blond hair. Normally he would have squirmed away, but he stood still until the vicar slammed the Bible closed, as if he sensed the desolation in me.

We all filed back to our cars in sombre silence. The January morning was grey and damp, and as I looked over the hill at the old farmhouse where Bill had spent his childhood and at the stark outlines of the bare trees which surrounded it, I thought of the gorgeous weekends when, still innocent with happiness, we'd drive there from London to see Bill's parents. On an afternoon swollen with spring, Bill had painted me running across their lawn and down the slope, my long, dark hair streaming behind me, my sundress billowy, an expression of both euphoria and terror on my face as I flew towards the headstones.

Now, beside my car, I fumbled for my keys.

'Gloria.'

I looked up. It was Jim, Bill's best friend from university. I'd never seen him in a suit before, except at my wedding. A huge pain rose in my chest when I saw how perfectly pressed his shirt was. It had been a standing joke that Jim wouldn't recognize an iron if he got burnt by one. There were tears in his eyes.

'Bill was the best of us,' he said. 'A real purist.'

'Yes.'

His shoulders shook. 'I thought I had things figured,' he said. 'But now – I mean ... Christ ... *Bill*. He didn't deserve ...'

His words dissolved as his face contorted with sobs. Its soft, pink vulnerability turned some long-rusted key within me, and I embraced him. 'I know,' I said.

2

'I know.' For one dangerous moment, palms against Jim's shoulder blades, I thought of my father.

'Mum.' Curran's small, plaintive voice. 'Gran needs to talk to you.'

We pulled apart. Still distraught, Jim walked away, raising his hand in farewell just as my mother-in-law put hers on my arm. 'Please come up for lunch,' she said, voice pleading yet cautious, as if she expected me to lunge at her, given the slightest provocation. 'That is, if you want company.'

I didn't, but her pale hazel eyes were so forlorn and the house over the hill held so many reminders of Bill that I nodded. 'I'd like that.'

A light rain drummed on the windowpane as I sat on the living room's plaid sofa with a quilt draped over my shoulders, my legs tucked under me, and my fingers wrapped around a cup of Earl Grey. Bill's father stoked the fire while his mother cleared the plates of roast beef and mango chutney from the table. I ran my tongue over my lips, remembering the gentle, sleepy hours of early evening when their son and I had lain beneath blankets, reaching our hands under the sheets to memorize each other as we listened to water pound on the roof and promised ourselves just ten more minutes before we'd get up to raise the drawn shades and start supper.

'Would you like some more tea, dear?' Bill's mother asked.

'Yes,' I said. 'Thanks, Louise.'

She came in from the dining room and handed me a second cup, gazing at me with a mournful look on her face. She stroked back a lock of my hair. 'My favourite daughter-in-law,' she said, a joke since I was her only one. Her eyes were red.

When we had first met, I had found her nervous, mousy, almost subservient in her eagerness to please, but I'd liked her despite her quirks. After twenty-one years with my mother the fashion goddess, I was delighted to meet a woman who answered the door wearing jeans with holes in them.

Now she sat beside me on the edge of a corduroy wing chair. 'Gloria,' she said, 'I want you to know that you're always welcome here. You'll bring Curran to see us, won't you?'

'Of course.' I glanced around. 'Where'd he wander off to?'

She laughed. It was the tremorous, broken laugh which had tumbled from my mouth countless times, the pained peal of a mother fighting to keep herself

4

under control. 'The darling. He volunteered to do the washing-up, can you believe?'

'Just like his father,' I said. I took a sip of the tea, then set it on the table. 'When I met Bill, my friends told me I'd hit the jackpot. An artist who could actually balance a cheque book and cook and clean.'

By the fireplace Bill's father wiped the moist corner of his eye with his thumb. He caught me watching him, and I smiled; he turned his head. I felt as if all day I had witnessed and validated the grief of others – Jim, Louise – while my own lay submerged, waiting to spring out, not in acceptable expressions of tears or eulogies, but in a frantic plea, an angry shout, fingernails scraped down an innocent cheek.

We heard a banging noise from the kitchen.

Bill's mother stood. 'I'd best go and check on him,' she said.

I watched the tail of the old workshirt she changed into flapping as she retreated. My eyes grew heavy. I spread the quilt over myself, curled up on the sofa, and stared at the wildflower pattern on the tea saucer before me until I drifted off to sleep. Drowsiness had always been my escape from pain. After my father, after the bullet, I'd slept for two days.

When I awoke I heard Curran and Louise talking

in the kitchen. Bill's father still sat by the fire. I hugged my knees and watched the flames and played a maudlin game of could-have-been, wondering if Bill, had his white cells not staged a coup, might have been like him at sixty. Would he have smoked a pipe and wrapped himself in green wool cardigans? Certainly he'd have been gentler than his father; he'd readily admitted that he was easier on Curran than his father had been on him. Even when he had every right to, Bill never raised his voice at our son. He had the amazing ability to convey firm, deep disapproval – whether it be over Curran's grade on an exam he forgot to study for or the way I treated my mother – with a few simple, quiet words, an arm placed knowingly across a shoulder. I would have snapped at Curran over anything – a door slammed, clothes left scattered on the floor – had it not been for Bill. *Don't*, he'd say, as his wide-knuckled fingers worked out the brutal knots of tension in my neck. *It isn't worth it. Relax.*

Bill's father cleared his throat now.

'There ... there are some old sketchbooks in the attic,' he said. 'Things of Bill's. You might have a look. Curran's interested in art, isn't he? Perhaps he'd like to see them.'

I rose and stood beside him in my now-wrinkled

black dress and stockings. I'd always been a little afraid of him, what with that gruff voice and pretentious name: *Edward Ladbrooke Burgess*. When I'd come here to dinner for the first time, he'd shaken my hand warmly, but his face registered pure disapproval of the fact that the girl his son had chosen to marry was not a gracious English flower, but a reticent American exchange student going through a punk phase. I didn't forgive him for his snap judgment, but now I longed to rest my hand on his shoulder and soften him with human touch.

'I'll go ask him,' I said.

We climbed creaky stairs in the darkness, ascending towards the gabled attic. 'Are there bats?' Curran asked.

'I don't think so,' I said, 'but if it'll make you feel better I'll go first and check.'

I gazed into the main space. Behind me Curran swayed without a rail to grasp and reached for me to maintain his balance, his hand against the small of my back. I thought of Bill's fingers stroking my spine, awakening my flesh.

'We're fine,' I said. 'No bats in sight.'

I guided him up the last few steps. The dusty

stillness of the attic was eerie, as if Bill had just run down to the kitchen for a bite to eat and would soon return to his charcoals and oils and brushes. I stepped around coffee jars and newspapers from the seventies, picked up a sketchbook, and sat on the window ledge to thumb through it. The first pencil drawing I came to was an image of a narrow-faced, dark-haired girl who at first glance looked like me. The caption beneath her read SARAH. Probably one of his first girlfriends, judging by the adolescent penmanship. I frowned and turned the page. The next sketch was a colour portrait of Louise, perfectly capturing her complaisant eyes and mop of brown hair. I grinned.

I flipped through a few pretty but dull drawings of ivy-covered trellises, outbuildings, and gardens. Then I leaned back and wiped the grimy window so I could look out of it. From where I sat, I saw the cemetery and its freshest grave.

'Do you remember,' I asked, 'when we'd come here to visit your grandparents and you'd always ask to go to the cemetery because you were afraid the dead people would get lonely?'

Curran pretended not to hear me. He skimmed his hands across the battered easel, the table draped with canvas, the dried colours encrusted on a palette.

Finally he spoke. 'No,' he said with a sharp, angry incredulity I'd rarely heard before in my mild, docile child. 'That's daft.' He shrugged. 'But I suppose I was little then.'

How quickly a child forgets, dismisses with a wave of his hand. Whole years obliterated. I was five; I'm eight now. A sage. Ludicrous.

Would he forget the sound of Bill's voice? Would the scent of his father fade from his memory?

When he'd been younger he'd adored the cemetery. He'd begged me to read him the names of 1800s stillborn babies that were inscribed on the cracked white tombstones, and soon he could rattle off the birth and death dates of all the beloved mothers, daughters, sons. He spoke of the dead as if they were friends with distinct wants and needs and personalities, and picked flowers to adorn their graves. 'Let's go see Hannah Cartwright,' he'd say, as if she were a lovable old aunt who'd greet him with tea and biscuits and open arms when he arrived. 'Can she hear us?' he asked once.

I swallowed. 'No, sweetheart,' I said. 'When you're dead you can't see or hear or do anything.'

'Oh,' he said, and wrinkled his eyebrows, mulling over the idea for a moment. Then he ran to find a person with a tall headstone whose ledge he could jump off.

Today he'd wandered away while Louise was asking me to lunch. I'd turned and seen him standing by Bill's grave, his head down. He was small in his brand-new black suit. His fair hair blew. The look on his face said: *so this is it.*

Now he fingered a box of pastels. 'Gran gave me this big lecture while you were sleeping,' he said. 'About how I'm the man of the house now, and I'm supposed to look out for you and not mind if you get a bit mental since you're sad.'

Please not again, I thought.

'Curran,' I said. 'Come here.'

He turned and came over to me, his expression solemn. I held out my arms. He leaned into them, resting his cheek against my shoulder. He smelled of chalk and peppermint and naïveté shattered.

'Don't worry about me,' I whispered onto the top of his head. 'Promise me you won't.'

Against the wool of my dress he nodded. I clutched him to me and closed my eyes. In my mind I was far from the farmhouse and its rustic charm. I was across the Atlantic Ocean, in the house of my childhood, an ivory palace full of chandeliers and spiral staircases and walls I couldn't brush my hand across and carpets I couldn't walk on in my shoes, and I was hearing a Vivaldi cello solo, my mother's screams, the terrible, mournful sounds of my father's weeping.

chapter two

When I'd been twenty-one, I'd boarded a plane to London under the guise of studying English literature in the land where it originated, but I'd really gone for two other, paradoxical reasons: to escape from my parents, and to see firsthand the frighteningly seductive country where my father had been born, and where my mother had fallen in love with him. During the flight, I scrawled a youthful, defiant declaration in my journal. 'Even if for some weird, creepy, Santayana-esque reason I end up marrying an Englishman and having his child,' I wrote, 'I swear to God that I will never, ever become as bitchy and unfulfilled as my mother or as sad and sick as my father.'

A month later, I met Bill. He was blissfully normal; I was aching for oblivion. At first I thought I'd have no trouble keeping my promise.

But now, after Bill's death, I sensed the awful aspects of my parents within me, sure as a pulse. The question which for years had lingered in the back of my mind jumped to the forefront of my consciousness: what if I *am* like them?

I needed details. I needed to hold the circumstances of their lives and mine with them, like tissue-wrapped angel statuettes shoved in a box and left untouched for a decade, mouths cracked and noses chipped, ceramic ivory lustre soured to a dingy yellow, their folded hands and wide-eyed beautiful stares subversive, wasted figures clasped to the heart then slammed at the wall.

And so I struggled to resurrect them. My mother, Caroline, was the one who set the rules about not walking on the carpet with shoes on or not brushing a hand across the wall. Jaw set, short blonde hair brushed severely off her forehead, she swished when she walked. Her strong, square features and mocking, pale blue eyes endowed her with a haughtiness which made her fascinating but kept her from being called pretty. She was one of those women who insisted on mascara and heels for a Saturday grocery trip, one of those rare chameleons who could be on the verge of a nervous breakdown when the phone rang and still answer it with an even-tempered 'Hello'.

She gave cello lessons at home, not so much because we needed the money but because she claimed she'd go crazy if she didn't have something 'nondomestic' to do. To say she was talented would be an understatement; she'd studied at Juilliard and gotten her master's overseas. She pined to join a symphony orchestra and travel the world, if only for the theatrics: first-class flights, roses in her hotel room, long, flowing black skirts to wear for performances, the pride of seeing her own intense face bent over the strings in a close-up shot broadcast on public television.

But she couldn't. She had me.

'I grew up in an age when success was a diversion for a year or two before marriage,' she told me once when I was older. 'You're lucky, Gloria. You can do what you want; there aren't any pretences. Back then, though, the only reason we strove like hell to get into a good school and earn the diploma was so we could entice men with our intellect. Ha.'

She never said outright that I was the tether keeping her from the concert halls of Paris and Vienna, but her resentment rooted itself in every pore, affecting the way she treated both me and her students. More often than not she drove them from the house in tears because of her criticisms, knowing her music had taken on the same numb timbre as theirs.

My father, Riordan, was so gentle by contrast that when I later thought of him I was reminded of the Jains, those men of India who sweep bugs from the sidewalks lest anyone tread on them. He taught chemistry at a nearby community college, and loved to recount tales of kids who almost blew the lab to bits. His dinner conversations were wild tangents on how every atom gets recycled, how nothing ever disappears.

'Just think,' he'd say, gesturing widely over the spaghetti, 'you – *you* – could have the atoms of Albert Einstein within your body.'

My mother would roll her eyes. 'Oh, for Christ's sake, Riordan,' she'd say. 'I can't tell relativity from chickenshit. You know that.'

Wondrous though my parents' exchanges were, they had a pattern which puzzled me. My father's earnest intensity met my mother's sarcasm like a hand desperately reaching to touch an averted face. They'd stare at their plates, scrape the last bites of food into their mouths, gulp water. By the time I was six, I'd mastered the art of talking to fill gaps, whether it be about what I wanted for Christmas or someone throwing up during social studies. Soon my mother would push her chair away from the table and announce she had a lesson in a few minutes. Then my father would murmur that his stack of tests wasn't going to correct itself.

While my mother complained if I knocked on her door while she was teaching, my father always left his study door open. I'd lean against the jamb and watch him grade in the green glow of his banker's lamp, one palm flat on the page, the other hand gliding out 72s and 85s and 90s, never in red ink because he was sure it caused students unnecessary anxiety. His face was thin and boyish in the light. Prematurely grey hair wisped in silver half-moons around his temples. 'Come on in, love,' he'd say, in that marvellous British voice which sent a delicious shiver up my backbone. 'Don't be shy.'

When he'd finished his work, I'd sit on his lap and draw lopsided hearts and stars and rainbows on his desk blotter while he told me stories about how life was before I was born. Basic facts became myth in that little room; our family timeline blurred to a watercolour mandala amongst the musty textbooks and cordovan leather. Mommy had been the glowing muse, vibrant with the scent of hope and gardenia perfume. She had taken his hands and forced him to live again; she had enveloped him in flames and burnt his pain to ashes as they danced into the morning. I pictured this: their bodies slowly revolving in smoky air, roles reversed, his cheek buried in her neck, her fingers caressing his back. 'And you lived happily ever after, right, Daddy?'

'Of course,' he said, and his voice never faltered.

His stories were reassurances. They balanced the sharp spaces between my parents' words, their jabs and pointed glances. The picnics, the leisurely walks through narrow streets, the afternoons spent painting their 'grotty' first flat in the Australian ghetto of London's Earl's Court, getting less paint on the walls and more on each other – all his nostalgias lulled me into a candy-coated haze which promised me that if happily ever after had been possible then, it was possible still.

In hindsight what shocked me wasn't the fact that I swallowed his sugary morsels of memory. What shocked me was the fact that, twenty-five years later, the truth remained nebulous. Did they really kiss in stairwells and giggle over the fortunes in their cookies at Chinese restaurants? Maybe, but in retrospect the pastel web my father wove felt like a blinder, a narcotic, a wistful man's skirting of actual experience. His recollections were dense whispers at the edge of my ear as I sat on his lap and drew, while we both struggled to convince ourselves that the exuberant angel he once knew and the elegant, fiery shrew across the hall screaming at little girls for horrible intonation were one and the same.

The only concrete evidence was photographs. They were taken in clumps like clots of blood, one event to a roll. My parents lying on their stomachs on a beach towel at Eastbourne, his arm dangled around her shoulder, their grins crooked. She wore a yellow bikini, and her mouth hung open, slack with laughter. My father gazed down, his nose sunburnt. A thermos (of lemonade? brandy? no telling what) lay between them. Another picture showed them caught in a doorway in a pinched embrace on New Year's Eve, he suited, she in velvet cloak and fur beret, cheek to cheek. Someone's noisemaker was stuck by his ear.

There were two other snapshots, however, which stuck in my mind for many years, mainly because of the fact that in both, my parents wore the same clothes, giving the pictures the Before/After quality of a ghoulish makeover.

In the first, they sat on a blanket in the grass, beneath a tree. In the right-hand corner the massive stone of a college building loomed behind them. They were on their knees, the remnants of lunch — what looked like the core of a Cox's Pippin apple, the ubiquitous thermos — spread about them. Once again his arm was around her shoulder. Her hand grasped his. He held her tightly against his chest, as if she might fly apart if he let go. Her head was tilted, and her eyes gleamed. She wore a white peasant blouse and a skirt dotted with wildflowers, dark blue or black — in monochrome, it was hard to tell. A girlish mischief I'd never seen in her shone on her face. My father looked the same as he did when I knew him, except that his hunter-green jacket with the leather elbow patches was new and his hair was darker, almost black as mine. His eyes were closed, chin down at an angle, lips poised to skim the side of her thin, smiling mouth. They looked giddy, my sweet, ravenous father and my mother who couldn't tell relativity from chickenshit but had a Fulbright to Oxford. Under closer scrutiny, though, it was obvious they were pulled by different desires, in opposite directions. My father itched to gather her against the rough fabric of his shirt and rasp, 'Don't leave me, don't you ever,' and while my mother glittered with photogenic playfulness, her body arched, she strained to tumble past him into a space of her own.

In the second photograph, taken a few months later, they were on the QE2, heading back to the States so my mother could hit up her rich relatives for money. They'd stay for decades, first near Philadelphia, in Bryn Mawr, where she'd grown up and would soon give birth to me in the steamy twilight of a summer evening. Later, lured by the modest promise of my father's teaching job, they'd relocate two hours west to another small Pennsylvania town, which my mother would describe as 'death by quaintness', charming to the point of suffocation, a far cry from London, cultureless, conservative. There, in a huge brick Colonial house funded by her parents, they'd languish in an upper-class-wannabe neighbourhood, slowly sinking down into the too-new elegance, learning to distrust each other. But they didn't know that then.

In both snapshots they wore the same skirt, the same jacket, the same smiles, but a subtle distance lay between them, so subtle the passenger who kindly captured them on film probably couldn't see it. My mother's face was fuller. Her eyes crinkled with an emotion too frustrated for elation, too ladylike for anger. Her hair, still long — she'd cut it off after she had me — was drawn up with barrettes, an impish, childlike touch, but some of it had come loose and whipped freely in the ocean air. She held a straw hat banded by navy grosgrain ribbon. My father held her elbow. There was a vacancy in his squinting gaze, a passive acceptance that they weren't sailing towards, but sailing away. They kept their backs to the deck railing, to the water, to the horizon.

And of course there was another crucial moment, one not suitable for Kodak. After I'd become a mother myself, and had known the perverse, maddening experience of raising a child, I thought of it often. I imagined the famished hour of my conception.

I pictured their bedroom with its cherry suite, its gold baroque mirror, its china baubles and doilies on top of the dresser. I saw him ease back onto the bed's heavy rose-coloured comforter, hands laced across his stomach as he waited for the moment when her stubby musician's fingernails would catch wool threads as she lifted his mulberry sweater. She stepped forward, knees against the mattress, and shoved her straight, glistening hair behind her ears. He watched her with a languid smile as she unbuttoned her cornflower-blue silk blouse, then her skirt, revealing the dip of her breasts and her quivery ribs, the empty bowl of her stomach and pinch of navel, the pomegranate cave which was her heart. 'Please,' he would say, voice pathetic; in my mind she would have red marks on her shoulders and back from where he gripped her so tightly. She'd slide down in an arc like a diver to meet him, bone over bone, because she was young and flattered and not yet a bitch and because she wanted to yield to him, to the swell in her blood like the thrill of a full orchestra.

Did he whisper to her that if she gave him the chance, he would make her life beautiful? Did she have any idea of his warped longing, his pain's magnitude? I thought so. After me, the merry clusters of photographs grew smaller and smaller.

chapter three

Those first few weeks after Bill's death, I expected to wake up each morning and find the windows smashed, our bedroom walls gutted, the whole city lost in the senseless echo of grief's reverberation. Instead I found only myself, curled up under a fortress of blankets, shivering, in the middle of the mattress.

When Bill had been in the hospital, I'd risen before my alarm every day, jittery with expectation and false hope, pacing barefoot on the cold floor before I went into the kitchen and gulped countless cups of black coffee while I made French toast for a still-slumbering Curran. Now, however, my drowse-heavy hand reached out by reflex to press the clock's snooze button two or three times as I dove back down into turbid oceans of sleep, awash in dreams of a shoulder to bury my face in, a body to coil around, until I felt small fingers shaking me, a small voice calling into the depths, *Mum, you must wake up* — Curran's fingers, Curran's voice, urgent, scared, sweet.

I could hear him slamming cupboard doors and opening and closing refrigerator drawers in the kitchen as I hurriedly yanked on my nylons and learned to anticipate his shout of 'I'm making you breakfast,' while I bent in front of the mirror, still blurry-eyed, to put on my lipstick. I'd come out to find him already dressed for school, hair better-combed than mine, homework and books already in his knapsack on the floor, a plate of buttered toast and a cup of amaretto, with cream and sugar, awaiting me on the table. 'Since when did you learn to make coffee?' I asked, yawning.

'Last week. Your lipstick is on crooked.'

I swiped at it with the side of my hand.

'Other side. There. It's brilliant now.'

He reminded me so much of Bill. I sat down at the table and picked at the toast. 'I'm not that hungry,' I said. 'Here, take some of it.'

'No,' he said, shaking his head. 'I ate already, and besides, you're getting dead skinny, Mum. You should eat more.'

I smiled absently. Slumped there, I felt like a passive verb. A child.

'What time is it?' I asked.

'Time to leave,' he said. 'I phoned Mrs Romdourl downstairs. She said I can go to school with Raj.'

He slung his knapsack over his shoulder and headed for the door, terribly small yet terribly wise in his navy-blue sweater. A shot of longing tore through me.

'Hold on a minute, love,' I said.

He turned. 'I need to go. We get black marks if we're late for morning assembly.'

Before, I'd always had to scream down the hall at him to get him out the door. *Quit poking around, or you'll be in trouble!* Bill would lope into the kitchen in his old faded robe, just up, and kiss me on the side of the neck, his mouth imprecise with half-sleep. 'A few black marks never hurt anyone, love. I had plenty.'

Now I held out my arms. 'Not enough time for a hug goodbye, at least?'

He ran over, embraced me hard. I closed my eyes, whole again, right again. 'You've got a button missing on the back of your dress,' he said.

'Don't worry about it,' I said. 'Go on.'

The door banged closed behind him. I felt down

my spine, found a spot of unadorned wool, rested my head on the table. I was already twenty minutes late for work. And he was right.

I taught English at a comprehensive school just outside of London. I'd stumbled upon my career guided by echoes and a sense of defiance; I'd seen too much of my mother's artistry wasted to want to emulate her, and chemistry was out of the question once I got old enough to debunk the farfetched magic of my father's theories. English, therefore, had seemed a viable choice for me in college, a sort of middle ground where articulateness and freakishness, finally, wouldn't be branded one and the same. The last thing I wanted was to become a floaty, surreal muse infatuated with language (my father's dream daughter), or a useless pedant bulldozing tight-faced through Bakhtin (my mother's object of contempt), so I'd been elated when I'd gotten the rather pragmatic job offer seven years earlier. I had summers free, got to banish the word *polyglossia* from my vocabulary, and learned incredible patience on the days I wanted to strangle every sullen fourteen-year-old who sat down in my classroom and proclaimed each work we studied 'a bunch of bloody rot'.

Their lack of decorum aside, most of my students and I got along well. They complained about my tough grading, but loved it when, on dreary winter mornings when none of us were in the mood for Chaucer, I let them lounge on top of their desks and just talk. 'Listen, you guys,' I'd tease the ones with the nose rings, 'I was around for the *real* revolution.'

They'd gasp and fight to defend their cherished quasi-individuality. 'No, you weren't,' they'd say, eyeing my suede heels and Marks and Sparks sweater with such suspicion that the next day I brought in a picture of myself at fifteen. The room rang with their howls of laughter at my rags and dyed hair and black lipstick, but after that, they bitched about their essay scores a lot less and paid attention to my lectures a lot more.

During the long ordeal with Bill, they'd displayed a gritty compassion of which I'd never thought adolescents were capable. They never commented on the way my hands shook while I handed back papers or the tremble in my voice when I read off that night's list of reading assignments after I'd gotten a call from the hospital. They asked about Bill often, with refreshing bluntness oddly similar to that of my son: 'Your husband, has he got better yet?'

'Not yet.'

Wicked yet shy smiles. 'Well, once he does we're throwing you a party.'

'God help us that day,' I'd say, broken inside, laughing.

Now, though, once they'd seen me come back a week late from Christmas break, hollow-eyed with exhaustion and ten pounds thinner, once they knew there wouldn't be any wild celebration, they were different. They still made their usual boisterous room-entering noises, and rolled their eyes at announcements of what to them were disgustingly early paper-topic deadlines, but they never joked anymore, never begged for a 'telling Chaucer to bugger off' session, as they'd referred to them when they thought I was out of earshot. Instead they concentrated on my lectures with a control so rigid it was eerie, and when they worked together in groups they actually whispered and kept on task as opposed to engaging in loud discussions of who pulled who on the secondary-school circuit the previous weekend.

Had this transformation been under other circumstances, I would have been delighted, but now I saw it as a subtle betrayal of trust, a terrible foray into the twisted world of adult social graces, as if, like Curran in his grandmother's kitchen, they had been advised to tread lightly with me, Mrs Burgess the mental, the literature instructor gone unhinged. Countless times when I wrote assignments on the blackboard or leaned over to read a student's introductory paragraph, I longed to whirl, to grab their tough-but-innocent shoulders, to cry out in a strangled, intense wail, 'I'm me, I'm still the hardnosed grader with the punk stories, still the one who can make you laugh and piss you off when I deduct for spelling, and we can still tell Chaucer to bugger off occasionally, I'm the same, grief hasn't transmuted me, don't you see?'

But sometimes I had trouble believing.

At night, taking the tube home, huddled inside my coat, I bit my fingernails to shreds and watched ubiquitous blonde girls in leather jackets hop on and off at stations, their bodies thin as mine but glowing, gliding effortlessly through the dull metal of the sliding doors while mine shivered, spluttered its refrain of cold, winter, loss, there is no escape. The blooming flowers of Northern Line graffiti swam before my eyes, their red-and-blue swirls reminding me of the bouquets in mid-wilt all over my living room, my dining room, my kitchen, and with them the people I had to thank for their kindnesses, their saccharine words, their carnations.

I tipped my head back. The world roared past me in the darkness. In my mind I gave myself instructions in much the same way as did the silky, disembodied voices on the tube platforms who gently chastised all passengers to mind the gap and cheerfully announced that the next station was King's Cross.

When the signs on the wall slow down enough to be read, when they stare at you, endlessly repeating ANGEL ANGEL ANGEL, that piercing word he was, you'll get up, you'll shove your way out, you'll mind the gap, you'll ride the escalator up to the turnstile in the slick brightness, your eyes will mist but you'll blink, pretend to read the ads for Harvey Nic's, Dillons, the Tate's latest international exhibit, oh Jesus that one will hurt but you'll keep on moving, you'll shove the card in the slot, watch it pop up, no wavering here, and then out into the open, into the murderousness of winter, you'll walk towards Upper Street, you will ignore the rosy-cheeked families of three, four, sometimes five but not often, not usually two, not ever two, you will look past the wool-sweatered husbands and their trench-coated wives who don't deserve them, you will grit your teeth if you have to and turn onto the side street that is yours, make your way up to the walk that is yours, to 10a Theberton, the round green door and frozen empty windowbox, slick streets and streetlamps aglow, it is like you dreamed it when you were twenty, it is like you dreamed it but with a piece cut out, oh Jesus this will hurt but you go up the front steps, you take the stairs two at a time, you are shivering, you want warmth, you want arms and fingers and voices and mouths to surround you, you're crying, you let yourself in, into 10a, you have minded all the gaps and watched for rapidly closing doors which when obstructed, you know, are dangerous, and you are home but you are alone, the flat is a mess, there are too many flowers, too much fecundity in the face of this barren hour of five o'clock, but you'll wave to your son when he barrels in, you'll smile through the wet mask of tears that has covered your face, you'll come inside. And I did.

In the evenings, after I had crouched on the edge of the bed and cried for what felt like the ten millionth time, after I'd peeled out of my stockings and dress and yanked off my earrings, I crawled into the bathroom's old claw-footed tub and soaked in water so hot it verged on painful.

There in the ragged comfort of walls' peeling paint and the half-glow of dim lights which shrouded the mirror, my shivers dissipated as my hair fanned out around me. As the water grew tepid, I thought briefly of winter afternoons stark with magic when, young, absorbed, I'd scrubbed the splashes of paint and turpentine from Bill's neck and shoulders in the same porcelain tub; he got so involved when he painted, with his whole body practically, his lack of inhibition both hysterically funny and admirable to watch. 'God, you're a mess,' I said. 'How do you get like this?'

He pretended not to hear me. 'Something a lot of artists don't understand,' he said, 'is the basic concept of ephemerality.'

'As a limitation?' I asked, running a hand gently through his hair. A cascade of green paint flecks rained down. 'Most attractive, love.'

He grinned, 'As a limitation, yeah, but also as progress. Part of doing anything creative is learning when to trash it. When to let go. Being able to work on something for five, ten years and then smashing it to bits because it doesn't work, because it's stale now, and then assimilating the dead good aspects . . . that's progress.'

Ephemerality. I had to laugh now, thinking about how naïvely I'd slid closer to him, rested my cheek against his soapy shoulder blades, and thought, *Screw the ephemeral, screw progress. I will never let go of this.*

Eventually I would hear the loud door slam that

was Curran coming upstairs from his friend Raj's (he had his own key now, now that I couldn't always be trusted to wake up and get home on time and be a concerned mother), and soon a yell of 'I'm making sandwiches; shall we have roast beef or ham?'

'Roast beef!' I'd yell back. 'And how many damn times do I have to tell you to come in quietly?'

It wouldn't hit me until I'd grabbed my bathrobe and headed down the hall to change into my jeans that lately I sounded like a frightening fusion of my parents' faults: my father's neediness, my mother's temper. And there would be Curran in the kitchen, still in his school uniform, dutifully spooning chutney. Fragile kiss on the cheek. 'Did you have a good day, Mum?'

I should be doing this, I thought, sitting down at the table and for the second time in one day watching him grab napkins, pour tea (he knew how to boil tea *and* make coffee? had Bill taught him that? or was it Louise during her postfuneral lecture?), slice more bread for me. He munched away at his sandwich, one leg kicking his chair – 'Stop it,' I said. 'I don't need a headache' – while I vowed to get up earlier in the mornings, to quit wallowing in tears and torrid water after work so I could be in charge again, if only for him. In Curran I searched for signs of my own quiet, perverse childhood, huge-eyed sorrows and disturbing precocities, but found none. *You see?* I told myself with the false brightness of rationale. The fact that he felt compelled to perform these small, tenderly executed duties, to make me sandwiches and alert me to my crookedly applied lipstick, wasn't what bothered me. What bothered me was the fact that, as with Bill, I had come to expect them.

One night in late January, I lay on my back beneath a red plaid quilt, shivering as I chewed one fingernail until the blood surged in my mouth. Light from a streetlamp outside spilled hieroglyphic shadow-symbols across the bedclothes.

The door opened. My breath grew tight. Every time I saw a hand on a doorknob, my body stuttered with delusional hope. But no. It was only my son. 'Mum,' he whispered, 'it's suppertime. Are you going to get up?'

I nodded and turned on my side, propping on one elbow. He sat beside me on the mattress.

'Shall I ring the take-away man for Chinese?' he asked.

'Sure.' I stroked his hair. He didn't squirm or

protest my touch, but rather sat still and looked away from me, his face alarming in its stoicism; I knew what he really wanted was to run down the hall and order sweet-and-sour prawns, yet he knew he had to indulge me. I drew my hand back.

While he made the call, I stumbled into the bathroom and splashed water on my face and tied back my hair. After a decade of living with the idiosyncrasies of British heating, I'd grown used to wearing two pairs of socks and enduring a perpetual slight chilliness, but following Bill's death I'd grown colder. I grabbed my robe from its hook and wrapped it around me.

The doorbell rang. 'My wallet's on the hall table, Curran!' I yelled.

After a short pause I heard him call back, 'I don't think it's the take-away man, Mum – he hasn't any boxes and he doesn't look very Chinese.'

'Well, that's nice and ethnocentric of you,' I said as I came into the kitchen. The man at the door, with short, gleaming black hair and disgustingly white teeth, laughed. In his silk shirt, black jeans, and Doc Martens, he looked like just another thirtysomething Islington trendy, a brand of creature even I, the romantic Anglo-American, couldn't hide my disdain towards. The memory-taste of vodka bobbed in my throat when I noticed the combat boots.

'Gloria Burgess?' he asked.

'Yes.'

'I'm Jascha Kremsky.' He offered his hand. Though I assumed from the name that he was Russian, his accent was hard to place.

'And your point is?'

'I'm a sculptor at a co-op in Chelsea. The ... the same one Bill belongs to. Belonged.'

'Oh. Come in.'

His name didn't sound familiar. Then again, there'd been so many in that group, so many who'd sat around our kitchen table with jumpy hands and excited voices and quasi-sophisticated chatter. The ones closer to him – Lorin, Sean, Taylor – had been at the funeral.

'Sorry I didn't ring first,' he said. 'I hate to catch you at such a bad time and interrupt your dinner, but since I was just in the area I thought I'd stop by.'

'You don't have to apologize,' I said, motioning towards a chair as I dropped into one next to it. 'Any time is bad around here lately.'

'I'm sure it is.' I liked the flatness in his voice,

the objectivity it held. No pity, no mournfulness, just acknowledgement.

'Would you like some tea?'

'No, no thank you. I'm fine.' He leaned back in his chair. 'What I've come to talk to you about is Bill's work.'

'His work?'

'Yes. Specifically the idea of a retrospective.'

'It's not usual for an artist to get a retrospective at the age of thirty-two, is it?'

'No, but Bill wasn't your run-of-the-mill artist, was he?'

His voice was soft, eulogistic, coaxing.

'Let me ask you something,' I said. 'Why now? Why not six months ago, when Bill was euphoric and sure he was going to survive, when he would have loved to do a show? Why not two months ago, when he was getting sicker but still creating? Why not the night before he died, when he was pumped full of morphine, for Christ's sake? Why the hell now?'

Jascha stared straight at me. I admired him for not flinching.

'There were some paintings,' he said, 'that Bill did in the last few months of his life. I've seen them at the co-op. They're extremely powerful and innovative, they're—'

'Enough criticspeak. I know which ones you're talking about.'

'What I'm getting at is that they have a lot of pulling power. Which is not to say that his earlier works are bad pieces, but would they attract large numbers of people? No. However, with the inclusion of his last paintings, especially under the circumstances, since they detail a man coming to terms with his mortality—'

'What you're basically saying is that the only reason my husband is worth a retrospective is because dead people are more interesting.' He nodded. 'That's the most repulsive, exploitative thing I've ever heard.'

The doorbell rang again. Curran, who'd been sitting and listening to our conversation with a mixture of fascination and fright, ran to answer it. This time it was the take-away man.

Jascha watched as Curran handed over a ten-pound note in exchange for a huge box and a plastic container of wonton soup. 'How old is your son?' he asked.

'Eight.'

His face softened. 'He's a cute kid,' he said, and

then returned to his persuasive speech, 'You must understand, Mrs Burgess, that no one's intention is to exploit Bill. We just have to hit the right time, the right climate.'

'Victim art,' I said. 'Controversy. I understand full well what you're saying, but I still think it's sick.'

'I'm sorry if this sounds harsh, but there is a commercial aspect to the promotion of art. One I don't think Bill fully realized or wanted to acknowledge.'

Yes. That was Bill — gentle, idealistic, art-will-conquer-all. The last few months, he'd come home from the studio with a daub of green on his cheek, a smudge of sepia across his nose. He'd speak in TV-movie clichés like 'I think I'm going to beat this thing.' I kissed him and said I was glad. Stupid, stupid darling. Did he really think he could stop leucaemic cells with a paint brush?

'It'll be big,' Jascha said. 'It'll be very tastefully done. We're hoping to get the Hayward or Whitechapel.'

At the counter, Curran struggled to get the lid off the soup. 'Watch what you're doing,' I said, 'or you'll splash it all over yourself.'

'Don't you think that is what Bill would have wanted?' Jascha asked.

41

'I know this is what Bill would have wanted,' I said, and stood. 'But I also know that any maudlin memorial or trendy display could never pay homage to who Bill was. He was too complex.'

'So you aren't giving us permission for the project?'

'You're very bright.' I led him to the door. 'Now I'd appreciate it if you'd get the hell out so my son and I can eat dinner in peace.'

He drew a piece of paper from his pocket and handed it to me. 'My number. In case you change your mind.'

'I don't intend to.'

He stepped outside, then turned around to say more. 'Mrs Burgess—'

I slammed the door on him.

After dinner I sat at the kitchen table and stared at the wadded napkins, the smudged water glasses, Curran's aborted homework, which was so illegible it looked more like the Cyrillic alphabet than a set of multiplication problems. I felt split open. My throat hurt even though I hadn't been yelling at Jascha.

One afternoon years ago, Bill and I had gone museum-trekking in the middle of winter and I'd forgotten my gloves. When we came home he sat me down on the red paisley couch in the living room, knelt before me on the floor, and massaged my numb hands. 'This is going to hurt,' he said, and it did. They were great stabs, those pains of regained feeling, and I felt them again now.

Curran padded back in, barefoot and fresh from his bath, clad in pale blue flannel, hair damp. A comb swung in his grasp. 'Come here,' I said. 'Let me get the knots out for you.'

He came and turned his back towards me so I could get the most unruly bit at the nape of his neck. His warmth comforted me. I ran the comb's teeth through the moist tangled curls, and saw Bill's hair, soft and brown and falling out in clumps.

Curran wriggled.

'Mum,' he said, 'if there's an exhibition of Dad's, can I go to it with you?'

'There isn't going to be an exhibition.'

He whipped around to face me. 'But you said that that's what Dad would have wanted.'

I set the comb on the table and took his face in my hands. 'Forget about it,' I said, and kissed his forehead. 'Put some slippers on and finish your math, all right?'

*   *   *

That night I had the dream.

I was standing with my father in total darkness at the side of the M6 motorway to Manchester. Suddenly two cars came from opposite directions, washing us in the terrible gleam of their headlights and slamming into each other. We saw the driver of one car, a young girl, fly against the windscreen, her eyes wide. 'Adrienne,' my father sobbed, and clutched me to him, burying my face against his chest and holding me there until I suffocated.

I'd dreamt the same thing for years. This time, though, I didn't startle out of sleep right away, like I normally did. I dreamt that Jascha Kremsky held my head under in the River Lethe, and I fought, unable to decide whether to struggle to the surface or let the water take me down, torn between the need to remember and the desire to forget.

chapter four

After a while my father tired of the stories about
my mother as muse. Then on our nights in the
study, he began the saga of Adrienne.

She'd gone to secondary school with him back in
Manchester. She'd sat in front of him in sixth-form
English, and during the class he'd stared at the
gorgeous dark hair she wore piled on top of her
head, all but one seductive wisp, which trailed down
the back of her high, classic neck.

He couldn't concentrate on Keats because of
her. She was afraid she wouldn't pass her A-levels
in Maths because of one dreadful chapter trip-
ping her up in calculus. He tutored her; she lent
him her meticulous notes. By exam time, they
were in love.

Like all my father's stories, it was waiflike, sweet,
and tinged with cliché, but as a child I loved it.

'Tell me more,' I begged. 'About her pretty-coloured sweaters, how she had one for each day of the week. About how she used to amaze the teachers by using such big words in class.'

Beautiful though she'd been, Adrienne had, like my father, also been a loner. 'She understood perfectly the difference between loneliness and solitude,' he said, 'and she was brilliant. For her, talking about existentialism and literary theory was ordinary conversation, natural as discussing what to have for dinner.'

Although I had no idea what he meant, I nodded happily and leaned my head against his shoulder, transfixed by his language and his tales of such a marvellous creature.

'She was delicate,' he said. 'Strong of mind, but that very strength gave her delicacy. I had to protect her. I had to watch out for her. She could have been taken advantage of easily.'

I couldn't imagine him ever protecting my mother.

'That woman was a gift,' he said. 'There I was, this tall, skinny lad, friendless, in threadbare sweaters with unkempt hair – and to think that she loved me, that she would be the one ...'

More than his other stories, these quickly degenerated into mumbled monologues on how undeserving he'd been.

'But you were both different. You were both alike,' I said, picturing the two of them, twin geniuses trapped in the grey maze of a northern city, sitting in a cold, draughty classroom and thinking solemn thoughts as they turned their heads from the teacher's too-easy lecture to stare out of windows spattered with rain.

'Yes,' he said. 'It was the two of us against the world, and we were winning.'

One night he showed me a picture of Adrienne. He took the second volume of the encyclopedia down from the shelf and flipped to the page with an article on Robert Browning, where he had placed the photograph. 'Her favourite poet,' he said. 'She said she loved him because he pursued communion with the world to the point of audacity. His friends used to think he was crazy because he ate flowers.'

'That *was* crazy,' I said.

'No, it wasn't,' he said. 'He wanted to take in everything.'

'Well, they must have tasted awful.'

He laughed and handed me the picture. In it,

Adrienne smiled, the soft smile of a girl who, like
her favourite poet, wanted to take in everything.
Her hair curled around her ears and down past her
fragile shoulders, and her face was bony and narrow.
She wore a pair of dangly glass earrings and a dark
sweater whose neck came down in a sharp V. Her
eyes shone.

'She looks a lot like me,' I said. 'I mean, she's
much prettier, but ...'

'Ah, child, you've got my talent for self-depre-
cation,' he said, and drew his arm around me. 'You
look exactly like her.'

I turned the photograph over. On the back Adrienne
had written him a message in handwriting so ornate it
looked like calligraphy. I struggled to read the words.
She'd quoted a stanza of 'Two in the Campagna':

Riordan —

I would I could adopt your will,
    See with your eyes, and set my heart
Beating by yours, and drink my fill
    At your soul's springs — your part,
my part
    In life, for good and ill.

Although R.B. would probably doubt me if he were here, I have, love, I have, and I shall never go back to seeing any other way.

– Adrienne

Later on, at college, I would analyze that poem, prattle for fifteen pages of explication about spiritual unity and elective affinity and how echoes of the piece's theme could be found in the work of Graham Greene, but at that moment as a nine-year-old all I grasped in the archaic phrasing was the sheer power of love. The dangerous kind of love that happens once and only once, that either heals or scars, melds or shatters.

'Does Mommy know about Adrienne?' I asked.

'She knows she existed, yes,' he said. 'She doesn't know how much I loved her.'

'Did you love her more than Mommy?'

He gazed out the open door. We heard a brisk request from across the hall. 'Could we take it from the second measure, *please!*'

'Adrienne was pure,' he said. 'Your mother is all veneer. She isn't real.'

'So why did you get married?'

'She was a warm body. She was there. She was

49

witty and sharp-tongued and eager, and I needed to forget.'

'Forget what?'

He leaned down and kissed the top of my head. 'That's another night,' he said, 'but now it's your bedtime.'

He and Adrienne had gone to Oxford together, two of only five from their class to be accepted, their faces shining and oblivious with youth as they stood on the train platform, Adrienne in a soft green floral dress with a cream-coloured shawl around her shoulders, my father in his one well-worn suit, waving to their families with relief at the knowledge that they, the gifted ones, wouldn't suffer their parents' proletarian fate, not with degrees in literature and chemistry. Then they dashed onto the train, grabbing each other's hands with giddy excitement as they watched the smokestacks of factories roll past, eventually giving way to the sombre lushness of a university town – or so they thought later on, his arms around her, his cheek against the back of her neck as she read passages from Joyce to him, curled up on the window seat of her attic bedroom while in the pubs the rest of Oxford's students laughed their ale-thick way through another pint of bitter.

Their final year there he asked her to marry him. Of course she said yes.

'We were so incredibly happy,' he said. 'We had the wedding set for July – we wanted the traditional June, but we knew we'd go barmy if we tried to get married during finals – and our whole lives figured out. We were both going to go on to graduate school, and she was going to teach and write – she'd already been published – and I was going to teach as well, and we were going to be academics for a while, a Renaissance couple, and then have children ...'

'Why didn't you?'

He sighed and rubbed his temples. 'She died,' he said.

It had been a Friday night in early December. He and Adrienne had planned to drive home to Manchester to see their parents for the weekend. My father had had to stay late to monitor a lab project, so that night she made the drive home alone.

'We said goodbye out in the quad,' he said. 'It was snowing a little. She had on a deep-blue scarf and a white beret. She glistened. She kissed me, and her mouth was warm in spite of the cold. "Don't torment yourself too much with the analysis, Riordan," she said. I wanted to pick her up and hold her in the folds of my jacket. I wanted to breathe her in. I told her to ring me up as soon as she got home, no matter what the hour, and to be careful. "When have I ever not been?" she said. And then she ran across the lawn, car keys jangling in her hand, coat billowing.'

'What happened next?' I asked.

She'd been about to turn onto the M6 when a car swerved across her path and hit her head-on. She'd flown against the windscreen with a motion so violent it had broken her neck, that high, classic neck at which my father had gazed with such rapture during sixth-form English. The driver of the other car – possibly drunk, but who was to say? – kept right on towards Birmingham on foot and was never found. Adrienne died instantly.

I trembled. While before the study had been cloaked in a soft warmth, it now felt harsh and cold. The glass which covered the top of my father's desk was the glass of the car's windscreen, and the glow from his banker's lamp became the gleam of oncoming headlights, the last thing Adrienne saw.

'Don't talk,' I said. 'I don't like this story any-more.'

'Why do you keep calling it a story?' he asked. It was the first time he'd ever spoken to me roughly. 'This is her life, *my* life.'

He put his head down on the desk and sobbed. It was a wrenching, pitiful sound; it dug into me and made me want to cry with him and at the same time make him stop. I wrapped my arms around him and pressed my cheek against the back of his neck. 'Please don't,' I whispered. 'Daddy, please don't.'

In a few moments he quieted. Slowly he rose up again, his face flushed and mouth contorted with pain. I grabbed some tissues from a box on the shelf behind me, and sat gingerly on his knee. With one hand I steadied his quaking shoulder. With the other I dabbed at his tear-stained cheeks. 'Please don't cry,' I said. 'You're scaring me. Please. That was a long time ago. It's OK now.'

In her music room my mother screamed, 'You call that vibrato?' while I blotted his face again and again, and still the salt trickled from his reddened eyes.

chapter five

A few days after I'd slammed the door in his face, I called Jascha Kremsky. 'You're the last person in the universe I expected to hear from,' he said.

'I owe you an apology,' I said. 'You wanted to have a calm discussion, and I behaved like a shrew.'

'I'm the one who should be sorry, seeing as I barged into your flat at suppertime and fed you a line of postmodernist crap when all you were expecting was Chinese food.'

I laughed.

'I had no right to act as if I knew what your husband would have wanted,' he said.

'No. You didn't.'

'But I'm still devoted to the idea of the retrospective. Not for the sake of controversy or trendiness, but for Bill.'

'How well did you know him?'

'Not very, I have to admit.'

'Then why are you so devoted?'

'Every day, Bill came into the studio ready to get down to business,' he said. 'He never sat around bullshitting about artistic responsibility the way the rest of us did when we were stuck on a piece and didn't know where to go with it. Bill always knew. And he never spoke about his art. Hell, we'd talk and talk about what we were going to do until the energy dissipated and we didn't do it, but not Bill.

'I'd watch him walk in,' he said, 'and he'd have on an old coat and a plaid shirt and a scarf tied around his head, after he'd lost his hair. Some days he only stayed half an hour, he was that weak, but he came.'

Behind me I felt Bill as a phantom lover, his mouth on my neck, hands sliding down my arms, dredging up the goodness within me.

'Mrs Burgess? Are you still there?'

I jumped.

'Yes,' I said, twisting the phone cord around my finger, 'and please, call me Gloria.'

'Gloria, I'd like you to reconsider.'

'Why do I get the feeling that you're not going to give up until I do?'

'Because I won't.'

'I don't know. It's just — it's not something I think I can deal with. You've got to understand. Getting up in the morning is hard right now.'

'I understand.'

'And I don't mean to offend you, but I've seen the kind of affected, marginally sincere stuff your group tends to put on, and I don't want it to be—'

'I'll give you full say in all aspects of the project, final approval of all decisions, but I'll try to make it as small of a burden on you as possible.'

I sighed.

'All right,' I said.

His voice filled with relief. 'Thank you,' he said. 'You won't be disappointed.'

About a week later, he asked me to come into the studio and look over the pieces he'd selected as possibilities, and I agreed to meet him there one night.

It was eerie going back to the place where Bill and I had first met. Sometimes when he worked there in the evenings, I'd meet him at the studio and we'd eat at a chip shop across the street. I'd always felt a little uneasy standing there in my big black coat with my hands stuffed in my pockets, an anomaly, a lone once-academic female in the midst of twenty male artists who scraped and banged and swirled away at marble, wood blocks, and canvas while loud rock music grated. Even when I had an enraptured Curran with me, I never thought of the studio as anything more than an annoyingly incongruous but vital backdrop to a life my husband loved. Now, however, with him gone, the place was imbued with an almost mystical significance, a wild energy which turned the track lights into radiant beacons and the industrial discord-songs into wrenching anthems.

When I arrived, I found Jascha sitting on the window ledge. 'You made it,' he said.

'Did you think I stood you up?'

'I wouldn't put it past you.'

He led me into a small room off the main workspace. Its shelves held a variety of audio-visual equipment. In one corner sat a cart with a television and VCR. On the far wall hung a movie screen.

'What, you didn't make me popcorn?' I asked. I'd forgotten that some of the group members were into film production.

Jascha laughed nervously. 'You amaze me,' he said.

'Why? Do you think that just because currently my life is hell I've lost all sense of humour? Granted, it was a bad joke ...'

He pulled a box off one shelf. 'We're lucky that we've got slides of all the work he'd done as a member,' he said as he set up the projector.

I sat on the faded green couch which smelled of ale and cigarettes and feverish idealistic dreams, and Jascha dimmed the lights and sat beside me. 'You realize,' I said in the darkness, 'that I won't be able to look at this as an art critic like you will.'

'Yes.'

'I won't be able to judge perspective, or form, or chiaroscuro.'

'I know.'

He clicked the first image onto the screen. The motion was almost comical, reminiscent of basement vacation showcases, only this time the slides weren't of the Grand Canyon or Hawaii, but my husband's inner landscape.

'I liked this one,' he said. 'I thought it was youthful, delicate. The colour's terrific.'

It was the painting of me running down the hill at Bill's parents' farmhouse in Lamberhurst.

'Is that you?' he asked.

'In my younger days.'

'Oh, come on,' he said. 'How old can you be? Twenty-nine? Thirty?'

I nodded. 'That wasn't long after we got married. It was the most innocent, ridiculously happy time of my life.'

'Ever?'

'Ever. We were drunk on each other. We were oblivious. We were saturated in the kind of joy that makes you think you're invincible, armoured, but really leaves you open to attack.'

'If you were so happy then, why does your face look so terrified there?'

'I'm not sure,' I said. 'I guess I've always been ambivalent.'

I rubbed my eyes. We'd been looking at slides for two hours, and we'd only advanced three years. I hadn't realized how prolific Bill had been.

'Are you OK?' Jascha asked. He touched my shoulder. I jerked up.

'I'm fine. Really.'

'Why don't we take a break?' he said.

We went into the kitchen, and I sat on the table,

still in my good silk skirt and heels from work, while Jascha rummaged through the refrigerator.

'I married the last man who was in this kitchen with me,' I said.

He glanced over. 'What?'

'Don't worry; I was only being reflective. It wasn't a warm-up to a proposal. Although I firmly believe that history repeats itself for those who let it.'

He grinned. 'Let's see,' he said, 'we've got half a head of lettuce, a bottle of mineral water, a beer—'

'Grab that. I'll split it with you.'

'Seriously?'

'Seriously.'

He poured two glasses, handed me one, and sat beside me. 'Does this bother you?'

'Would I be doing it if it did?' I took a sip. 'Actually, it does. It hurts the way every reminder of him hurts. Living without him, though ... that's what really bothers me.'

I leaned back and laughed.

'I suppose you think this is funny,' I said. 'Or at least mildly amusing. Here you are, wanting to do something very controlled, very logical, a *project*. And you have to deal with me, the melo-dramatic widow.'

'I don't think it's funny,' he said. 'Though I must admit, when I went to see you I never expected you to chew me out in your bathrobe.'

I stared down into my glass. 'It's so strange,' I said, 'but since Bill's died I feel like I'm becoming the very woman, the very mother, I swore I'd never become. People I talk to – my sweet Indian neighbour who lives below me and watches Curran sometimes, the other teachers in my form – keep telling me how strong I am, how well I'm coping. But I'm not. I'm dangerous. Because grief is essentially selfish. Grief is essentially hunger.

'God, the person I swore I'd never be, the things I swore I'd never do! Every day I'm amazed at the soap-opera actress who's me. I find myself getting maudlin. Of course I'm allowed to, but … I find a sweater of his draped across a chair and I cry. I set out three plates instead of two. All that Monday-night-movie shit.

'Bill was my anchor. My friends used to tease me; they said I was emotionally dependent, but I could never explain to them just how Bill made me feel. He was a man who inspired light-ness, who made you feel as if whatever badness you had in you was purged. Whatever wrong you'd done or had done to you was forgotten, forgiven.'

Jascha watched me with a pensive look, mentally recording every detail while maintaining the kind, probing gaze of a psychoanalyst – *go on, continue, yes, of course, every nuance is relevant, every thought matters.*

I set down my glass. 'Well, this isn't helping us to choose paintings, is it?' I said.

'No,' he said. 'Look, maybe we'd better call it a night. We can finish another time.'

I checked my watch. 'You're right. I ought to get home to my son.'

I slid down from the table and smoothed my skirt.

'You do understand,' I said, 'that despite what I told you, Bill was not a saint?'

'Yes,' he said. 'I do.'

'So there really is going to be an exhibition, Mum,' Curran said as he crawled into bed. 'Can I go to it?'

'I don't think so,' I said, and sat beside him.

'Why not?'

'Oh, it'll be boring.'

'How do you know?'

'I've been to shows before. They're just a bunch
of people standing around drinking wine and acting
like they're smarter than they are.'

'I don't care.'

'We'll see,' I said. 'At the rate the plans are
progressing, you'll be twenty before the exhibition
opens.'

He lay back on the pillows, face soft and perfect
with satisfaction. 'Then I can go and drink the wine
no matter what you say,' he said.

I laughed, and held out my arms to him. 'I love
you,' I said, and breathed in his scent of talcum
and freshly washed hair that sent splinters into
my heart.

'I love you, too,' he mumbled. I closed my eyes
and felt him quiver in my embrace. He's one-half
Bill, I thought; he could *be* Bill, in that twisted logic
– the logic of atoms—

'Mum,' he said, 'please turn out the light.'

I let go of him and sat up. Lately I'd sensed in
myself a desperation, a clinging desire driving me,
and in him an impatience, a sullen silence born of
anger. Most of the time I played strong and he played
well-behaved, but who knew, who knew?

I reached to switch off the lamp. I glimpsed my

hand – a mother's hand, a madwoman's hand – and it scared me. 'Sweet dreams,' I said. The words tasted like gravel.

chapter six

After I heard the story of Adrienne's death, I began to have nightmares about her. I saw her hand fly up in protest, and her eyes widen with terror as her neck snapped like a doll's. Sometimes it would be me in the car, driving towards my death. I'd wake just before the awful metallic sound of the crash, my nightgown drenched with sweat, my breath a pronounced rasp. Still delirious and drowsy, I'd climb out of bed, stumble towards my parents' room, and wrench open the door.

Incredibly enough, it was my mother who crawled from the sheets and came to me, glimpsing my mute three a.m. anguish. Night softened her. She didn't complain about being awakened, but instead put her strong, bony hands on my shoulders and led me back to my room. 'It was only a dream,' she said over and over, her voice hypnotic, as I lay on my back on the mattress and gripped her warm fingers and stared at her calm face, thinking, *I am not Adrienne.*

But in the hours of daylight I wondered. What about what my father had said at the dinner table that one night? If my mother could have the atoms of Albert Einstein in her body, couldn't I have those of Adrienne? Wouldn't that answer the question of why my father indulged my mother as if she were an insolent child, and why he saw me as his brilliant adult confidante? Wouldn't it explain why he gazed at me with a look of such sad, pitiable yearning?

Saturday afternoons I spent curled up on the sofa with one of his textbooks, in search of answers. I marvelled at the pictures of mushroom clouds and electron configuration diagrams, trying to pronounce the words. *Valence, cation, nucleotide.*

'You think that stuff's terrific, don't you?' my mother yelled over the din of pots and pans as she started supper in the kitchen. 'Give yourself time. Then you'll see that being erudite won't get you anywhere in this world. Good God,' she muttered, 'it's hard enough having an academic for a husband, but to have one as a daughter ...'

Much as I loved what I read in books, I didn't like school. It was a huge, daunting place, with spiderweb hallways and too many scents of other people, too much noise and grime. Up until the point I entered school I had been used to an encapsulated universe of tasteful wallpaper and Mozart and debated aesthetics, an intimate universe in which I had to deal with the idiosyncrasies of just two people. Suddenly I was thrust into a huge maze with five hundred other children from more rural, less pretentious surrounding neighbourhoods who weren't like me, and not only was I expected to endure this bewildering injustice, I was also supposed to enjoy the mass herdings from classroom to cafeteria, then back again.

I resented the teachers who assumed that all children were bright-but-dumb, cheeky souls whose lives had no complexities, to be pacified by rewards of smiley faces drawn on papers and stamps on hands, to be reprimanded by a simple time-out or, in more extreme cases, a walk up the hall to the principal's office for a swat. I hated the other kids' squabbles, their stupid contests as to which homeroom lined up for lunch the straightest and quietest, thereby earning extra recess time.

Most of all, I hated the other girls in my class, whom I looked at with the same mixture of fear and longing as I did my mother. They had perky names like Becki or Mindi, little monikers with precious spellings, and wore anklets adorned by ruffles and roses and barrettes with streamers. They carried pink zippered pencil cases and monogrammed bookbags. They sat in the front row and did their work well enough to make the teachers happy, but not with such zealous perfection that they risked ostracism. They were full-lipped, saucer-eyed girls who talked incessantly of being fashion designers, interior decorators, models. They gushed. They shrieked. They traded cupcakes at lunch and braided each other's hair, exuding a pouty, flirtatious sensuality on the edge of innocence. They were flighty, but they were good girls, secure and complacent in their little circles, and I ached for their kind of careless, happy alliance.

However, a thick veil, an integument invisible to me but apparent to everyone else, separated me from them. Perhaps it was my reticence. Perhaps it was the fervour with which I threw myself into my schoolwork, as if the manipulation of numbers and the stringing together of sentences were wars won only by gold stars and excellent report cards. No matter what the reason, I was alone.

My parents argued frequently about me.

'She's gifted, Caroline,' my father said. 'She's lonely and starved for intellectual contact.'

'She's a child, for Christ's sake!' my mother said. 'I won't have her turned into a little pedant. She needs to learn that the world can be cruel to intellectuals.'

'I think we should put her into private school.'

'No.'

'We've got the money.'

'It's not an issue of money or affluence or whatever you want to make it. The fact is, she's a sensitive kid and she needs to toughen up. She needs to face facts.' Something in her voice told me she wasn't ready to face the facts of her own life.

But my mother won. So I went to school and listened to the good girls giggle and I read *The History of the Atom* on the playground and came home in tears. My father would gather me into his arms and stroke my hair and whisper, 'Shh, shh, angel, you've just got to bear it, but remember that you're better than them.'

He told me that I shouldn't waste my time on such imbeciles, and so we remained apart, the good girls and I, the studious one with the long, dark hair who spent her days huddled over her desk.

71

In a way it was a relief not to have to talk to anyone.

Cloying, affectionate, my father was the one who turned to me, but my mother was the person to whom I wished to turn. I feared her, that was true, but my fear was laced with a potent idolatry. She was a mulberry-and-mauve floral goddess, a Laura Ashley-clad amazon, and I desperately wanted to be close to her. Sometimes when she gave lessons, I peeked through a crack in the door and watched the tantalizing motion of her wrist as she moved the bow across the strings, and a wild fluttering resonated deep inside my chest.

I wanted to tell her to join the biggest, most famous orchestra there was. I wanted to put my arms around her neck and smell her scent of talcum powder and rosin and cologne. I wanted to run my fingers beneath her jaw and feel the angry pulse that throbbed there, but I could never get close enough, and I never dared try.

My mother's attention was a rare gift when it happened. Every once in a while she'd cancel her Saturday appointments and decide we needed an afternoon out. She'd tie a gauze scarf in her hair, grab her credit cards, and we'd drive to another small town, about an hour away from ours, whose livelihood revolved around a massive, Colonial-style complex of a department store and gallery and French restaurant. She'd turn on classical radio on the way over, and we'd have contests to see who could guess the composer of the piece first – 'Debussy, no, Bartók, wait, Liszt!' we'd shout before the throaty-voiced announcer would spit out the title of the work.

Before punk came along, I never had the obsessive concern with clothes my mother did – even as an adult I was happy to live in a few simple black dresses – but on those afternoons I was so enraptured with the fact that she had devoted her whole day to me that I let her drag me by the wrist from rack to rack without comment. Much as she scoffed at 'slaves of fashion', in a neatly divided world of departments and price tags she was in her element, the stylized opposite of my father and me, flourish and flair masking her anguished bitterness as she laughed and smiled and made a fool of herself. 'What do you think? Is it me?' She'd bat her eyelashes comically, after she'd plunked a chartreuse wide-brimmed hat on her head and tossed a leopard-print cape around her shoulders.

I'd giggle as the grey-haired salesladies stared at us in horror.

She'd try on delicate sundresses that made her look like an eighteen-year-old, and black evening gowns with heavy gold collars ('I look like fucking Nefertiti, don't I?' she'd whisper with glee), and then we'd go up to the children's section. 'Do you like this?' she'd ask. 'And this?' Everything I showed the slightest flicker of interest towards she'd sling over her arm, and we'd barrel into a fitting room with about ten garments over the limit.

The closest I ever came to my mother was in those locked cubicles with no space in which to turn. She didn't nag me for wadding a skirt in a heap or chastise me for fumbling with buttons the way she would have at home, and she didn't insist on critiquing how the outfit hung on me or how I had the frame of a matchstick. She'd just lean against the wall with her arms crossed, watching me out of the corner of her eye, her head turned and her expression wistful.

If I struggled with the straps on a pinafore or wrestled the zipper on a dress, she'd kneel behind me and help with slow, careful fingers, and then she'd lean her chin on my shoulder and stare at our reflections in the mirror. 'You know, there are people in this world who would kill for your bone structure,' she'd say, and I would feel hopelessly happy.

Then we'd go get our purchase rung up; she'd shove her card across the counter at the cashier and make some remark like, 'My husband'll kill me for this one,' though we knew he wouldn't. Navy-and-gold plastic bags swinging in our hands, we'd run breathlessly across the street for lunch at a place that had an amazing dessert cart and required an extensive knowledge of fork etiquette. She'd order a few glasses of burgundy, enough to make her face flush, and every few minutes she'd reach over the table and squeeze my hand and say, 'We should do this more often, huh?'

On the way home a cozy silence would envelop us. I'd rest my cheek against the windowpane and watch townhouses, Amish farms, identical neighbourhoods slide by. She kept her gaze on the road, but there was a looseness, a sloppy calm around her which probably came from alcohol but which I attributed to contentment.

When we'd pull into the driveway, she'd stop the car, move across the seat, and draw me into her arms. 'You had a good time today?' Her voice would be numb, brittle. 'Yeah?'

I'd nod, head buried in the folds of her blazer.

'You love me? Do you?'

Her hand would nervously stroke my back as if it were disconnected from the rest of her body. I'd nod again.

She'd let go, move away, ready to grasp the door handle. She'd chew her lip. She'd say, 'OK.'

After that we'd go inside and dart up the stairs before my father could glimpse what we got – 'It's a *surprise*,' we'd say in histrionic whispers – and spread all we got out on her bed. The room was enshrouded in the dim, comforting glow of early evening and the lights of her vanity mirror, and shadows flickered on the wall from the headlights of cars that turned in the cul-de-sac outside. I'd put on the new dress or skirt or sweater, and she'd French-braid my hair and let me put on her lipstick. We didn't laugh or talk or even look at each other.

When she was done making me look like I was twenty, she'd turn me around and stare into my face. She'd rest her hand against my cheek, and her eyes would blink very fast. 'You're just like your father,' she'd say, not with admiration or distaste, but with simple regret, as if she knew that that fact was capable of making me do something sad.

She'd smile, then, and I'd smile back, and then we'd go back downstairs, her palms on my shoulders, and I'd turn before my father in the new outfit. He'd gush his approval, and I'd keep it on all through dinner. Even when the tension came between them, I was still too happy to sense it. I wanted those evenings to go on forever.

chapter seven

❧ 'Sometimes I'm amazed that the world still
 turns,' I said to Jascha one night. We sat in
the chip shop across the street from the studio. We'd
decided to eat supper before we tackled more of the
slides. 'I know that sounds solipsistic, but ... There
was an idea very popular in the Middle Ages called
the correspondence theory, and what it basically said
was that one man's agony could send the universe
into a tailspin. You see it in Shakespeare a lot, and
I've talked to my classes about it, but I never truly
understood its appeal until now. Because to me, a
world without Bill should spin out of control. I want
floods. I want fires. I want earthquakes.'

Munching on haddock, he gazed across the table
at me with the same expression of alarmed curiosity
I often saw on my son's face.

'I feel terrible thinking like that,' I said, 'but I can't

help it. I walk home from work and see lights aglow in windows, and I want to scream. I imagine a million couples kissing and talking and eating tandoori in a million warm rooms above my head, and I seethe.'

I looked out the window. A small girl of about seventeen walked past on the street. She had short, scraggly blonde hair and wore a big beige coat. As she passed, she gazed at us wistfully. She must have thought we were lovers.

'I think one of the worst aspects of Bill's death,' I said, 'is that I have to face up to the nature of my love for him, the nature of our relationship when he was alive. I used to think that it was pure, the only thing of real purity in my life. To Bill, I wasn't odd or a rebel or antisocial, all those labels I'd worn before I met him.'

'Isn't that what love is about? Lack of pretences?'

'To me it is,' I said. 'But I can't escape this nagging feeling of . . . having used him. Of giving so little and taking so much. There was a time last fall when he came down with an infection – his immune system was weak from the drugs – and a bad fever. Not nearly as bad as the last one, but awful enough to land him in the hospital and make mortality cross my mind. He lay drenched with sweat. He twitched.

He thrashed, and I held his hand. It was like pinching the string of a balloon in two fingers while it bobs wildly in the wind. Do you know what I said to him? I said, "You sure as hell better not die on me, honey, because if you do I'll go even crazier than I am now." Oh, I meant it as a joke, and he took it as one. Laughed in the midst of his fire. But to think that I didn't offer words of comfort, words of reassurance – that I was too worried about how I'd go on if he left me ...'

'That was a legitimate worry.'

'You sound like him,' I said. 'Always humouring me. "Oh, no, love, nothing wrong with that, burn the house down if it'll make you feel better."'

'Damn right I'm humouring you. If I don't, there won't be a retrospective.'

I laughed. 'You have no fear of telling it like it is, do you?'

'I see no reason to tell it otherwise.'

I toyed with a chip on my plate. 'And then there was the matter of Australia,' I said. 'As long as I could remember, Bill had been attracted to aboriginal culture, the whole Dreamtime concept. For years he fantasized about going into the bush. We seriously considered a trip, but we had Curran and not much money. When he was in the hospital last fall, when there was some question as to whether or not he'd come out, I told him, "Bill, you make it through this, and I'll take you to Australia, I promise."

'Well, he made it, but we never went. It would've been a stupid move on our part, anyway; what if he got sick while we were there? But I never tried. Never looked into the cost of plane tickets, or an itinerary. Almost nine years he held me together, and I couldn't even call a damn travel agent about a vacation in Australia.'

'I think you're beating yourself over the head for crimes you didn't commit,' Jascha said.

'Of course I am,' I said. 'This guilt over a spoken sentence and a broken promise is stupid. A soothing word or a trip wouldn't have saved him. But after he's gone ...'

I sighed.

'I don't know how to explain Bill and me,' I said. 'I don't know if language exists to explain us.' With him I had a feeling of absolute *knowing*. Not the cliché of lovers-as-one who finish each other's sentences, but the sensation that Bill's gestures exploded from my hands, that I'd stepped into his body as easily as I'd walk through a rice curtain. He was my elixir, my addiction. I knew it was perverse to think of the man I loved as a drug, but it was true. He sang in my bloodstream. He touched me, and I was lulled. He coaxed the words onto my silent tongue. You get loved like that, and you're bound to become selfish. You're bound to wonder how you'll survive when that love's gone.

Jascha leaned forward, napkin in hand. 'Hold still,' he said. 'You've got ketchup on the side of your mouth. Let me get it.'

His thumb brushed my cheek. Under the table, I dug my fingernails into my palms. I clenched my teeth so I wouldn't cry out. I knew it was silly, that he wasn't Bill no matter how gentle his fingers were, but still my shell-shocked body pined for hands to slide down my arms and awaken me with their firm touch.

He said, 'Let's get back to work, shall we?'

We walked across the street and settled into our dim, musty room. I took off my shoes and sat on the couch with my knees drawn up and my arms encircling them, my skirt spread around me. My stomach churned with dread as Jascha joined me, as slide by slide we advanced out of the bright, carefree years and into the last few months of my husband's life.

'The next painting is incredible,' he said. 'It's the best piece of his I've seen.'

Noticing the date of completion scrawled in the lower right corner of the slide, I gasped. 'He never showed me this.'

On the screen, dark, murky colours reminiscent of Munch glared at us. In the foreground of the painting gnarled, sinister black hands pulled Bill down into a greenish-brown grave as his mouth contorted into a scream. On the far left stood Curran and I, dressed in black. I glowered, shoulders hunched, my too-red lips drawn back in a possessive snarl as I clutched Curran to me, my too-long fingernails grazing his small waist. He ducked his head against my shoulder in the hope of escape, but with my free hand I kept his face turned towards the horror, ignoring his eyes glazed with fright.

'Oh, God, Bill,' I said.

'Not a very flattering portrait, is it?' Jascha asked.

'No,' I said, 'but it might be a true one if I'm not careful.'

'What do you mean?'

'I've seen grief flatten a marriage,' I said. 'I've seen

it subvert the way a parent looks at his child. I don't want that to happen to me as a mother. I can't let it happen.'

He gestured towards the painting. 'Why portray you like this, then?'

'There's always the desire,' I said.

'What desire?'

'To chicken out. To give up that creed every mother follows, the one that says, Be strong, be strong at any cost. Put your son's needs and your son's pain ahead of your own, even if your own threatens to swallow you. Find his mittens for him, cook him his favourite supper, help him with his homework, when what you really want is to drop to your knees and bawl.'

'Are you afraid you'll chicken out?'

'Terribly. I always have been.'

'Did Bill realize that?'

'Until I saw this painting, I didn't think so,' I said. 'He was so oblivious, you know? Oblivious to a fault. He slept through thunderstorms, while I lay there in the dark and watched the curtains billow, the lightning flash.

'Right after Curran was born, I'd burst into tears all the time. Bill would sit beside me and stroke my back. "What's wrong, love?" he'd ask, and I'd say, "Nothing ... now." He'd laugh. "Well, then, what have you got to cry about?" That's how he was. Cheerful. Naïve. Forgetting that light throws shadows. I could never make him understand that it was the future I wept for, the wrong things that could happen later.'

'But he saw the future, what could happen, and painted it here.'

'Yes,' I said softly. 'Yes, he did.'

'Gloria, do you mind if we use this? Would it bother you?'

'No,' I said. 'Go ahead.'

'You're sure?'

'I'm sure.'

'Let me check the title on it,' he said, and leaned over to skim his list. 'Here we go. *Necessary Madness.*'

'*Necessary Madness*,' I repeated.

'Yeah. I wonder what that's supposed to mean.'

'Self-preservation,' I said. 'When you're drowning, you'll clutch anything. Because you have to. You have no other choice.'

'Even if it's madness?' he asked. 'Even if your very effort to survive might make you lose your grip?'

'Even then.'

By the time I got home it was ten o'clock. I found Mrs Romdourl on the living-room sofa, reading in the lamplight.

'He went to bed about half an hour ago,' she said.

'How was he?'

'Fine.'

'Did he do his homework?'

'Without my even asking.'

I took a ten-pound note from my purse and handed it to her.

'Oh, no,' she said. 'I can't take this. Save it for yourself.'

'Don't argue with me, Deepa,' I said. 'You give far too much of your time to me to go unrewarded.'

She smiled and patted my arm, then left. I slipped into Curran's room and sat beside him on the bed. He slept on his stomach, one elbow and one knee hanging off the mattress's edge, breath sticky. In the glow of the night-light shaped like a sailboat, I gazed at him and remembered myself as a twenty-three-year-old who had just been handed seven pounds of new life wrapped in a blue blanket dotted with bunnies, who had cradled his skull in her cupped palms, stared into his primitive, sapphire-coloured eyes, and shaken with the burden. I remembered Bill, who'd sat beside me on the bed, his arm around both of us. Euphoria and amazement captured his face when Curran gripped his finger. 'Wow, oh, *wow*,' he'd said.

And we had given him his own name. No litanies for the dead. No entrapment the way I had been trapped, not even out of reverence.

Now I watched my son's translucent eyelids flutter, and heard him sigh in sleep. Gently I turned his wrist over and ran my fingertip down his milky-blue, unblemished vein. How easy it would be to furrow his pale, downy brows with confusion, to feed him my agony disguised as sugary icing, to seduce him into rebellion.

chapter eight

When I exploded into adolescence, I felt like a walking bomb, a tangled mess of too-long arms and legs and stark hungers. The idea of having a catty legion of friends to gossip and fight and try on eyeshadow at drugstore make-up counters with struck me as anathema to my whole being. When I walked through the halls at school with my hair raked into a hurried top-knot and with a leather knapsack stuffed full of compulsively neat notes slung over one shoulder, lost in the labyrinth of varsity sports banners and locker-openers' chatter, I was convinced that I'd been tattooed with a million epithets of difference, their indelible marks glistening, stamped on my skin: *dark, weird, crazy*. I was bones when the universe demanded flesh; black turtlenecks and ripped jeans when the watchwords were soft sweaters and vivid skirts, shakily cerebral in the face of the comfortably visceral.

My father said, 'Don't worry about it, love. You're ahead of your time. You're perceptive.'

My mother said, 'Why don't you join Student Council?'

He got me through Honours geometry with an A; she invited bubbly, vacuous girls to sleep over in an attempt to get me a social life. Those terrible evenings, I cringed at the sound of the doorbell, while she glided in a classy column dress and pumps across the polished wood floor of the foyer to let in bitch after bitch who squealed with amazement at how huge our house was and ran up and down the spiral staircase all night, making microwave popcorn and bouncing on the guest bed. Under the guise of brushing my teeth, I'd lock myself in the bathroom and listen to them argue over who was the hottest guy in British Literature class while I stared at my pale face and longed to smash the mirror.

After the next day's breakfast, though, it would all be over, their slouch socks and nightshirts and overnight bags picked up off my bedroom floor, their cereal bowls cleared from the sink. My mother would swish smugly around the kitchen and hum, pleased with herself for being such an attentive mother. 'Wasn't that fun?' she'd ask.

'That was a farce,' I'd say, 'and you know it.'

Her face would crumple, and before she could protest I'd storm down the hall. My father's study would be cloaked with the golden glow of a Sunday morning. He'd look up from his desk, motion all five feet eight inches of me onto the edge of his chair, and slip his arm around me. 'So have the banshees left us?'

'Hopefully forever,' I said with a laugh. 'No more comparative studies of every high school male within a fifty-mile radius.'

He smiled. 'And who was deemed most worthy in your opinion?'

I leaned my head against his shoulder. He stroked back a lock of my hair. I could feel him breathing. The loneliness fell from me easily as water. 'None of them,' I said.

When I was fourteen, punk came out. Suddenly subversion was validated. I bought the boots, the chains, the rags. I painted my fingernails black and cut my hair and dyed it so that in the light it glimmered purple. I joined the school radio station, headed by

anarchists, and during our meetings in the lecture
room after class, we'd sit on tables and make out
playlists while listening to the Clash, agonizing over
the need for revolt, and discussing how one could tell
a person's political affiliation by the colour shoelaces
he wore in his Doc Martens. We threw basement
parties which lasted until all hours.

Amazingly, throughout this I still managed to keep
a perfect grade-point average. After station meetings,
I'd get one of the members who had a car to drop
me off at my father's college, and I'd do research
for history papers in the library until his final class
of the day let out. He'd find me seated on a couch
with my black leather feet propped on a glass table,
my face buried behind a *Rolling Stone* or *Newsweek* once
I had finished my academic reading.

Then we'd drive downtown to an Italian restaurant
we liked, which had teal-coloured walls and fresh
flowers on each table. As she handed us our plates
of linguine with shrimp marinara, the waitress would
stare at us, the grey-haired father with a Shetland
wool cardigan draped around his shoulders and the
sullen daughter in the garish plaid skirt and fishnet
stockings. While I devoured a slice of rum cake,
my father would stroke my free hand and tell me

stories about his colleague's pregnant sixteen-year-old daughter. 'You know that I'll support you no matter what decisions you make,' he said, his pale, gentle eyes daring me to do something bad.

Every time I stayed out late, he met me at the door and led me upstairs, arm slung around my shoulders, finger against my lips to silence my thick-tongued laughter. He sat on my bedroom carpet and helped me with my Latin homework at two a.m. When I got drunk, his soft hands held my skull steady over the bathroom sink as I retched, and when my knees wobbled down onto the tile, he picked me up and carried me into bed, pulling back the sheets with one hand and laying me on the mattress.

'I'll tell your mother it was something you ate,' he said. I nodded, my throat still in burn from the vodka, the lyrics to 'Anarchy in the UK' floating through my brain as fitfully I dreamed of England. He bowed his head, folded my fingers over, and pressed my knuckles to his mouth. I knew he was thinking of Adrienne.

My junior year I started going out with Mike, a senior and fellow radio station member, who wore a studded leather jacket and had spiky, bleached hair.

He had been kicked out of three private schools, and lived down the street from me, in a lovely old Victorian house. Unlike me, however, he had sweet, unassuming parents.

One night in December, I walked over to visit him when his family was out shopping. We sat on the green camelback sofa in his living room. I stared at the candles on the Christmas tree, and their soft light stirred in me a thousand apologies, a longing for home. He lit a cigarette, took a drag, and passed it to me. I inhaled and tried not to cry.

'You're lucky,' I said. 'Six more months and you'll be out of here.'

'Not if I don't pass Advanced Comp.'

'Well, if you aren't so fucking stubborn and let me proofread for you, maybe you will.'

He laughed. Turned my chin to face him. 'You're a madwoman,' he said.

I moved closer so that my knees touched his. I put my hands on his shoulders and dug my fingernails into his neck. 'Mike,' I said softly. 'I'm scared of myself.'

'You shouldn't be,' he said, and pressed his mouth to mine. By some voracious reflex, I slid back and unbuttoned my skirt. We dropped to the floor. My spine stung as I hit the rug. I grabbed fistfuls of his shirt. His zipper rasped against my bare skin. I bit my lip. Tasted blood. His face swam above my head as he shoved himself inside me.

Afterwards, he leaned down and kissed me roughly on the neck. I rose and put my clothes back on, and then we stood at the kitchen counter and ate his mother's Russian tea cookies as if it had been nothing, numb, defiant.

That night I walked home with my black wool duster coat clutched around me. The sidewalk and the road shone with a dusting of snow, and lights glowed in each house I passed. I thought again of Adrienne, Adrienne who in her white beret had glistened on the quad at Oxford on a night like this. I balled my fingers into fists. I'm not her, I told myself. I'm not that pure, intellectual darling.

I let myself into the house and made it halfway up the stairs when I heard my father call. 'Gloria? Is that you?'

'Yeah, Dad.' Sighing, I came back down and stood in the doorway of his study. 'I'm home.'

He set aside his stack of chem labs. 'I was worried,' he said. 'I didn't know where you were.'

'I'm sorry. I just went down to Mike's.'

'You didn't tell me.'

'I told Mom. She was in the middle of a lesson, so she probably forgot. She said it was OK as long as I came back by ten.'

'But I didn't know.'

'For Christ's sake, Dad. I said I was sorry! At sixteen you don't think I have the autonomy to walk a block away from you? Or is it fine to run off if it's our little secret, but if my mother's involved, forget it?'

He motioned me inside. I sat beside him and rested my head on my arms on his desk. I felt sticky, wrung-out. 'What's wrong, love?' he asked.

He reached out and gently stroked my hair. It was such a simple action, but it felt more painful than thrashing to the floor with Mike had.

I said, 'I don't know.'

One night that winter, Mike dropped me off and, warm with liquor, I stumbled up the slick, icy front walk. Fashionable though they were, my combat boots had miserable traction, and I fell flat on my face on the porch. I crawled on my hands and knees to the door, grabbed the knob to pull myself up, and fumbled for my house key. It wasn't there. I rang the bell. My mother answered, her floral silk robe wrinkled, her hair rumpled for once.

'Get in here,' she said. 'Now.'

I stepped inside and slumped to the floor.

'You're drunk,' she said. 'You're rip-roaring drunk, aren't you?'

'Of course not, Mommy,' I slurred. 'I've got complete and utter control of my mental faculties, can't you see that?'

She grabbed my wrist and dragged me to my feet.

'Look at yourself,' she said.

I stared down. Blood from a gash on my chin dripped onto my Sex Pistols T-shirt and the black turtleneck I wore under it. My nylons had ripped, and the skin was torn on both my knees.

'Come on,' she said, and led me into the bathroom. 'It is two-thirty in the morning, two-thirty in the fucking morning, Gloria Merchant, and I really don't appreciate this.'

She sat me down on the toilet seat and rummaged through the medicine cabinet. 'We might as well start with your chin. Jesus. How'd you do this to yourself?'

'Fell,' I mumbled. I leaned back against the wall and closed my eyes.

'Don't fall asleep on me, damn it.' She held my head still as she bandaged my chin. 'You'll live, but not without a scar, I'll bet.'

She knelt down and dabbed my knees. I winced at the peroxide's sting. 'Yes, I know it hurts,' she said, 'but maybe you ought to think about that next time before you try to down the whole bottle, hmm?'

I nodded.

'Revolt.' She stood and put the peroxide and the box of bandages back in the cabinet, slamming the door. 'I never had a chance for any goddamned revolt.'

I staggered to my feet. She shoved me back down and put her hands on my shoulders. 'Wait. I'm not done with you yet,' she said.

I stared up into her blurry face.

'Listen,' she said, 'your father may let you get away with this shit, but I won't. You are too intelligent to do this to yourself. I don't ever, ever want to see you like this again. Do you hear me?'

'Yes,' I whispered.

'You can whine at me all you like about my being the bitch of all bitches, but that won't change the fact that I love you and won't let you wreck your life.'

She hauled me up. 'Now I want you to get upstairs and go to bed.'

She went into the kitchen for a glass of water, and I crept into my father's study. I turned on the banker's lamp, went to the bookshelf, and took down the B volume of the encyclopedia. I turned to the page with Robert Browning, and there Adrienne lay, smiling softly at me. 'You idiot,' I said. 'You didn't have to drive to Manchester for the weekend. You could have stayed with him.'

I laid the book down and searched through the desk drawer for a pair of scissors. When I found them, I sat cross-legged on the floor with the photograph and hacked away at Adrienne until she was a mess of black-and-white strips.

'Gloria,' my mother said from the doorway, 'what the hell are you doing? I told you to get to bed.'

She came inside and sat before me.

'Sweetheart,' she said, 'why are you crying?'

I looked up. My mouth twisted with sobs. Salt spilled down my cheeks.

'Oh, God,' I said. 'He'll kill me. I've got to put it back together.'

With one arm she pulled me against her and kissed

my forehead. 'I'll help you,' she said. We sat there on the floor for an hour, silent, our hands touching as we used up a whole roll of Scotch tape repairing his idol.

chapter nine

One Friday night I stood at the stove, stirring a pot of stew, watching the potatoes and carrots as they swirled to the motion of my wrist, and I thought: I have kept my promise. I am neither a Riordan nor a Caroline. I respect my son's youth. I iron my blouses, but don't mind if they wrinkle. I wear mascara, but don't hyperventilate if it runs. I experience loss, but I still function.

I hummed as I set out two bowls, two spoons, and two napkins. In the living room, Curran laughed at some banal show on television. *You hear that?* I asked myself. That soft, sweet, high-pitched laughter of a child? He is yours, but he is not you. He is intelligent and inquisitive, but he does not read chemistry text-books or come home in tears. Of course he's grieving, inside he aches, but he will be fine, and you have done well, do you hear? You have done well ...

I returned to the stove and gave the stew a final stir. Too hard, I realized, because the next thing I knew, the pot tipped and clattered to the floor, drenching me and the linoleum, and it was Friday night in the city I'd grown to love, and the flat was swollen with warmth, and Bill was not in my arms.

'Curran!' I screamed. 'Curran, help me!'

He rushed into the kitchen. He put out his hand to stop me, but I skidded to the floor, slamming my back against the oven. Pain knocked the breath from me. I sat there, stunned, soaked amongst vegetables, and began to cry. I put my hands over my face as the sobs ripped me.

'Mum? Are you OK?'

I lifted my head. Bit my lip. Reached out my hands. 'Come here, baby,' I whispered. He knelt beside me. I saw stains from the splattered broth on his jeans when he shifted, and they made me cry harder.

'Don't worry,' he said. 'I can help you clean it up.'

'No, no, you don't have to, angel,' I said. 'Just hold me. Please, please, please just hold me.'

He put his arms, his tiny little arms, around me. 'Tighter,' I whispered. He hugged me so hard my ribs hurt. He kissed my burning forehead.

'Mum, I'm hungry,' he said.

'I know you are, sweetheart,' I said. Snot trickled from my nose down to my mouth. On the television, an audience roared with laughter.

I closed my eyes and sent silent messages to my son: your chromosomes are one-half composed of the penchants and desires and scents and hopes and superstitions of your father, the man I shared a bed with, but you are not him. And I won't expect you to be. I'll never hurt you. And I said that, 'I'll never hurt you,' into his ear, on the kitchen floor, over and over, as if repeating the words like a mantra would keep me from doing it, from hurting him.

After a while he untangled himself from me, and as he retreated into the bathroom, I heard his footsteps and then the delicious sound of running water. He came back and sponged my flushed face with a wet washcloth. 'Thank you so much,' I said.

I was on my hands and knees, scrubbing the last splotches of stew off the floor, when the doorbell rang. Curran called, 'It's Jascha!'

'Jesus, Mary, and Leopold Bloom,' I said, and grabbed the counter to pull myself to my feet.

'Another chaotic dinner?' Jascha asked.

'You could say that,' I said. 'Seeing as I'm wearing it.'

'I just came by to get your approval on the final list of paintings,' he said, 'but why don't I take you both out?'

'Could you?' He nodded. 'You're sweet. Thanks.'

'No problem.'

'Give me a minute to change, and I'll be ready.'

I went into my bedroom and pulled on jeans and a big black sweater. In the kitchen I heard Curran ask, 'You're a sculptor? Are you really?' I glimpsed myself – red-eyed, swollen-faced – in the mirror, and scowled at the woman I realized I'd never been before.

We ate cheap sandwiches at a coffee house near the university, and then walked up and down the familiar streets from my college days: Leigh, Gower. I pointed out places to them. 'See that café? I used to waitress there.'

'I can't imagine you waiting on *anybody*,' Jascha said.

'I did, though,' I said. 'Worked illegally. Got tons of free food. Oh – that pub over there, the one with the patio on the roof, was where we all got drunk after finals.'

I thought of the pub's dimness, its chattering voices, the smell of ale on breath and skin. And me, sick of *de rigueur* nonconformity yet clinging to it like a life raft, on the far edge of belonging.

Next to Jascha and Curran, bundled in my coat, I wondered how passers-by saw us. Windblown, out for a walk in the crisp air on a cold February evening, a dark-haired couple, fashionably casual, and their solemn blond son. I jammed my hands into my pockets and pretended that it was the truth.

We took the tube back to my flat. Jascha sat in the kitchen while I put Curran to bed. He looked small and wan, propped up on his pillows. 'Tonight,' he said, 'when we went out and you showed us all the old places where you and Dad used to go, I wanted him to be with us so much that ... well, this is daft, but I imagined that Jascha was Dad — I mean, I know he's not, he's lots different, but I just thought maybe I'd feel better ...'

'I know, love.'

'The thing was, I *did*. And I felt bad then because it wasn't right. It wasn't right for me to be happy when Dad's gone and you're so sad.'

'No, Curran. Listen to me,' I said. 'It's perfectly all right. You don't have to worry about me or Dad.

If you're happy, well, you just scream out the window and tell the world that you are at two in the morning, if you feel like it.'

He giggled. 'Can I really?'

'Well, not at two in the morning. We don't want to wake Mrs Romdourl.' I leaned down and kissed him.

'You still smell of vegetables,' he said.

I went back into the kitchen and with a sigh slumped into a chair across from Jascha. 'Something tells me you're bothered by more than just the fact that tonight you dumped half of Sainsbury's fruit and veg on yourself,' he said.

'Damn it,' I said, 'why do you always insist on making me laugh when I want to cry?'

'"Excess of sorrow laughs; excess of joy weeps."'

'Blake.'

'Could you stop being the English teacher for a second?'

'What's that supposed to mean?'

'That if you'd quit analyzing every move you made and every one you contemplate, as if your life's a piece of poetry to be explicated, maybe you'd feel better.'

I stared down at my nails, I'd bitten them down to

nubs. Loneliness generates bad habits. In the past few weeks I'd begun to smoke again, something I hadn't done since I was a teenager. I gnawed my lip and the skin around my fingers until they bled. Voracious. Bill had been like that, those last few months he was still energetic. He'd come up behind me as I washed dishes, run his hands through my hair, grab great fistfuls, graze his mouth against my ear, his breath hot, as if he knew he had to get his senses full of me before the end.

'Gloria?'

'Yeah?'

'I've got the list made up if you want to see it.'

'OK.'

He slid the list across the table. I read over his selections.

'I've got no problem with what's here,' I said. 'My qualms mostly lie with your presentation.'

'There'll be no unnecessary hype. Just the necessary madnesses.'

'That wasn't funny, Jascha.'

'I know it wasn't. I'm sorry.'

I rubbed my forehead. 'When I had my little culinary disaster,' I said, 'I sort of snapped. This front I've been keeping up fell from me like the pot did off the stove. And Curran, poor thing, came in and said, "Mum, I'll help you clean it up." He sat down on the floor and held me. He put a wet rag to my bloated, fevered face and told me not to worry, when he should have been in the other room watching cartoons and waiting for me to bring his supper on a tray.

'But it's so easy to do without Bill here to ground me. It's so easy to say, "Darling, make Mummy a sandwich for supper, she feels awful right now," to say, "Come here, give me a hug, I've had a rotten day." The other night I said to him, "Curran, we *are* going to get through this, aren't we?" He looked at me and he said, "Mum, I don't know."'

'Don't you think you're blaming yourself too much? He seems pretty well-adjusted to me.'

'Sure he does. He goes to school, he plays video games with his friend who lives downstairs. Maybe he's a bit quieter, a bit more pensive lately, but he's always been that way. He just scares me ... The grief of a child is so buried. It pops up in the softest, most incongruous moments. Like tonight. As I was tucking him in, he said that he felt ashamed to be happy when I'm sad like this. Do you know what that feels like, to know that your son can't be happy because of you?'

I thought of Louise lecturing him in the kitchen after Bill's funeral: *You're the man of the house now, and you mustn't mind if your mum gets a bit mental.*

'You're his mother,' Jascha said. 'Of course he wants to help you. Of course he wants you to be happy when he is.'

'But there are too many fine lines,' I said, 'and I've never been one for tightrope-walking.'

I didn't tell him that Curran had pretended he was Bill, or that I'd walked with my fists stuffed in my pockets all night so I wouldn't reach for his hand, or that I'd wanted to simply because I didn't feel right walking the university streets, the streets of the early days with Bill, without someone's fingers laced through mine.

chapter ten

I graduated second in my high school class, which meant that I had the distinction of being the school's first purple-haired salutatorian. At commencement I gave a speech about the importance of individuality in a turbulent world. My father wept. My mother complained about the stadium's heat.

I went on to major in English at a small, liberal college in New York with a reputation for being too artsy and sexually perverse for its own good. While there, I mellowed a bit. I grew my hair and let it fade back to its natural colour. I kept my affinity for combat boots, but also developed one for long, gauzy skirts. 'I am surrounded by erudite people,' I wrote to my father. 'I even have deep conversations in cafés and coffee houses with some of them, but I still can't shake my feelings of apartness.'

My senior year, I got accepted into a foreign-exchange programme in London. My father drove up to see me before I left. He sat on the edge of my bed and watched me with a desolate look on his face while I packed jeans and heavy sweaters.

'My God,' he said, gesturing towards the textbooks and clothes and pizza delivery boxes on the floor. 'Caroline would go absolutely barmy if she saw this place.'

'Why didn't she come with you?'

'Lessons. She had lessons.'

'Right. I should've remembered her selfless dedication to scaring the shit out of poor, defenceless little fourth-graders so they'll play in tune.'

'Gloria. It's better that she's not here. That way we can talk in peace.' He grinned.

'But she could've tried. She could've given up one damn afternoon.'

The door swung open. It was Beth, my room-mate. Her cropped hair stood up in tiny green spikes, and she wore a T-shirt that said FUCK ART, LET'S KILL. My father twittered. For a moment I was embarrassed, ashamed of him, even, that gaunt, stoop-shouldered man who sat surrounded by Cure posters.

'You're leaving already?' Beth asked.

'My flight's at two.'

'Are you excited?'

I nodded. 'Beth,' I said, 'this is my father, Riordan Merchant.'

He extended his hand. 'Hello, Beth,' he said. 'I must tell you, my dear, that I've had a secret desire for hair like yours for years, but I've also a wife who'd slap me with a messy divorce if I ever tried to emulate it.'

Beth smiled. 'Well, in that case, I'd stick with the colour you've got.'

'You don't know my mother,' I said. 'Tell him to go for your hair, Beth.'

They both laughed. 'We'd best be off,' my father said.

I turned to Beth. 'I guess I'm out of here,' I said. She held out her arms, and we hugged. We hadn't been that close — we'd only been room-mates for a month — but I was seized with one of the short, intense bursts of sentimentality I always felt when faced with the kindnesses of those who I'd thought cared nothing.

'You've got to write to me and tell me all about your exploits with those British men,' Beth said.

'What's this about British men?' my father asked.

Beth giggled. 'Your father is so cute, Gloria,' she whispered in my ear. 'He looks like Anthony Hopkins. And he's charming.'

'Yeah, well, he's my father,' I said.

On the way to the airport, he and I were silent. It was only when we sat waiting for my flight to be called that the words came.

'You don't know how much I want to go along,' my father said.

'Why? To be with me or go to London?'

'Both.'

'Come with me, then.'

'I think they just announced your flight,' he said.

We stood. He had tears in his eyes as he took my hands.

'Promise you'll write me,' we said in unison.

'Owe me a beer,' I said.

He laughed. 'When Caroline's not looking, that is. But seriously, love, you will write, won't you?'

'Of course. I'll be writing you the second I'm in the air. You know that.'

'And ring me up as soon as you get the phone number to your flat.'

I nodded. 'I'd better go.'

He put his arms around me and stood there with his chin on top of my head.

'Dad,' I said, 'if you don't let go of me right now, I'm going to miss my plane.'

He drew back. 'Sorry.'

'Don't look so sad,' I said, and leaned up to kiss his hollow cheek. It was the last time I would see him alive.

I lived in a big, bare flat on Leigh Street, near the university, with three other girls: Meg, an actress who wore too much eyeliner and high heels with jeans; Sarah, a delicate mystic who played guitar and burned scented candles; and Pandora, a fellow American, with dyed red hair and a wicked laugh, who'd changed her name from Rebecca out of principle. While not at class, we lounged around playing with Ouija boards and debating Marxist versus liberal feminism. 'I'm intoxicated with the city, with its greyness,' I wrote to my father. 'As for my own ... I don't know.'

One weekend Pan suggested we go down to Chelsea and see an artists' co-op a friend of hers was in. It was a huge, minimalist place with harsh lighting and hardwood floors, but the others gushed over it as Nick, the cropped-haired friend with an earring, led them on a tour, showing them quasi-African sculptures and 'postmodernist' pottery. I sat on the windowsill in my boots and a long black dress and cardigan, shivering.

The front door swung open with a gust of leaves and night air. A man came in wearing an old field coat and a pair of loafers whose stitching was almost shot. He waved to some people who milled in the studio, gave a perfunctory nod to Pan and the girls, and sat on the floor beneath me as if he'd known me my entire life.

'Bill Burgess,' he said, and offered his hand.

'Gloria Merchant,' I said. 'You work here?'

'Yeah,' he said, stretching out his legs. 'But I try not to have pretensions about it.'

'So you're not into those "dysfunctional double boilers" or whatever Nick said those pieces of scrap metal are over there?'

He grinned. 'God, no. My paintings and I are disgustingly normal.'

I tipped my head back and laughed. 'I'm glad.'

'I take it you despise pretension, too?'

'I do ... but that doesn't mean I'm not living pretentiously.'

He gestured towards Pandora and Meg and Sarah. 'You mean in their kind of way?'

'Exactly,' I said. 'They're great girls. Terrific fun. But I'm not like them. I'm a loner, I guess.'

'By choice?' he asked.

'I don't think so,' I said. 'Although I may make my loneliness worse.'

'Nothing wrong with solitude,' he said. 'Until you find that person, the one who accepts, who understands.'

I pulled my cardigan in tighter.

'Say,' he said, 'you look cold. Want some coffee?'

He led me into a small, grungy kitchen. The fluorescent strip of light above the sink hummed. I blinked at the brightness, remembering Adrienne, seeing her again in my mind, her features terrified blossoms in the headlights. I thought of myself as a sad, pitiful girl trying too hard to be rebellious, as a child who fought to brush away her father's tears before they fell. I leaned against the counter and drank my coffee, feeling ashamed as I gazed at Bill over the rim of my mug.

'Better?' he asked.

I nodded. Set the saucer on the Formica. We reached for each other at the same time, cueless. I rested my chin on his shoulder. He ran his hand over my back. We could hear someone chiselling away at a block of marble in the studio. I closed my eyes and imagined it was me he was shaping.

After a few soft moments, we pulled apart. He didn't smile or speak. I wanted to pull him back against my flesh, breathe him into me.

'Gloria?' Meg called from the main space. 'Are you coming?'

I turned my head. 'Give me a goddamned minute, would you?' I yelled.

He laughed under his breath. Then, filled with purpose again, he pulled a piece of paper off a message pad by the phone, dug a pen from a stash in an empty coffee jar on the counter, and wrote down his number. The motion of his hand seemed to take a millennium, but the digits came out in a broad scrawl. He handed the slip of paper to me, folded my fingers over. There was no hint of smugness, or even expectation, on his face. Only pure offering.

We turned and walked back to the studio. The girls stood before me with Nick: coy Sarah in her batik dress, high-cheekboned Meg in her tunic and miniskirt, and Pan just Pan with her ripped jeans and messy hair.

'So what were you doing with Bill Burgess in the kitchen?' she chirped on the way home.

'Drinking coffee and no more,' I said. 'Get your mind out of the gutter.'

That night I went straight to my room without saying another word. I crawled into my pyjamas and into bed before anyone could entice me into a Tarot card session or an impromptu drink round. Through the wall I heard the sounds of pillows flying, shrieks, a lamp knocked over. I lay still, hollow yet satisfied. Moonlight bloomed a lush shadow on my upraised palm.

I called him a week later. I got one of his room-mates first. Then there was the sound of the television and running water and finally his voice. 'Hey,' he said. 'I was wondering when you'd ring.'

'I didn't want to bother you,' I said.

'Well, you aren't bothering me,' he said. 'Come over for dinner. It's a grotty madhouse, but one of my mates makes a dead good boil-in-the-bag curry.'

I laughed. I couldn't help it. It was his voice, that voice so casual and yet so earnest, making me buoyant.

'What?' he said. 'Have you seen a particularly amusing side of curry I haven't?'

'No,' I said. 'In fact, I love it. And I live in a grotty madhouse, too. But I wouldn't mind seeing yours.'

I went over that night. The flat was in Earl's Court, small and dark and dingier than mine. We sat in the kitchen as the curry boiled. The room was tiny and yellow, with overgrown plants hanging in the bay window and an ugly plastic cloth on the table, but as the darkness closed in around us and steam rose in the pot on the stove, a drowsy warmth surged through my veins.

'So where's the marvellous mate-who's-a-chef?' I asked.

'At the co-op.'

'Do you always kick your room-mates out when you've got a girl over?'

He laughed. 'There haven't been that many.'

'Oh, come on. A nice boy like you.'

We took our bowls of curry into the living room and sat on a ratty brown corduroy sofa. We talked about art and our futures and the subtle madnesses of our parents and the insincerity of people. Soon it was ten-thirty.

'Damn,' I said. 'I promised Sarah that tonight I'd help her study for her philosophy exam.'

We stood, and he walked me to the door and handed me my coat. I put it on. 'It's been lovely,' he said.

He reached out his arms and drew me into them. I lifted my head, and he smudged his lips across my mouth. I ran my fingers through his unkempt brown hair and darted urgent kisses along his jaw. I shrugged out of my coat and let it fall to the floor.

'I thought you had to help one of your flatmates revise,' he whispered.

'She can wait,' I said, and buried my face in his neck.

Towards morning, in a bed that wasn't mine, I woke to the sound of rain. I lay there and stared at the outline of Bill's back and thought *This is gorgeous, but it won't last long*. I wanted to lift myself up with my palms and lean over to kiss his broad, slumbering mouth, but I must have fallen back asleep before I could do it, because when I opened my eyes again he was curled beside me, shoulder pressed to mine, and the rain had grown into a full-fledged storm, the windows were rattling with thunder.

*   *   *

Those days I was stupid with happiness. On Saturdays we went to the Tate and marvelled at the Hockney paintings in the gallery, then ate seedcake in the restaurant downstairs, each time trying to find something new on the mural of Epicurania. I tried not to think about the wild, despairing timbre which coloured my father's latest letters.

'I've committed emotional manslaughter,' he wrote. 'I'm not what your mother wants, she's not what I need. What I need is gone, gone, and all I'm doing is hurting everyone else, making them into replacements for her ...'

One evening he phoned me while I was at Bill's. I took the call in the bedroom. Bill lay there and grinned at me.

'Dad,' I said. 'Hi.'

'I've been trying to reach you for days, but you've been out.'

'I've been pretty busy.'

'A girl gave me the number of where you are now when I rang your flat. Meg, she said her name was.'

'Meg. Yeah.'

'How have you been?'

'Terrific. I've got a lot of friends.'

'And your studies are brilliant as usual, I hope.'

'I wouldn't call them that, but I'm doing all right. It's tougher here.'

'I told you it would be.'

Bill sat up and leaned against my back. He toyed with my hair.

'Gloria? Are you still there?'

'I'm still here, Dad.'

'I miss you terribly.'

Bill brushed his lips against my neck.

'I miss you, too. Is Mom being her usual self?'

'Unfortunately. Friday-night dinner parties with histrionics over whether the rose-coloured candles match the mauve table-cloth. Gloria, I just don't know what I'm going to do. I ...'

While he rambled I tossed the phone into the air and caught it in my hands a few times. Bill burst out laughing. 'Shut up,' I said, and clamped my hand over his mouth. 'No, no, not you, Dad. Bill's just being incorrigible.'

'Who's Bill?'

'The artist I met in Chelsea. I told you about him. Don't you remember?'

'Oh. Yes. Bill.'

'Listen, Dad, I've really got to go,' I said. 'I'll talk to you later.'

'You were nice,' Bill said when I hung up. 'Do you always treat your own father with such callousness?'

'No,' I said. 'In fact, I've catered to him for the last twenty-one years. I think it's time I stopped.'

He smiled. 'Come here.'

Later, staring up at the ceiling, I thought: it's come full circle. Here I am, just like my mother, on my back on a bed in a dishevelled flat in Earl's Court, with a gentle, delicious-voiced man above me.

chapter eleven

When I went to pick up Curran at Deepa's after work one night, I found the usually noisy flat draped in a guarded hush. Raj, who was eight, answered the door. 'Curran's in the lounge,' he said, sombre-voiced, and jerked his thumb in my son's direction.

Curran sat on the Romdourls' tweed sofa, head in his hands. Deepa sat at his side with her arm around him. 'Your mum's here,' she said.

He looked up. His left eye was blackened.

'Please don't be mad at me,' he said.

'There was a fight at school,' Deepa whispered. 'A note from the teacher's in his bag, explaining it.'

'Come on,' I said to him. 'We'll go home and talk about this.'

Upstairs, in the kitchen, I read the note and sighed as Curran ran down the hall and slammed the door to his room. I waited until I heard the creak of the bedsprings before I went in and sat next to him. I stroked his back.

'Want to tell me what happened?'

'Why should I? You read all about it.' His words were muffled by the pillow.

'Mrs Cunningham didn't give me your side of the story.'

He lifted his head, and I winced at the sight of the dark streaks that radiated from his eye like the rays of a cruel sun. 'We were outside,' he said. 'It was almost time to come in for maths, and I was standing against the wall, talking to Raj, doing nothing to vex anyone, really. All of a sudden, Nigel Clark – he's massive, and he always teases me – ran up and grabbed hold of me and punched me in the eye. Well, Raj told me, "Ignore him, Curran, or you'll have worse trouble," but I couldn't. I just got so mad. Because it wasn't fair. It wasn't fair that Nigel could beat me up like that when I was minding my own business. So I went for his nose. I never thought there'd be so much blood ...'

The phone rang, 'Christ,' I said.

It was Jascha.

'I absolutely cannot talk right now,' I said. 'Give me half an hour.'

I went back to Curran. 'Who was that?' he asked.

'Jascha.'

'Are you going to marry him?'

I laughed. 'What a question!'

'Are you?'

'Goodness, no. We're working on the retrospective, that's all.'

'But will you get married again, ever?'

I sighed. 'Does the thought of that bother you?'

'A bit.'

'Well, I can't give you a definite yes or no,' I said, 'but if I do find someone else, I think it'll be a long time from now. OK?'

'OK.'

He flopped onto his back.

'Mum,' he said, 'are you mad at me?'

I folded my hands in my lap and stared down at them. I drew in my breath, and struggled to discern between several answers which spun through my head. No, that's what Riordan would have said. No, that's what Caroline would have said. Where were the words which were mine?

'No,' I said. 'I'm not mad at you. I think you had every right to be angry, because you're right. Life hasn't been fair lately. However, that doesn't give you an excuse to use Nigel Clark as a punching bag, even if he did hit you first. Promise me you won't get in trouble again?'

He closed his eyes, and nodded.

'That still looks pretty swollen,' I said. 'Stay here, and I'll get you some ice.'

I went back to the kitchen and called Jascha. 'What was it this time?' he asked. 'Not another collision with the stockpot, I hope.'

I told him about the incident at school.

'*Your* child did that? Tiny, quiet, unassuming Curran?'

'Yes.'

'Wow.'

'When I first heard what happened,' I said, 'I wanted to kill the little son of a bitch who gave him the black eye.'

'But you can't fight his battles for him. You can't keep him cloistered.'

'I know.'

'What made him do it? Other than the fact that some eight-year-old psychopath jumped him, I mean.'

'He said that he just got mad at the unfairness of things.'

'Poor kid.'

'He also asked me if I was going to marry you.'

Jascha chuckled. 'And your response?'

'No fucking way, sweetheart.'

'Figuratively speaking.'

'Of course. So, what did you want to talk to me about?'

'Galleries.'

'Galleries?'

'Yeah, you know,' he said, 'little places to hang works of art in . . .'

'Cut it out. What about them?'

'Targeting ones that might be interested in Bill's work.'

'And?'

'Like I said earlier, we're probably looking at the Hayward or Whitechapel. Tate's out of the question. Too big. Bill's not that established.'

'Right,' I said.

'What do you think?'

'Let's avoid the Hayward. Bill hated it. He called it a big concrete monster.'

'And Whitechapel?'

'That's very ethnic, very young, sort of East End-y, isn't it?'

'Mmm-hmm. David Hockney had his first show there, I think.'

'That sounds good,' I said. 'I've got to go. I promised Curran I'd bring him some ice.'

I wrapped two pieces in a paper towel and carried them down the hall. When I stepped into his room, I found him curled up on his side, sobbing. I sat beside him. The ice numbed my shaky hands. A lump rose in my throat, and I swallowed it down. I set the paper towel on the nightstand and gathered him into my arms. 'Go ahead and cry, love,' I whispered. 'You go right ahead.' In the faded light of early evening we sat on the bed, and I held him, the same way that, with no questions, no obligations, I had been held, in Bill's arms.

chapter twelve

One January afternoon during my exchange year in London, I got a phone call telling me that my father had gone into his study, closed the door, pointed a gun at his head, and pulled the trigger.

I went back into the living room where I'd been taking notes on the sofa, and with one swipe of my wrist knocked the books to the floor. I knelt in the middle of the room and jammed my knuckles in my mouth. In the bathroom, Pandora sang along with a Kate Bush album as she shampooed the dye into her hair, and Meg screeched, 'Christ, would you turn down the bloody music?'

The doorbell rang. It was Bill. He picked his way around the strewn papers and got down beside me. He smelled of wool and fleece, aftershave and goodness. 'Hey,' he said softly. 'Hey, love, you OK?'

I made a tiny noise deep in my throat. Wordlessly I

pushed aside his shirt collar and put my cheek right next to his warm skin. On Pan's stereo Kate Bush wailed, *Do you know what I really need? Do you know what I really need?* and there on the floor he put his arms around me. We stayed like that for I don't know how long, barely breathing.

He took me back to his flat. We had peasant supper that night, soup and thick bread. He tore the crusts off his and swished them in the bottom of his bowl. As he scooped them into his mouth, broth clung to his chin. He looked like such a child that I wanted to laugh.

Instead I burst into tears. I sobbed so hard it hurt, it felt like I'd never be content in my own body again. He drew me around the side of the table and pulled me into his lap. I pressed my face against his neck. I wanted to dive beneath his skin. He kissed the edge of my mouth. I said, 'Don't let go of me.' We sat there in the kitchen until midnight, when he carried me into his bed.

Two days later, I woke. Morning sunlight hurt my eyes. I lifted my head from the pillow and glimpsed Bill by the door.

'You're getting up,' he said.

I turned my face away from him and drew my knees to my chest beneath the quilt. 'No,' I said. I slid my tongue over my cracked lips, moistening them.

'Yes,' he said. He came into the room and stood beside me. With one hand he tossed the quilt back. I curled tighter. My teeth chattered. My calves spasmed with little shivers. I shook my head.

'Come on.' He slung his arm around my shoulders and hoisted me up. I collapsed against him as he led me around the bed. Suddenly I felt conscious of the vinegary taste of too much sleep in my mouth and the grease in my hair. 'You're going to take a shower,' he said, voice steady, 'and I'm going to make you breakfast, and then when you're awake we'll talk.'

Grip tight, he guided me into the bathroom and turned on the shower. Its spray blasted me with cold droplets through the parted curtain. Tears filled my eyes. I gazed down, fingers numbly working up the buttons on my nightgown. He put his hands on my shoulders and kissed my forehead.

'You're going to have to trust me,' he said, 'when I tell you that sometime you're going to feel like living again. Can you trust me?'

I swallowed, and nodded.

'OK,' he said. 'I'll be in the kitchen.'

I stood trembling beneath the water for an hour, face in my hands. When I got out, I grabbed Bill's robe from a hook on the door and put it on. It was a faded cranberry colour, imbued with his scent. I felt calmed as I padded into the kitchen. I sat down at the table and rested my head on my arms.

'It looks clean for once,' I said.

'That's because everyone else is at class.' Bill stood at the stove, making omelettes. He grinned. A bright yellow nimbus glowed around his features. The room was so golden and gorgeous I felt as if I might break.

'What day is it?' I asked.

'Thursday.'

'You have Advanced Life Drawing this morning, don't you?'

He nodded.

'Can you miss it?'

'I need to be here. That's all that matters.'

'But—'

'Don't worry about it, love.'

He brought a plate over, sat down across from me, and watched me eat. I hadn't realized how starved I'd been.

'Your mother called,' he said.

'Oh, Jesus.'

'She was lovely, very cordial, very businesslike. Not the virago I expected.'

'That's her. Still Miss Manners in the face of grief.'

I looked away. At the dishes in the sink, the sign penned in Bill's handwriting and taped above the counter: IF YOU GET IT OUT, PUT IT BACK. Below the order one of his room-mates had scrawled SOD OFF, NEATFREAK!

'The funeral's tomorrow,' he said.

'I know, I want to go, but—'

'It's all taken care of. Your mother wired money and I got a plane ticket. You leave at noon today.'

'But my classes – The new term's just begin-ning—'

'I talked to Meg. She can straighten it out at university. She's bringing your things over, and I'll take you to the airport.'

I sighed. 'What would I do without you?'

'I should ask the same question,' he said.

On the hour-and-a-half drive north from Baltimore later that night, I sat curled up in the front seat of my mother's car, sluggish with jet lag and newborn grief, head against the frigid windowpane. It wasn't until we passed the bright blue sign grinning WELCOME TO PENNSYLVANIA that she finally spoke.

'I found him,' she said.

She paused for a moment, then continued.

'He stayed home from work that day. Tuesday. Sure I thought it was odd, not like him at all, but I figured he'd just needed a break. You know how absolutely devoted to those scatterbrained kids he is. Was.'

She turned a corner, and in the sudden glow of a streetlamp her features gleamed. Her slender, manicured hands gripped the steering wheel. Her wedding ring shone.

'I'd gone out on an errand in the morning. Had to pick up some theory books I'd ordered from the music store. When I got back, I was in a really good mood. I guess it was the snow glistening on the ground, the way your face and your fingers get all flushed when you come in from the cold. So I went and knocked on his study door to see if maybe he wanted to go downtown for lunch. But I got no answer.'

I closed my eyes.

'There he was, on the floor. Flat on his back. His wrist splayed, the pistol beside him. Blood and brains everywhere. Like pain had melted his entire face.'

'Don't say any more, Mom.'

'I thought you'd want to hear this. I thought you'd need to know.'

'Please. Just don't talk.'

'After all, he's your father, and you two were so close, I can't see why you wouldn't—'

'Shut up!'

She clenched her jaw. In the darkness I glimpsed a spasm of nameless emotion — shock? pain? relief? — wrench its way across her face like a sharp ripple in silk. She turned again, onto our road, and I watched the elegant but ostentatious hodgepodge of houses — contemporary redwood, sprawling stone, precise neo-Colonial — slide by us. Through picture windows, bay windows, French doors, I caught sight of slender girls in fuzzy sweaters, doing their homework at expensive cherrywood tables in their brightly lit dining rooms, talking to their boyfriends in their warm custom kitchens, phone cords twined around their delicate fingers as they whispered banal love-words and lifted pale gorgeous eyes to monitor the snow's fall on their lawns.

'So is it good to be home?' my mother asked softly.

'No,' I said.

We snaked up the driveway, and with the touch of a button beside her the garage door opened, its backward-scraping motion a sort of surreal magic to my exhausted eyes. After she parked the car she just sat there. The key still in the ignition. Her profile blank.

'Thanks ... thanks for postponing things a day for me,' I said. 'I know it must've — must've been hard.'

'Don't thank me. You had to be here.'

She leaned down and rubbed her temples, features tight, then with a shuddering noise halfway between a sob and a sigh dropped her head in her hands. I thought of touching her shoulder, of the strangled cry in my own throat which, if released, might reach her, this sad, stricken other woman. But then she lifted her chin, my mother again.

'I'll have to get the rug cleaned,' she said.

As we walked back to the car after the burial the next morning, all I could think about was taking off my nylons and ending the hurt and seeing Bill again. 'Why did you wear those awful army boots?' my mother asked. 'They look awkward with a dress, and given the occasion they're disrespectful.'

'If you'd shown respect to a person who'd needed it years ago,' I said, 'there'd be no need to have this occasion.'

She bit her lip and turned her face away. Pain cramped her laugh lines, those slight wrinkles which were misnomers since I had trouble recalling her laughter. In mourning colours she looked ashen. She should have been wearing cream and mulberry and rose. I should have been in my flat studying for an exam on Virginia Woolf, Bill's head in my lap.

But we weren't.

The minute we got back to the house, I tore upstairs and out of my clothes, ripped the pins from my hair, and collapsed on my bed. I screamed into the comforter so she wouldn't hear me, and then I put on jeans and a heather-blue sweater, things I knew she'd like, and went downstairs again. The outfit made her smile as I came into the kitchen.

'Mom,' I said. 'About what I said earlier. I didn't mean to insult you.'

I couldn't explain to her how what she considered

disrespectful in me was what my father had encouraged most. I didn't dare tell her that in a mean way, an honest way, a subtle way, what I had apologized for was the truth.

'Hey, I've made stupider statements in my life, believe me,' she said. 'It's OK.'

She lit a fire in the den fireplace. I lay down in front of it, wanting to curl up and sob everything out of me until I was parched and new again, calmed by the flickering flames. I went over Woolf's dominant metaphors in my mind, analyzing them. I was on the angel whose heart gets shattered by an inkpot when Bill called.

My mother brought the phone to me; she thought I was asleep. She touched my shoulder. Her face was all glowing shadows. Its concern made me think I could love her, but part of me still cringed. I waited until after she left the room before I put the receiver to my ear.

'Hi,' he said. 'How are you doing?'

I closed my eyes. 'Talk to me,' I said, 'just talk to me.' He did. His voice was a narcotic, a protective membrane encircling me through the transatlantic wire. On my fingers I counted off the number of hours until I'd be in London.

*　　*　　*

He met me at Heathrow and took me to a Chinese restaurant in Bloomsbury, and we sat at a candlelit table adorned with wax roses. He quizzed me on *To the Lighthouse*. I kissed him and tasted the sweet-and-sour sauce on his lips. This is home, I thought. I'm never leaving here again.

After we ate, we walked up and down Gower Street in the slick, shining darkness. He laced his arm through mine. 'I want to marry you,' he said.

'I want to *be* you,' I said.

'So I take it you agree?' he asked, laughing.

'Unequivocally,' I said.

The next night I told the girls while we washed dishes. They shrieked and wrapped their arms around me.

'What, no ring yet?' Meg asked.

'Go easy on him, he's a starving artist,' said Sarah.

'Next time, I'd marry for money, though.'

'Shut up, Meg,' I said. 'There isn't going to be a next time.'

'Have you picked a date?' Sarah asked. 'Have you made any plans?'

'I've only been engaged for twenty-four hours,' I

said. 'Give me a break. Although I definitely know I'll be recruiting you wild women as bridesmaids.'

'I'm sure as hell not going to wear anything flouncy and pink!' This from Pan by the drying rack.

'Very funny,' I said, and threw a dishtowel at her.

Eliciting a positive response from my mother wasn't as easy.

'You've known him two months and you want to marry him?' she asked.

'Yes.'

'Don't you think that's rushing things?'

'For some people. Not for me.'

'You sound like you're being impulsive.'

'So were you.'

On her end of the line there was silence.

'How long did you know Dad when you got engaged?'

'Three months.'

'I rest my case.'

'But, Gloria,' she said, 'that didn't—'

'Didn't what?'

'That didn't work out.'

'Finally! Twenty-three years it takes her, but she speaks the truth at last!'

'Cut the theatrics,' she said. 'I don't want to argue with you.'

'Neither do I.'

'But are you sure about this?'

'Would I be doing it if I weren't?'

'I did.'

'Mom. Stop. I love Bill.'

'You may believe you do, but let me ask you this: do you love him, or are you just tempted?'

'Don't belittle what I feel.'

'I'm not. I just know how it is. To be tempted. To be charmed by an accent and an earnest face and a vicious need.'

'He's not another Riordan, damn it!'

'Did I say he was? All I'm asking you to do is make sure you know what you want to do and do it for the right reasons. Be careful.'

'Mom, don't lecture me. You made the same decision I did when you were my age.'

'Which is exactly why I'm lecturing you.' She sighed. 'Listen, I know you didn't call me to get my approval, but I just don't want you to make my mistakes.'

'It's not a mistake. If you ... if you could only meet him. Seriously. Come here, meet Bill, and you'll know.'

'Is that an offer I'm hearing?'

'Yes. It is.'

'Bill,' she said. 'Is he complicated?'

I knew exactly what she meant. Bill had his quirks, his paradoxes, his idiosyncratic range of emotions and secrets like anybody, but he wasn't that. *Complicated* meant capable of betrayal, full of bad hunger, façades, a man like a Chinese puzzle.

'No,' I said.

'Thank God,' she said. 'I didn't mean to interrogate you. If you're happy, that's all that matters.'

'If I put in a quarter, will you say that again?'

'Oh, Gloria. Please.'

I laughed. 'No, really, Mom. You're too classy for clichés. If I told you that I spent my teenage years as a murderess, chopping up men with pickaxes and burying them in the backyard, would you still say that as long as it made me happy, you approved?'

'Hell, no. I'd get you incarcerated. Now, your father, on the other hand—'

'Would have dug their graves for me,' I said softly.

In June I flew back to the States to graduate, *summa cum laude*. Bill came with me, and we drove to New York City with my mother, who took us to the Russian Tea Room. She chattered and laughed and grabbed Bill's arm all through dinner, looking younger than I in her strappy heels and filmy pink dress. After a few glasses of champagne she launched into tales of my childhood, which Bill endured with a wry smile. 'You know I'm incredibly proud of her,' she said, 'but it does surprise me that she's gone on for a degree in English. You should have seen her when she was six. Bill — curled up with a stack of her father's chemistry textbooks, amused for hours. It was adorable.'

I kicked her under the table. She didn't flinch.

'I thought for sure she'd major in the sciences, the way she loved them then, the way she adored her father. They were quite ...' She paused. 'Quite kindred spirits.'

'Gloria's told me,' Bill said.

'I'm sure,' she said. 'But anyway, I should have expected. Gloria tends to surprise us. She's always been a bit of a rebel.'

'A successful rebel,' I said under my breath.

Bill heard me. 'Well, it's a dead good thing,' he

said, laughing as he stroked the inside of my wrist, 'because thanks to Nora Barnacle here and her final thesis, I now actually have a bloody clue as to the point of *Finnegans Wake*.'

My mother beamed. When Bill got up to go to the bathroom, she leaned across the table before I could chastise her for her askew storytelling and whispered, 'All my doubts are gone, Gloria. You've got fabulous taste.'

'I never thought I'd hear that from you,' I said.

'I must admit, I'm a bit jealous,' she said. 'He's an angel, absolutely sweet. Plus he's got great teeth – for an Englishman, that is.'

I snorted. 'Mom, you're awful.'

'I try.' She smiled, then leaned back in her chair and crossed her arms. She turned her head to gaze at Bill as he made his way towards our table. She blinked hard. Her lip trembled. She said, 'He's what Riordan should have been.'

On the flight home, Bill said, 'Your mum is smashing. From what you told me, I was anticipating some middle-aged martyr with a monstrous ego.'

I laughed. 'You've got to understand that all the skeletons in my mother's closet are tightly zipped in garment bags,' I said, and rested my head on his shoulder and slept until we landed.

And so we got married and had a baby and bought a nice little third-floor walkup in Islington before the area got fashionable, and thought we'd live happily ever after.

   But it wasn't that simple. We forgot the Jim Jones/ Santayana creed. Yes. The one about condemning the past and being doomed to repeat it.

chapter thirteen

Two months after Bill died, my mother called and told me she wanted to come to England. 'You've got to be kidding me,' I said.

For years she'd tried to reach across the Atlantic Ocean to me through the contents of a box, an envelope: flowery, elegant cards on my birthday each July, expensive sweaters at Christmas time, cheery letters, presents for Curran. She'd flown to London but once since my permanent move there, and then only for the weekend of my wedding. All splashy florals and affectation, boyfriend on her arm, she waltzed from guest to guest in Bill's parents' Lamberhurst garden while silently I stood beside Bill, her careless kiss numb on my cheek, and swore I'd never let her set foot in the sanctuary of our flat on Theberton Street.

When Curran was born the following March, I begged Bill to be the one to call her from the hospital. 'I'm exhausted,' I said, running a hand through my tangled hair as I leaned down to smudge my lips across my newborn son's fragile forehead. 'I can't deal with her right now.'

'You weren't too knackered to talk to *my* mother,' Bill said.

'I know, but please, just do this for me, all right? She likes you. She won't interrogate you.'

'OK, love,' he said, shaking his head as he went out into the hall.

He came back ten minutes later. 'How was it?' I asked.

'You make it sound like talking to her is torture.'

'Sometimes it is.'

'Well, it was fine. More than fine. She's so bleeding excited I had to tell her goodbye about five times before she'd hang up. She wants to come and visit. When you've had time to rest, she said.'

I yawned. 'All right. I'll have to take about fifteen years, then.'

'Crikey Moses, Gloria,' he said, sitting beside me on the bed and taking Curran from me so I could comb out my hair in earnest, 'why won't you meet her halfway?'

'I refuse to rearrange my life for someone who's so gushingly in denial.'

'Suit yourself,' he said, 'but I still think you're being terribly ridiculous.'

I flipped my hair upside down and worked out a particularly bad snarl, then lifted my head, leaned over, and drew him to me, two fingers beneath his chin. 'You go through eight hours of labour and see if you aren't,' I said, and kissed him, a hard *I'm-back-from-hell* kiss, deep and long. Just then, Curran twitched in sleep. I laughed and gathered him back into my arms, pressed my cheek to his warm scalp, and thought: *mine*.

When I carried him into our flat for the first time two days later, there were four messages on the answering machine. I listened to the first one — *'Gloria, I'm so happy for you, and I'd love to . . .'* — and then hit the ERASE button.

'You can be really cold sometimes,' Bill said from the doorway.

'So can she,' I said.

But she kept trying. Once a week, at first, then every two weeks. I left the machine on, or had Bill field her calls for me. 'Tell her I'm in the shower,' I said, towelling off my wet hair in the kitchen. 'Tell her I'm hormonal and crazy because of Curran and I need a nap.'

'You're still going to be using that excuse when he's twenty, aren't you?' he asked.

'Probably,' I said, and skulked out of the room, arms wrapped around myself, feeling miserable.

One late December afternoon, after the calls had trickled down to one every six weeks at best and I figured she'd given up, the phone rang. Bill got it. I kept my back to him, down on the floor in the living room with a then nine-month-old Curran. Bill came up behind me, put his hands on my shoulders. 'Gloria,' he said, 'don't you think it's time you stopped this game?'

'What do you mean?'

'You know what I mean. Your own sodding mother is on the phone wanting to wish you a happy Christmas, and here you sit hiding out like she's your worst enemy.'

'That's not a bad approximation.'

'Look,' he said, 'I'm not going to referee this one anymore.'

'All right,' I said, and grabbed his arm to pull

myself up off the carpet. Curran's eyes widened, inquisitive. 'Back in a bit, darling.'

'Yeah, Mom,' I said, picking up the kitchen phone.

'Gloria,' she said, voice high-pitched with a fusion of delight and hurt. 'Sweetheart, almost a year of not talking to you, and this is all I get, "Yeah, Mom"?'

'Motherhood chinks away at your ability to articulate. When you spend all day with someone who has a five-word vocabulary, you don't exactly quote Shakespeare anymore.'

She laughed, but then turned clenched. 'That's not what I meant, and you know it.'

'Mom. Damn it. I don't have time for this.'

'For me.'

'No. I didn't say that ... I mean, yes, I'm busy, I have a life over here, I have a child, I—'

'You have a mother.'

'When she feels like being one.'

'Gloria, for Christ's sake, I'm trying to—'

'Trying to what?'

'To start over.'

'What a coincidence. So am I. Well, there we go, Mom, that's just perfect. You've got your new life with your smart little condo, your ever-so-hot lawyer, your first chair in the symphony orchestra, and I have mine with Bill and Curran. Now why can't we see this on the same wavelength? We move on, we respect boundaries, we make no strained attempts at warm fuzzies.'

'Damn it, Gloria, can't you see that I never had a chance—'

I heard a loud thud, and Curran crying in the next room.

'Mom,' I said, 'I have to go. Curran needs me.'

Her voice softened. 'How is he?'

'He's gorgeous,' I said.

'God, I'd love to see him.'

'Well, who knows,' I said sweetly, angry panic rising like steam inside me as Curran's wails battered my ears. 'What with that lovely piece of meat you had draped all over you at my wedding, you could find yourself in my position pretty soon – you're still young enough, and, Jesus, how old could he have been, twenty-four, twenty-five? Or is he an artifact now?'

'Don't go there. Don't even think it. You live like I did, Ms "I Have Complete Control of My Life Now That I Married an Englishman", you live one fucking year like I did, and you will never begrudge me the happiness I have right now again.'

'Gloria?' Bill called from the living room.

'Mom,' I said, swallowing hard, 'I'm hanging up the phone in about five seconds, so if you want to get any messages of holiday cheer out of the way, you'd better do it now.'

'Merry ... Merry Christmas,' she said softly.

I hung up and slammed my fist down hard on the kitchen counter, then went back in to Curran and Bill. They stared at me with bemused expressions from where they sat on the oriental rug, Curran in Bill's lap.

'What happened in here?' I asked.

'His usual "I'm-trying-so-bloody-hard-to-walk-but-I-can't" spills,' Bill said, stroking back the damp blond strands of Curran's hair, which gleamed reddish-gold in the light from the Tiffany lamp behind him. 'What happened in *there*?'

'Mudslinging, honey,' I said. 'Pure and simple.'

'Did you clean up the kitchen?'

I smiled and sat down beside him. 'Not yet.'

He noticed my reddened knuckles, and touched the side of my face. 'Gloria, you really ought to give her a chance.'

I leaned up to kiss the top of his head. 'You are the world's biggest peacemaker, and I love you for it,' I said, 'but you have just got to understand that my mother and I are destined to be at each other's throats forever.'

'Yeah, well, do it quietly,' he said. 'You were scaring Curran.'

I held out my arms to my son, and he beamed. 'No more yelling,' I said. 'Mummy promises, OK?'

My own mother and I wouldn't hear the sounds of each other's voices again until after Bill was dead.

Now I drummed my fingers on the kitchen counter, hesitating before I spoke for fear that I'd burst out in either a laugh or a scream.

'You have *got* to be kidding me,' I said again.

I could hear her on the other end of the line, sharply drawing in her breath.

'I just want to see you and Curran,' she said.

'Please, not this game again.'

'Gloria, I only thought that after Bill you might need ...'

I'd sent her a brief letter, scratchy with shock, right after his death. I hated to do it, but she and Bill had liked each other, and I'd always felt a compulsion to let her know, at least perfunctorily, about the major events in our lives: my new job, Bill's work on an experimental show, Curran's excellent marks. I never expected her to respond with a request — or was it an offer?

She paused.

'You don't want me to come, do you?'

'Well, after all the shit we've been through over this one—'

'I know it won't be easy, and maybe I'm asking too much, but I'd just like to—'

'Jesus, Mom, don't do this to me! You really think I need this stress right now?'

'Only you would think of an honest conversation with your mother as hazardous to your mental health.'

'Only you would believe that after countless brawls with you I could just banter away blithely and say, "Sure, catch the next plane from Baltimore to London, no problem."'

Her voice tightened. 'We don't have to be this way, you know. We can work through this, we can make things better. Or at least try. That's all I want. A chance.'

'Yeah, well, that's very noble, and if you put a

gun to my head' — I winced at my own choice of words — 'I'd have to agree with you, but you've got to understand something.'

'Yes,' she said, slightly breathy, waiting for the great confession, the blissful moment of closeness.

'I am an absolute fucking mess. I can barely scrape dinner together without losing my mind, much less patch up every splintery relationship in my life right now.'

'I know.'

Do you really? I wondered, rubbing a hand across my eyes.

'Mom, I'm tired,' I said. 'I can't play the flawless hostess.'

'You don't have to. I can help you, honey, I'd be glad to, I mean, God, if you ever need someone to take over with Curran when he gets on your nerves, I'd love to volunteer, after all I haven't seen him—'

'You had to work that in there, didn't you?' I said. 'Look, if you want to come visit us, then come visit us. I'd like to end this charade once and for all.'

'Oh, I'm so glad. I can book a hotel somewhere if you want. I know there isn't exactly a dearth of them up where you are, but if it'll make things easier for you—'

'No,' I said suddenly, surprising myself, 'it's all right. You don't have to do that. You can stay here.'

'Really? You're sure it won't be any trouble?'

Mountains of it, I thought. 'I don't think so. Just don't expect the Savoy.'

She laughed. 'I'm performing in my concert series until April thirtieth, so I'm aiming for the first week in May, if that's all right.'

I told her it was, hung up the phone, and returned in a what-have-I-done stupor to the table, where I'd been grading papers. The phone rang again. It was Jascha.

'Good news,' he said. 'I got Whitechapel.'

'You're kidding.'

'I'm not.'

'For when?'

'May. We open the fifth.'

I groaned.

'What's wrong? I thought that was terrific, considering how most places are booked into the next century.'

'Oh, it is, but my mother's probably coming to London that week.'

'What's the problem with that?'

'Just ... everything.'

'You sound like you could use a stiff drink.'

'Hell, yes.'

'I know the perfect place for one,' he said. 'I'll be over.'

I sent Curran down to the Romdourls', and Jascha took me to a restaurant called Nikita's on Ifield Road. We sat and sipped lemon vodka.

'Could I ask you something?' I asked.

'Sure.'

'Why are you so damn nice to me? You buy me dinner, you sit and listen to me ramble, you kindly validate every word I say. Why do you take the time, other than because I'm the executor of Bill's estate? Do you want to sleep with me, or what?'

He laughed, then grew pensive.

'I take the time,' he said, 'because where you are is where I've been.' He looked away. 'So, what's the deal with your mother?'

'My mother,' I said, 'is fifty-three but looks forty. She's skinny and stylish and blonde and a brilliant musician. She eats at French restaurants every night of the week and lives with a younger man.'

'She sounds cool.'

'Oh, she's very cool,' I said. 'Ripened by age. In control of her life for the first time. In bloom.'

'So why disparage her?'

'Because she wants us to be pals. She'd love for us to trade recipes and clothes, to whisper conspiratorially and grab each other's hands when we're excited, to have deep conversations about the mysterious bonds of blood and bone one moment and bitch about how long it takes to clean the bathroom the next.'

'And that can't happen?'

'No, it can't happen. I can't be her best friend right now, because she wasn't my mother when I needed her to be.'

His eyebrows furrowed.

'You're confused, aren't you?' He nodded. 'Well, then, I think it's time for a little story.'

We paid the bill for the drinks and went outside. 'Let me give you the abridged version,' I said. 'When my father was at Oxford, he was engaged to a beautiful genius. She died. My mother came over on a Fulbright. She was angry and frustrated; he needed a pair of strong arms around him. They got married, went back to the States, and guess who was born of their misguided passions? My mother became a bitch. My father became a parasite. Night after night I listened to him weep, blotted the tears from his swollen eyes, and she let me carry the burden. When I was twenty-one, I came to London. Three months later, my father put a bullet in his brain, and her marvellous life took off from there.'

'Aren't you oversimplifying things?'

'Of course I am. Of course I know it wasn't all her fault, and in a way I feel sorry for her. Her parents wanted her to marry a morally upstanding young man; she only wanted to make love to a cello. Do I blame her for pulling away from him, for being angry? No. Do I fume when I think of how she left me unprotected, the victim of a sort of emotional incest? Yes.'

We walked along in silence for a while. The effort to verbalize that which felt wordless, to clarify the ambiguous, sent a tiredness through my veins.

'There's a story by Joseph Conrad,' I said, 'in which a young man of one tribe loves a girl from another. He and his brother hatch a plan for the two of them to sail away and elope, and as they're about to push the boat from the shore, these angry tribesmen, out for blood, approach him, and the boy has to make a decision to stay and save his brother, keeping his loyalty intact, or to climb into the boat where the girl he loves waits.'

'And who does he choose?'

'The girl.'

Jascha chewed his lip in silent meditation.

'I did it without a thought,' I said. 'Shoved off from the shore, gave up my allegiance to my home, my parents. With Bill, I rowed towards the sun. I honestly believed that I'd find "a country where death would be forgotten".'

He put his hand on my arm. 'You look cold,' he said. 'My flat's just down the street. Do you want to go in for a bit?'

In his living room's cluster of black leather couches and sling chairs, amongst pyramid-shaped lamps and metal sculptures, I sat next to Jascha, hands folded in my lap, head down so I wouldn't look at his face and shatter.

'It's funny,' I said, 'but I finally understand what my parents did, because I'm doing it.'

'How do you mean?'

'Well, one time when I was about nine, I guess, I asked my father why he married my mother if he didn't love her as much as he had his fiancée who'd died, Adrienne, and he said, "She was a warm body. She was there. I needed to forget." At the time I thought that was a mean, callous thing to say, but now — shit, now I know what he meant, and why, because I feel his need, the irrationality of it. I wake up every morning to a half-empty bed. And you know what's awful? You know what's so terrible, what right now I'm thinking?'

'No.'

I laughed. I laughed, and trembled. 'Right now,' I said, 'I'm sitting here and thinking. I'm thinking that I want to kiss you, I want to kiss you just so I can remember how it felt, and, Christ, what am I saying? You aren't Bill. You aren't Bill.'

My hands flailed in inept gestures. My lips curled back in a sob as tears slid down my cheeks.

'I've got to stop crying,' I whispered. 'I've got to stop, but ... Why, damn it? Why not a drug dealer, why not me and him? I would've given him my marrow. I would've gladly killed anybody.'

He moved closer, reached out his hand.

'Don't touch me,' I said. 'Please don't touch me, because if you touch me, I'll explode, I'll detonate, I'll turn to you, I'll be dangerous, I'll do something desperate, and, oh, God, Jascha, I know why they did it, I know how it feels to hurt so bad you want to hurt somebody, and where do I go from here? Jascha, I'm scared ...'

He put his arm around me and drew my cheek against his shoulder. 'I'm sorry,' I said. I stared up at his face and thought how easy it could be — lift my chin, reach out my fingers, press my quavery mouth to Jascha's, find oblivion, beg him to save me.

'Don't be,' he said.

'When we were at Nikita's,' I said, 'you told me that the reason you take time to listen to me is because you've been where I am. What—'

'About four years ago,' he said, 'my wife and five-year-old daughter were killed in a car accident.'

I closed my eyes. Thought of the Shelley poem I'd used with my fourth-form students as an example of metre gone awry. Death is here, and there, and everywhere.

'I used to watch you,' he said, 'on the nights when you met Bill at the studio. You'd have on a long black dress and a big baggy coat, and your hair would be gathered up except for one little curl that escaped right here' — he touched my jaw — 'and you'd have Curran with you. Bill would drop what he was doing and run over, excited as a child at the sight of the two of you, and he'd put his arm around your waist and you'd all walk out for fish and chips, and as much as I respected him as an artist, God, how I hated him then, for what he had, that gorgeous, happy triangle, that glistening, flaunted safety ...'

He laughed. It was my dangerous laugh. Help-me-I'm-falling.

'I hate to admit this,' he said, 'but you occupied my thoughts a lot then. I felt silly — I mean, I hadn't said a word to you, and didn't even know your name. You were just Bill's American wife. Still, I looked for pieces of Marianne in you, and found them: the way you kept your head down with a wry smile on your lips, the motions of your hands when you spoke. Why do we do it, Gloria?'

'I don't know.'

'I still try,' he said. 'And it's been years. All those TV-movie-type-things you say you do? I do them, too. I see a little dark-haired girl wearing a pink ruffled dress in Hyde Park, and I whirl, the syllables of her name slide from my throat. "Elizabeth," I cry, and the poor thing's eyes widen. "Mummy, why'd that man call me that? Doesn't he know my name's Anna?"'

'And toy stores, oh, Jesus, don't even let me get

near one. I walk past Hamleys, and I hear her saying, "I want this, Daddy, and this, and this," and I think, it's her birthday soon, she'll be nine, or should be, and it won't be long before she turns to boys in leather jackets who run their fingers down her spine, and like a fist uncurling, she'll ripen ...'

'Despite what people say, it doesn't get any easier, does it?'

'After a while there's a sort of dulling, a dulling that has to happen if you're ever going to get out of bed in the morning and do laundry and make breakfast without bursting into tears. I used to read newspaper stories of kids who'd fallen into frozen ponds and stayed submerged for half an hour, forty-five minutes, an entire hour, and lived. "How do they do it?" I wondered then, but now I know, because grief isn't much different than their survival. After you reach a certain point of unbearable cold, there's a mechanism of shutdown. Blood slows. The organs and passions go sluggish. You do what you have to, and you do it well.'

'Necessary madness,' I murmured.

'Right, and then all of a sudden you'll settle into a comfortable chair to read, and the sun will slant across the page. You'll swell with joy, you'll think you've never before seen a thing of such beauty, and then you'll remember: I did, I *did*.

'So, in answer to your question, no. The pain becomes more subtle, but there's nothing easy about this.'

'When Bill was at his sickest,' I said, 'and the possibility of his dying was at its strongest, I told myself I was lucky. Better for it to happen slowly, I reasoned. Better to know, to have time to prepare myself, to prepare Curran for the fact that in a matter of weeks or months he wouldn't have a father. Stupid of me, wasn't it? Because there's no "better" way to die. Death isn't qualifiable.'

I lifted my head from his shoulder and fumbled through my purse. 'I need a cigarette,' I said. He smiled as I leaned back, lit one, and inhaled.

'When you told me about the Conrad story,' he said, 'it reminded me of the questions I face. Questions of loyalty, of the ethics of rowing away, so to speak. What do you do when your Siamese twin stops drawing breath? Do you carry the dead body fused with yours, drag it the rest of your life, or do you plant your feet firmly in the earth?' He sighed. 'My wife and my daughter are phantoms, and

I don't know whether I should hold on to them or reach for something tangible.'

'That's what I'm afraid of,' I said.

'I know,' he said. 'Hell, when you were being your usual cynical self at Nikita's and asked me if I wanted to sleep with you, I almost said yes.'

'You didn't.'

'I did. And then I thought, "Just because she's attractive and going through the same agony you are, that's no reason to throw yourself at her. One good fuck won't magically make your lives better."'

'No,' I said, 'it won't.'

I checked my watch.

'It's getting late,' I said, and stood. He walked me to the door and handed me my coat. I shrugged into it and pulled on my gloves. 'Thank you for the drink,' I said. I took his face in my leather-clad hands and kissed his forehead.

'What was that for?' he asked.

'For being there,' I said. 'For giving me hell's highway map.'

I turned to leave, and he caught my arm.

'Gloria,' he said. 'That story about the couple in the boat. You never told me the ending.'

'They have a few years of bliss,' I said, 'but then

the woman dies with a raging fever and the man is forced to contemplate his choice.'

'They never find a country where death can be forgotten.'

'No,' I said. 'There is no such place.'

chapter fourteen

When Bill suddenly grew pale and tired, we brushed off his symptoms, attributed them to working too hard. It wasn't until he joked about having a map of the world in bruises on himself that I insisted he see a doctor, and even then I wasn't overly concerned. At the worst, I expected him to come home with a bottle of iron pills and orders to eat more leafy vegetables.

The day of his appointment was gorgeous, a harbinger of spring, the colours of the sun and sky so crisp it hurt to look out the window at them. Curran was downstairs with Raj, so I had the flat to myself as I did the breakfast dishes. While I dried them, I was struck with a rare, delicious flash of euphoria, of cohesion: I'm thirty years old, I've got a wonderful, gentle artist for a husband and an adorable, bright little son, and I'm perfectly all right with myself. This is incredible. This is my life.

Then I heard Bill's key in the lock and the sound of his tossing his jacket over the back of the living-room couch. He came into the kitchen, walked up behind me, wrapped his arms around my waist, and rested his cheek against my neck. I sensed a solemnity, a sadness in the way he held me, and so I stared at the jars full of herbs perched on the sink-ledge to steady myself: a focal point, like in labour. 'Gloria,' he said. 'I need to talk to you.'

He sat me down at the table. He leaned forward, elbows on the Formica. His pale grey eyes gazed into my face as if he were fighting for solid ground, fighting not to shatter. He opened his mouth to speak. I wanted to reach across and brush my detergent-soaked fingers over his lips, stop the words from flying out. He said, 'He thinks it might be cancer.'

Eclipse. My vision swung out of focus. Blood surged through my ears with a roar. I skimmed my hands over the tabletop and braced myself for the terrible fall, but it never came. The sun and the sky and the breakfast dishes and the herb jars were still there, and my husband still sat before me in his plaid flannel shirt, holding my wrists, telling me not to worry as he rambled on and on about medical advances and bone-marrow biopsies and not jumping to conclusions just yet. Then Curran burst back in, blond and breathless, babbling about the new game Raj just got, and we had to smile, we had to nod, we had to pretend. We forced our voices into the high, cheerful register of parents bent on deception.

That night I tricked myself into believing that I would crawl into the cocoon of sleep and wake up the next morning to find Bill whole and smooth and unblemished, with no traces of the day before in sight.

Instead I woke to a brightness that drove my eyes closed again, and the truth so heavy it was like a pair of giant hands pinning me to the mattress. I stared at Bill's shoulder blades and willed myself not to cry.

After a while I propped up on one elbow and leaned over to look at his face. He slept with his mouth slightly parted, breath light as a child's, body slack with pleasure and unconscious abandon. I marvelled at the wild asymmetry of his too-broad features, his passion-roughened brown hair, the pale curve of his neck and the throbbing vein that ran down it, as yet unscarred, a blue river. How, I wondered, could someone so perfect possibly have such vileness blooming inside him?

When he woke, he turned over, rested his hand against my cheek, and pulled me closer so that our foreheads touched on the pillow. We stared into each other's eyes, not with the languid drowsiness of love, but with full knowledge of the grave turn our lives had just taken.

On the first day of spring, a man sheathed in white shoved a needle into Bill's hip and drew out a syringeful of his marrow. I had a fourth-form class at the time, and was trying to explain T. S. Eliot's concept of the objective correlative to a group of uninterested fifteen-year-olds, but I couldn't stop thinking about the long, thick metal piercing flesh.

I called home after lunch.

Bill answered. I'd begged him to let me pick him up at the hospital, but he'd insisted he could get home on his own. 'Hi, love,' he said. His voice sounded thin.

'How are you?'

'Fine. A little sore.'

'How was it?'

'Your usual garden-variety agony.'

'Bill, please. How was it really?'

'Painful. Dead painful. Long.'

'Do you know when we'll get the results?'

'Day after tomorrow, probably.'

'Will you be all right until I get home?'

'I'll be fine.'

'You're sure? Because if you want me to, I'll leave early. It won't be a problem.'

'Don't worry about me.'

'I can't help it.'

'I know, but try not to, OK? Whatever happens, happens.'

Sometimes I thought we were locked in our roles, handcuffed to certain attributes: Bill the protector, Bill the optimist, Bill the rock, the endomorph, all flesh, and me the protected, off-kilter, fatalistic one, all bones and angles.

'Gloria? Are you still there?'

'Yes, but I'd better go. I've got a class in five minutes.'

'I love you,' he said.

'I love you, too.' The parroting, the reverberation, one sentence, tiny, compact, driving the voice into a higher pitch, curving the lips back in primeval cry — *I love you; you must live!* — and splintering me, splintering me, oh, don't hang up, please not that click, that finality.

I drifted through the third-form class, the sixth-form class, instructions and assignments and criticisms tumbling from my mouth, my gaze fixed not on my students but on some far-off plane, all my energy cathected upon one glowing objective: must get home to Bill, must get home to Bill.

I found him propped up on pillows on our bed, reading a book on Edvard Munch. He grinned, and patted the edge of the mattress. I slipped out of my heels and sat beside him. He held out his arms. I leaned into them, breathed him in like oxygen, inhaling the scent of his skin: warm, earthen, but with a foreign undertone of antiseptic, of crackly examining-table paper. He stroked my hair and rested his chin on the top of my head. 'My angel,' he said. We stayed there like that for a while, in the soft glow of the lamplight. A gentle rain drummed on the windowpane, and I thought, *Whatever happens, happens*.

Later I made tea, and we sat cross-legged on the quilt and drank it, passing the same cup back and forth. We talked about the Munch book, about the shy, nail-biting girl in my fifth-form class who was a published poet – anything to keep our minds off the phone call which would jangle us from our contentment, knock the walls down, signal the end of the world.

It came two nights later. I sat at the kitchen table, helping Curran fix mistakes in his school composition. When the phone rang, it felt as if a firecracker had exploded inside my chest and was now burning its way through my body, but I stayed calm, stayed still and poised with my pen while Bill answered. 'Look at this one, here, darling, it isn't so hard to change. You have down "t-h-e-r-e house", but which word do you need?'

'The other one. T-h-e-i-r.'

'Brilliant. OK. Let's check the next sentence.'

As I scanned, I listened to Bill. 'Yes,' he said. 'Yes.'

I pulled my chair closer to Curran's and put my arm around him. 'The rest of this looks great. Better than a lot of the papers I get.'

He giggled. 'Really?'

'Really,' I said, my lips against the curve of his ear.

'How soon?' Bill asked. I looked up. 'Yes, of course, I understand.'

He hung up the phone. Bit his lip.

'Curran,' I said, 'why don't you take your paper and get ready for bed? Could you do that for me?' He nodded and headed down the hall with a perceptive sort of obedience which I saw often in him and found frightening.

Bill and I stared at each other.

In those few seconds, I felt my skin peel away, felt every layer of me reduce to reddish-black blood and glistening bone. My whole body contracted. In my husband's face I saw the shock, the numbness, the truth.

And then I was falling, hurtling through empty space and into the black. Of all possible nightmares, that one is the worst. If you dream you're falling and you don't wake up, then you die. But I was already awake.

We had it all laid out for us. Like a medical Tarot.

The next night we went to the oncologist's office and sat amongst his obligatory ocean of books and papers and the smell of leather and despair. I stared at the diplomas on the walls. Bill put his hand over mine. Dr Levitch, our card reader, twisted the cap on his fountain pen and told us about risks, reasons to be glad, dangers.

Bill's body was in a state of revolt. Like a rebellious teenager drunk on the taste of power, one immature myeloblast had gone on a rampage. The only way to destroy it, and its army of warped copies, would be to pump his veins full of toxic chemicals. They would nauseate him, ulcerate him, make him lose his hair. Fire with fire. Either way, Bill would get scorched.

The first round of treatment was set to begin the next day. There was no time to waste. The meter was ticking. Ten days in hell, a brief respite, then back again, and again, and soon it would be summer, all locusts and lushness. Three shots at the white corpuscle legion, and then we'd wait. And hope for a remission.

'Survival rates are good, but there are no guarantees,' said Levitch. 'A relapse is always possible. Shutdown of other organs, overwhelming infection ...'

Of course there are no guarantees, I thought as I leaned back in my chair. *There are never guarantees with anything.* When Bill drew me into his arms that first time in the studio kitchen, I didn't know whether he would heal me or crush me, but there he sat, with me still, listening to the tale of what lay ahead.

It was almost seven by the time we took the tube home. On impulse we stopped at a chip shop on

Upper Street. We sat at a table by the window and ate the haddock straight from the paper. Bill, for once, was silent. I watched him, my love with his grease-stained fingers and worn coat, and my anger boiled. I wanted to reach across the table and into his blood so I could kill every poisoned cell inside him.

We took a long time to eat, trying to preserve the grimy simplicity of the moment. Bill put his arm around me as we walked up our street in the darkness. We saw a light on in our son's window. I trembled to think of him pulling on his pyjamas in an empty room, watching the clock with a child's unbearably slow perception of time. Bill's grip on me tightened. 'What do I tell him?' he whispered in my ear as we came up the front steps.

'The truth,' I said.

And so, fingertips touching, we sat on Curran's bed, one on either side, and in the gentle blue-tinged light explained the cruelties of the body to him. He lay beneath the sheets and gazed at us. 'Dad will get better, though,' he said. 'Won't he?'

I opened my mouth. Bill spoke before I did.

'I can't make that kind of promise,' he said, 'but I will try my hardest to stay here with you.'

At that point I went out in the hall and wept.

Later I sat on our bed and watched him undress, thinking, *This is the last time I will see this body unscathed, unbrutalized, free of pain.*

'It's not a death sentence,' he said, folding his jeans and hanging them over a chair.

'No.'

He sat down beside me. I turned one of his hands over and ran my finger across his palm. Across the lifeline.

'It's not like the flipping 1940s,' he said, 'when you were just taken home to die and had no hope.' He swallowed, repeated himself as if doing so would convince either him or me or both of us. 'It's not like that.'

'Of course not,' I said.

In a few hours, I thought, *he will be weak and broken and sucked dry in a sterile white bed, head spinning.*

He winced as accidentally I stroked a splodge of purple on his skin, a nascent bruise. An unnamed country.

'Bulgaria,' he said, and grinned.

'Bill,' I said, 'what are we going to do?'

He flopped onto his back. 'We're going to live,'

he said. 'Now come here. I've got ten nights without you ahead of me.'

And so I rolled over, into his waiting embrace, and when his hands reached beneath the thin fabric of my nightgown, I whispered *I love you, I love you* into his hairline, as if love were enough, as if love were armour, as if love were an amulet which could plunge us into light and out of darkness.

chapter fifteen

 My mother met me at Heathrow with good
   intentions and too many suitcases, throwing
her arms around me as if thirty years of our lives
never happened. She babbled as we headed towards
customs. 'God, I can't wait to see how the city's
changed, and *you*, just look at you, you're lovely –
not that I ever expected you not to be, but you had
to get out of that punk phase, that's all ...'

I didn't look at her. If I looked at her, there
would be bloodshed or tears, so I nodded at her
every word – yes, Mom, of course – and kept my
gaze on the sign we were approaching, the one which
read NOTHING TO DECLARE.

We took a taxi home. She grew solemn. There were
no more brittle jokes like the one she'd whispered
in my ear about hiding her Uzi before the airport

security check. She was a graver version of my mother, that woman who sat beside me in a pink wool suit and pumps, legs crossed, blonde curls stiff with perfection. She leaned against the door, body curled as if wounded, face turned towards the window. She had a run in her stocking. I thought I'd scream for joy.

While I lugged her bags inside, she ran about the flat, investigating my decor. 'These are beautiful,' she said as she fingered a pair of mosaic votives on the living-room table.

'Camden Passage,' I said. 'Five pounds. Get yourself some.'

'And your kitchen!' she said, gesturing towards its wallpaper border of *trompe l'oeil* plums. 'It's cozy, it's precious, it's—'

'Dirty,' I said, and with a sigh set down her last suitcase. It was so like her to rhapsodize over things that didn't matter. 'God, Mom, you're only staying a week. You didn't have to bring your entire wardrobe.'

'I know, but I like to be prepared.' She snorted and held up a jar which read ASHES OF DEAD LOVERS. 'Where in the hell did you get this?'

'From the girls in my old flat. As a gag gift at my bridal shower.'

'And you kept it?'

'Out of sheer sentimentality. It's in terrible taste, though, especially given our family history, don't you think?'

She looked away. 'Maybe I'd better go unpack my things.'

Sprawled on my bed, I watched her sort her clothes. Hanger by hanger her mauves and powder blues and beiges encroached upon the blacks and dark greens in my closet. She said, 'I hate to kick you out of your room.'

'I don't mind.' The couch would be tight and soft, like an embrace. I'd volunteered to take it so I wouldn't have to face the taut expanse of sheet on Bill's side of the mattress.

My mother hung her last blouse and lined her shoes up in a row. She sat beside me, a little smile on her face. She patted my knee. She smelled like guilt and floral perfume. 'I think we really needed this,' she said.

Jascha called me two days later.

'Day after tomorrow,' he said. 'You ready?'

'I think so, but I can't say I feel any sort of thrill. It's going to be hard.'

'I know.'

Since our conversation that night in his flat, those two words had taken on a whole new power. They were no longer silence-fillers, no longer patronizing.

'How's life with Mommy dearest?' he asked.

I laughed. 'No catfights yet. We're very civil, considering our history of screaming matches. I feel as if soon there'll be a shift, a fracture, something will happen, the masks will drop off our faces, and we'll either collapse in each other's arms or kill each other.'

'If you plan on the latter, please do me a favour and wait until after May the fifth.'

'I'll try. And Jascha, she took us to Le Gavroche. Fucking Le Gavroche. Do you know how much that costs?'

'More than anyone should have to pay?'

'Exactly. I don't even like French food, and poor Curran, he thinks macaroni and cheese is a big deal, so he was awestruck, scared, really. Later he said to me, "I know it'd hurt Gran's feelings if she heard this since she spent so much money, but I didn't like it there. There were too many different forks and I was afraid I'd spill something."'

'How's he dealing with all this?'

'Oh, he thinks Caroline's neat. A real switch from Bill's mother. The other day he told her, "I think you look younger than Mum," so now she adores him. They look eerily alike.'

'Are they coming to the retrospective?'

'I don't know. I mean, I hate to bar my mother from the thing, but ...'

'She can come. I don't mind. I'll behave myself around her.'

'I'm more worried about Curran.'

'He wants to see it?'

'He's obsessed with it. I hate to tell him he can't go, but then again I have to consider what might happen if he did. The paintings, they're ... what if he saw *Necessary Madness* and thought ...'

'I can't decide for you, Gloria.'

'No.'

'But listen, I was thinking ... about the opening ...'

'Yeah?'

'You might not like this, but I thought maybe it would be a good idea if you wrote a brief bit, you know, something to read for that night.'

'Oh, for God's sake. You want me to play the tragic widow? Give a eulogy? No.'

'Come on.'

'I'll be on display. I'll feel stupid. I'll be there rambling and making an inarticulate fool of myself and of Bill.'

'You can articulate his work and his life better than anyone else.'

'I guess so, but—'

'Please. Just a few words.'

'Jesus. Jascha ... I don't know ... I mean, if you really want me to, I can, but don't expect a tearjerker or a master's thesis, OK?'

'Thanks. I'm sorry to stick you with this so late.'

'It's all right.'

'Oh, and good luck with your mother.'

She came in as I hung up the phone. 'Who was that?' she asked.

'The person who's working on the retrospective with me.'

'The sculptor?'

'How did you know?'

'Curran told me. "He's dead good," he said. "He took us out to eat the night Mum tipped the pot off the stove and got a bit mental."'

'Yeah. He did.'

'Are you going out with him?'

'Jascha? Hell, no.'

'You sound a little too vehement for me to believe you.'

'Would it have bugged you if I'd said I was?'

'No, it's just that with Curran—'

'Oh, OK. Now you fight valiantly for the welfare of the child. Now you waver, you worry.'

'Gloria, please. I was only trying to make the point that so soon it might put Curran in an awkward position. That you should think of him.'

'You think I don't?' I said. 'You think that twenty-four hours a day, every word I say and every move I make doesn't undergo scrutiny, isn't subjected to the question of "How will this affect Curran?" You're a fine one to talk, seeing as five months after Dad died you were waltzing back out on the rebound.'

'That isn't fair,' she said. 'You were older. You were living your own life.'

'But it still bothered me.'

'The situation was different. I had a right to do that.'

'So what you're telling me is that because your marriage was awful, you were justified in fluttering on to someone else, but since mine was good I should pull out the black veil and bear my grief alone the rest of my days.'

'Stop it. I don't want to argue with you. That's not what I came here for.'

'If I hear you say that one more time,' I said, 'I'll scream. I don't want to argue with you, either, but I've lived with you long enough to know that doing it's the only way to find my mother inside this polished acquaintance who's standing before me. And I'm sorry if I have to be raw, and I'm sorry if I ruin the ambience of your London vacation, but the reason why I was so vehement about not seeing Jascha was because I am so fucking scared that I will before I'm ready. Are you satisfied now?'

She turned her back to me, but I could tell she was wiping her eyes. 'I never did any dances on Riordan's grave,' she said.

I took off work the next day. It pained me to think of her wandering the city alone, even though she'd insisted she still remembered its layout, and I felt bad about having made her cry.

'Do you need a dress for this exhibition?' she asked that morning at breakfast.

'No, Mom, I don't need a dress. I've got a black velvet one I bought a few years ago.'

'Velvet? In May? Oh, honey, you really need to give up that black fetish. Let me buy you something different.'

I sighed. 'I take it you want to go shopping.'

'Gloria,' she said, 'is the world round? Of course I want to go shopping.'

We went to Harvey Nichols, and she bought me a long, cranberry-coloured dress, simple but dramatic. 'OK,' I said, 'you put me through the classy Caroline Merchant routine. It's my turn.'

'Uh-oh. Where are you taking me?'

I smiled. 'To a place with studs and leather.'

She gasped as I led her inside a store that looked more like a warehouse. 'London Calling' blasted over a stereo system, and she laughed at me as I mouthed the words and steered her from rack to rack. She looked relieved when I grabbed a black pleated skirt, but then her eyes widened when on top of it I piled a black lace top, a white T-shirt snipped to rags, and a leather vest. 'No more,' she said.

'Just wait, this'll be fun,' I said. 'Accessories next.'

I picked up fishnet stockings, a pair of Doc Martens, and a studded choker, then got a pink-haired girl to open a fitting room. I leaned against the wall and listened to my mother fumble and swear inside it.

'Gloria, these boots are killing me,' she said. 'How could you stand them?'

'Revolution wasn't supposed to be comfortable.'

There was a brief pause, and then she said, 'Oh, Jesus.'

'Let me see.'

'There's no way I'm coming out in this.'

'Come on. You've seen me drunk; I can see you in leather. Open the door.'

She stepped from the cubicle. We burst out laughing at the same time. Doubled over, we hobbled to the larger triptych of mirrors.

'I wish I had a camera,' I said.

'Look at us,' she said. 'We've reversed.'

I gazed at our reflections: my mother in rags with her boots half-laced, me in my long skirt and silk blouse, minimalist but tasteful in comparison.

'You're right,' I said, 'but for the full effect we'd have to give you spiked hair and a nose ring.'

'Could you imagine? Think of me at a symphony concert in this. Of course a short skirt of any kind with a cello is pushing it.'

'Do you want me to buy you the choker?' I asked. 'You've spent so much on me, I owe it to you.'

'Sure,' she said. 'It'll be a little souvenir to show David.'

We grew quiet then. David was her thirty-year-old lawyer.

As we walked out into the street, she said, 'You've never seen the place where your father and I lived, have you?'

'I've been to Earl's Court, yeah. Bill used to live there.'

'I meant the actual flat.'

'Oh, that, no.'

'Would you like to?'

I nodded.

We took the tube there and walked past scores of fast-food restaurants. My mother's face fell. 'It's so ... touristy,' she said.

'It's thirty years later,' I said.

'There,' she said suddenly, and pointed her finger across the street. 'See it? On the second floor?'

'Yes.'

It looks so ordinary, I thought. Gingham curtains. Shapes, the silhouettes of people's bodies inside, moving from couch to kitchen table to bed and then back again, unaware that in those rooms my parents had experienced their brief flicker of happiness.

'There was cabbage-rose wallpaper in the bedroom,' she said. 'I'd wake up to that, and his head against my shoulder ... I wonder if it's still there. Maybe I should ring the bell, ask if I could have a look around.'

'No,' I said.

She turned. 'And over here,' she said, 'was where we'd sometimes walk to a little diner for breakfast.'

'Looks like it's a gay bar.'

'No kidding.'

We walked back towards the tube station.

'Did you love him?' I asked.

'Yes,' she said. 'No matter what you might like to think, no matter how cold and unfeeling he may have made me out to be, yes, I did.'

'But all those years ...'

'I know. We were separate, we were together alone. But you've got to understand that your father—'

'Wanted you to be someone you weren't.'

'Exactly.'

'But you could have listened to him. You could have been there.'

'I could have, you're right. After a point, though,

when the flattery turned cloying, and his rich murmur of "I want to exist for you" faded to a desperate bleat of "I want you to exist for me," it got hard.'

'That's a pitiful excuse, Mom. That's selfish.'

She nodded. 'I realize that love requires a certain selflessness, but your father asked for the wrong kind. What have you got if you're loved for what you offer and not who you are?'

'Grounds for divorce.'

She laughed. 'Good girl.'

'Then why did you stay with him?' I asked.

'He was safe,' she said. 'In his own quiet, warped way he idolized me. And there's enormous, seductive safety in idolatry.'

'The thing that I don't understand,' I said, 'is why he had to be like that. What makes some people recover from grief with boundaries, with strength, while others falter? I mean, much as I yelled at you yesterday, I have to admit that I admire how you've gotten on with your life. What made you able to do it, and not him?'

'I don't know,' she said.

I thought of my father and Adrienne, and the whole affair – the brilliant, pretty girl killed in a car crash before she could marry her fiancé, the shy, sensitive young man crushed by his loss — seemed too hokey to be real. But it had been. There had been that photograph with the quote from 'Two in the Campagna'.

'Have you got enough money for the tube fare?' my mother asked.

'More than enough,' I said.

When we got home we dumped all our bags on the couch and sat on the rug to cut the price tags off what we'd bought. 'Where do you want to go for dinner tonight?' my mother asked.

'Nowhere,' I said, poised with the scissors. 'You and Jascha Kremsky have got me so spoiled I'm forgetting how to cook. I need practice.'

'Do you mind if I turn on the radio?'

'Go ahead.'

She knelt by the stereo and fiddled with the dial.

'Remember the contests we used to have,' she said, 'to see who could guess the composer first?'

'Yeah.'

Music swelled from the speakers. She turned her head in my direction, daring me to get it right.

'Debussy,' I said, and lit a cigarette.

*   *   *

That night, when she and Curran had gone to bed, I sat at the kitchen table with a blank sheet of paper in front of me, and tried to write the speech Jascha had asked for. After half an hour, all I'd done was scribble a childish proclamation of maiden initials and futility: *G. M. loves B. B.*

So what? I thought. Love wasn't a cure. Love couldn't outwit death.

Soon my English-teacher instincts kicked in, and I began to scribble full sentences. At one a.m. my mother came out in her nightgown.

'Did the light keep you awake? I'm sorry.'

She sat beside me. 'It's late,' she said. 'You've got circles under your eyes. You should get to bed.'

'I have to finish this. It's for the retrospective.'

She tucked a strand of hair behind my ear. I thought of her firm hands on my shoulders, leading me back to my room after the nightmares when I was six, pulling me to her on the floor of my father's study when I was bloody-chinned and sixteen.

'Sweetheart,' she said, 'your fingernails.'

'What about them?'

'They're bitten down. They're awful.'

I looked up from my page and was about to

remark that the state of my manicure was the least of my worries, but I stopped. Finally I understood her language. The talk of tube fares, dresses, gnawed nails — all wails of warning to a dark daughter, oh, you're slipping and I can't catch you, no matter how hard I try, no matter how sweet my grasp.

chapter sixteen

Most of the spring, Bill had lain in a hospital room with the shades drawn. In the evenings I sat beside him and graded stacks of students' exams while he slept. I'd be halfway through a kid's complaint that 'Araby' wasn't a 'real' story when he'd moan, and I'd scrape my chair over closer to the bed and hold his now-bare skull over a blue basin while he retched.

Afterwards, gasping, he lay back on the pillow, and I sponged his bile-stained mouth and hot face. He gazed first at me, then at the tulips on the nightstand. His exhausted eyes said, *Someday I'm going to paint this.*

In June, after the last round of treatment, I took him home. A week later, when he got the results of his bloodwork, he pulled me up from the table and waltzed me through the flat.

199

'I take it you're in remission,' I said.

'For an American, you're pretty damn bright.' He kissed me. 'Yes, my love. We're safe.'

'Right now, you mean.'

'Right now, yeah.'

'How long do you have to be in remission before you're cured?'

'Five years, Dr Levitch said.'

'Five yea——'

He put his hands on either side of my face and brushed his thumb over my lips, silencing me. 'Shh, shh, don't trouble yourself with it,' he said. 'Think about today.'

I smiled.

'There you go. That's better,' he said. 'Oh, God, I can't believe this. I want to get out of the city. I want to breathe wild air. Let's go to the seaside. Do you want to?'

'Well, if it's all right with Dr Levitch, I guess——'

'Brilliant. Smashing. OK. Curran,' he yelled, 'get your things together. We're going on holiday.'

'This very minute?' came a call from the other room.

'This very minute.'

'Bill, come on, don't be silly,' I said. 'I'm a mess,

look at me, I haven't even had a shower, and the kitchen—'

'Forget the bleeding kitchen,' he said. 'We're free.'

He turned and walked to the doorway, then ran back and kissed me again. 'We're going to the seaside!' he yelped, and did a little leap into the air.

'You amuse me no end,' I said. After he left, I slumped to the floor and laughed until I cried.

We drove to Dover and rented a guesthouse overlooking the beach. 'You mean I get my own room?' Curran asked.

'Yes, you get your own room,' I said, 'but no beer and no loud parties, OK?'

'OK,' he said, giggling, and ran upstairs to check it out.

That night, while Bill got ready for bed, I stood on the balcony and watched the ferries make their way across the Channel, sending shards of light into the darkness. I wrapped my arms around myself.

'Honey,' Bill called, 'are you going to stay out there pretending you're Matthew Arnold all night?'

'No,' I said, and came inside.

He sat on the edge of the bed in his boxers,

shoulders hunched. For the first time, I realized how thin he'd grown. I ran a finger down his ribs. He shivered at the salt air. 'I'm sorry,' I said. 'I forgot to close the door.' I went back and shut it. When I returned his teeth began to chatter. I untied the cardigan from around my waist and wrapped it around him. As I did so, my hair spilled over his bare scalp, I wanted to hold his ravaged body inside me so that, by some trick of the womb, I could let him grow again and begin over.

He drew me onto his knee. 'I don't want to go back,' he said.

'Neither do I.'

'I feel like London's ground zero, the epicentre of an earthquake,' he said, 'and if we just keep going, if we cross the water to France, and then further on into another country, pushing past borders, we'll get away from this thing. Remember when we went to Nice, right after we were married? Remember how great that was?'

I nodded, and thought of afternoons in an air-conditioned hotel on the Riviera. I'd wash the salt and sand from my hair, slip a pink sleeveless nightgown over my head, and crawl into bed beside him, droplets of water still clinging to my skin. Sunburnt, we'd doze, his head on my breasts, my palm on his back, until dinnertime, when I'd open the curtains.

'It would be so easy,' he said, 'to wake up Curran and take a ferry, to pretend our enemy were here and we could escape it, you know? But the enemy was inside me. And it could come back.'

I stroked his collarbone. 'This is a switch from the happiness dance you did earlier,' I said.

'I'm scared.'

'So am I.'

Later, as he slept, I lay awake and listened to him breathe. I touched his face and he stirred a little. I put my palm to his chest, and it rose and fell. *Surely this counts*, I thought. *Surely this luminous moment matters*. And then I slid my knuckles down his side, down to the marrow, to where I knew that, despite the safety of numbers and reports, the terror would soon grow again, a thousand white cells coagulating deep in his hip.

The next morning I woke, reached across the sheet, and found it bare. Panic swelled inside my chest. I rushed out of bed and gazed around the room. Empty. I checked my son's room, the bathroom, downstairs. 'Oh, Jesus, Bill,' I said, and ran back up, heart pounding.

Then I saw that the door to the balcony was slightly ajar. I shoved it open and stepped outside. Ocean air whipped strands of my hair into my mouth, and I pushed them back. I shielded my eyes from the morning sun and stared down onto the beach.

Suddenly I glimpsed him. He stood with a towel around his shoulders in ankle-high water, barefoot, his trunks soaked. 'Cold but terrific,' he yelled.

I burst out laughing. It was one of those moments – tender, cinematic – which makes you feel as though you might shatter.

'You scared the shit out of me!' I yelled back. 'Get up here.'

Curran stumbled into my room and onto the balcony. 'What's going on?' he asked.

I put my arm around him. 'Your father's being a lunatic,' I said.

He said, 'Then he's definitely well now.'

It rained that afternoon, I curled up on the sofa and read, while Bill and Curran went to Tesco's for groceries. They trooped back in with their bags, soaked.

'Look at you two,' I said. 'Drowned rats.'

'I jumped in every puddle,' Curran said, unpacking apples and cheese and a packet of Hobnobs.

'So I can tell by your shoes. And did you sneak in those chocolates?'

'No. Dad said I could get them.'

'Well, OK, but no sugar highs, please, and put on some socks. That goes for you too, Bill.'

Bill grinned. 'Yes, Mum.'

As they turned to go upstairs, I drew them both to me. 'Things can only get better from here,' I said.

Three glorious summer months. Of singing, of parks, of Bill's bruises faded. And then the bomb.

In September he relapsed. We tried to ignore the signs: blood in the sink every morning from his raw gums, pain in every bone, a host of new purple countries — Madagascar, Sri Lanka, Mozambique — which appeared on his arms. But we couldn't, and so on a day crackly with fall I took him back to St Pancras for the same ten-day routine with the blue basin. This time, though, when I brought him home he was so drained that he leaned on my shoulder coming up the front walk, and the weather had turned colder, sharper.

Still he went to the studio. He'd arrive home smelling of turpentine and triumph, so worn he'd flop onto the couch and sleep through dinner. I'd sit on the floor and listen to him snore while I graded exams. Around nine he'd wake and lie there, silently playing with my hair as I debated who got extra credit. 'Sweetheart,' I said, 'you shouldn't work so hard.'

'You don't understand,' he said. 'You know the saying about running for your life? Well, I'm painting for mine.'

I laughed. 'I'm sorry. I don't mean to make fun of you, but that just sounded like the name of a game show, the way you said it.'

'Yeah, it did, now that you mention it,' he said, and put on a deep-throated announcer's voice. 'Now, live from the BBC, it's ... "Paaainting for Your Life".' And he laughed so hard he scared me.

One November night he rolled against me in sleep, and I startled awake. He threw his arm across my chest, in not an embrace but in a desperate reflex. His limbs twitched. Sweat glittered in tiny globules on his creased forehead. He licked his cracked lips and let out a moist moan. He had a musky, iron smell, all agony and perspiration. I held him still and pressed my wrist to his cheek.

With one hand I whipped the blankets back and thought: water. I propped him up, twined my arm around his waist, and led him down the hall to the bathroom. When I flipped the light switch, he lowered his head, rubbing his eyes, and cried out. He leaned against the sink. His fingers fumbled with buttons as I knelt on the linoleum to adjust the faucet. My knees ached. My knuckles hurt. I tested the water, making it cold enough to stand. I looked back and saw him slumped on the floor, back to the wall, chin down at an uncomfortable angle, eyes closed, pyjama top half-open.

I guided him to his feet and held him there, easing the plaid flannel fabric off and down, sensing his shame at an intimacy born of dependence, not passion. I steadied him so his knees wouldn't buckle as he stepped over the rim of the tub. He kept his face turned away from me, gazing instead at the cracks in the wall tile.

There, on his back, he lay in the icy water. It made ripples over his yellow-black bruises. He tipped his head back, my fingers supporting it as if he were an infant, and for a moment smiled with sheer cool pleasure.

With a washrag I sponged the hollows of his neck and then swished the cotton through the water. Waves pulsed across his chest. His breath came in deep, ragged shudders. I sat and swished, sat and sponged. Slowly the shock hit his body. His shoulders quivered. He raised his hand, and with one thumb stroked the same place on my neck I'd bathed on him. The water dripped a wet splotch onto my nightshirt. 'Thank you,' he said.

Later, dressed again, he sat on the edge of the bed and I took his temperature. In the lamplight I strained to read the mercury. 'Shit,' I said. 'A hundred and two. It's back up again.'

He curled up on top of the quilt. 'I'm going back to sleep,' he said.

'No, you're not,' I said. 'Not until I call Dr Levitch.' We'd been warned that the drugs would make him susceptible to infections, which, though seemingly trivial, could be dangerous.

Dr Levitch confirmed that this was one of them, so at three in the morning I helped Bill into his coat, shook my son awake and with a thousand apologies deposited him at Deepa Romdourl's, and drove Bill to the hospital. Between starched sheets he lay, parched and gleaming, as I sat beside him until dawn broke, and kissed his fevered wrist over and over, and made wild promises about Australia.

When he came home, he was so weak that at dinner his first night back, I had to hold the fork to his lips. He ate a few bites, then ducked his head against my shoulder and sobbed, 'I'm sorry, I'm sorry.' I patted his back. Curran stared at us, horrified. I motioned for him to leave the room.

Bill looked up. He made a noise deep in his throat. His mouth was so ulcerated that he had difficulty speaking more than a few words.

'Don't strain yourself.' I tore the edge off one of my lesson plans. 'Here. Write it down.'

I put my hand over his to steady him. In a shaky scrawl he wrote in all capital letters: I DON'T WANT TO DIE. DAMN IT!

'Of course not,' I said. 'And you won't, sweetheart. This was just a setback. Dr Levitch said it might—'

Before I could help him, he grabbed the pen again

and wrote: YOU AREN'T GOD, YOU DON'T KNOW.

'No,' I said, 'I don't.'

Those late-fall nights. We lay in bed, slightly shivery, loving the crispness. Moonlight turned him silver. I traced his mouth with my fingers and thought: winter is coming, my angel, and we will have to gorge ourselves now before the famine.

He told me once how, during his fever, he'd seen me standing at the foot of his bed with my black hair swirling around my face and my head swathed in a nimbus of hues, vibrant reds and purples and blues, stained-glass church-window colours, like the woman in Russolo's *Perfume*. He'd screamed and screamed and tried to reach me, but couldn't.

'You had a temperature of a hundred and four degrees,' I said. 'You were hallucinating.'

He wrapped his arms around me. 'I don't care,' he said. 'I don't ever want you to be out of my grasp.'

That night at dinner, Curran asked, 'Do dead people remember?'

*   *   *

He went to the studio for the last time on a Saturday afternoon in mid-December. I drove over to pick him up. He came out in old jeans and a Navajo-print blanket coat, a red scarf tied around his bald head. 'How'd it go?' I asked.

'Dead good.'

From the back seat, Curran said, 'Are you going to be famous, Dad?'

'I sure hope so,' he said.

That was the day he finished *Necessary Madness*.

Christmas. The pipes froze. We made love beneath three quilts and drank coffee. His teeth chattered. The world was all holly berries and howling wind. He kissed my temple and said, 'There will never be another moment quite like this.'

The next day, Boxing Day, he woke feeling miserable. He had a slight fever, but neither of us worried about it. We figured he was just tired from the holiday rush. I gave him some aspirin and promised to keep Curran out of his hair, and, satisfied, he slept.

In the afternoon, though, he grew worse. He thrashed, sweating, breath raspy. I had to hold his head still to keep the thermometer under his tongue. I turned my back to him and read the mercury. My jaw dropped.

'It's ... it's not as bad as last time, is it?' he asked.

Quickly I swung around to face him. 'Oh, no, not at all,' I said, 'but just to be safe I think I should call Dr Levitch.'

I stood. He grabbed my hand and pulled me down beside him. 'Stay here,' he said.

'It'll only take a minute,' I said, and kissed his forehead.

In the hall I passed Curran. 'Do me a favour, love,' I said, 'and go sit with your father while I call the doctor.'

'What's wrong?'

'He's got a bad fever.'

'Will he be OK?'

'I think so, but he's worried. Go on.'

I was about to call Dr Levitch's home number when I heard a scream from the bedroom.

'Mum! Mum!'

I ran in and found Curran crouched on the floor in tears. On the bed, Bill's eyes rolled back in his head as his limbs jerked with convulsions.

'Get up,' I said to my son. 'I want you to get up and call an ambulance. Now.'

He scrambled to his feet and down the hall while dumbly I just stood there, longing to touch Bill even though I knew I shouldn't, aching for a way to make him realize I was with him, a way to say, *Even in your most paralyzing pain, way down in your deepest darkness, my darling, I am there, I am there.*

chapter seventeen

The morning of the retrospective, I went into Curran's room and told him he couldn't go. He threw a pillow at me. 'I hate you,' he said.

'Go right ahead and hate me, then,' I said, and closed the door behind me as I left.

My mother and I did the breakfast dishes to the sound of his sobs. 'Don't you think you're being too harsh with him, Gloria?' she asked.

'No.'

'But he's so interested in art, and he idolized his father so much—'

'I've made up my mind. He's not going.'

'Why?'

'Because Bill's paintings are like autopsies. They detail thoughts and emotions that as an eight-year-old he shouldn't have to deal with.'

'He's intelligent, though.'

'And still a child.' I handed her a plate to dry. 'Besides, he's got to learn that the world can be cruel to intellectuals, doesn't he?'

She looked down. Blinked hard.

'You love to push the knife in deeper, don't you?' she said.

'No. I just want the truth.'

I leaned up to put a glass back in the cupboard, and she touched my arm. 'What?' I said.

'Trust me,' she said. 'You aren't another Riordan.'

As night fell, I grew nervous. I picked at the roast beef sandwich on my supper plate and bit what little nails I had left. My mother sat across from me with a bowlful of water and her make-up bag, intent upon turning them into fabulous daggers. 'Mom, come on,' I said. 'This isn't about me. This is about Bill. No one will notice.'

'I know,' she said, and smiled.

I didn't protest, understanding that this was one of her odd stabs at closeness.

'The first exhibition I went to that had Bill's work in it,' I said, 'was one right after Curran was born. Of course I was nervous and self-conscious about how I looked after that, plus I had this inflated idea of myself as the artist's wife, a dark, chthonic figure for all the photographers to snap pictures of, so I ended up sorely disappointed. There was no press in sight. It was dimly lit and smoky and trendy, and Bill seemed like the only person in the room with any shred of sincerity about his work. I felt like, Christ, why bother, what's the use of this charade? But now, this time ... I don't know what I'll feel.'

'Hold still. There's no way I can push your cuticles back while you're gesturing wildly.'

'Sorry.'

'What time do you leave?'

'Eight.'

'Are you going by yourself?'

'No. Jascha Kremsky's taking me.' I sighed. 'Drop your eyebrow back down, Mom. It's nothing symbolic.'

'But won't that look as if—'

'Yes, it might, but I don't care. I can't go alone.'

'Yes. Of course not. You shouldn't.' I winced as she filed the edge of my thumbnail. 'Just out of curiosity, do you think he's interested in you?'

'He's not a lecher. He's gone through the same thing I have.'

She looked up. 'He has?'

'Yeah. Worse, actually. He lost his wife and daughter.'

'Oh, God.' She rifled through her assortment of bottles.

'Pick a subtle colour, OK? I'm not exactly in the mood for "fuck me" red tonight.'

'Would you stop swearing like that?' Her tone admonished me, but then she grinned. 'I left that shade at home, anyway.'

After she finished her polish job, I went into my room, slipped on my stockings, and pulled out the cranberry Harvey Nichols dress. I'd just stepped into it when I heard a tentative knock at the door.

'Come in,' I said, expecting it to be my mother asking if she could work on my hair next.

It was Curran, his head low with shame. He'd steered clear of me all day.

'Hey, kiddo,' I said. 'What's up?'

'I – I'm sorry,' he said. 'I really don't hate you.'

'I know,' I said, and touched his hair.

'Can I stay in here for a while?'

'Sure, if you promise not to throw any more pillows at me.' I struggled with the zipper on the back of the dress. 'Damn, it's stuck. Could you get this for me, Curran?'

He clambered onto the bed, swept my mother's robe aside, and on his knees pulled the zipper up the whole way. His small, soft hands rested briefly on my shoulders. 'There you go, Mum,' he said.

'Thanks, love.'

I sat before the mirror and pinned up my hair. As I leaned forward to put on lipstick, I glanced sideways, waiting for some filament of Bill to materialize behind me on the bed and fiddle with his tie or advise me on which necklace I should wear.

But, no. There was only the pale orb of my son's face.

'Someday,' he said, 'could I see Dad's paintings?'

'When you're older.'

'Are they good?'

'I'm no art critic,' I said, 'but they're honest, and that's all anyone can ask for.'

'Gloria,' my mother called from the kitchen. 'Jascha's here.'

I fumbled for my earrings, stepped into my heels, and gave Curran a kiss, then went out to meet him. 'Your mum's incredible,' he said as we walked down the front steps.

'Yeah, well, she acts like this is the fucking prom.'

He laughed as he opened the passenger door of his car for me. 'Sorry,' he said, 'but I forgot the corsage.'

I went to nibble the corner of one polished nail as he got in beside me, but then balled my hand into a fist and stared out the window.

'You look nice, by the way,' he said.

'Thanks.'

'What's wrong?'

'Nothing. I – I just – I'm afraid of this.'

We drove the rest of the way to Whitechapel in silence. 'Oh, God,' I said when we got there. 'I didn't expect this many people.'

'Don't worry,' he said, and took my elbow as we went in.

At the entrance, there stood a rackful of pamphlets printed with somebody's analysis of each piece. I grabbed one and stuffed it in my purse, thinking I'd give it to my mother. Another little souvenir for David.

Inside, the crowds were thick. Less noise than I was used to permeated the gallery. There wasn't the usual off-the-subject chatter about the warmth of the wine, the difficulties of arranging publicity, or the latest independent film at the Everyman Cinema. People filed past the paintings with the studied silence of academics, glasses clutched in their hands, their black garb for once truly appropriate. I looked down at my dress and felt like a bloodstain, a siren wailing. Make way for the widow.

Bill's friend Jim came over and embraced me. 'Gloria,' he said. 'I'm so glad you let us do this.'

I smiled weakly.

'So how have you been?' he asked.

I made a wavering motion with my hand. 'I'd be a liar,' I said, 'if I told you that I'm doing fine, but things are a bit better.'

'That's good. You know what they say about time—'

'Healing all wounds, yes. But not without scar tissue, believe me.'

I expected him to laugh, but then remembered that he wasn't Jascha. Behind my shoulder, a flashbulb went off. I jumped.

'Jesus,' I said. 'Are there photographers here?'

He nodded. 'From *The Times*.'

'I'm not one for self-flattery,' I said, 'but to be

safe maybe I'd better get out of the line of fire. Good to see you, Jim.'

I waved to him, and then wandered to the end of the line. Might as well look, I thought, and be anonymous for a while. I twisted my wedding ring and swallowed hard as I passed the Lamberhurst painting. I tried to keep my gaze rapt but cool, and found I couldn't.

Jascha broke through the throng and came over to me. 'Gloria,' he said. I stood with my arms wrapped around myself, gazing at a portrait Bill had done of our son, and didn't hear him. He moved to touch my shoulder, but instead his fingers brushed my neck.

I startled. 'Yeah?'

'We're about to start the – the, ah, presentation in a few minutes,' he said. 'I just wanted to let you know.'

'Do I have enough time for a drink?'

'Sure. You need one?'

'Violently.'

'OK.' He pointed to a table. 'Right next to that woman in maroon.'

I went over, took a glass, and stood against the wall. I had to admit that Jascha had done a good job. The backdrops were stark, simple, free of hype. White, the colour of the cells which had gone wrong.

A young man joined me. He cleared his throat, sipped his drink, pushed his dark hair out of his eyes. A wise-ass art student, no doubt – probably the Royal Academy.

We stared at the line of people snaking past the canvases, snaking towards the end of Bill.

'Isn't this amazing?' the young man asked. 'Isn't it incredible how his paintings parallel his illness and resulting death?'

'There is no parallel to death,' I said. For a moment I considered throwing my drink in his face.

He glanced over at me. 'Did you know Bill Burgess well?'

'I was his wife.'

Jascha waved from across the room. 'Excuse me,' I said, and walked over to him.

'Just a second, and we'll be ready,' he said. 'What's the matter? You look like you could murder someone.'

'I had a little run-in with the intelligentsia.'

'Fun, fun.'

'Listen, there aren't going to be any newspaper types in hot pursuit of me, are there?'

'No, why?'

'I don't think I can answer deep questions.'

'You won't have to.' He led me over to a platform which had been set up with a podium. A murmur rustled through the crowd as it trickled towards us, and then there came a call for silence. Jascha climbed the steps and took his place. He adjusted the microphone, which gave the telltale squeak those things insist upon emitting in moments of high tension. *Please don't joke*, I thought. *Not now.*

'Good evening,' he said. 'We're here tonight for a bittersweet gathering, one of both celebration and mourning. Celebration, because there's joy inherent in the showcasing of an artist who deserves to be showcased, and mourning, since that artist could not be here with us to take pride in his work.

'I'm sure most of you are aware that Bill Burgess died of leucaemia on January fifth of this year. You'll notice that I said "died", and not "passed away" or "left this earthly sphere" or any other euphemism commonly employed in order to mince around death. To use one would have been to deny what Bill's art was about: the truth, bare, controlled in its expression. In a time when pretension encroaches upon us, isn't it important to reward the unpretentious?

'And so we have done our best to honour Bill Burgess. Many have invested time and energy in this project, but those who deserve special thanks include all at the Whitechapel Gallery ...'

As he spoke, I gazed at his black hair slicked firmly in place, at his flamboyant purple tie, at his eyes as they darted from us to the paper then back at us again. I imagined him as he must have been as a child – hyperactive, mischievous, smooth-talking, but painfully well-intentioned. I smiled.

'. . . and also the members of the Chelsea Emerging Artists' Cooperative, particularly Sean Kennedy and Jim Welsh. Most important, I want to thank Gloria Burgess, Bill's widow and executor of his estate. Without her kind permission, this retrospective literally would not have been possible, and without her insight it would not have been as fitting a tribute to Bill. I've asked her to share with us a few thoughts on his work and his life. Gloria?'

Shaking, head down, I made my way up the steps, holding the folds of my skirt in my sweaty fingers so I wouldn't trip. Jascha nodded to me, and, before he left, squeezed my hand hard behind the podium. I stared out at all those intense, expectant faces, and tried to think of the tricks they'd told us to use so we'd relax while giving speeches back in high school Oral Communications. Look at the wall. Picture your audience in their underwear.

I tucked a strand of hair behind my ear.

'Hi,' I said. 'I've ... I've got to admit that this whole concept gets me nervous, and I've got to warn you that what I'm about to say is neither a tear-stained eulogy nor an art history dissertation.

'What can I tell you about my late husband? Well, I could tell you that he patterned himself after Munch and, in his earlier, more conventional and less troubled years, Hockney, that he was kind to a fault, that he longed to go to Australia. I could give him to you in a slurred catalogue: artist-lover-husband-father-angel-protector-visionary-*dead*. I could get confessional and tell you how he was there for me, how in my darkest, most poisoned moments he was willing, so willing to pick up my wrist and suck the poison from the wound, to take the risk of holding the venom in his mouth those first few dangerous seconds.

'But that wouldn't suit the task at hand. My cries of "I remember" wouldn't give you a true picture of Bill or his art, because memory distorts. It slips and spirals and gets lost in the private code of the one who remembers, her loose jargon of allusions, symbols.

'I think Bill realized the perils of this. He was not a man of grey. He saw the world in brightness and coherence. The universe was simple and gorgeous to him, and he wanted to capture it all, to pick it up and devour it easily as you would a piece of fruit – or flowers, if you're Robert Browning.' A few people laughed. 'This is not to say that Bill was blindly idealistic. He understood full well the chiaroscuro of living; he just chose not to dwell on it. Sometimes I wonder if his belief in the inherent goodness of things made it easier for awful ones to befall him.

'I'm not an artist by any means, but I do have a decent background in poetry, and when I think of the importance Bill's art held for him during his last few months, I'm reminded of a prose poem the Russian poet Anna Akhmatova placed in one of her books under the title 'Instead of a Foreword'. In it she tells of standing numbly in a prison line in Leningrad, and of a woman who whispers to her, "Can you describe this?" Akhmatova replies that she can, and some semblance of a smile slips over the shell of the woman's face.

'Like Akhmatova, Bill equated his art with his survival. One time he told me, "I am painting for

227

my life." In a physical sense, this statement is of course naïve, impossible; all the canvases hung here tonight cannot resurrect him from the dead. But Bill knew that being a witness, that depicting the fear and doubt and terror of his struggle to live, was the only way to survive. Thank you.'

I stepped down to applause. As I pushed through the crowd, I heard whispers. 'So she's the woman in number thirty-six ...' 'And wait, look here, he probably meant to portray her in number eighteen, too ...'

I ran to the rest room and splashed cold water on my face. My breath came in frenzied gasps. My eyes grew wet. I stared at myself in the mirror, glared, and thought, you are going to have to do better than this.

I sat on a folding chair by the sink and lit a cigarette. A girl came out of one of the stalls. Perky, short blonde hair, challis-print dress. Probably another art student. Oh, neat. Let's go see the death paintings.

'Your mascara's running,' she said.

'Oh. Thank you.'

I rummaged through my purse for a tissue and watched her leave. God, is that woman ever unhinged, I heard her thinking.

Stop, I told myself as I wiped my eyes. You told your son he couldn't punch Nigel Clark just because he was mad at the unfairness of what happened, so don't be a hypocrite and go making monsters of everyone because of it. She was a nice girl. A kind girl. She wanted to keep you from embarrassing yourself.

I reached for another tissue and instead pulled out the retrospective pamphlet. I turned to Number 38, *Necessary Madness*, and skimmed its description. The words blurred. 'Harsh, stark ... symbolic of the parent-child ... evokes questions of ... perversity of grief ... those who go on ...'

Those who go on, I thought. Yes. We who have to live, to remember, to breathe after the loved one's last drawn breath. What about us? Where do we go when we go on?

We have several choices.

On one end of the spectrum, we can refuse to go on. We can pull a Riordan Merchant, whether it be with a knife, a bottle of pills, or a gun. Entranced by thoughts of reunion, driven by desperation, we can cop out. Fade to black. Bang. Crash. Game over. Enough people left hurting to rival the magnitude of our pain, the pain we swore no one could surpass.

Or, if we still want to watch the sun rise every morning, or are squeamish about plotting our own deaths, yet we feel on the verge of collapse, we can lean on others. Do it for decades. Become a sort of mournful moocher. Expect our children to blink back their tears and catch our salty rivers of them in their trembling cupped palms. Notch our scars into the skin of their unscarred bodies.

And what if we're afraid of inflicting pain? What if we're afraid to feel it ourselves? Then it's deep-freeze time. Automatic pilot. Psychic Novocain. Get up-brush our teeth-wash our hair-make breakfast-go to work-come home-eat supper-fall into bed. Don't think about it. Don't let the love or the anguish creep in. And then when it explodes, we are caught out in the open, no shelter, no mask, bones lit up, flesh torn.

There's got to be another option, I thought, *but what?*

'I don't know,' I said aloud. I tossed the pamphlet in the trash, and then, cigarette in hand and regulation smile in place, went back out to the gallery.

The rest of the night was nebulous. I remember having three more drinks and telling a reporter to get out of my face, and then all of a sudden it was eleven-thirty, and everyone else was filing out into the night air, and Jascha and I stood alone in the empty brightness.

We stared at each other. I wanted to run from him, wanted to run through the maze of paintings to its end and find Bill waiting there, his arms open, his grin wide as he said, 'Ha. Fooled ya, didn't I?'

Jascha took my arm. 'We'd better go,' he said. As he led me out, I glanced over my shoulder at the canvases. So clean and neat, so boundaried.

'Are you happy now?' I asked when we got outside.

He looked up as he unlocked the car. 'What in the hell is that supposed to mean?'

'You got what you wanted, didn't you?'

'Why are you being so bitter?'

'Answer my question, and I'll answer yours.'

'Yes,' he said. 'If you mean that I put together a good retrospective and it went smoothly, yes, I got what I wanted.'

'So are you happy now?'

'No.'

I gulped. A tear slid down my cheek, and I batted it away.

'What's wrong?' he asked. 'Was it the exhibition?

Did I do anything out of line? Was there something in it we hadn't discussed that you didn't like?'

'No, no,' I said, 'not at all. For a minute there during your little speech, I thought you were going to tell some story about me, like, "And then I wound up in the flat of this crazy bitch who came to the door in her bathrobe, and ..."'

We laughed.

'I liked it, though,' I said. 'It was great. Very dignified. Very Bill.'

He touched my wet face.

'So what's with this?' he said.

'Because – because he isn't—'

'Isn't here.' He sighed. 'Yes. Oh, God, yes.'

He brought his hand down, and I grabbed it. He moved closer. I brushed my lips across his. They were quick, starved empathy kisses – *I know, I know.* He reached his fingers up to the base of my skull, and yanked the combs from my hair. When we pulled apart, strands of it were in his mouth.

'Sorry,' we both mumbled.

I leaned forward and wrapped my arms around him. 'Owe me a beer,' I said against his neck.

'What?'

'You owe me a beer. Didn't you know that's what

you're supposed to say whenever you and someone else say the same thing at the same time?'

'No. I didn't.'

'Well, you do now.'

He stroked my back. 'Honey, you don't need any more alcohol,' he said.

'Yeah. Next thing you know, I'll be kissing a complete stranger.'

'I lied,' he whispered into my hair. 'I'm not sorry.'

'Neither am I. Mixed up. Guilty. But not sorry.'

We leaned against the car door, his arm around my waist, my head pressed to his shoulder.

'You know,' he began, 'I think Bill would have—'

'Shh,' I said, and put a finger to his lips.

'That's right,' he said, 'I'm forgetting how, the last time I tried to tell you what Bill would have wanted, you slammed the door on me.'

'Don't talk.'

And so we stood there, silent in the darkness, holding each other, and as I watched the late-night traffic pass by and thought of my parents, I told myself, *We're not making their mistakes. We're not like them.*

* * *

233

He drove up to my building and we sat in the car for a while. I had a smoke.

'You really ought to quit that,' he said.

'Yeah.' I glanced past him and into the windows of my flat. All dark. 'I'm surprised my mother's not inside with a stopwatch. "Gloria, you've been out there with him for ten minutes! There's something going on between you two, I know it!"'

He laughed. 'What, does she think there is?'

I nodded.

'Well, there is, isn't there?'

I tipped my head back. 'You don't waste any time, do you?' I said. 'I ... I don't know what to call what just happened. There's no convenient Greek name to assign it. Maybe it was meaningful, or maybe it was a mere rush of hormones at an East End car park.'

He reached for my free hand. I slipped it from his grasp and ran my fingers gently over the back of his neck. My nails shimmered next to his skin.

'Gloria,' he said. He leaned towards me, lips parted. His eyes shone.

'No,' I said. 'Not now.'

'Do you need me to walk you up?'

I shook my head.

'Can I call you?'
'I can't stop you,' I said.

I went upstairs and stumbled into the kitchen, feeling my way through it so I wouldn't have to turn on a light and wake anyone. I banged my shin on the table, and clamped my hand over my mouth to muffle a scream of pain as I limped down the hall to my room.

Inside, I took off my heels and padded over to the closet, where I pulled out my pink French Riviera nightgown. It was an expensive one, and so had lasted all those years. By the light from the window I unzipped my dress and pulled off my stockings, ever aware of my mother asleep on the bed. I prayed she wouldn't see my bent figure, all glowing flesh, drunk, vulnerable. There was a bruise on my leg.

'Tanzania,' I murmured.

'What?' came a moan from the direction of the pillows.

'Nothing,' I said. My hands rose to my loose hair, and I fought to remember where I'd stuffed the combs after Jascha had pulled them out. I went back to the closet and found them shoved in my coat pocket. I threw them on top of the dresser. They stared up at me: gilded, innocent.

I thought of the slippery, ephemeral feel of Jascha's skin beneath my fingers, the salty, caustic taste of his mouth, the thick haze of his musky scent — all veneer, all polish, all fire, a foreign country, while Bill had been bland, visceral, smelling of oatmeal soap, earthen, like a homecoming. I took off my earrings and put them in my jewellery box. After a moment of hesitation, I left my wedding ring on.

I stealthed past my slumbering mother and down the hall. On my way to the bathroom, I passed my son's room. His door was ajar. I tiptoed past and stood by his bed. I stared at the pale, round half-moon of his cheek and listened to the steady, even rhythm of his breathing. He stirred. When he glimpsed me, he rocketed up, his hair rumpled.

'Mum,' he said. 'The exhibition. How was it? Were there famous artists there? Were there newspaper people?'

I smiled. 'Here,' I said. 'Move over.'

He wriggled to the other side of the mattress, and I crawled under the covers and put my arms around him. He rested his chin on my collarbone.

'You smell of smoke,' he said.

'Yeah. Pretty awful, huh?'

'You should stop. If you don't, your lungs will turn to rubbish.'

'I know. Jascha's been bugging me about that, too.'

Speaking his name felt like both a benediction and a betrayal.

'So tell me about the exhibition,' Curran said.

'It was nice,' I said. 'It fit your father.'

'Will there be an article about it in the paper?'

'Probably. There were reporters there.'

'Can I read what they wrote about Dad when it comes out?'

'Oh, if you insist.' I kissed his forehead. 'It'll mostly be journalistic babble, though.'

'I won't mind if I can't understand some of the words. I'll just ask you. You're a walking dictionary, Mum.'

I laughed. 'What, not a thesaurus?'

'That too. Do you think Dad will be famous now?'

'That's not for me to decide.'

'I think he will. Did you give a speech about him?'

I nodded.

'I wish I could've been there to hear it,' he said.

'I know you do.' I stroked back his damp hair. 'You'd better get back to sleep, love. It's one in the morning.'

'Really?'

'Really.'

'Wow,' he said.

I climbed out of bed and tucked the blankets back in around him. The image of us from *Necessary Madness* synapsed briefly through my brain, and I pushed it away. No, I thought. That will not be him. That will not be me.

After that I went into the bathroom and removed my eye make-up. I was about to blot off my lipstick when the nausea hit me. I leaned over the sink and turned on the tap to cover the sound of my throwing up four glasses of wine and my dinner.

My mother came in just as I wiped my mouth with a towel. I caught sight of her face in the mirror as she stepped behind me and put her hands on my shoulders. For a moment I expected her to yell at me — *It is one in the fucking morning, Gloria Merchant, and I really don't appreciate this* — but she didn't.

Instead she turned me around and gazed into my eyes.

'Gloria,' she said.

I ducked my head and rested my cheek against the smooth, cool curve of her neck. 'Mom,' I said, 'tell me that I'll make the right choices. Tell me that I'll be brave enough.' Clad in floral silk, she smoothed back my tangled hair and stood barefoot on the linoleum tile and whispered, *You will, you will.*

chapter eighteen

London froze during Bill's last winter. I saw my breath each morning when, still in my nightgown, I crouched on the edge of our bed and dialled the hospital to hear if he'd survived the previous night. My lips moved in silent prayer as the wind howled, rattling casements.

Weary but polite voice on the other end of the line:

'Yes. He's stable.'

Yes. A tiny snip of a word, but at that moment the most euphoria-inducing statement in the English language, the seven a.m. pivot upon which my life turned. *Yes* sent blood to the surface of my skin and pushed warmth into my icy fingers as I dressed in the grey dawn, pulling on layers of wool, wanting to open a window and lean out into the street and scream, 'My husband is alive!'

Instead I'd go down the hall to wake Curran. He moaned when I slid my hand beneath the covers and shook his shoulder, but within seconds he always sat up and asked, 'Is Dad all right? Can he come home?'

'Not yet,' I said.

'Well, when?'

'I don't know. The drugs they're giving him take time to work.'

'That's bollocks,' he said as he climbed out of bed. 'They should make him better' – he snapped his fingers – 'like that.'

'Don't swear,' I said, but part of me agreed with him.

He complained each time I took him downstairs to Deepa's for the day. 'Why do you get to see Dad, but I don't?' he asked, kicking at her welcome mat as we waited for her to let us in.

'Because there are rules that say you can't.'

'Those rules are daft.'

'I know, but be patient. You'll see him soon enough.'

I didn't tell him about the one exception to the rule: he could come with me if his father was dying.

∗   ∗   ∗

In Bill's hospital room we were encapsulated. The room was a white jungle, sticky with the heat which rose from him. Every morning at nine I stepped inside, closed the door, took off my coat and scarf and gloves, sat down on a hard-backed chair, and gave up all citizenship in the outside world. For hours I didn't move. Nightfall slanted across us, darkening the thin blanket that covered him, and not until then did I stand and reach above his bed to turn on the light, a glowing strip eerily similar to the spotlights in the galleries where his paintings once hung.

We didn't say much. When he and I spoke it was through raised eyebrows, brushing of thumbs, fingertips stroked in the hollows of palms, those necessary languages, those alternate tongues. He dozed, and I gripped his free hand, the one that wasn't numb from being stuck with needles, and waited for the mercury to drop. By spring, I thought, he'd be home. His hair would grow back. He could sleep in the sun on the balcony. We'd make real plans about Australia and drink mango tea, and only safe things would blossom.

When night crossed the border into morning, he

gazed at me tenderly and rasped, 'Go home. You must be exhausted.' At that point, had he in that cracked voice told me to slice my flesh into ribbons, I would have gladly done it.

I stood again and bent to embrace him. His frail arms encircled my back. 'Angel,' he said. The word stabbed me, but still I went through the motions of strength, said all the calming murmurs: *yes, I'll be back tomorrow, yes, I'll send Curran your love.* Anguished scream caged, held inside for the goodbye kiss. Later, during the tube ride home, the wail tore its way through my body as I sat in the cold, gleaming darkness and licked my lips to taste the salt of his sweat on them.

Leaving him. The determined speedwalk down the corridor — *don't look back* — and into the rotunda, past the nurses charting every cell multiplied, every cell lost, in the dusky hush at their stations. Into the elevator. Fists clenched tight. How many times did I watch the grimy mirrored doors slide towards each other and lift my hand to push the button which kept them from closing at the last instant? How many times did I choke down my desire to career through the halls, knocking over medicine carts, leaving fallen interns in my wake, all to rush to his room and put my ear to his chest, to whisper, 'I'm here, I'm here,' to make sure his heart was still beating?

Before I left, as I stood in the parking lot, I always turned around and peered up into the window I knew was his, comforted to see a white shard of brightness inside it. He slept with the light on, like a frightened child, never wanting to be in darkness, ever. I strained to glimpse his profile, the outline of his bare skull, whatever fragments I could. I hated to think of him alone, at any uncomfortable angle. What could I do? What sign could I give him? A wave would have been too cheerful, a blown kiss too melodramatic. Powerless, limbs thick with fatigue, I picked my way across the asphalt as the icy air assaulted my flushed face and the wind blew all traces of his scent off me.

Each night I collected a drowsy Curran from the Romdourls', leading him across a den carpet littered with Christmas toys, and put him to bed, then sat at the kitchen table and went over the plans for my second term before I snatched four or five hours of sleep.

At three o'clock one morning, my son came

out in wrinkled pyjamas and asked, 'Why is God so mean?'

On the thirtieth I decided to send Curran to stay with Bill's parents for a few days. I couldn't keep burdening Deepa, who had two children of her own to worry about. I explained to him that this way would be better for all concerned, but still I had to drag him to the car. 'Better for who?' he screamed. 'Better for you, you mean!'

He quieted as we drove to Lamberhurst. I didn't try to reason with him; the roads were so slick that if I spoke I feared I'd lose control. When I pulled in the driveway, he unbuckled his seatbelt and let it fly back with an angry snap. He rested his cheek against the cold windowpane.

'Is Dad going to die?' he asked.

'We're all going to die, Curran.'

'Don't be stupid. You know what I mean.'

'I can't tell you,' I said. 'The doctors say he isn't in great shape right now, but then again they said that last time—'

'So he might get better, or he might not.'

'Yeah.'

'I hate not knowing.'

246

'I do too, love.'

He scrawled his name backwards on the frosted glass.

'I want to be near him,' he said. 'And you. I don't want to be way out here where I have no idea what's going on.'

'Curran,' I said. 'Look at me. I'm going to call you every day, and you'll know what's going on. Promise.'

'You won't lie, or make things sound happy when they aren't?'

'Of course not. And if anything important happens, anything at all, I'll have Gran bring you back to the city.'

'That second?'

'That second.' I motioned him across the seat, and he slid over to me. He shivered. I drew the folds of my coat around him. We sat like that for a few minutes, his face against my neck.

As we went up the front walk, a light snow began to fall. I leaned my head back and caught a flake on my tongue. 'Tastes like rum and Coke,' I said.

He laughed. 'That's disgusting, Mum.'

He turned around and gazed at the fields and outbuildings which surrounded the house. His face

247

was bright and red with cold. He looked so small holding his suitcase. 'When I leave here,' he said, 'either Dad will be home or he'll be dead.'

New Year's Eve. Bill's fever went down enough to put him in good spirits. He begged the nurses to sneak him beer. *He'll get through this*, I thought. *How sick can he be if he's pleading for some Guinness?*

'I talked to Curran today,' I said.

'Yeah?'

'Yeah. He was all psyched because Gran was going to let him stay up till midnight.'

He laughed. 'I miss him.'

With jittery, sweat-soaked fingers, he toyed with a few strands of my hair.

'Resolutions,' he said.

'Sweetheart, last time I checked it was still this year. Aren't you being a bit premature?'

'No harm in that. Go ahead, tell me yours.'

'OK,' I said. 'Let's see. I resolve ... to be as utterly perfect and goddess-like as I have been thus far in my life.'

'Shut up.'

'You asked for it. No, seriously, I resolve to stop taking advantage of people, not to yell at the fourth-formers no matter how pesky they get, and to quit cowering behind intellectual bric-a-brac.'

'You're too hard on yourself.'

'Yeah, well, it beats egoism. Your turn.'

'I resolve to get out of this place,' he said, 'to get well, and to live with my arms flung wide.'

He fell asleep soon after that. I woke him up at 11.55 and sat on the edge of his bed, and we turned on the television and rang in the new year. He leaned over and kissed me. 'Everything is possible tonight,' he said.

The next morning I got a call from the hospital. His fever had shot up to one hundred and six degrees. Any higher than that would be alchemy. Any higher than that would kill him.

Deep inside his smouldering haze, my husband slept, limbs suffused with fire. Outside, the sky turned blue-black. Streetlamps flickered on. People drew their coats in tighter and took the tube home. Rain sloshed in gutters, and still he burned.

Bill lay with his head turned towards me on the pillow. Lost weight had sharpened his features, given them angles, made him look harsh and hungry. Heat softened his flesh. He was all purpled wax-paper skin, both an infant and an old man. Taped to his wrist, inside a scarred vein, lay a needle attached to a thin line of tubing which dripped antibiotics into him.

I once read a story about Houdini and his wife, and how they planned his stunts together. Before he departed, he'd give his wife a goodbye kiss in front of the crowd, and she'd slip him a key to unlock his chains. I loved that image of her, pale, dour-faced in a wide-brimmed hat, the way all women seemed to look at the turn of the century, her cheeks flushed with anticipation as she leaned forward to feel the brush of his lips, the cold metal waiting on her tongue.

Night after night I sat beside Bill, feet close together on the grey-flecked linoleum floor, fingers twisted around a tissue in my lap, head tipped back. I longed to take his head in my hands and press my mouth to his, to give him the chance for freedom.

The third day of the new year, I walked into his room to find him thrashing. I rushed to the side of his bed and reached out a hand to touch him, but he shrank back. 'Who are you?' he said. 'I don't remember you. You aren't supposed to be here.'

'Bill,' I said, 'it's me. Don't you—'

'Get out of here!'

In tears, I ran into the hall and begged someone to find me Dr Levitch. 'When he's in pain, he gets disoriented,' he said, hands on my shoulders. 'Go take a walk and calm down. We'll give him some medication, and in a few minutes he'll be fine.'

I did as he suggested, and then returned to find Bill asleep, curled up, his back to me. He gleamed with sweat and innocence. After a few minutes, he woke and turned over.

'Hi,' he said softly. 'What's wrong? You look like you've been crying.'

I told him what had happened.

'Oh, God,' he said. 'So this is how bloody awful it's become.'

That night, shivering, I went up the front steps of my building in the darkness and thought, *I want this to be a movie.* I want to lean back in my red plush seat with a plastic carton of popcorn and watch this awful story unfold, and know I am no part of it. I want to weep at the scene of a woman in a black coat who walks into her empty flat to call her son in a farmhouse miles away, but I also want the reassurance of a sudden garble in the sound, a sudden splotch on the screen, to remind me that her agony is just on film. Most of all, I want

251

to leave the theatre and find my husband waiting for me on the sidewalk, snow in his hair, mouth frosty against mine, arm snug around my waist as he asks, 'So, how was it?' I want to walk out of this life like I'm walking out of a room. I want to be anyone but me.

January fourth. He woke in such pain that the day revolved around morphine. In the afternoon Dr Levitch motioned me into the hall. 'I don't think he'll pull out of this,' he said.

There were no hysterics, no melodramatic exchanges. He just touched my arm gently, and I nodded. We gazed at each other, Levitch and I, like two conspirators whose plot had failed, two idealists whose hero had fallen.

After he left me I went to one of the banks of phones and dialled Bill's parents in Lamberhurst.

'Louise,' I said, 'you'd better bring Curran.'

She drove to the hospital right away. I watched my son come out of the elevator, head down, hands stuffed in the pockets of his royal-blue winter jacket. He ran to me. I hugged him hard, then sat him down on a bench outside Bill's room, my arm still around him.

'Either it's good or it's bad,' he said. 'Tell me which.'

'Well,' I said, 'your father is in a lot of pain, and his fever is very bad. Not many people with a fever as bad as his survive.'

'But he could.'

'He could, you're right, but the chances are slim.'

'So Dad's probably going to die.'

I nodded.

He toyed with the zipper on his jacket. 'Can I see him?'

'That's why you're here, sweetie.'

'Gran said that sometimes he's confused. She said I should be careful.'

'There's no need to worry. Just don't say anything that might upset him.'

'Will he know who I am?'

'Of course.' I squeezed his shoulders. 'Stay only a few minutes, though, OK? We don't want to tire him.'

He stood and turned to me. 'Aren't you coming along?'

'No. You deserve a bit of time alone with your father. Don't be scared. Go on.'

He went inside Bill's room, and softly closed the door. Louise sat beside me. We stayed there in silence until Curran came back out, face tight, eyes wet. Louise and I both stood. I bent down and kissed his forehead. He slipped one hand into his grandmother's and one into mine, and then we went to the cafeteria for supper. Over tuna-fish sandwiches, our knees touching beneath the table, he leaned forward and looked into my face and said, 'That was the last time I'll see Dad, wasn't it?'

After Curran and Louise left, I went back to Bill and sat beside him. Off and on we both slept.

At one in the morning he lifted his head, panicky, and called out, 'Gloria.'

'Yes.'

'You aren't going to leave me, are you?'

'No. I'm going to stay right here, love.'

'All night?'

'All night.'

His features relaxed. He lay back on the pillow. There was no more of his usual talk about how I must be knackered, how I should get home. He smiled. 'Good.'

With one hand he patted the mattress. I got up

from my chair and sat on the bed. Fumbling but instinctive, he brushed his fingers across the sheet until they met mine. I grabbed on tight. 'Don't let go,' he said.

For the next sixteen hours, I didn't move. I couldn't look at Bill's face. Instead I stared at a frayed thread on his pyjama top, at its pearly buttons. I wanted to rip them open with both hands, put my head on his chest, and feel the muted throb of his heart inside his ribs, but I didn't. I might cry. I might hurt him.

At three o'clock in the afternoon he reached up, pulled me down until his lips were at my ear, shoved my hair out of my face, and whispered in a dry rasp. 'What?' I whispered back. Though I couldn't hear him, I hated to make him repeat himself; at that point every word that came from his parched throat was a sacrifice.

'Please,' he said. 'Something for the pain.'

He stared at me. I saw a sudden cramp in his gaze, like the tightening of a belt. His skin was liquid.

'OK. Hold on.' With my free hand I reached for the cord that hung above his bed, and punched the call button with my thumb. In a few moments, the door swung open. A white-clad figure stepped inside.

Bill blinked at the light from the corridor. The nurse
went to the side of the bed and injected the glistening
painkiller fluid into the IV line. Bill moaned a little.
She gazed over at me.

'Let me know if there's anything else I can do,' she
said softly. Her curly blonde hair was pulled back so
tightly I could see the vein at her temple throbbing.
The tag pinned to her blouse said REBECCA. I
remembered that that had been Pandora Brennan's
original first name, and thought of my Leigh Street
days, their angst so deliciously trivial.

The nurse left, and Bill sank back on the pillows.
He coughed. It was a loose, scraping sound. He
gagged a bit, tried to speak, but all that came out
was a futile creak.

'Water,' I said. With a tiny jerk of his chin
he nodded.

I leaned over to the nightstand and picked up a
full Styrofoam cup, careful not to press in too hard
and risk its implosion.

With one hand I held it, and slid the other beneath
his head to raise him. He fought, the lines in his
forehead going deeper, saying, No, no, let me do
it, fighting for those last small shards of autonomy.
I put the edge of the cup to his lips. He drank in

fragile, quick gasps. His whole skull bobbed with the effort. My hand jerked, and the water slopped down his throat, over his collarbone. He smiled. It was a crude, minuscule smile, but I almost cried to see his face gleam as it broke open with pleasure.

The cup's edges had gone moist and cracked. I leaned across, tossed it in the wastecan.

'You've got circles under your eyes,' he said.

He reached for my hand, straightened it, lifted it to his mouth, and kissed my fingertips. Two hours later he was dead.

That night I took the tube home from the hospital and walked for a while on Upper Street. My hands cramped with coldness even though I stuffed them in the pockets of my coat, and my face stung. As I passed pubs and kitchen-gadget stores and wine bars, I thought, *Oh, God, there's no one here to hold me this time. It's happening again.*

I was crying by the time Deepa Romdourl let me into her flat. She smelled like flour and silk and homecoming, and draped a soft brown arm around me. I leaned against her shoulder and gasped long and hard, my tears of sheer exhaustion staining her peach sari.

She sat me down in the kitchen, patting my hair maternally before she turned to wash dishes. I rested my head on my arms and squeaked my thumb over the plastic tablecloth as I watched Curran, sprawled on his stomach on the den sofa. He'd stayed with her since school had resumed. It was almost ten o'clock. Bill had died at five.

Meanwhile Deepa's daughter, Vari, lounged on the floor beside my son, doing her algebra homework in front of the television. 'Sodding polynomial,' she muttered. Her mother frowned. Curran sat up, rubbed his eyes. I stood. Went over to him. Knelt down. He mumbled something drowsy about Dad, was his fever still bad? Leaned his head on my collarbone. His palms were hot at the back of my neck. I wondered if he could sense it, the palpable aura of morphine and last wishes that clung to me, but I didn't answer him. Instead I helped him to his feet and mouthed to Deepa, 'You're a saint. Really.'

I led Curran back to our flat, keeping him close to me as I flipped every light switch: the one to the living room, the hall, his bedroom, mine. I bit my lip as I guided him, all moans and yawns, into a pair of blue flannel pyjamas. He slid under the covers, and I pulled them up to his chin and kissed him good night.

Then I closed his door behind me and tore out of my clothes and into an old shirt of Bill's, and then I crawled between a pair of freezing sheets, and somehow, I don't know how, I slept.

The morning after was a Sunday. That got me. The air was so soft and quiet with luxury that any moment I expected Bill to come in with unkempt hair and the Arts section of the *Observer*.

I heard the sound of feet padding to the bathroom and back. I waited until I heard a creak and the rustlings of bedclothes before I slid from beneath them.

Curran didn't open his eyes when I sat beside him. I shook him a little. He jerked. The sweetness, the anticipation in his gaze – more snow to cancel school tomorrow? Dad's gotten better? – cut into me.

I swallowed.

'Listen, love.' I said. 'Your ...'

The kind euphemisms, the gentle lead-ins, reduced themselves to a rough gag in my throat. I'd forgotten to put on my robe, and shivered. I clutched his hand.

'Curran,' I said. 'Your father died last night.'

With one convulsive snap he wrenched himself

away from me, back turned, his cries dulled by the pillow he buried his face in, palm flung upward. Little-boy tears displaced themselves as tremors along his spine. I reached out to touch his shoulder and he flinched. Now I knew where the phrase 'break the news' came from. Even the air that circled between us seemed fractured.

I got up and went into the kitchen and made a cup of coffee. I sat at the table and drank the amaretto and gave myself orders: inhale, exhale, I waited for the scream of aloneness to overtake me.

chapter nineteen

The morning after the retrospective, I woke on the couch, groggy and dishevelled, to the sound of a ringing phone. My mother got it. I lay back and listened to her perky, polite voice as it drifted towards me from the kitchen. 'I'm sorry, but she's asleep right now ... Yes, that was a long night, wasn't it? ... Shall I have her call you? ... Right, right, of course. Goodbye.'

She came into the living room and sat on the floor beside me.

Her face glistened in the sunlight. She wore a tiny gold heart around her neck. I'd never noticed it before. Probably a gift from David. I rubbed my eyes.

'Who was that?' I asked.

'Jascha.'

'Oh, God.'

'He wants you to call him.'

I sat up and yawned. 'I'm sure he does.'

Her features tensed with concern. 'Gloria, what happened?'

'I don't know,' I said. 'I mean, objectively I can tell you, but emotionally I—'

'You want to talk about it?'

'Not really.'

I got up and went into the kitchen before she could ask another question, then poured myself a glass of orange juice and called Jascha.

'Hey,' he said. 'How are you?'

'I'm slowly regaining my mental faculties, thanks.'

'I think we need to talk.'

'Yes.'

'Can I take you to lunch?'

'Today?'

'Today.'

I watched my mother fold the sheets and blankets that had fallen off the couch.

'Gloria?' Jascha asked.

'Yeah?'

'Are you mad at me?'

'No. At myself, maybe. But not you.'

'Listen, if you're tired, or you don't want to, I'll understand, but I really think we should—'

'OK.'

'Where do you want to go?'

'It doesn't matter. Pick somewhere.'

'Can I trust that I'll find you suitable to be seen in public with by around, say, noon?'

'You can.'

I went back into the living room. 'Mom,' I said, 'would you have any great qualms about watching Curran for an hour or two this afternoon?'

She looked up. 'No, why?'

'Jascha's taking me to lunch.'

She opened her mouth to speak, then closed it again and returned to tidying.

'You don't have to fold all that,' I said. 'Really. I can take care of it.'

She smiled. 'I don't mind.'

'Well, I'm going to run and take a shower, OK?'

I walked to the door and then turned. 'Mom,' I said.

'Yes?'

'I'm sorry if I've been treating you more like a baby-sitter than a houseguest.'

'What are you talking about? He's my grandson. We have a lot of catching up to do.'

Jenn Crowell

'I know, but—' I swallowed. 'I just wanted to say thanks. You've helped me out.'

She pushed a lock of hair behind her ear, and for a moment I saw the girl in the wildflower-print skirt at Oxford. 'You're welcome,' she said.

After a shower, wrapped in my robe, I stopped by my son's room and stood in the doorway. Draped in pale-gold light, he lay with the blankets tucked around his chin, his face soft, his tiny, slender fingers outspread on the sheet. His breath made the sound you'd expect a flower to make as it opens. I wanted to run to him, and drop a thousand gentle wake-up kisses on his cheek, but I stayed still with my arms around myself.

Curran, I thought. Loving you, raising you, being both your parents now, is the acid test by which my strength is measured. Every time I hunger, every time my numb tongue crawls towards the feel of the open mouth of a stranger, every time my flailing arms and legs reach to wrap around the waist of a man who is not your father, I promise I will think of you. Of your hazel eyes filled with tears, of your silent face, cramped with anger.

* * *

That afternoon Jascha took me to a place overlooking Hampstead Heath. We sat on the terrace and ate simple pub grub, bread and cheese and Branston pickle. He had a copy of the *Sunday Times* with him, and he spread it out over the table and paged through the Culture section.

'The article's in here,' he said.

'So soon?'

'Yeah.'

I looked away as eagerly he read. 'You're in the third paragraph,' he said. 'They called you "shaky but statuesque".'

'I hate New Journalism. Was it brutal?'

'Not too bad. "Bill Burgess's works strive relentlessly for an expression of the archetypal, sometimes with clichéd overstatement, sometimes with astounding power."'

'Stop. I don't want to hear any more.'

He folded the paper. 'Gloria,' he said. 'About last night.'

I stared down at the table and shredded a paper napkin between my fingers. 'God, that sounds funny,' I said. 'Like some line from a soap opera. As if it were some vague, incredible blur of passion. *Last night.*'

'But it wasn't funny.'

265

'No.'

He leaned back in his chair, rubbed his forehead.

'I feel like such a predator,' he said. 'Here you are, widowed only four months, and—'

'I'm not some trembling forest waif.'

'I know you aren't. But it's just the idea that I would—'

'That I could—'

'Yeah.'

'It was both of us. You know that. It wasn't like a sporting event, where we'd be able to run an instant replay, have it all measured, a matter of time or distance or whatever. "Oh, yes, it was . . . him, making the first move with a lead of two thousandths of a second."'

He laughed. 'Has anyone ever told you that you're really fucking weird?'

I took a sip of water. 'Everyone in the world except Bill, actually.'

We paid for our lunches – or, rather, he did, despite my protests – and took a walk through the Heath.

'There's this part of me,' I said, 'that keeps asking, "So what? You're in the same boat. You're both lonely. Go ahead. Go for it." Then there's another part of me that wants to laugh last night away, pass it off as silly tipsiness.

'And of course there's the voice of the wedding ring, the voice of guilt that whispers, "Oh, but poor Bill, poor darling Bill, you mustn't betray him." There's nothing adulterine about what happened. Bill is *dead*. He's lying in a grave in a Lamberhurst cemetery. He can hardly object. So why does it feel like a betrayal?'

'The vows only go up to "until death do us part",' Jascha said softly. 'They don't give us any rules for what we should do after that, do they?'

We sat down in the grass. On Parliament Hill, a thick-waisted father in an olive fatigue sweater stood behind his slender denim-clad son, hands over his hands as they guided a kite into the air.

'Since your wife died, have you ever had another relationship?' I asked Jascha.

He shook his head.

'Not in four years?'

'Four long years,' he said. He reached up and ran his fingers across my hairline. I grasped his hand and drew it away.

'You want an answer, don't you?' I said. 'You

want it to be straight and concrete and boundaried; either I'm in love with you, or I just want to be your friend, or I never want to see you again. But I can't give you an answer.'

I gazed down and rubbed a worn spot on my jeans.

'You don't know how easy it would be,' I said, 'for me to fall in love with you. You're an artist, you're honest, you're empathetic, you've got a sense of humour ...'

'You're not so shoddy yourself.'

'But—'

'What?'

'I'm afraid. Of forgetting Bill – I mean, my God, it hasn't even been six months, and the sound of his voice—'

'Is slipping.'

'Yes. Yes.' I sighed. 'That's the hardest part of all this. You understand.'

'But is that reason enough for us to get together?'

'I don't know.'

I checked my watch.

'Do you need to go home?' he asked.

'Yeah, I promised Caroline I'd be back by three-thirty.'

We turned to each other.

'Listen,' I said. 'I can't – I can't make any big decisions right now. I don't want to hurt Curran, and I don't want to rush myself. So could we just – could we just live in limbo for a while?'

He leaned over and hugged me.

'Beats living in hell,' he said.

When I came home, I found my mother and my son sitting on the living-room carpet, playing invisible instruments – violins, cellos, oboes – as they listened to Radio Three.

Curran put down an imaginary bassoon and said, 'Did you have a nice lunch, Mum?'

I nodded.

'Did Jascha have a copy of the paper? The one with the article on Dad's paintings?'

'Yeah.'

'Did you save it for me?'

'It's on the kitchen table.'

He jumped up and ran to get it. I sat beside my mother. 'You look like something's bothering you,' she said.

I leaned back against the sofa. 'Mom,' I said, 'when you first met David, was it hard?'

'Yes,' she said. 'Exhilarating, delightful – because he possessed a bluntness, a vigour, your father never had – but still hard.'

'Did you feel guilty?'

'Yes ... and no. You were right to yell at me the other day, Gloria. Because too many times I think I used the wretchedness of our marriage, the fact that your father was so unhappy—'

'More than unhappy. He blew his brains out.'

'OK, unstable, then. Neurotic. Suicidal. Whatever. But I used that fact as an excuse, a rationale, really. Because I felt freer than I ever had in my life after your father died.'

'Did you ... did you look for pieces of Dad in David? Did you try to make David into him?'

'No. No. In fact, I was deliberately attracted to David because he wasn't like Riordan. I knew too well the dangers of trying to make people over.'

'The way Dad tried with us.'

'Yeah. I never – I never again want to lead the kind of life I led with him,' she said, 'but when things between David and me get tense, or in certain moments, like when you and I were in Earl's Court that afternoon, I just ... I just want to bring him back, to breathe good breath into

270

him. I want him here in fragments: his excited hands, his voice that was like fingers stroking the pain away from a bruise. Sometimes I wonder if there was anything I could have done – should have done – that would have saved him.'

'Come on, Mom. You were distant, sure. But he wouldn't have been satisfied. Not even if you'd thrown yourself at his feet. Because you were the wrong woman.'

She looked away. Mozart poured into the room, and with her thumb she smoothed a wrinkle in her silk skirt.

'How much did you know about Adrienne?' I asked.

'When we were at Oxford together, he mentioned to me that his fiancée had died earlier that year. It worried me, the fact that his love for me had a desperate tinge attached to it, but—'

'You let your worry slide.'

'I did. He was so vibrant, and intense. In hindsight I saw that that intensity was dangerous. I should have taken my nagging feelings more seriously, but when you're in love, do you psychoanalyze your lover?'

'Of course not.'

'After you were born, he said you resembled her,

and you did. The same dark hair. The same grave eyes. "She is Adrienne reborn," he wept. I got angry at him then. "For Christ's sake, Riordan," I said, "she isn't her." He wanted to name you Adrienne, but I refused. I didn't want you to carry those obligations on your shoulders.'

I thought about that act of refusal she had performed. How could I thank her? Not the same way I had for the cranberry-coloured dress and the dinner at Le Gavroche.

'But I did,' I said. 'Later.'

She gazed at me.

'I know,' she said.

'Did you know it then?'

She gestured at me helplessly. 'I – I had an idea,' she said. 'I mean – after the whole deal with the name, the way he obsessed about how you looked like her, I had an inkling, and I was scared – scared that you might ... that you might not be safe—'

'So why did you let him be a parasite?'

She dropped her head in her hands, massaging her temples as if the emotional strain of finding the answer had crossed into the physical realm and given her a headache.

'You don't want to answer the question, do you?' I asked.

She swung back up.

'No, but I have to,' she said. 'I let him because I was over-burdened and I wanted what he had. What you had, even.'

'How do you mean?'

'You two were . . . singular. You had your passions. You were able to have them without guilt. Chemistry . . . lost loves . . . James Joyce . . . punk rock . . . whatever they were.'

'And you didn't. Because you were trapped raising me and teaching.'

'Not trapped. Culturally conditioned, definitely, and stuck sometimes. But I could've said no to all that in the first place, had I been stronger. That's the worst part, knowing I wimped out.'

I heard Curran banging drawers in the kitchen.

'What are you doing?' I yelled.

'Looking for scissors.'

'They're in the drawer to the left of the sink. What do you need them for?'

'I'm cutting out the article.'

'OK. Be careful.'

'You have no idea how hard it is for me not to be a part of your life,' my mother said.

'What are you talking about? You're here, aren't you?'

She sighed. 'You know what I mean. Eight years. Eight years I write to you, and hope, and—'

'And what?'

'You don't write back.'

'I did.'

'A scrawled page every six months.'

'I'm sorry my English degree failed you.'

'Why are you being so bitter?'

'Why are you?'

'Because I love you. Because I want to be a part of your life.'

'I understand that, but what you want can't happen overnight. It can't be all fun and laughter and togetherness.'

'But – but that day – the day we went shopping . . . that was fun, wasn't it?' Tears glistened in her eyes. 'Wasn't it?'

'Mom,' I said. 'Oh, Jesus, Mom, please don't cry. It was. It *was*. Don't cry. I'm being mean. I'm sorry.'

A frantic, pacifying tone crept into my voice, and,

remembering my father, I grew silent. She recognized my panic, and put a hand on my arm.

'No, Gloria,' she said. 'I'm the one who should be sorry.'

'Stop. I hate these apologizing marathons. We're both sorry. Let's get over it.'

She laughed. 'Good call.'

'Bill always liked you,' I said. '"Come on, love," he'd say. "She's your mother. You ought to keep in touch with her." OK, I said. I'll send her a little postcard like the ones from the gynaecologist's they send as a reminder when it's time for an appointment, to remind her that I still care. He didn't think that was very funny.'

She grinned.

'I understand what you said,' she said, 'about things not happening overnight. Maybe I do expect too much too soon. You will write to me and keep in touch after I leave, though, won't you?'

I nodded.

'I really think being together here has drawn us closer, don't you think?'

'Yes,' I said.

After that I went back into my room and slept. I needed time to lie on my back, on my own bed, and fall into oblivion, to digest my feelings towards Jascha and Caroline inside a cocoon of blackness.

When I woke again, the flat was draped in the softness of early evening. I got up and followed the sounds of my mother and son's voices to the kitchen. I leaned against the door with my arms folded, watching them.

My mother stood at the stove, where Bill used to stand, wearing the green apron Bill used to wear, the sleeves of her pink blouse rolled up. The soup she ladled into bowls was steamy and hot. I gazed at her hands steadying each bowl, holding its rim, and a part of me cried out, blood rushed into my fingers. I wanted to lean against her. I wanted to thank her. For vegetable soup. For trying. She looked over, smiled. Her face was thin, every bone pronounced, girlish. 'You're up just in time,' she said.

The three of us took our bowls to the small Formica table and sat down. Our knees softly touched. The steam warmed our faces. We ate in silence, crossing a border together into a room where the end was only the beginning.

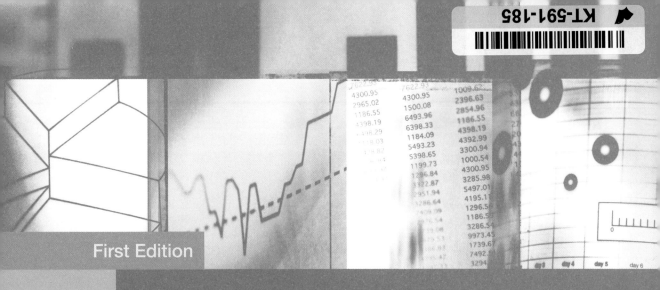

First Edition

Public Sector Financial Management

ANDREAS BERGMANN

FT Prentice Hall
FINANCIAL TIMES

An imprint of **Pearson Education**
Harlow, England • London • New York • Boston • San Francisco • Toronto • Sydney • Singapore • Hong Kong
Tokyo • Seoul • Taipei • New Delhi • Cape Town • Madrid • Mexico City • Amsterdam • Munich • Paris • Milan

Pearson Education Limited

Edinburgh Gate
Harlow
Essex CM20 2JE
England

and Associated Companies throughout the world

Visit us on the World Wide Web at:
www.pearsoned.co.uk

_____

First published 2009

ISBN 978-0-273-71354-8

British Library Cataloguing-in-Publication Data
A catalogue record for this book is available from the British Library

Library of Congress Cataloging-in-Publication Data
Bergmann, Andreas.
   Public sector financial management / Andreas Bergmann. -- 1st ed.
      p. cm.
   Includes bibliographical references and index.
   ISBN 978-0-273-71354-8 (alk. paper)
   1. Finance, Public -- Management.   2. Finance, Public -- Accounting.   3. Managerial
accounting.   I. Title.
   HJ9733.B47 2009
   352.4 -- dc22
                                                         2008026801

10 9 8 7 6 5 4 3 2 1
13 12 11 10 09

Typeset in 9/12pt Stone Serif by 73

Printed and bound in China
EPC/01

The publisher's policy is to use paper manufactured from sustainable forests.

Public Sector Financial Management

We work with leading authors to develop the strongest
educational materials in management, bringing
cutting-edge thinking and best learning practice to a
global market.

Under a range of well-known imprints, including
Financial Times Prentice Hall, we craft high quality print
and electronic publications which help readers to
understand and apply their content, whether studying
or at work.

To find out more about the complete range of our
publishing, please visit us on the World Wide Web at:
www.pearsoned.co.uk

Contents

3 Public sector budgeting and management accounting 43

4 Public sector financial accounting and reporting 70

About the Author

Andreas Bergmann is Professor of Public Management at Zurich University of Applied Sciences, and a member of the International Public Sector Accounting Standards Board. He has management degrees from the Universities of St. Gallen and Lancaster, and a doctorate in economics and management science from the University of St. Gallen. He was the Director of the Institute of Public Management from 2000 until August 2008, and is currently Associate Dean of the School of Management. He has acted as a scientific advisor, in the area of financial management, to all levels of government, in various countries, and to international organisations. His research activities focus on the international convergence of public sector financial management.

Preface

For a long time public sector financial management has been the domain of highly specialising professionals, quite a few of them economists, blended with a smaller group of statisticians, accountants and lawyers. Each of these professions had their own approach and each of these approaches had its own rigorous scientific foundation. The only downside was the lack of an overarching concept that would bring them together. This textbook tries to bring them together from a managerial perspective.

Although public sector financial management is taught in many tertiary courses around the world, there are only very few textbooks covering this matter. Teaching on tertiary level does not necessarily require a textbook, but a textbook can help by providing what the French call *fil rouge,* a thread that ties the various pieces together. The current reforms of tertiary education introducing comprehensive syllabi for each course certainly encourage the use of a textbook. And a managerial perspective certainly fits best with the syllabi of other courses taught at business schools or faculties.

Such a managerial perspective is also needed if public sector financial management is to play the role it is assigned as part of many reforms of public sector financial management, both in developed and developing countries. There is a high degree of consensus on the potential that public sector financial management has as an enabler for wider economic and political reforms. International organisations such as the World Bank have put strong emphasis on public sector financial management as an enabler of economic prosperity. However, quite often the enabling alone takes much of the momentum and the scarce resources. It would be a very satisfactory result if this textbook helps to improve the effectiveness of such reforms.

Obviously, there are more specialised titles that drill deeper in some of the concepts presented here. More depth is of course needed to fill specialists' positions within the relevant ministries and agencies. In the references there are hints for further reading in this direction. This title is also not focused on one single country or jurisdiction. Public sector financial management is still to some degree different from one country to another. Beside some convergence, which can be observed and will certainly decrease the differences, it is up to the lecturers or the readers to fill the jurisdiction-specific content.

The other dimension this book tries to cover is the international one, including international organisations, which recently have become major players in this field. This not only as strong supporters of reforms on the national and sub-national level, but also increasingly in the management of their own organisations. Although management of international organisations is rarely taught in tertiary education, an increasing number of graduates with a public management focus are hired by international organisations. They, as well as practitioners, contribute to the reforms in these organisations.

April 2008

Dr. Andreas Bergmann
Professor of Public Management
ZHAW School of Management

Acknowledgements

We are grateful to the following for permission to reproduce copyright material:

Exhibits 1.2 and 2.5 from Gross Public Debt (2006) as defined in the Treaty of Maastricht, *OECD Economic Outlook no. 82*, © OECD 2007; Exhibit 2.1 from General government outlays in percent of GDP nominal (OECD definition), *OECD Economic Outlook no. 81*, © OECD 2007; Exhibit 2.3 from Public Expenditure of Education in percent of GDP (year 2004), *OECD Education at a glance, 2007*, © OECD 2007; Exhibit 2.4 from Gross Debt in percent of GDP (OECD definition), year 2006, *OECD Economic Outlook no. 81*, © OECD 2007; Exhibits 4.2 and 4.3 from *Government Finance Statistics Manual 2001* http://www.imf.org/external/pubs/ft/gfs/manual/pdf/all.pdf, Statistics Department, IMF, 2001; Exhibit 8.1 is reprinted by permission of the Swiss Federal Office of Transport; Table 8.3 adapted from *Financial Statements of the Government of New Zealand for the Year Ended 30 June 2006* http://www.treasury.govt.nz/government/financialstatements/yearend/pdfs/fsgnz-jun06.pdf, Government of New Zealand, 2006; Exhibits 8.10 and 8.12 adapted from UN Population Division Database, 2006 revision http://esa.un.org/unpp/p2k0data.asp, United Nations, 2006; Exhibit 8.4 © Raumgleiter GmbH, Zürich.

1

Public sector financial management

Learning objectives

- Describe the scope of public sector financial management.
- Identify the goals of public sector financial management in practice.
- Understand the tasks public sector financial managers are accomplishing and the way performance can be assessed.
- Understand and improve structures in the field of public sector financial management.
- Describe the use and limitations of integrated approaches.

Key terms

Accounting	General government sector	PEFA
Assurance	Government financial	Public sector
Auditing	statistics	Treasury
Budget	Internal control	

Public sector financial management has been an area of considerable and constant development over the last 25 years or so. Not many other areas of management have enjoyed so many different proposals for improvement. Many of these have disappeared as quickly as they have emerged. Others have persisted for some time, but were strictly limited to a few countries as they were influenced by a specific country's culture or sometimes even by a limited number of outstanding individuals making their case limited to the boundaries of their personal influence. Some concepts were closely following private sector models, yet others were tailor-made for specific public sector institutions, for example international organisations or school districts.

Only the new millennium has, alas, brought some consolidation to those developments. International standards have been created or greatly improved in some core domains such as public sector accounting or government financial statistics. After a wave of new concepts in private sector corporate finance during the 1980s and 1990s, the new millennium brought a sharper image of the core concepts, which then became increasingly accepted in the public sector. A precondition for this consolidation was the acknowledgement of the prevalence of the public sector itself. During the first enthusiastic years of privatisation this was less clear, as the *raison d'être* of the public sector was challenged by famous economists[1] and not less famous politicians.[2] Now, it is generally accepted that the government has to supply public goods such as stability and security and also at least a minimum level of services such as health and education. The controversial discussions have clearly shifted upward to the question which variety and standards of services are still essential. This has made it clear and undisputed that, yes, also in future there will be a public sector that needs to be managed. This, of course, includes management of its financial resources.

This consolidation of ideas and concept was conditional for this book. It is following this internationally accepted 'mainstream' rather than emphasising the still existing, uncountable specialties in the various countries and entities. As they may be relevant they should be provided by teachers or instructors.

1.1 Umbrella for the matter of finance in public sector entities

Many textbooks are dealing with specific matters such as public sector accounting, to name only one of the possible options. This book follows a more holistic approach including the specific matter but not without acknowledging their role in a wider system. This wider system is called public sector financial management, as there is the assumption that the system is to be managed. This should not be seen as some kind

---

[1] Milton Friedman to name only one.

[2] Margaret Thatcher, Ronald Reagan, to name only two.

Exhibit 1.1 Public sector

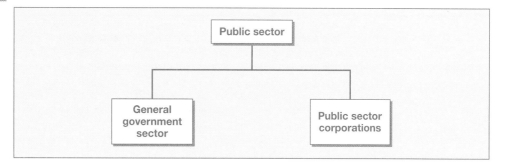

of managerialism, but rather as pragmatic description of reality. Although in an ideal world, perhaps, there would be no need to manage public sector finances, there is no empirical evidence of the ideal world. All public sector entities are affected by external and perhaps also internal shocks, which need to be absorbed without damaging the entity's mission.[3]

Talking about entities raises the issue of what is a public sector entity? The System of National Accounts (SNA) as well as the European System of National Accounts (ESNA/ESVG) define the various sectors of the economy and include the principles delimitating the sectors.[4] According to this internationally recognised definition the public sector includes the general government sector (often briefly referred to as government) as well as public sector corporations (see Exhibit 1.1).

The entire public sector is controlled by a country's citizens and the government. For public sector corporations this generally means that a majority of their share is held by the country or its government. However, public sector corporations generate more than 50 per cent of their revenues from market activities, i.e. selling goods and services to customers.[5] In addition international organisations should also be considered to be part of the public sector, at least if they are set up by various nations or governments, rather than non-governmental organisations. In fact many of them, i.e. the European Union, merely add an additional level to the general government sector. Although this addition to the general government sector is not generally supported and also not based on the SNA, actual financial management practices in virtually every field covered by this book make a clear case for adding them to the scope of public sector financial management.

Definition

Public sector financial management
Public sector financial management is any activity in order to analyse, structure, set objectives and implement measures in the field of finance, if the entity addressed is a government of any level, a corporation controlled by the government or an international organisation set up by various nations.

---

[3] Some readers might even want to assure existence of the entity itself. However, at least at sub-national level, it is evident that various forms of organisation can be feasible.

[4] EUROSTAT (1996) 31.

[5] The customers may include the government, if both parties have an option to sell/buy, i.e. telecom services from a government-owned telecom corporation to the government are usually considered to be market transactions.

Example   Public sector entities

> Most countries have different levels of state or government. For instance the United States of America have a federal government, 50 state governments and about 87,000 local governments, such as counties, cities, municipalities, school districts, etc.[6] Germany is organised in a similar way, having a federal government, some 16 states (*Länder*) as well as various local governments (*Landkreise*, *Städte*, *Kommunen*). Federal nations are based on sovereign states or provinces. Other countries, such as France or Japan, have no sovereignty below the national level, but still maintain lower levels of administration, rather than lower levels of government, as they have no or very little legislative power, but still some autonomy fulfilling their executive tasks. The administration of all levels of territorial government is usually referred to as the 'general government sector' or 'GGS' (as we shall see in Chapter 4 there are a few other entities within the GGS, but for the sake of simplicity we restrict it to territorial entities).
>
> All governments of all levels own some corporations. These may be railways, telecommunication companies, postal services, banks, insurance companies, airlines, utilities, etc. It is controversial both in politics and economics how feasible government ownership of commercial firms is, but very few countries have taken a clear stance for privatisation. Examples are the United Kingdom or New Zealand, but even these countries have maintained ownership in a relatively small number of corporations (e.g. the Royal Mail or Air New Zealand). Even more so if entities on the borderline between commercial and non-commercial activities, such as schools, universities or hospitals are considered, because they often make more than half of their revenues on the market. Such government owned enterprises, which are operating on a market, are public sector corporations.

However, opening an umbrella called 'public sector financial management' is not undisputed. Many countries and also some international organisations have a long tradition of splitting the responsibilities in the field of public finance between various entities, including Budget offices, Treasuries, Ministries or Administrations of Finance, Comptroller's offices, Controlling or Accounting units and sometimes even central banks.[7] Behind such an extensive division of labour are basically two ideas. One is emphasising the limitation of power ('checks and balances') while the other is advocating differences in the relevant qualification ('skills'). Although the checks and balances approach is not in contradiction with the idea of an umbrella system including various sub-systems, the skills approach is, in a way, as it supposes critical differences between the various tasks or institutions. The tasks and institutions will be dealt with more closely in Sections 1.2 and 1.3 of this book. However, practical evidence shows substantial and permanent friction at the borders of such systems and therefore suggests treating them as sub-systems under the umbrella of public sector financial management.

Example   Examples of friction between the sub-systems of public sector financial management

> **Government financial statistics v. public sector accounting**
>
> The production of government financial statistics (GFS) is dependent on a constant flow of data from public sector accounting. This is the major source for their statistics. However, the

[6] Source: www.census.gov/govs/www/cog2002.html.

[7] This list is not exhaustive.

economists usually working at GFS units and the accountants working at their units in most countries do not cooperate closely. This makes GFS vulnerable to misperceptions and errors. On the other hand, accountants regularly complain about additional work that needs to be done 'only for the statisticians'. Looking at it from a broader perspective reveals that both are producing information for the very same decision makers. It is also generally accepted that it is possible to design accounting systems in such a way that they will produce feasible data for the statistician without any downside for the accountants. This interaction is evidence for both being part of one system.

Budgeting v. Treasury

While budget entities and staff have the sense of being policy makers, the Treasury people are said to have the whole perspective of finance in mind, with the downside of being 'number crunchers'. However, there is no use of a budget if it ignores the whole picture and there is no use of the whole picture if it is not on the political agenda. Again, looking at them as part of a whole is adding value.

Bringing finance and management together in the public sector context is a more recent idea, based on various reforms under the name of new public management (NPM), which have numerous and important financial implications. They equally affect accounting, budgeting and reporting.[8] Guthrie et al. even suggest calling it new public finance management rather than new public management.[9]

Public sector financial management, in the context of NPM pursues different goals. A widely accepted classification is the one used by the World Bank:[10]

1 **Fiscal management.** Flows (revenues, expenditure), positions (assets, debt) and risks.
2 **Resource allocation.** Allocation of resources according to the policy priorities.
3 **Value for money.** Economy, efficiency and effectiveness.

While the third goal introduces the ideas of NPM, the first two are more traditional. The first goal will be discussed more in detail as part of Chapter 2, while the second and the third goal shall be looked at in Chapter 3 of this book. As a part of the umbrella nature of public sector financial management, however, they should be observed together.

1.2 Task-based approaches

This book is based on a broad, systematic conception of public sector financial management. But this does not mean that various aspects or approaches should not be treated adequately. In fact, the systematic approach allows for sub-systems. They can either be structured by tasks or by institutions. The task-based approach is hereafter considered first.

---

[8] Caperchione, E. (2006), FEE-PSC (Fédération des Experts Comptables Européenes' Public Sector Committee).
[9] Guthrie, J., Olsen, O., Humphrey, C. (1999) 211.
[10] World Bank (1998) Chapter 2.

1.2.1 Public finance

Public finance is part of economics. It deals with the financial decisions of public sector entities. Traditionally it includes the following issues:

- **The economic basis of government activity.** What is the economic rationale behind governments? Why should they exist? What should/shouldn't they do?
- **Government expenditure.** How should budgets/funds be allocated between various types of expenditure? How should expenditure be controlled?
- **Government financing including taxation and debt financing.** What kind of taxes are fair taxes? What levels of government debt are sustainable?

Public finance is at least trying to give a comprehensive picture of the entire economic activity of the public sector. It is doing so through the government financial statistics (GFS) which are part of the system of national accounts (SNA). Public finance is, in comparison with public sector financial management as a whole, less focused on decision making. It is working in a similar way like other sector specific fields of economics, such as the theory of households or the theory of enterprises. Although it is sometimes considered to be a special field in addition to macroeconomics and microeconomics, much analysis is undertaken by using microeconomic models. In fact, the public sector is only one of several actors in an economy, although one of substantial size and importance. The main concepts of public finance are thus highly relevant for public sector financial management.

In welfare economics, the analysis of government activity starts from the market perspective. Markets are generally efficiently allocating goods and services through a price mechanism (exchange and product efficiency). However, in some cases markets are likely to fail. This is the case if consumption of goods and services is either non-rival or exclusion of free-riders is for some reason or other not possible.[11] Non-rivalry means that the consumption by one person does not prevent the consumption of the very same good or service by others, because the good or service is still there after the consumption by the first person. Good examples are defence or radio broadcasting.

Practically more relevant are examples of non-exclusion, in which theoretically someone could be excluded from consumption, but exclusion is not enforceable. Consider policing. Of course it would be possible to exclude one part of the population, but in most countries this would clearly breach the constitution. It would also lead to anarchy and violence, perhaps even to the destruction of the society. Exclusion of some citizens is, therefore, not even for those who would not be excluded, a feasible option. If either non-rivalry or non-exclusion applies, the market is bound to fail, as the marginal cost and consequently the price equals zero. This in turn will bring any private supply to an end. Thus the government has to step in and supply such goods and services itself. The goods and services are then called social goods/services or public goods/services. They make up for the adverse results of market failure, if the kind of market failure leads to insufficient supply.

In real life things are not always as clear cut. It is rather controversial if, for example, higher education or state-of-the-art health care are classed as public services too.

---

[11] Stiglitz, J. (2000) 53 ff. See also Musgrave, R., Musgrave, P. (1989) 42 ff.; other reasons for market failure, such as external cost, are not prompting additional supply from the government, rather the contrary. Natural monopolies due to barriers of entry including very high capital requirements may lead to additional supply from the government, but more likely to nationalisation of existing suppliers.

Economists say they would at least qualify as merit goods or services, which are not necessarily produced but at least promoted through various government interventions including grants and other financial aid. In the case of merit goods or services the government tries to compel individuals to consume. However, the concept of merit goods is not nearly as sharp as the one of public goods and therefore provides little guidance. It is also subject to criticism, as the idea of merit goods is referred to as paternalism.[12] In practice, the decision as to which goods and services should be supplied by the government is more a political than an economic one. Furthermore there is a third option, not allowing governments to produce the goods and services themselves, but buying them on behalf of the citizens from private suppliers.[13] In fact governments face a 'supply or not supply' and additionally a 'make or buy' decision.

The second issue considered in public finance is government expenditure. Here the main issue is the government's share of the entire economy. There are various ways to measure this:

- government expenditure as a percentage of the gross domestic product (GDP);[14]
- tax revenues and social security contribution as a percentage of GDP; and
- tax revenues as a percentage of GDP

Obviously all the three quotas measure something different and can be useful in their way. In fact the second and the third do not measure expenditure at all, but revenues. The value of the first is generally the largest and the value of the third the smallest, because governments have other ways to finance their expenditure, including increases of the debt or fees charged to citizens. However, the three indicators are frequently used in the same context and eventually confused or even abused. The share of government expenditure can be critical for economic growth because of potential crowding out of private activities. Due to globalisation it has also become increasingly critical for the competitiveness of a nation. International investors are generally more reluctant to invest in economies with a large share of government expenditure, as they expect high taxes or other collections from government, if not at present, then in future, in order to refinance the public debt.

In many countries, namely the member states of the European Union, the focus has shifted from the total share of government expenditure to the share of the government deficit as part of the GDP. One of the criteria stated in the Treaty of Maastricht caps government deficits at 3 per cent, with some exceptions. The convergence criterion of the EU will be examined more closely in Section 2.3.4.

The third issue of public finance is government financing including taxation and public debt. During much of the last century the focus was clearly on taxation, creating a classification for the various forms of taxes (i.e. direct, indirect, on flows, on wealth etc.) and developing principles of 'good' or 'optimal' taxes.[15] Good taxes are taxes that are fair, cause minimal disruption or side effects to the economy and minimal cost for collection.

Recently, the issue of public debt has (re)emerged, certainly because it has reached an increasingly dangerous size in many countries. Economically a public debt means a shift

---

[12] Stiglitz, J. (2000) 86 ff.

[13] Schedler, K., Proeller, I. (2002).

[14] Rosen, H. (2002) 11 ff.

[15] Stiglitz, J. (2000) 550 ff. See also Musgrave, R., Musgrave, P. (1989) 211 ff.

Exhibit 1.2   Gross public debt (2006) as defined in the Treaty of Maastricht

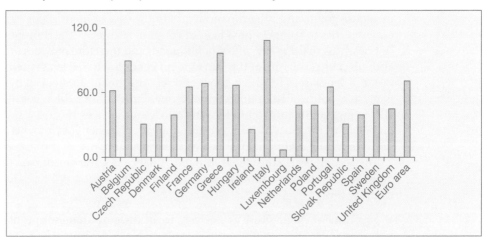

Source: Gross Public Debt (2006) as defined in the Treaty of Maastricht, *OECD Economic Outlook no. 82*, © OECD 2007

of the financial burden to future periods. This is uncritical if the debt is steady or growing more slowly than the economy, i.e. the burden from earlier periods affecting the current period equals the one shifted to the next period. However, if the debt is growing faster than the entire economy a larger burden is shifted to future periods and generations. This is clearly not advisable, at least not in the long run over the entire business cycle. Therefore a 60 per cent cap has been imposed by the Treaty of Maastricht. Exhibit 1.2 shows gross public debt as a percentage of GDP in 2006, as defined by the Treaty of Maastricht.

It is interesting to note that the general definition of public finance, supporting decision making about financial issues, is very much the same as the general definition of corporate finance. However, the areas covered are slightly different. While the public side seemingly has to give a justification for its economic activity and is mostly concerned with (current) expenditures and revenues, corporate finance is concerned mainly with capital expenditures (investments) and their risk-return pattern. While this clearly reflects the actual priorities of decision makers in the respective sectors and is therefore currently adequate, it should not be taken for granted. Governments are making investment decisions and many of them, notably large-scale strategic projects, are risky. There is no good reason for governments to make their decisions on a different basis. Different return expectations or payback periods can be adjusted by using different parameters. Investment and risk should be added as a fourth and fifth issue of public finance, in order to adequately cater for the decision makers' needs.

1.2.2 Public sector financial planning

Public sector financial planning has long been synonymous with budgeting, meaning the financial planning and authorisation for the next year.[16] Unlike in private sector enterprises, the budget is not only a tool to deploy strategic plans, but also part of a formal,

---

[16] This text uses the term year, acknowledging that different countries or entities are using different concepts (i.e. calendar year, fiscal year, hydrological year, etc.). By using the term year, it is meant to be a 12-month period.

legal authorisation of any expenditure. In many countries the budget is called a law and is approved in the very same way as a new law, in order to reflect this status. Thus it is available to the general public and by no means secret. It still contains strategic elements, as it is based on the government's programme or platform.[17]

However, it is generally accepted that a one-year budget is not sufficient. Most public sector entities around the world have therefore introduced longer-term financial plans or multi-year budgets. Financial plans often cover the time until the next scheduled election, but at least three and often up to five or six years. The legal authority of long-term financial plans is usually less strong than that of one-year budgets. This allows for the necessary adjustments when the planning is reconsidered on a rolling basis, i.e. the next year is adjusted and becomes the budget while one year is added at the long end. Multi-year budgets usually cover two years, but sometimes up to four. They are equally authoritative like one-year budgets, but give the entity some additional flexibility in spending. Multi-year budgets are particularly common in international organisations (e.g. the United Nations).

During the year, many public sector entities have started producing forecasts. Because there is less pressure from the investors, some of these forecasts are for internal use only; others are presented but attract less attention in the general public than, for example, a profit warning of a listed company.

Another issue in the field of public sector financial planning is performance-based budgets. Other names include output- or outcome-based budgets. The main idea is to shift the focus of financial planning from organisational structures to results. The underlying assumption is that the citizens are more interested in service levels than in the internal organisation of service production and delivery. For example, they are interested in how much is spent for higher education and whether these funds are really reaching the students, rather than which university or department is getting which share. Performance-based budgets usually are not presented by nature of the revenues and expenditures (i.e. payroll, interest), but only by product groups or service groups. For obvious reasons performance-based budgeting is more common in entities that are large service providers than in others that are working more behind the scenes.

1.2.3 Public sector accounting and financial reporting

Public sector accounting used to be a mere record keeping of budget execution. As political decisions are made when drafting and approving the budget, relatively little importance or attention has been attributed to budget execution and thus to public sector accounting. Public sector financial reporting, as a function in its own right, is an even more recent phenomenon. Traditionally, the main focus was on the statement of financial performance (which is known in the private sector as 'profit and loss statement') or the statement of cash flows. In fact many governments and international organisations are still on a cash basis of accounting, which means that only inflows or outflows of cash are recognised.[18] Considering the vast amount of assets and liabilities that are on a statement of financial position ('balance sheet') rather than on a statement of financial performance, but also off-balance-sheet positions like contingent liabilities, this is

---

[17] The expression for the strategic plan of a government varies from one jurisdiction to the other. But it is generally accepted that governments have strategic plans and the budget makes reference to it.

[18] In contrast, public sector corporations, like their private sector equivalents, generally adopted full accrual accounting many years ago.

clearly inappropriate. This is the main rationale for moving beyond mere budget execution reporting into fully fledged financial reporting. The financial statements should include balance sheets, statements of financial performance as well as the more traditional and often budget-related cash flow statements. Looking at such a comprehensive system makes it more urgent to move to full accrual accounting. That is why the introduction of full accrual accounting is on the agenda of many governments around the world. This is also an important part of the mission of the recently developed International Public Sector Accounting Standards (IPSAS). Both the basis of accounting and the IPSAS will be examined more closely in Chapters 4 and 5.

The second issue in this field is related to the performance-based budgets mentioned in Section 1.2.2. A mere financial accounting, not to mention a cash-based one, is insufficient to report the basis of products rather than organisational structures. It has become necessary to calculate costs or perhaps even prices for specific goods and services. Private sector enterprises and public sector corporations have, of course, faced this challenge at a much earlier stage and introduced management accounting to respond to this need. Governments, and to a lesser degree international organisations, are still adopting such systems. In many cases these systems go well beyond the need of performance-based budgeting and should be considered fully fledged controlling systems. However, more advanced management accounting or controlling systems can still be found in countries with some tradition in the field of performance-based budgeting.[19]

But public sector accounting includes a lot of back-office tasks. With the increase in size of governments, international organisations and public sector corporations the complexity has grown steadily. Large-scale IT solutions are required and implemented. Process management becomes a crucial aspect. In most countries and international organisations more than 80 per cent of the project budget for the adoption of full accrual accounting is spent on the IT side.[20] But also the operational costs are substantial and should be managed carefully, as they are part of the overhead, not immediately adding value to the citizens. However, there is some practical evidence that countries with sound public sector accounting also have a sound financial performance.[21]

1.2.4 Public sector controlling

The developments in the field of public sector financial planning and accounting have created a new task which is best captured by the expression public sector controlling. With a public sector increasingly developing from pure policy maker to a large-scale service provider, long-term financial plans and shorter-term budgets are no longer sufficient to control the organisation. There is a need to set lower level goals and objectives, both in respect of finance and performance. Even if there is no performance-based budget, performance needs to be considered at this lower level.

Let us take the example of schools: in many countries they are governed by the states or provinces. Yet there are several school districts within one state and several schools

---

[19] Examples include Australia, New Zealand, Austria, Germany and Switzerland. Germany is somehow a special case, as it is well advanced in respect of performance-based budgets, but lying behind other developed countries in respect of accrual accounting.

[20] Examples include Canada, France, Switzerland, the European Commission, the United Nations.

[21] Well-known examples are Canada, Sweden, Australia and New Zealand. All were troubled financially before improving their government accounting and all four have become very good performers since then. However, the sample is too small and other potential influences too strong for empirical evidence.

within one school district. Obviously there will be a state-level budget and – if performance budgeting is in place – overall performance goals and objectives. The financial side includes overall operational and investment expenditures. The performance side perhaps includes student numbers, learning achievements, and deliverables of reform projects and so on. Now this is all far too general for the headmaster at the individual school. She/he needs to be given figures, but perhaps also performance goals adjusted to the size, type and catchment area of the school. The results also need to be compared against these adjusted objectives and goals. Perhaps the management of either level needs to be advised on measures to be implemented. This, of course, would not be needed if the ministry consisted of just a minister and a few aides. But public sector reality around the world is – with a few exceptions, such as parliament's offices – closer to one of a service industry than pure politics.

The delimitation between the two more traditional tasks of public sector financial planning and public sector accounting and the more recently developed task of public sector controlling is obviously not a huge divide. All three need to work together closely. With the emergence of public sector controlling, the financial planning could more clearly focus on the political level, leaving the management to controlling. Accounting is a vital preparer and provider of information for financial planning and controlling alike.

1.2.5 Public sector assurance

Most practitioners would rather call this auditing than assurance. However, the term auditing is slightly misleading in the public sector context, as the scope of 'audits' is generally not the same as in the private sector. As only relatively few public sector entities make a difference between internal and external audit, the two are blurring. The objective of an audit, taking it from the International Standards on Auditing (ISA), is 'to express an opinion whether the financial statements are prepared, in all material aspects, in accordance with an identified financial reporting framework'.[22] This reflects the objective of an external audit of financial statements and is also what is in the various textbooks on auditing.[23] Perhaps the term assurance, which is now also used as a name for the professional service firm's business lines performing audits, is less biased towards external audits and therefore should be used in the public sector. It reflects any measure to increase the confidence of the user in the information provided, financial and other statements, both internal and external.

Definition	**Assurance**
	Assurance is any measure undertaken by independent and mandated professionals to increase the confidence of the user in the information provided.

The task list of public sector assurance staff (commonly called 'auditors'), many of them employed by audit offices rather than professional service firms, includes the audit of financial statements but goes well beyond. Most of them are supposed to give an opinion on the economic use of resources and on compliance with all kinds of laws and

---

[22] ISA 200.

[23] e.g. Hayes, R., Dassen, R., Schilder, A., Wallage, P. (2005) or Whittington, O.R., Pany, K. (2003).

regulations (not only the ones relevant for the presentation of the financial statements). Sometimes this even includes the power for judicial decisions in administrative matters. According to the Supreme Audit Institutions grouped in the International Organisation of Supreme Audit Institutions (INTOSAI), in its Lima declaration, the task list includes internal and external audits in the form of legality, regularity and performance audits.[24] The core of this declaration is on the independence of auditors or, as we may rather call them, assurors.

As in public sector accounting the field of public sector assurance also has experienced the emergence of international standards. The International Standards on Auditing (ISA), which have been there for quite some time, have undergone a major overhaul, mainly as a result of the profession being hit by various scandals, such as Enron or Worldcom. They are supposed to apply equally for the private and the public sector. The revised standards include public sector-specific guidance in the body of the standard, while earlier standards refer to a public sector perspective (PSP) section at the end of each standard. In fact many public sector auditors are adopting them. Public sector-specific issues are addressed by auditing standards that the International Organisation of Supreme Audit Institutions (INTOSAI) started to develop and issue in 1998. First, auditing standards (AS), in respect of financial audits but also in respect of performance audits, are issued. On the national level the standards are translated and adopted either through national standards or directly. Contemporary audit standards are emphasising the need of thorough planning of the audit, including the clarification of the mandate (i.e. full audit or more limited review), identification of risks and issues, and the development of an audit programme, which reflects the needs identified and increasingly the documentation of the findings. Such a structured approach obviously improves the results, but also the cost associated with the audit.

More recently, public sector assurance has also been influenced by the issue of internal control. Although governments and international organisations, less so public sector corporations, have been exempt from new legislation including the so-called Sarbanes-Oxley Act in the United States of America, this has clearly influenced their work, including recent reforms. In Europe an initiative of the European Commission on internal control called Public Internal financial Control (PIfC) is evidently also influencing the further development of assurance.

1.2.6 Internal control

Most public sector entities have had internal control in place much before the professional discussion started. Any payments to third parties are traditionally being scrutinised in a sophisticated process, in order to avoid false payments or even fraud. However, the traditional emphasis was clearly on payments and not much else.

Sadly, public sector entities also had to learn that their risks go well beyond inappropriate payments. In many cases compensation for environmental damages or the work-out of pension plans by far exceeded the damage caused by unruly payments. This should not be an invitation to drop all the checks on payments, but to face other, perhaps more substantial risks as well. Internal control, which is the responsibility of the most senior management level, should acknowledge and address all the current and future risks in a comprehensive system.

---

[24] INTOSAI (1977) Sections 3 and 4.

Beside the obvious influence from the Sarbanes-Oxley Act, public sector entities are frequently referring to the COSO-framework (Committee of Sponsoring Organisations of the Treadway Commission). In the European Union (EU) as well as in the so-called candidate countries, preparing themselves for accession to the EU, the Public Internal financial Control (PIfC) initiative is very much determining the development of internal control. All three, the Sarbanes-Oxley Act, the COSO-framework and the PIfC initiative, will be examined more closely in Chapter 6.

Perhaps it is worth noting that control and controlling are slightly different concepts. While control has very much to do with supervision and compliance, controlling is more process oriented and should provide vital support to the management in deploying its strategies. Control is more reactive and controlling more proactive. Control is about checks, controlling about goals and objectives.

1.3 Institutional approaches

Public sector financial management can also be looked at from a different perspective, the institutional one. It is indeed strongly influenced by reputable institutions such as treasuries, ministries and so on. Even the more recent task-oriented approaches, like the introduction of international standards in various fields, had to go along with the institutions. This sometimes meant that the role of the institutions was in need of realignment. This section takes a closer look at the more traditional as well as the potential future roles.

1.3.1 Macroeconomic control units

The term macroeconomic control unit is not one from real life; it is rather unlikely that you will find a unit bearing this name. However, there are usually units responsible for a macroeconomic oversight and decision making. They usually include a statistics sub-unit, which is responsible for the preparation of the national accounts and, for the sake of public sector financial management, more importantly, government financial statistics (GFS). As the government's most obvious option for macroeconomic policy is fiscal policy, the only one that is solely in its hands, macroeconomic control units generally exercise substantial influence on public sector financial management. Major decisions about spending, the generation of revenues and even debt are unlikely to be made without the formal or informal approval from those units.

Macroeconomic control units are either part of the Ministry of Economic Affairs or the Ministry of Finance. Their mission is clearly a country's economy as a whole, with the government being only one of several important actors. Macroeconomic policy is not one of the objectives of this book, as there is a variety of textbooks with excellent coverage of this issue. Therefore macroeconomic control units are not considered in close detail, despite their impact on public sector financial management.

1.3.2 Budget offices

Traditionally at the core of public sector financial management there is much to say about budget offices. Obviously their core responsibility is the preparation of the next year's budget, which is then submitted to the cabinet[25] and finally to the parliament[26] for final approval. However, as mentioned in Section 1.2.2, contemporary budgeting goes beyond the one-year time horizon and includes longer-term financial plans or perhaps even multi-year budgets. They are also within the responsibility of budget offices.

Adjustments to budget are a further responsibility of importance. As public sector budgets are a legally binding authorisation for any spending, they need to be adjusted more frequently than private sector ones. Even if additional spending is absolutely undisputed, i.e. after natural disasters, most jurisdictions would require a formal adjustment to the budget. Budget execution sometimes is in their responsibility, but more likely is not, as the treasury or in some cases even accounting units take over from the budget office once the budget is approved.[27] Obviously small entities, especially at the local level, don't have such a sophisticated division of labour; they rather have one single unit responsible for budget, accounting and treasury activities.

They have attracted particular attention from academics as well as the Organisation for Economic Cooperation and Development (OECD). The attention OECD has paid to budgeting is unparalleled by other issues. Clearly it has driven the development of budget offices in the developed countries and elsewhere for many years. Recent issues are also discussed in Section 1.2.2.

1.3.3 Accounting offices

Accounting offices are – not surprisingly – responsible for the accounting. However, many public sector entities have a long tradition of decentralisation. Accounting is one field that is, in many cases, highly decentralised. Almost certainly ministries and independent entities like universities are doing their own bookkeeping. In still very numerous cases even lower ranking departments or units have their own accounting team. Beside tradition the main argument for such a structure is the, somehow understandable, fear that more centralised units might take some of the funds secured in the budget process away when it comes to budget execution. However, there are not many other reasons. In other words, a coherent accounting policy, as well as investment in IT systems and operation costs, stands against a decentralisation. In fact, public sector corporations tend to have centralised accounting – like their private sector counterparts. Anyway, the management of accounting is challenging in both ways. A great emphasis lies on process management and, in recent years, IT. Especially in a decentralised environment accounting units are also likely to have a normative role. They develop and issue guidelines, sometimes even standards, which need to be observed at least by an inner circle of public sector entities (i.e. budget entities).

The other challenges brought by recent years are a greater interest in the presentation of financial statements, rather than just bookkeeping, and a move to full accrual. The latter is still in development in many countries. Surprisingly, the national level seems to lag behind lower levels of government, at least in Europe.[28] Also, international organisations have only recently embraced the concept of full accrual accounting, with OECD, NATO and the

---

[25] And/or the president in some countries. At lower levels of government it can be some sort of council. International organisations usually have some kind of board of directors or a secretary general.

[26] At lower levels of government it can be some sort of council or in very small local governments even a meeting of the electorate. International organisations usually require approval by their general assembly.

[27] At least some kind of treasury (see Section 1.3.4).

[28] Lüder, K., Jones, R. (2003) 20 ff.

EU spearheading the movement with others, including the UN, following closely. These developments have raised the importance of the normative role of accounting offices.

In some countries, but not all, accounting offices are also responsible for the preparation of government financial statistics (GFS). This has the indisputable advantage that they generate the relevant information. However, as Section 4.5 shows, there is a difference between the entities covered by GFS and the scope of entities covered for financial reporting purposes. In most countries national or state government may not consolidate lower levels of government, as they enjoy at least some independency and, in a federal system, even some kind of sovereignty. But they are clearly part of GFS. On the other hand, some commercial entities controlled by the government may be within the scope of (consolidated) financial reporting, but fall out of GFS. It is therefore not very obvious that the preparation of GFS should be within the responsibility of accounting offices. Other models allocate this task to statistical offices; although this is not yet very common, it may be worth considering.

1.3.4 The five kinds of treasuries

Almost every jurisdiction has an institution that is called a 'treasury'. But in almost every case their role is different. Five main streams can be observed – obviously with some variations, but still fairly consistent. In these five streams the treasury takes a very different role. The five streams are:

1 **Financial affairs in government.** In some countries the treasury is in fact a ministry and the treasurer or secretary of the treasury is a member of the cabinet of ministers. The treasury then comprises all the other functions or roles described below. Examples: many continental European countries use the term treasury when describing an array of different tasks in fiscal politics, and financial management in English.

2 **The revenue and borrowing side of the government.** In some countries, the treasury is still on government level, but more focused on raising the revenue and borrowing from the capital market, for which there is a ministry of finance responsible for the spending side. Example: Australia.

3 **Top-level financial management.** Other countries have a ministry of finance as well as a treasury. The ministry is then responsible only for financial politics, especially fiscal politics. The treasury is providing professional financial management services and advice to the ministry of finance and other entities. It is also managing the government-owned enterprises, if they are considered to be an investment, rather than mere providers of public services. Example: New Zealand.

4 **Budget execution.** In other countries the treasury is still at high level, but responsible only for the budget execution, including accounting, and not for the budget preparation and planning. Example: many countries in Eastern Europe and Central Asia.

5 **Management of financial instruments.** In other countries the treasury is responsible only for the management of financial instruments, especially cash and cash equivalents. They deal with cash pooling and short-term investments in or borrowings from the money market. Sometimes, they are also involved in longer-term financial instruments like government bonds, especially if it comes to risk management, for example the hedging of interest rates or foreign exchange risks. Example: Switzerland.

The fifth option corresponds to the concept in many private sector corporations, while the earlier four are quite different from the private sector. Public sector corporations tend to follow the fifth option, while for governments it is a question of legal tradition.

As the term treasury is apparently used in very different ways, caution should be exercised when conclusions are drawn from the institutional arrangement of the treasury. Such conclusions could very well become different if the institutional arrangement is different. As the examples show, this is the case even in otherwise relatively similar countries. In an international context the term should be avoided altogether as it is a major source of misunderstanding.

1.3.5 Auditor general offices

Some jurisdictions require audits by external, independent auditors. Their work is very similar to the one of private sector auditors, giving an opinion about the presentation of financial statements and not much else. In these jurisdictions the external auditor is supplemented by an internal auditor, who is responsible for compliance and operation audits, especially those addressing the internal control.

However, in most jurisdictions there is an auditor general office, taking responsibility for both external and internal audits. This office is sometimes called the chamber of accounts. Their independence is granted, as they are directly reporting to the parliament. The auditor general is usually elected by the parliament. In some countries, including France and Germany, the power of the auditor general office goes even further and includes some judicial power in matters of public sector financial law (they are called *court de comptes* and *Rechnungshof* respectively).

1.4   Integrated approaches

Both the task-based and the institutional approaches are supported by practitioners and academics alike. They are suitable for assisting the definition of strategies, processes and structures in the field of public sector financial management. The only downside of the task-based approach, and even more so the institutional approach, is its inherent tendency of separation rather than cooperation. Task owners and institutional staff tend to put the case for their task or institution over the system as a whole. This may occasionally obstruct perception of issues and hinder the setting of priorities. That is why integrated approaches have been created.

1.4.1 The PEFA PFM performance measurement framework

Major international donor countries[29] and international financial organisations[30] have jointly developed the so-called PEFA PFM performance measurement framework. PEFA stands for Public Expenditure and Financial Accountability, while PFM stands for Public Financial Management. The PEFA framework, as it is often briefly referred to, is basically an assessment tool; however, it obviously gives an overview of public sector financial management as it tries to overcome the traditional segmentations. The framework is supposed to be used both in a self-assessment and an assessment by international experts. It is therefore also a common basis for dialogue. It has been developed because the

---

[29] The United Kingdom, Norway, France, Switzerland.

[30] The World Bank, International Monetary Fund, European Commission, The Strategic Partnership with Africa.

performance of public financial management has been identified as critical factor in the 'implementation of policies of national development and poverty reduction'.[31]

If there are flaws in public financial management, other areas of development such as education or infrastructure are likely to be biased by misallocation of funds and even criminal practices such as corruption. Good financial management is a precondition for other areas of development. However, the PEFA framework should not be perceived from a developing nation's perspective only. In its technical section the framework itself makes no reference to development issues at all; and also the set of indicators refers to development issues only in a very limited number of cases. From a technical perspective the framework is applicable to any jurisdiction and, in fact, there are plans to use it in highly developed countries as well. The only difference to be expected are higher scores in some areas. However, many indicators are equally challenging for the developed world.

The PEFA framework identifies six critical dimensions of performance of public financial management.[32] These are:

1 **Credibility of budget.** The budget is realistic and implemented as intended.
2 **Comprehensiveness and transparency.** The budget and the fiscal risk oversight are comprehensive and fiscal and budget information is accessible to the public.
3 **Policy-based budgeting.** The budget is prepared with due regard to public policy.
4 **Predictability and control in budget execution.** The budget is implemented in an orderly and predictable manner and there are arrangements for the exercise of control and stewardship in the use of public funds.
5 **Accounting, recording and reporting.** Adequate records and information are produced, maintained and disseminated to meet decision-making control, management and reporting purposes.
6 **External scrutiny and audit.** Arrangements for scrutiny of public finances and follow-up by executives are operating.

Contemplating the six critical dimensions, it is quite obvious that much emphasis is placed on budgeting, which is not only the starting point, but also subject to four out of six dimensions. Budgeting is critical, as it is not only the driving force of the controlling cycle, but also the closest link to the non-financial world of policy making. However, as all six dimensions are given equal importance, the PEFA framework is also giving high prominence to accounting and reporting, as well as assurance. Thus it clearly departs from the traditional budget-over-everything-else idea and recognises the shortcomings of this idea. As a matter of fact, there are plans to extend the non-budget sections of the framework.

The PEFA framework itself is relatively slim and comprises a mere six pages in its English edition. But there is a comprehensive annex 1 providing a set of 28 public financial management performance indicators as well as 3 indicators on donor practices. In fact, the three donor practices are perhaps the only sections that are of less interest to developed countries – except of course for their development agencies. Table 1.1 gives an overview over the 28 plus 3 indicators.

Although the PEFA framework is not actually a management tool for the public sector financial manager, it gives a good overview of the state of the art in the various fields

---

[31] PEFA (2005) iii; available for free download at www.pefa.org.
[32] PEFA (2005) 2.

Table 1.1 Overview of the PEFA PFM performance measurement framework indicator set[33]

	A. PFM-out-turns: credibility of the budget
PI-1	Aggregate expenditure out-turn compared to original approved budget
PI-2	Composition of expenditure out-turn compared to original approved budget
PI-3	Aggregate revenue out-turn compared to original approved budget
PI-4	Stock and monitoring of expenditure payment arrears
	B. Key Cross-Cutting issues: comprehensiveness and transparency
PI-5	Classification of the budget
PI-6	Comprehensiveness of information included in budget documentation
PI-7	Extent of unreported government operations
PI-8	Transparency of inter-governmental fiscal relations
PI-9	Oversight of aggregate fiscal risk from other public sector entities
PI-10	Public access to key fiscal information
	C. Budget cycle
	C(i) Policy-based budgeting
PI-11	Orderliness and participation in the annual budget process
PI-12	Multi-year perspective in fiscal planning, expenditure policy and budgeting
	C(ii) Predictability and control in budget execution
PI-13	Transparency of taxpayer obligations and liabilities
PI-14	Effectiveness of measures for taxpayer registration and tax assessment
PI-15	Effectiveness in collection of tax payments
PI-16	Predictability in the availability of funds for commitment of expenditure
PI-17	Recording and management of cash balances, debt and guarantees
PI-18	Effectiveness of payroll controls
PI-19	Competition, value for money and controls in procurement
PI-20	Effectiveness of internal controls for non-salary expenditure
PI-21	Effectiveness of internal audit
	C(iii) Accounting, recording and reporting
PI-22	Timeliness and regularity of accounts reconciliation
PI-23	Availability of information on resources received by service delivery units
PI-24	Quality and timeliness of in-year budget reports
PI-25	Quality and timeliness of annual financial statements
	C(iv) External scrutiny and audit
PI-26	Scope, nature and follow-up of external audit
PI-27	Legislative scrutiny of the annual budget law
PI-28	Legislative scrutiny of external audit reports

▶

---

[33] PEFA (2005) 9.

Table 1.1 *(Continued)*

	D. Donor practices
D-1	Predictability of direct budget support
D-2	Financial information provided by donors for budgeting and reporting on project and program aid
D-3	Proportion of aid that is managed by use of national procedures

as well as the relationship between the fields. Perhaps one should keep in mind that it was started from the budget perspective and therefore this dimension is still somewhat dominant. There are also a few conceptual issues, such as the implications of federal structures or various degrees of consolidation, to be resolved on the level of the framework. But nevertheless the PEFA framework gives a comprehensive idea of the issues to be addressed.

1.4.2 Accounting models

Many continental European and a few Asian countries have a tradition of what is called an accounting model. There is no equivalent either in the private sector or in the anglo-saxon world. Accounting models, unlike accounting standards, are based on an economic model of the government sector. They usually follow the state of government financial statistics (GFS) at the moment of their creation but go well beyond that. They include the budgeting and planning as well as detailed accounting procedures (similar to standards) and a binding chart of accounts (CoA). Despite their name they go well beyond accounting. Sometimes they go as far as fiscal policy guidelines, prescribing how specific investments or their replacement should be financed. Accounting models have their main importance on the local level as superior levels of government may influence their financial management in a very comprehensive manner through accounting models. They are sufficiently detailed to serve as an instruction for practitioners, even if they are not professionally educated.

However, accounting models help to overcome institutional barriers on higher levels as they require close cooperation of the various tasks and institutions. Their downsides are more or less significant compromises which had to be made in order to achieve a single accounting model comprising all the various perspectives. This obviously attracts criticism from the proponents of each of those perspectives. By their nature, accounting models also have a tendency to overemphasise some details.

Example   Example of an accounting model

> **The Swiss Harmonised Accounting Model (HAM)**
>
> The HAM was issued for field testing in 1977 and became effective with a few amendments in 1981. It was designed by committee under the auspices of the Conference of State Ministers Finance, the body that formally recommended its implementation to all states (*cantons*) as well as local governments. It was based on the government financial statistics of

▶

Example	(Continued)

that period and introduced an accrual basis of accounting. An updated version, acknowledging the developments over the last 26 years, including performance-based budgeting and the emergence of the International Public Sector Accounting Standards (IPSAS), was released in 2008.

The best overview of the HAM can be given by looking at the interaction of the various budget statements and financial statements. Theoretically the statement-oriented structure of HAM and the corresponding chart of accounts (CoA) can be used for the drafting of long-term financial plans, approving one-year budgets, bookkeeping under the year and then again for the presentation of the financial statements. Hence, HAM not only provides accrual accounting, but also accrual financial planning and budgeting.

HAM is based on the basic concept of (corporate as well as public) finance, that any investment can either be financed through surpluses, depreciation or capital issued. As equity is usually unavailable for public sector entities, capital issued is either loans or bonds. In order to depreciate the assets, investments need to be activated.

Exhibit 1.3 gives an overview of the statements under HAM. Exhibits 1.4 to 1.6 show the interaction of the statement of financial performance and the statement of investment in the three scenarios of debt financing, payback of debt and equilibrium.

Exhibit 1.3	Overview over the various statements under HAM

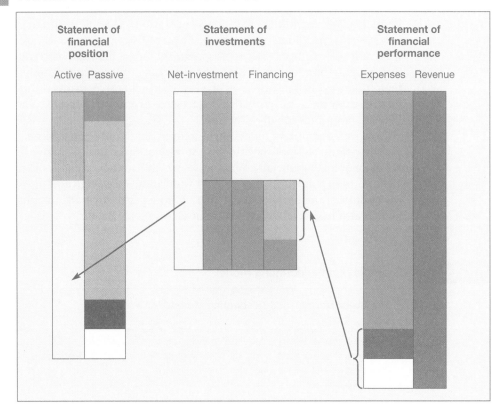

Exhibit 1.4 Investment financed by depreciation, surplus and new debt

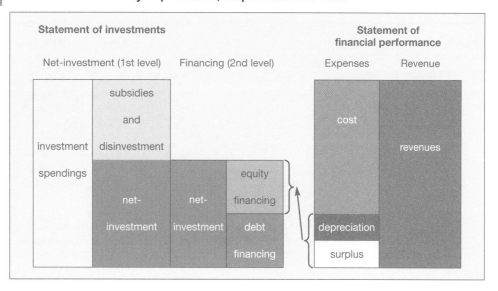

Exhibit 1.5 Investment financed by depreciation and surplus. Excess surplus used for paying back some of the debt

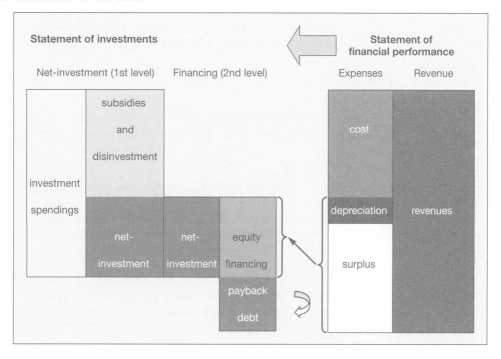

| Exhibit 1.6 | Equilibrium: investment financed by depreciation and surplus |

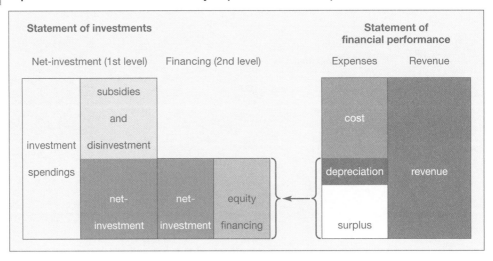

Work assignments

1 Take a list of public sector entities in your country and assess whether they belong to the general government sector or whether they are public sector corporations.

2 Some of the most controversial issues in the discussion about public or private provision are energy supply and public transportation. In both cases show which are the arguments from welfare economics that are used for both opinions, in favour of public provision as well as in favour of private provision.

3 Discuss the relative importance budgeting has had and perhaps still has in public sector financial management.

4 The PEFA PFM performance measurement framework has been developed for the assessment of developing countries' public financial management. Why is the public financial management so relevant for developing countries? Is it possible to transfer this relevance to highly developed countries?

5 Accounting models, such as HAM, emphasise the flow of money in public sector entities. Let us take the example of a local school (or school council), which receives CU 1 million per year from the Ministry of Education, CU 0.1 million from fees, donations, etc. and runs at operational costs of CU 0.9 million. It owns a 20-year-old school building, which was constructed for CU 9 million and has a useful life of an estimated 30 years. There is a mortgage loan of CU 0.5 million on this property. The school building needs refurbishment and expansion, representing an investment of CU 2.5 million. This will expand the useful life to another 20 years. The Ministry of Education will contribute a non-repayable grant of CU 0.5 million for the extension. Show how the money flows using HAM or another model from your jurisdiction. Will the school be able to make the investment? Is it sustainable to increase the loan?

Interface to national concepts

In this section, at the end of each chapter, there is a list of the concepts that should be followed up in each jurisdiction in which this textbook is used. The concepts listed may vary substantially, but should be found in some way or another.

1 Check the organisational structure of public sector financial management:
   - by levels of government (i.e. what is the role of local governments, state governments, national governments?); and
   - by entities (i.e. are there public sector corporations, agencies, departments?).

2 What is the division of labour between various entities (i.e. treasury, ministry of finance, budget units, accounting units, auditor's offices, etc.)?

3 What is the deficit and debt situation of the various public sector entities/levels of government?

4 Are there any accounting standards, models or frameworks – either in place or under development?

2 Public finance

Learning objectives

- Describe and question the concepts that public finance offers in the field of public sector expenditure.

- Classify public spending and income appropriately.

- Describe the current issues of public sector income.

- Describe and apply the concepts that public finance offers in the context of public sector deficit and debt.

- Discuss the implications of the Maastricht criteria.

- Show, from a public sector financial management perspective, the relevant gaps in public finance.

Key terms

Convergence criterion	Expenditure	Golden rule
Debt	Expense	Maastricht criteria
Deficit	Fee	

Public finance is a traditional part of economics. As such it offers thorough analysis of the public sector's economics. Obviously a single chapter cannot substitute an entire textbook – many of which are at hand in the field of public finance.[1] Instead this chapter highlights the aspects that are crucial for public sector financial management as well as some areas of interest about which the traditional theory of public finance remains silent.

It follows a logical order comprising all financial transactions, including spending and income, as well as the bottom line of the two, deficit (or surplus) and debt. This corresponds to the main outline of public finance textbooks.[2] It follows a more traditional approach, not taking into account the latest research, which is in the field of behavioural public finance, as the results are rather tentative and consequences in the field of public sector financial management are not clear, as yet.

2.1 Public sector spending

Public sector spending is obviously very attractive for politics. No wonder public finance devotes a substantial part of its work to this. As public finance is part of economics, its main interest goes to total spending, i.e. the government's part of the economic cycle. It does not care too much about public sector corporations, as they are usually part of the larger private sector corporations sector. Neither gives too much interest to international organisations, which simply represent part of the exchanges with foreign entities. Perhaps this section should be called government spending rather than public sector spending. However, as we shall see, the suggested impact of the scope issue is far larger than it should be. Other shortcomings include the delimitation between consumption and investment.

2.1.1 Macroeconomic impact

In a simple macroeconomic model governments get their money from households and corporations. They spend it on what is called government consumption. Thus governments are part of the economic cycle; in fact government spending is part of the national income or, measured on the supply side rather than the demand side, the GDP measured by the expenditure method:

$$GDP = C + I + G + X - M$$

where GDP stands for the gross domestic product, C for consumption, I for investment, G for government spending, X for revenue from exports, M for imports.

Thus, an increase in government spending leads, *ceteris paribus,* to an increase of the national income. However, the models assume that this increase is rather a shift from

---

[1] More recent widely used ones include Rosen, H. (2002) *Public Finance,* New York: McGraw Hill, 6th edition; or Stiglitz, J. (2000) *Economics of the Public Sector,* various editions, New York/London: Norton, 3rd edition.

[2] Rosen, H. (2002); Musgrave, R., Musgrave, P. (1989).

Exhibit 2.1 General government outlays as percentage of GDP nominal (2006)

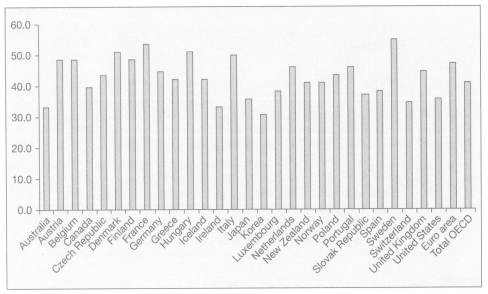

Source: General government outlays in percent of GDP nominal (OECD definition), *OECD Economic Outlook no. 81*,
© OECD 2007

private sector consumption or investment to the government, because governments either tax consumption or borrow money from private sector investors. That is the reason why most attention is given to the proportion of government spending in relation to the national income or GDP, i.e. the fraction of the cycle that is channelled through government's hands compared to that which is handled by individuals or corporations.

As we can see in Exhibit 2.1 in most countries about a third of the cycle is going through the government's hand. Whether this is a little or a lot depends very much on the political opinion. However, most politicians would shy away from large increases, as this would mean that the government is taking an ever increasing role in the economy. In fact, this is a kind of crowding out.[3]

However, the delimitation between the sectors is crucial. Let us take an example. A local government has a utility unit that takes care of the distribution of supplies, i.e. electricity, gas, water. As local governments are a part of the general government sector, the spending of this unit will count as government spending and be part of the government's share of the economy. If this unit becomes incorporated, but still owned and controlled by the same local government, it becomes a public sector non-financial corporation. In the national accounts the spending of such utility corporations are added to the corporate sector. Thus the very same spending is no longer government spending, although very little, economically, has changed. The example should not be considered as a privatisation, as ownership and control are still entirely in the hands of the government. But the same example also holds in the opposite direction. An investment by the corporate utility obviously counts as an investment, but the very same investment of the utility, which is a government unit, counts as consumption.

---

[3] Crowding out is generally used for any kind of government activity driving private actors out of the market. This can apply either to the market of goods and services or to the capital market. Where the government can influence the money supply it may also happen due to inflation.

Another area of inconsistency is social insurance. Social insurance clearly is part of the general government sector, thus their spending counts towards government spending. However, in many countries at least some social security schemes are run by private corporations, i.e. insurance companies. They count as social security because they may be mandatory and subject to rather strict government regulation. But the money flows through private sector entities and is therefore not counted as government spending. Similar stories can be told about Public Private Partnerships (PPPs).[4] If a motorway is constructed and operated by a private corporation in lieu, and under a concession of, the government, government spending is likely to be much smaller in early years, i.e. during the construction of the motorway, but higher thereafter, during its amortisation. Many of those PPPs have reached a size that makes it likely that the share of government spending in relation to GDP is affected.

If such inconsistencies were purely academic, it would be one thing. But they are not. If we later look at the Maastricht criteria, they may decide about compliance and in the case of non-compliance lead to hefty fines to the respective country. But they may even be troublesome internally, even at a local level. The incorporated but still fully owned utility from above incurs various risks, like any business but also any government unit. As with any other corporation their shareholders are ultimately carrying this risk – but their only shareholder is, no wonder, still the government. Thus by removing the utility out of the general government sector, transparency has clearly been reduced.

Public sector financial managers are regularly involved in such transactions, at the borderlines between government, public sector corporations and private corporations.

2.1.2 Classifications

Obviously information about a country's government's economic activity is essential for decisions in the field of public sector financial management, as well as on the political level. However, with all the pitfalls and inconsistencies mentioned above, it is rather doubtful whether both the politicians and the managers get the right information and eventually make the right decisions.

Therefore this book clearly advocates three developments that are driven by the ongoing reform of the government financial statistics (GFS). These are that:

1 Public sector corporations should be considered separately from their privately controlled equivalents. Any data, notably the government's share of the GDP, should be calculated with and without them.
2 Also for governments, investments should be distinguished from consumption.
3 Expenditure should be distinguished from expense.

These developments of course slightly increase the volume of data, but decrease the complexity for the decision makers, as they would have all the relevant information.

This book makes a strong case to distinguish between investment and consumption. But what is government investment like? It is no different from private sector investment: investment means the purchase of assets which are to be used more than just once for the production and delivery of goods and services. The idea of a more-than-once use is, for accounting reasons, usually extended to one period, thus investments are assets to be used

---

[4] Sometimes also called Public Financial Initiatives or – with a slightly more narrow meaning – Service Concessions.

over more than one period. This is no different from the private sector. Consider a school building used for a public and a private school. In both cases such a building will be used to deliver educational services over many, perhaps 30 to 40, years. Thus it is pretty obvious that a public school building is equally an investment. Of course, for some assets, e.g. IT equipment, useful life will be a few years only, but it is still an investment, as it is used for the delivery of goods and services over this shorter period of time.

Definition	**Expense**
	An expense is any consumption of net asset/equity by the operation of the entity or just the time going by. It results in a decrease of assets or an increase of liabilities.
	Expenditure
	An expenditure is any outlay of money to pay for expenses, invest into assets or pay back liabilities.

This distinction immediately leads to another one: expenditure and expenses. Expenditure is an outflow of cash or cash equivalent, while expenses are any kind of consumption or outflow of assets or increases in liabilities. Thus the concept of expense is much more comprehensive. It also includes increases in payables, depreciation, raises in obligations etc. Obviously, the concept of expense is an accrual concept, while expenditures are in the cash basis world. We will see in Chapter 4 the differences between the two. At this stage, considering public sector spending, we have to reckon that the traditional concept of public finance is based on expenditure, but this is falling short of the entire economic reality. Taking up the example of the school building again: the entire expenditure for purchasing or constructing the school building takes place in the very first year. But the school building is not consumed in the very first year, but over its useful life of 30 to 40 years. Thus expenses are much lower than expenditure in the very first year, but higher thereafter, as every year uses part of the entire useful life. Thus expenses equal the consumption of the entity.

In order to classify public sector spending or, as advocated by this book consumption and investment, there is the obvious option to do so by nature. By nature means that the classification follows the nature of the transaction, which usually is strongly influenced by the transaction's economic and legal classification. Very common classes of nature in the field of consumption spending include salaries/payroll, rent, repair and maintenance, interest, depreciation, etc. In the case of investments it includes property, plant and equipment, infrastructure, financial investments, etc. This classification by nature is useful for some decisions. For instance, if the government is considering adjustments to the wages, it is indispensable to know which part of its spending is wages. Important also are interest payments, especially if they reach a size that gives any potential for discretionary decisions. This is regularly the case for heavily indebted countries.

The other useful classification is by function. Obviously one needs to know how much is spent for education, defence, social welfare, etc. For politicians the functional classification is usually even more relevant than the classification by nature, as it is closer to the political agenda. It is quite unlikely to find repair and maintenance in any party's programme, but you can certainly find education or health. In order to standardise the classification by nature, the United Nations created a system called 'classification of functions of governments' (COFOG). Although most countries are committed to COFOG, you may find minor differences from country to country. Exhibit 2.2 shows the official COFOG on its top level. Lower levels are also defined, but more difficult to adopt in the various

Exhibit 2.2	Classification of functions of government (COFOG)

01	General public services
02	Defence
03	Public order and safety
04	Economic affairs
05	Environmental protection
06	Housing and community amenities
07	Health
08	Recreation, culture and religion
09	Education
10	Social protection

Exhibit 2.3	Public expenditure on education as percentage of GDP (2004)

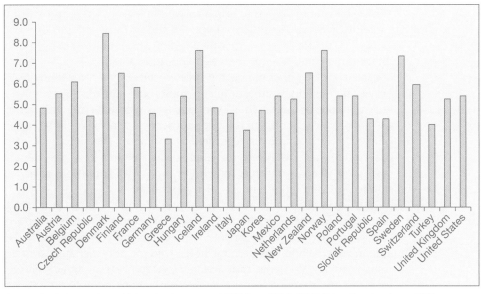

Source: Public Expenditure of Education in percent of GDP (year 2004), *OECD Education at a glance, 2007,*
© OECD 2007

countries, as organisational structures may differ substantially. For example, in education some countries have a system called K12, i.e. 12 years of mandatory schooling, while others have fewer years but formal vocational training after completion of a mandatory school education (so-called 'apprenticeships'). In some countries teacher training is part of university education, in others it is not and so on. In federal republics like Germany, the United States or Switzerland, structures differ even from state to state. That is why most countries depart much further from the international standard on lower levels of classification.

This classification by function is quite helpful if spending for each function should be determined and compared to other countries. Such comparisons are often used to assess the competitiveness of countries, i.e. by comparing their spending for education. This is shown in Exhibit 2.3.

2.2 Public sector income

Public sector spending, of course, needs to be financed somehow. Public sector entities normally have two main options, income and debt. Either the spending is covered by current proceedings ('income') or debts are to be increased. It is as simple as for any household. In this section only income will be considered, leaving debt to the next section.

2.2.1 Macroeconomic impact

As mentioned in Section 2.1.1, the public sector is part of the economic cycle. It takes its income out of this cycle, either from private households or corporations. There are two basic options to do so:

1 taxes and transfers ('revenue from non-exchange-transactions'); and
2 fees ('revenue from exchange transactions').

While any kind of tax has to be paid regardless of any service provided by the public sector entity, fees are usually linked up with the delivery of goods or services. More generically taxes should therefore be called revenue from non-exchange transactions and fees, on the other hand, revenue from exchange transactions. Of course, fees are also sometimes considered to be unfair in size, but they are due only if some kind of service is requested. Let us take schools as an example. A substantial part of the tax revenue most certainly goes to public schools.[5] Thus even taxpayers who have no children or send their children to private schools will pay taxes for schools. On the other hand, school fees have to be paid only if a child is registered at a school. The same lack of exchange can be observed for many transfers, e.g. money allocated to a local government. Obviously this case is less clear, as transfers sometimes come with conditions attached (i.e. the obligation to provide a set of services, such as schools).

In macroeconomic literature the impact of non-exchange and exchange transactions is usually considered to be the same. The money is taken away from consumption and saving/investment by private households and corporations. It reduces the disposable income. While this perhaps holds true for non-exchange transactions, it is questionable for any exchange transaction. Developments in public sector management have increased the share of such exchange transactions by holding entities accountable for their output and often making them charge fees for it. Thus what is the economic difference if you are charged, for example, a tuition fee by a public school or a private one? Perhaps none, because in both cases you are paying for the services delivered. If you do not like it, you have the option not to buy it and keep your disposable income for other purposes. Obviously the public sector was less of a service firm when the macroeconomic theories were drafted than nowadays.

2.2.2 Classifications

While a very broad classification has been made in the previous section, this should be explored further at this stage.

---

[5] Public means operated by the government, government agency or the like. (At least one very large country, India, uses the term public schools for private ones.)

First, taxes. Taxes can be divided into direct and indirect taxes. Direct taxes are those that are directly taxing the economic potential of individuals and corporations. Most countries have in place income taxes for individuals and corporate profit taxes. This is in contrast to indirect taxes, which instead tax each individual's or corporation's use of resources. Most countries have value added taxes (VAT) or government sales taxes (GST) in place, and some also have property taxes. They do not reflect the economic strength but rather the actual spending or the ownership of a particular asset, for example property. Obviously direct taxes pursue the goal of redistribution from the more to the less affluent individuals and from the prosperous to the not so prosperous corporations. This is supposed to add more fairness to the society, although it might damage the incentive of success. On the other side indirect taxes more simplistically claim the governments' share of the economic cycle. This, of course, makes no differentiation between rich and poor when it comes to basic supplies, which are therefore sometimes exempt from indirect taxes or taxed at lower tax rates. As both direct and indirect taxes have their advantages and downsides, most countries have adopted a system that includes both types.

Other tax classifications make a difference between flows (income) and substance (wealth), which is taxed. Although this may look similar to the direct-indirect criterion at first glance, it is not. Both direct and indirect taxes can be on flows or substance. Direct taxes not only address income (flow) but in some countries also wealth (substance). Indirect taxes prominently address sale of goods and services (flow) but also property (substance). Taxes on substance are less persuasive from the economics standpoint, as they are using up the substance. If there are capital gains, this is obviously not so bad, but in periods of devaluation, for example after a collapse of a price bubble, things are particularly bad. They are also more likely to change the government's share of the economic cycle, as they do not adjust to changes of the economic activities. That is why more recent tax reforms have decreased or abolished taxes on substance in many countries.

Duties both from customs and internal sources have frequently been classified as fees, as you get some sort of permission (i.e. to import goods) in exchange. With the emergence of indirect taxes, this argument has weakened, as one could basically classify most taxes as some kind of permission (i.e. to sell or buy). Actually, the service given in exchange of duties is not particularly large (i.e. opening the gate) and clearly not equivalent to the value of the duty paid. For economic purposes duties should be classified as taxes.

Other non-exchange transactions include transfers from one government to the other or also to private entities (i.e. grants, subsidies). As mentioned before, in some cases, especially grants, conditions are attached, which brings them dangerously close to exchange transactions. However, in many instances these conditions are not enforceable. The last class of non-exchange transactions are fines. Obviously they do not give permission to break the law and are clearly non-exchange.

Obviously fees can also be classified: as in private sector firms, they are usually classified along the various kinds of goods or services provided in exchange. In fact, most public sector entities are multi-product firms, which deliver a series of different products to the public. Besides the obvious option of creating an entity-specific classification, the COFOG, introduced in Section 2.1, is also applicable to revenues. Thus fees generally can be classified by function.

2.2.3 Current public sector income issues

Traditionally public finance gave much attention to the idea of 'good taxes'. However, the increase in fees being charged for various services has attracted more attention recently. New or increased fees are often criticised as hidden taxes.

Analysing this issue, there are two questions behind it. First, is the fee replacing a former tax? Second, is the fee adequate? The first question can be answered only in the respective context. Usually the documents on which the decision makers based their decision should give an answer. It is more difficult to find the right answer if the fee was introduced as part of a package, including various changes to the tax system and fee structure. As a matter of fact, such package deals may have an even result as a whole, but not for each and every individual. For example, the introduction of a fee for garbage collection may go hand in hand with a tax cut of the same total amount, but for those producing a quantity of garbage that exceeds the average, the fee will exceed the savings on the tax side. However, this is likely to be on purpose, as fees should be an incentive to reduce the amount of garbage.

The second question is more difficult to answer. Usually fees, like taxes, have to be based on a law or a decree. Sometimes this piece of legislation specifies which costs should be covered by the fee and which not. While direct costs, i.e. transportation and incineration of the garbage, are usually not disputed, the following cost components may be more controversial:

1 overhead costs, i.e. cost for management, administration, perhaps marketing;
2 depreciation, i.e. cost for the replacement of property, plant and equipment;
3 interest on invested capital; and
4 a profit, i.e. an increase in net assets/equity of the entity collecting the fee.

Item 1 is a question of delimitation. Most people would agree that overhead costs related to fee, i.e. garbage removal, should be in, but those unrelated, i.e. general environmental protection policy, should be out. The borderline needs, of course, to be defined. Items 2 and 3 clearly should be covered by a fee, as property, plant and equipment are necessary to fulfil the task. Thus capital and replacement needs to be paid for. Item 4 depends largely on the risk structure. If the entity collecting the fee has to carry operational or financial risks, they clearly need to have an appropriate level of net assets/equity. On the other side, if the government (or somebody else) is taking any risk, there is no need for equity on the entity level.

2.3 Public sector deficit and debt

Obviously even more important than the spending and income sides is what results in the bottom line. This can be either a deficit or a raise in debt.

2.3.1 Macroeconomic impact

Primarily a deficit means that the government is spending more money than it is taking out of the economic cycle; a surplus on the other side means that more money is taken out than spent. Such a difference may be on purpose, in the short term, if the government plans a fiscal intervention in order to support the economic cycle (deficit) or cool it down (surplus). Whether fiscal policy is a feasible measure or not is disputed among economists and politicians alike and cannot be resolved here.

But obviously the long-term impact depends very much on how the deficit is financed. It can be financed either by using up the net assets/equity that has accumulated in boom years, or by increasing the debt. Obviously the latter has more impact on the economy, because the government is borrowing from the private sector. This can lead to

Exhibit 2.4   Gross financial liability as percentage of GDP nominal (2006)

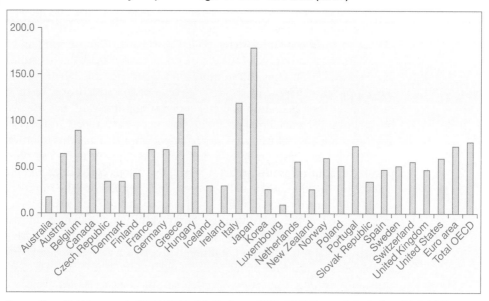

Source: Gross Debt in percent of GDP (OECD definition), year 2006, *OECD Economic Outlook no. 81*, © OECD 2007

crowding out of private sector investments, which of course contradicts the initial in-tention of the government, which was to support the economy. However, the risk of crowding out is much smaller if there is an excess supply of capital. Many industrialised nations have experienced this situation for a period of time, characterised by very low interest rates. But there is also a negative impact of debt financing on the government side. Higher debt means higher interest payments. Interest payments reduce the poten-tial for discretionary spending. Highly indebted countries are more likely to be unable to cater adequately for the needs of their population and economy. The financial liability of countries can be seen in Exhibit 2.4.

Another economically interesting feature of debt is the intergenerational transfer. If current spending, and to a lesser degree also investment, is financed by debt, there is a transfer of the economic burden to the next generation, as it is assumed they will have to pay back the money borrowed. This is obviously true if money borrowed is used for current spending. It is probably fairer if it used for investments, for example in infra-structure, of which the next generation can take advantage and also use. The idea of a 'shift of burden' from one generation to the next is disputed among economists, as some argue, following Barro and Ricardo, that rational actors would anticipate this shift and hence save the money today, because they know they have to pay tomorrow. Buchanan, on the other side, doubts such rational behaviour. In fact, there is little practical evi-dence for Barro and Ricardo's view. The shift of burden to the next generation is there-fore at least a strong argument against an increase of debt.

Finally, as Stiglitz makes the point, the effects of debt also depend on what the money is used for.[6] If it is, indeed, used for investments, which prove valuable for the future production of goods and services, it may be feasible. But if it is used for pure consump-tion or abandoned projects, it is clearly not feasible.

---

[6] Stiglitz, J. (2000) 782.

2.3.2 Measurement of deficit and debt

The definition of a deficit, the difference between spending and income, if the spending is larger, does not suggest how many measurement issues there might be. The main trouble comes from the still widely applied cash basis of accounting and the only slightly better situation in respect of the distinction between investments and consumption (see also Section 2.1.2). Thus still in quite a few countries the deficit is really cash payments out minus cash payments in. This leaves not too much of a technical measurement problem, as the calculation is pretty much straightforward, but the result is likely to be biased towards coincidental payments for long-term projects and a lack of recognition of anything that has not triggered any payments, as yet. Thus this traditional deficit should rather be called a cash drain (or a cash flow if it happens to be a surplus). Obviously, it is possible to adjust this unsatisfactory result by various corrections and present an adjusted deficit. But this does not usually increase the credibility of the numbers presented.

More promising is really full accrual accounting. The above-mentioned cash payments are, of course, still presented, but obviously in a statement of cash flows. The bottom line of the operational cash transaction is called cash flow or cash drain. The deficit on the other side is equal to the difference between expenses and revenues and – due to double entry – also the change in net assets/equity. It reflects an excess of the economic consumption over the economic income. And vice versa for surpluses. The difference between cash flow/drain and deficit/surplus equals the non-cash transactions, such as depreciation and provision. This mechanism can be illustrated by the so-called indirect method of calculation of the cash flow:

surplus (+)/deficit (−)
+ non-cash expenses (i.e. depreciation, newly made provisions)
− non-cash revenues (i.e. unrealised capital gains, dissolved provisions)
= cash flow (+)/cash drain (−)

Because depreciation is usually by far the largest position in the non-cash transaction, the cash flow (+) is sometimes used as proxy for the funds available for investment. However, caution should be exercised if a large part of the cash flow is made up by provisions, as they are not supposed to be used for this purpose.

The other aspect of measurement that needs to be addressed is also one already discussed in Section 2.1.2: the scope of entities included. Unfortunately, the public sector has a long tradition of not including less prosperous entities in the calculation of deficit, perhaps not even in the calculation of debt. So-called funds are quite a popular instrument for such scoping out behaviour. Obviously, these funds will then run a deficit and accumulate a debt – both not being part of the deficit and debt presented in the budget or the financial statements. Examples include social welfare funds or funds for large-scale projects such as the new, extra long rail tunnels beneath the Alps in Europe.

2.3.3 Targets

As we have seen in the previous two sections, both deficit and, even more so, debt are no good to the economy and the public sector entity itself. Thus there are good reasons to limit both to a rather modest level. But how much is still tolerable? These are questions that are answered as part of the first of the three goals of public sector financial management introduced in Chapter 1, the fiscal management goal.

Table 2.1	Targets for deficit and debt

	In case of recession	Average over the entire economic cycle	Long term
Deficit	Max. equals the amount of depreciation	0 (zero)	0 (zero)
Debt	Max. increase equals the usual decrease in boom periods	0 (zero) real increase, amount should be less than the value of long-term assets	Less than the value of long-term assets

As we have seen, there might be some macroeconomic reasons to allow a larger deficit in times of recession, rather than in boom periods. Economists refer to the first one as being 'in the short run' and the latter 'in the long run'. Unfortunately the term 'in the short run' ignores the conditions attached, i.e. it should be taken advantage of only in times of recession, and the term 'long run' suggests that much time may go by until this is the case.

The targets shown in Table 2.1 reflect the economics behind deficit and debt. In the case of a deficit, we have seen that it is tolerable only during a recession. But also then it should not exceed depreciation, as this would mean that there is borrowing of finance for current spending, which is a clear case of the shift of burden hypothesis. Over the entire economic cycle the deficit should be zero. There is no surplus needed either, as public sector entities are not-for-profit organisations, which do not have to pay dividends or provide a decent return on investment.

Debt, on the other side, should be increased only during a recession, very much for the same reason as the deficit. Over the economic cycle there should be no increase, or perhaps an increase equalling only a small inflation rate. If this target is not met, the initial financial situation at the beginning of the next economic cycle is worse than at the beginning of the previous cycle.

As for any private sector borrower, long-term debt should be covered by collateral, i.e. a long-term asset. Assets have a positive value in the public sector if they provide either a future economic benefit or, more likely, a future service potential. For instance, a school building is valuable if it can be used on purpose, i.e. for education on an ongoing basis. If the asset has such a positive value, it is also fair to future generations if at least a part of it is financed by a loan. Obviously the future generation will have to pay off the loan, but may use the asset at the same time. On the other side, loans that are not backed by assets are clearly more critical. They have to be paid off equally by future generations, but there is no asset that can be used at the same time. Thus long-term debts should be equal to or less than long-term assets.

These targets, which collectively are sometimes referred to as the 'golden rule', are very challenging for many public sector entities.[7] But unless there is a sound expectation of future windfall gains, it is very hard to find arguments against it. Such windfall gains may, in a very few cases, result from unexplored natural resources, but for most of the countries and public sector entities there is no realistic expectation of such future windfall gains and thus the targets are the only reasonable way to proceed.

---

[7] HM Treasury (2004) 4.

2.3.4 Example: the Maastricht criteria

Perhaps the most internationally famous and recognised examples of deficit and debt targets are the Maastricht criteria, set up by the European Community (EC) in 1992 as part of the treaty on the formation of the European Union (EU). Those debt and deficit criteria in Article 121, along with macroeconomic criteria, are the prerequisite for any country to join the so-called Economic and Currency Union (ECU) and introduce the euro as their national currency. While the former members, such as the United Kingdom, had the option to abstain from joining the ECU, even if they were in compliance with the criteria, new members of the EU are obliged to meet the criteria after a transitional period and then join the ECU.

Article 121 includes four criteria:

1 **Price stability:** the inflation rate should not exceed the average of the three ECU countries with the lowest rate by more than 1.5 percentage points.
2 **Public finance:** shall be looked at more closely hereafter.
3 **Exchange rate:** within a specified bandwidth for a minimum of two years.
4 **Long-term nominal interest rate:** maximum two percentage points above the average of the three most price stable countries.

For the sake of public sector financial management, obviously only the second criterion is particularly relevant and shall therefore be looked at more closely. This criterion is further specified to include two measures:

● Government deficits should not exceed 3 per cent of the GDP.
● Government debt should not exceed 60 per cent of the GDP.

Obviously, both measures are based on the general government sector (GGS) and therefore do not include public sector corporations. In fact, many countries moved entities, which formerly belonged to the GGS, out of it and privatised them, at least partly. However, the more detailed rules also had to prevent subsidisation of such units, as this would clearly be against the substance of the treaty. The same needed to be done for various other issues, including measurement. As we have seen in previous sections of this book, the terms deficit and, less so, debt are subject to different interpretations. Exhibit 2.5 shows the gross public debt as defined in the Treaty of Maastricht.

Compared to the more generic targets in the previous section of this book, the Maastricht criteria are rather generous, though they are easier to measure and compare. It is possible under the Maastricht criteria to run a deficit in the long run – although this most likely would lead to a conflict with the debt criteria. However, it may take much longer than one cycle to reach this limit. The debt criteria are less generous, as it is, exactly like the previous section, emphasising an absolute limit for the debt. However, there is no incentive for countries to stay below that maximum level, which is again more generous than the proposal in the previous section. However, this is clearly less of a concern than the deficit, which may be well beyond sustainable levels for far too long.

2.3.5 Sovereign wealth funds

The preceding part of this section has, for good reason, given the impression that the main problems are deficits and debt. As a matter of fact, this has been the situation in most countries for many years and has therefore been addressed by the public

Exhibit 2.5 Gross public debt (2006) as defined in the Treaty of Maastricht

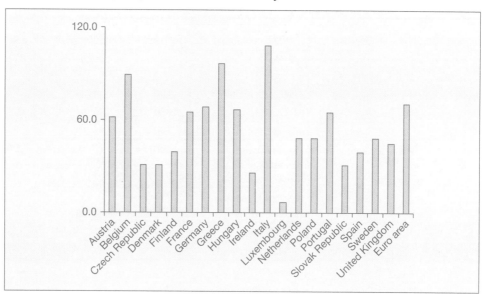

Source: Gross Public Debt (2006) as defined in the Treaty of Maastricht, *OECD Economic Outlook no. 82*, © OECD 2007

finance theory over centuries.[8] But also today's fiscal politics, including the Maastricht criteria, are still focused on deficits and debt, as they may jeopardise economic stability and prosperity.

Surpluses are less of an issue, perhaps because they are less frequently observed, or because they are perceived in a more positive way. But what should be done with surpluses? Should they be used to pay back debt or rather to lower taxes? Does it make any difference if the debt is at high levels or at low levels? Is it sensible to put surpluses aside for future distress situations? Public finance theory remains quiet about this unless a really high level of debt is involved, which of course should be paid back as soon as possible, at least down to a more sustainable level. What is more sustainable might be defined by the targets discussed earlier. It is also quite widely agreed that one-time gains, e.g. proceeds from privatisation, should be used to pay back debt. The same holds true for proceeds from the exploitation of natural resources.

The more recent economic history has, however, seen countries experiencing long periods of surpluses and their creation of sovereign wealth funds (see Table 2.2). These countries traditionally included oil rich countries such as Norway and many countries in the Middle East, especially the United Arab Emirates, but in more recent years countries such as Australia and New Zealand have joined in. However, New Zealand and, to a much lesser extent, Australia do not fit into this petrodollar fairy tale. They both have mixed economies where public sector surpluses are generated by means other than oil supply.

As Exhibit 2.6 shows, the surpluses varied substantially from one year to the next, which is due mainly to the proceeds of privatisation projects, one-time gains from the

---

[8] An early work worth mentioning is Smith, A. (1776) *The Wealth of Nations*.

Table 2.2 Sovereign wealth funds (non-exclusive, sorted by assets, based on Morgan Stanley and own research)

Country	Fund	Assets in billions US $		Year of inception
United Arab Emirates	ADIA	875		1976
Singapore	Temasek Holdings	100	combined	1974
	GIC	330	430	1981
Norway	Global Pension Fund	300		1996
China	State Foreign Exchange Investment Corp	300		2007
Kuwait	Kuwait Investment Authority	70		1953
Australia	Future Fund	40		2004
USA (Alaska)	Permanent Fund	35		1976
Russia	Stabilisation Fund	32		2003
Brunei	Brunei Investment Agency	30		1983
South Korea	Korean Investment Corporation	20		2006
New Zealand	Superannuation Fund	10		2002
Azerbaijan	State Oil Fund	1.4		2001

Exhibit 2.6 Development of the GGS surpluses/deficits in Australia and New Zealand

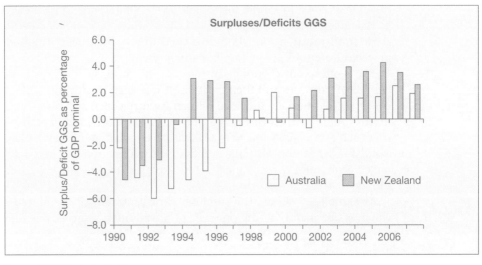

Source: OECD *Outlook*, No. 80.

Exhibit 2.7   Development of the government debt in Australia and New Zealand

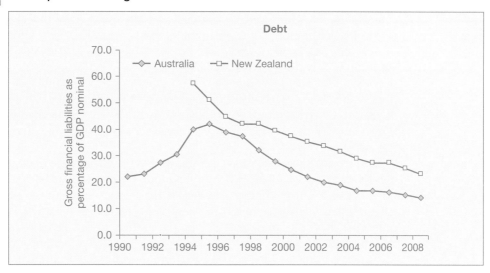

Source: OECD *Outlook*, No. 81.

sale of mobile phone licences or proceeds from natural resources. But both countries show substantial surpluses since the mid to late 1990s. As Exhibit 2.7 shows, they have used their surpluses to pay back debts, both achieving significant reductions of over 50 per cent.

In this situation both New Zealand and Australia created so-called sovereign wealth (or reserve) funds, an instrument that had been used mainly by oil-rich countries before. The sovereign wealth funds were created in a situation only where the debt had been reduced well below the level of similar countries. The OECD average gross financial liabilities have been around or above 70 per cent of the GDP since 1995.

However, the build-up of funds did start before the debts were fully paid back. The funds built up are dedicated to 'rainy days', which, in the case of Australia and New Zealand, are defined as the demographic change that will affect these countries later on.[9] This includes unfunded parts of old-age pensions, but also health costs which, like in most countries, are funded on a pay-as-you-go basis and likely to increase in future. They are supposed to reach a significant proportion of the country's GDP; in the case of Australia's Future Fund, a target of AU$100 billion, which would represent more than 10 per cent of the country's GDP.[10] However, considering the rapid build-up, even higher levels are very likely. The New Zealand Superannuation Fund officially targets NZ$109 billion by 2025, which would represent roughly 80 per cent of its actual GDP.[11] Perhaps it should be added that both Australia and New Zealand already have had relatively large funded schemes in place, even before the sovereign wealth funds became operational in 2003 in New Zealand and in 2005 in Australia.

But are sovereign wealth funds a feasible solution? Traditionally, economists – especially the supply-side breed – would argue that such compulsory savings would

---

[9] *The Western Australian* (23 January 2007) 11.

[10] Collett, J. (2007) 38.

[11] www.nzsuperfund.co.nz (29 January 2007).

weaken demand by charging excessive taxes. But although there is no rigorous empirical work available, yet, there are clearly no signs of weakening economic prosperity in those countries building up sovereign wealth funds. Thus such an empirical finding would be very unlikely. This might be due to traditionally very low levels of savings rates, especially in Australia, and rather low tax rates in both countries. But the low savings rate argument holds only for Australia and the tax rates are not exceptionally low, either. Thus there is at least some practical evidence from the macroeconomic perspective that surpluses should – as suggested by conventional wisdom – be used to pay back debt first and be used to brace for future economic distress situations, rather than being used to cut taxes. However, this conclusion has not been subject to more rigorous economic evaluation, as yet.

Most recently, the discussion has reached some of the more prosperous of the developing countries, e.g. Thailand.[12] There yet another flavour is added to the discussion, as it is not government surpluses that are targeted (the Thai government currently runs a budget deficit), but rather the central bank's foreign exchange reserves. In Thailand, and some other countries, they are at levels no longer required to stabilise exchange rates, which is their primary purpose.[13] Thus the foreign currency reserves become available for capital investments, similar to the abundant government surpluses, although – following contemporary monetary theory – it should not be the government but the independent central bank that decides on the use of the assets. But it is quite possible that yet a few additional countries, which until recently have had the reputation of being borrowers and not investors, are about to embrace the idea of establishing a sovereign wealth fund.

On the microeconomic side, sovereign wealth funds have come under scrutiny, as they are playing an increasingly important role in financial markets.[14] While some funds, like the New Zealand Superannuation Fund, are limited in their investment decisions by high ethical standards, other sovereign wealth funds, such as the Australian Future Fund, have no such provisions. It is argued that if such funds should help a country to brace for future social and environmental challenges, the least contribution they could make would be to invest more wisely. Groups like the Ethical Investment Association suggest that sovereign wealth funds should observe the Principles of Responsible Investment[15] released by the United Nations in 2006.[16] Other sovereign wealth funds have attracted some concern from a nationalist standpoint, as they became major investors in large blue chip companies in North America and Europe.[17]

Anyhow, the phenomenon of long-lasting surpluses needs to be added to the public finance repertoire, even if the majority of the country is still struggling with the much more familiar and better researched deficits and debt.

2.4 Bottom line

The bottom line section, introduced here, summarises the chapter's most important aspects from the public sector financial management perspective, without going back into the discussions.

---

[12] Chaitrong, W. (2007) 1B.

[13] About $80 billion in mid-2007 in the case of Thailand.

[14] Collett, J. (2007) 38.

[15] www.unpri.org.

[16] www.ethicalinvestment.org.uk/modules.php?name=News&file=article&sid=106.

[17] *Economist* (2008) 11.

Public finance clearly has been the driving force of public sector financial management for many years. However, traditionally it has substantial shortcomings in respect of the scope of entities considered as well as the accrual basis, including the notion of investments and expenses, rather than just expenditure. More recent developments, namely in the field of government financial statistics, make up for some of these shortcomings.

However, public finance provides sound concepts of classification, including classification of function of governments (COFOG), and important target rates for sound public sector financial management, including maximum deficit and debt concepts. The Maastricht criteria of the European Union (EU) are perhaps the most well-known and discussed examples of such targets. This book advocates more restrictive targets, with a maximum deficit being equal to depreciation and to being levelled out over the cycle. Debt should not increase in general and always should be covered by collateral on the asset side.

Relatively new and unexplored is the issue of long-term surpluses. There is some practical rather than empirical evidence that such surpluses should be used for paying back previously accumulated debt and then, as soon as the debt has reached a sustainable level, start building up sovereign wealth funds. However, the topic is, unfortunately, left largely uncovered by traditional public finance theory and research.

Furthermore, there are a few remarks from a practical perspective that highlight behavioural aspects, such as policy making or compliance with regulation. More recent work in the field of public finance has analysed such behavioural aspects more in depth.[18] This work is ongoing and has not reached a generally accepted level of consensus, despite substantial progress including Nobel prizes awarded to behavioural economists. But behavioural economists are still the 'new kids on the block', as McCaffrey and Slemrod put it quite adequately. In order to influence public sector financial management more clarity is needed. Most likely to be affected are the areas of financial planning and reporting, as they are most vulnerable to behavioural biases. Although there is no direct relationship between the two, behavioural public finance could be seen as a basis for the trend towards standards, which is discussed in later chapters of this book.

Work assignments

1 Explain the difference between spending, expenditure and expense.

2 This textbook takes the view that the difference between expenditure for investments and expenditure for consumption matters economically. Look for arguments against such a differentiation and discuss these.

3 Explain why taxes, fines and other transfers are non-exchange transactions.

4 Explain why most concepts of public finance, including the one in this chapter, encourage targets over an economic cycle rather than in the shorter run.

5 Unlike the Maastricht criteria this book advocates a balanced budget of the economic cycle and a long-term debt smaller than the value of the long-term assets. Describe the short- and long-term effects of such a rigorous fiscal policy.

6 Discuss the idea that the public sector should accumulate surpluses to cater for future financial distress situations.

---

[18] McCaffery, E., Slemrod, J. (2006).

Interface to national concepts

1 Look at your country's government financial statistics.

2 Check on target rates actually followed by your country and compare them to the targets proposed in this book as well as to the Maastricht criteria.

3 Is there any sovereign wealth fund, i.e. a state fund or agency investing capital, in your country? It is very likely that such an institution uses a name other than sovereign wealth fund.

3

Public sector budgeting and management accounting

Learning objectives

- Suggest a sensible time horizon for budgeting.
- Understand and interpret the different perspectives of budgeting.
- Identify the various stages in a budget process.
- Appraise the advantages and difficulties associated with the concept of performance budget.
- Distinguish output, outcome and impact.
- Develop a draft concept management accounting system for a public sector entity.

- Draft a proposal for a benchmarking project in the public sector.
- Take a position in the discussion about accrual budgeting.
- Describe the role of assurance in budgeting.

Key terms

Accrual budgeting	Full cost	Outcome
Benchmarking	Incremental budgeting	Performance budget
Budget	Impact	Product
Contribution margin	Marginal cost	Zero-based budgeting
Financial plan	Output	

Budgeting is perhaps the most popular and elaborate part of public sector financial management. It captures, in this broad sense, most of the financial decision making in public sector entities. Other approaches with a broader notion, including the balance sheet or the discounted cash flow method, to assess investments are increasingly considered, but clearly they do not have the dominant role that budgeting still plays and is likely to play in a foreseeable future. Associating budgeting with management accounting is a very mainstream approach on the private sector side; however, for the public sector it dates back to the early 1990s and is still fairly new in practice for some entities as reforms take their time. But it is an essential part of any control cycle and thus indispensable for public sector financial management.[1]

3.1 Functions of budgeting

Reviewing our findings in Chapter 1, we have identified financial planning and controlling as two of the core tasks of public sector financial management. This is sometimes even emphasised by an institutional setting which includes distinctive organisational structures for budgeting and controlling. In this chapter the two are brought together under the umbrella of the term budgeting. This is an attempt to bring planning and control as closely together as they should be, rather than overstating the accurate technical distinction made in Chapter 1. In fact, talking to professionals very likely would reveal that all is part of a complex process called budgeting. We have also seen in Chapter 1 that budgets are, at least in their short-term version, more authoritative in the public sector than on the private side, as they are the legal basis for any financial transaction and thus conditional in a legal sense.

Hence, budgeting comprises the following functions:

1 short-term planning;
2 short-term authorisation;
3 medium- to long-term planning;
4 control; and
5 budget reporting.

---

[1] Jones, R., Pendlebury, M. (2000) 21.

Short-term planning usually includes the next budget period which is, in many cases, one year.[2] Where multi-year budgets are in place, what is discussed under the short-term planning function applies to this multi-year period, if not mentioned otherwise. Short-term planning is the most detailed and yet most binding form of financial planning. It includes:

1 expenses;[3]
2 revenues;
3 investments; and
4 finance transactions, i.e. new loans.

Thus short-term financial planning can be presented in a budget statement of financial performance and a budget cash flow statement. Technically it is also possible to prepare a budget statement of financial position, i.e. a budget balance sheet, but this is less common and also less needed, as it does, per definition, not present any transactions and is therefore not a basis for authorisation. However, it can be useful for control purposes, as it may be linked with targets, such as a reduction of debt. The short-term planning function is not prescriptive for any form of budget, both the more traditional ones by nature and institution and the more recent performance-based ones. As a matter of fact, short-term financial planning includes all three perspectives, regardless of which is used for the authorisation. Even if there are performance budgets in place, expenses, revenues, investments and finance transactions need to be planned by some institution and this planning includes various line items by nature.

The perspectives of budgeting, discussed hereafter, mainly influence the second function, short-term authorisation. In many jurisdictions, the next one-year or multi-year budget becomes a law once it is approved. This law is as binding as any law and can be enforced by all means of law enforcement. Even if the jurisdiction does not issue a formal law, only authorised transactions may be made by the public sector entity and its management. There are generally some exceptions for emergencies, such as natural disasters. They are sometimes defined in the constitution or in budget laws. In many jurisdictions there are also exceptions for the case that budget approval is delayed. It is recommended to allow non-discretionary transactions, such as the provision of services on previous levels, in such a situation. Although the budget is usually prepared by the management of the public sector entity, its approval is almost always in the hands of a legislative body, usually the parliament.

Other bodies eligible for budget authorisation may include top-level supervisory boards or, in direct democracies, often found on the local level, even an assembly of the electorate. In this distinctive top level, democratic authorisation was first introduced during the French Revolution as an essential part of democratic control. The then new constitution of 1791 moved the power to authorise the budget to the legislative body.[4] However, it is often neglected to say that this top level authorisation does not remain the only one. A top-level budget is always very general and needs to be allocated further down to individual units or individuals responsible. This, of course, is subject to prior approval on the top level, but nonetheless not to be neglected. The allocation of

---

[2] Calendar year or other 12-month periods defined in each jurisdiction.

[3] In practice perhaps only expenditures, but as discussed in previous chapters this generally is considered to be insufficient for the purpose of financial management.

[4] http://www.assemblee-nationale.fr/histoire/histoire-1789.asp.

budgets should also provide for some margin to cover unexpected variations. However, if they exceed the margin, supplementary budgets or budget adjustments need to be authorised at the top level.

In contrast to the short-term financial planning and authorisation, medium- to long-term planning may be less legally authoritative, but it is definitely more strategic. The kind of approval that is required varies a lot between jurisdictions. In some it is just a planning tool, in many others it needs to be approved by the government, in some even by the parliament. It is the most important tool to deploy strategic goals into objectives and provide the necessary means for their pursuit. Its importance may be illustrated with the school building discussed earlier in this book. Obviously, a school district has to cater for the needs of its constituency. Thus forecasting student population is essential. If large-scale residential construction is taking place, it is likely that – with a time lag of a few years – student population also will rise. Perhaps additional facilities are needed. Obviously, it is not possible to build a new school within one year from the first idea to full operation. Therefore it needs to be anticipated in medium- to long-term planning. This obviously includes the investment itself, i.e. the school building, but also how this investment should be paid for, i.e. issue of loans, fund raising etc. Further down the road operational costs also need to be planned for, again including their funding. Thus medium- to long-term planning is highly critical for the successful provision of services in the future. It provides some kind of momentum for change and is therefore of substantial importance for the political and the management level alike.

All the short- and longer-term planning is obviously useless if the plans are not used for management decisions. Such decisions traditionally pursue the first two goals of public sector financial management, fiscal management and resource allocation. The preparation, the making and the execution of such decisions is called control. This is a circular concept that always leads back to new decisions. Because of the two potential loop-backs this circle is sometimes called a double loop circle and the achievement is portrayed as 'double loop learning' (see Exhibit 3.1).

While the management may, of course, insist on previous goals, it may also adapt those goals to a changed situation and new needs. Even if one does not consider the

Exhibit 3.1 Controlling cycle with double loop learning

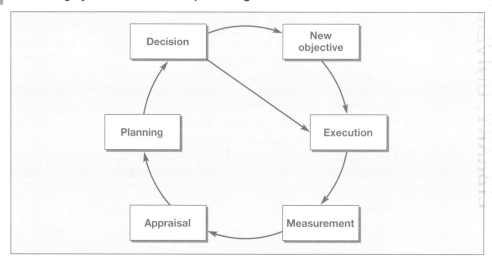

Table 3.1 Overlapping cycles

	For year 0	For year 1	For year 2	For year 3	For year 4	For year 5
In year 0	Execution & under-year controlling	Short-term planning & budget approval	Mid-/long-term financial planning	Mid-/long-term financial planning	Mid-/long-term financial planning	Mid-/long-term financial planning
In year 1	Preparation of financial statements & reporting	Execution & under-year controlling	Short-term planning & budget approval	Mid-/long-term financial planning	Mid-/long-term financial planning	Mid-/long-term financial planning
In year 2		Preparation of financial statements & reporting	Execution & under-year controlling	Short-term planning & budget approval	Mid-/long-term financial planning	Mid-/long-term financial planning
In year 3			Preparation of financial statements & reporting	Execution & under-year controlling	Short-term planning & budget approval	Mid-/long-term financial planning
In year 4				Preparation of financial statements & reporting	Execution & under-year controlling	Short-term planning & budget approval
In year 5					Preparation of financial statements & reporting	Execution & under-year controlling

double loop learning option, there are plenty of overlaps and options in the cycle. The main complexity comes from the parallel of usually two, perhaps even three, years. While the short-term plans made and approved in year zero for year one will be executed and subject to under-year controlling, year one also includes the preparation and approval of year two budget. In year two, while year two budget is executed and year three budget prepared, year one financial statements are prepared and reported. And this does not yet account for medium- and long-term planning. This complexity not only causes distress to textbook readers, but even more so to public sector financial management and even politics. Table 3.1 may help to illustrate the issue. Each column reflects the tasks fulfilled during that year.

The last, often neglected, function of budgeting is budget reporting. Budgets are not yet published in all countries, although western democracies generally consider this as a basic function of budgeting.[5] But apparently there is, even in those countries with a long

---

[5] Some countries present budget information only in civilian areas, but restrict the presentation of budget information in military/defence areas.

tradition of budget reporting, a much greater emphasis on the ex-ante preparation and approval of budgets, than the ex-post budget reporting.[6] This certainly is due to influence, which goes well beyond pure financial management, that may only be exercised ex-ante.

As we have seen before, medium- and long-term budgets have substantial strategic implications. In the short term, the momentum of ex-ante budgeting may be somewhat smaller, but still greater than ex-post. Thus why should anyone bother about ex-post reporting? Because ex-post budget reporting tells a lot about the quality of financial management. Consider two entities, one anticipating and responsive to any changes and rarely facing budget hardships, the other always asking for supplementary budgets or adjustments and always right at the edge of breaching the budget. Obviously the first entity will earn more credibility for its financial management. This may, bottom line, influence their borrowing capacity or at least the level of the interest rates. Thus the actual should be compared to both the first approved and the final, perhaps adjusted, budget. This comparison should be presented as part of the financial statements.[7]

3.2 Perspectives of budgeting

Budgeting includes not only a time dimension, but also different perspectives. The term perspective should indicate that it is rather a different picture of the same thing, than a truly different thing. Obviously there cannot be materially different budgets for the same organisation; however, there are substantially different points of view that can be taken.

3.2.1 Functional perspective (including the product perspective)

For the matter of politics, but also for strategic management issues, the most interesting perspective is the functional one. Functional means that expenses, revenues, investments, etc. are determined for different groups of products. This definition is different from the definition of functions in management science and the practical use in private sector corporations.[8] Products are the intended results of the public sector entity's activities, i.e. services delivered to the public or other entities, legislation drafted or executed. If the group of products is very broad, they are usually called functions. For governments as a whole, the COFOG presented in Chapter 2, Section 2.1, is a common list of functions. Obviously for individual public sector entities this list would be far too general. But also individual entities can look at their budgeting from a functional perspective, if you consider, for example, different types of school in a school district (e.g. primary, intermediate and high school), various services delivered by a hospital (e.g. emergency, surgeries, maternity, etc.) or the police (e.g. investigation, intervention, prevention).

The functional perspective is a very strategic perspective because it refers directly to the output of the entity. It plays an important role in the second goal of public sector financial management, resource allocation. Thus decisions may include increases or

---

[6] The important distinction between ex-ante and ex-post budget stages has been introduced by Hughes, J., *PSC* (2004) 1.

[7] In fact, IPSAS 24 does not prescribe any ex-ante budget procedures, but requires the presentation of an ex-post comparison between the approved and final budgets, and the actual amounts.

[8] In private sector corporations and in management science the term function is used for the various tasks, e.g. marketing, human resources management, accounting, etc.

decreases in the provision of that output, the quality of the output, introduction or increase of fees, investing in improved facilities, etc. They are reflected in the financial plans by increases or decreases in expenses, revenues or investment. They are also the basis for benchmarking with other entities. However, as we shall see in Section 3.5.2, even relatively minor differences in the definition of the function or the product are likely to deteriorate the results substantially and make benchmarking a difficult exercise.

Under the new public management (NPM) style reforms the focus has shifted from the top-level functional perspective into product groups or individual products, as this is more likely the level fiscal politics are willing to address. Perhaps fiscal politics simply does not want to spend 'more on education', but wants to determine which part of the education budget should be favoured, i.e. it makes a lot of difference whether the money goes into pre-school or tertiary education, although both are part of the function called education. Thus performance-based budgets, as discussed in Section 3.5, in some way fall under the functional view in a wider sense.

3.2.2 Budgets by nature

For managerial decisions, and only occasionally for political matters, the perspective by nature is essential. By nature means that expenses and revenues are classified by their characteristics. It is rather the input than the output that is contemplated. Examples include traditional line items such as salaries, maintenance and repair, interest, depreciation, revenues from fees, from taxes, etc. The political interest is usually limited to the development of the main items such as salaries (i.e. salary increases) or tax revenues (i.e. total tax burden). However, on the more operational management level, even much more detailed line items need to be appraised and influenced (e.g. expenses for IT services or sick leave). This is the case even if the main focus of the more senior decision makers is on the functional perspective. There is a lot of misperception in respect of the different focuses, sometimes even leading to claims that budgets by nature are redundant. However, as the example of salaries or taxes shows, this is not even the case on the political level. It is really a matter of different focuses.

Technically speaking, budgets by nature are aggregated to budgets by functions, not the other way around. On the lowest level of aggregation, there is budget by nature for a specific product. This is called a product budget. Various product budgets are then added up to groups of products and then to functions. Aggregation is not simply adding up, but also eliminating transactions between the various products, e.g. if some courses provided by a university make up a degree programme, the simple addition of the courses plus the total of the degree programme would lead to a double count. Thus the courses should be counted only once.

3.2.3 Institutional perspective

As those preparing budgets are generally organisational entities, i.e. institutions, there is also an institutional perspective. A single institution will often produce different products, e.g. school districts operate different types of school, a hospital provides different services. Obviously the individual product budgets may not only be aggregated to product groups and functions, but also to a budget of an institution, e.g. a hospital. This obviously is needed for the management of this institution. It may also be a basis for the allocation of funds between different providers of the same services, e.g. different hospitals within a state.

This approach of aggregating product budgets to institutional budgets is, from an economic and managerial position, the most sensible one. However, in practice you may observe that institutional budgets are in fact the first ones to be drafted, usually based on previous years' budgets plus a wish list for the upcoming ones. This is called 'incremental budgeting'.[9] This approach is widespread in practice. However, its downside is obvious. It is likely to carry forward errors and inadequate decisions, impedes changes that are necessary due to changes in demand, the environment or the policy, and is a major source of inefficiency and ineffectiveness. Obviously, incremental budgeting does not preclude a systematic analysis, which may make things a little better, but even this is done only in very few organisations.

3.3 Initial, approved and final budgets

What has so far been described as budget preparation and approval includes more than two steps. Higher levels of aggregation, both in the institutional and the functional perspective, require more steps. Aggregation is not only a technical process of adding up and eliminating mutual transactions, but also should include an appraisal of the results. Although, for example, all product budgets, which are essentially budgets by nature, may be sensible from the individual perspective of the product, the aggregation may reveal a lack of capacity or an insufficient efficiency overall. Or the budget may look feasible for one department, but not for the entire company. In larger and more complex public sector entities, such as hospitals, universities or entire ministries, this is likely to cause half a dozen or more iterations until the budget gets its first sign-off, the one from the management. This aggregation of budgets is shown in Exhibit 3.2. A budget signed

Exhibit 3.2 Aggregation of budgets

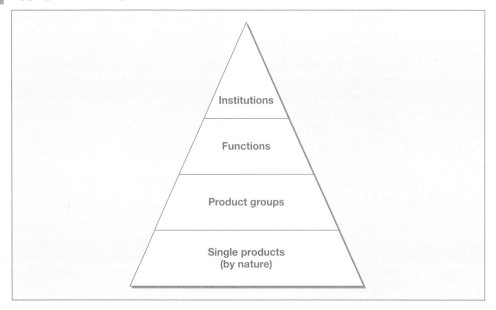

---

[9] Jones, R., Pendlebury, M. (2000) 64 ff.

off by the government or the management is called an initial budget. The preliminary steps are drafts only.

In order to manage the process to get an initial budget, the management should issue guidelines including targets to the preparers. Such guidelines usually specify aspects such as rates of increase in output and important inputs such as salaries. At least where part or the entire cost is to be covered by fees, it is likely to require the level of coverage or even the profit margin. The latter is often observed where public sector entities produce by-products which come out of the scope of public goods and services and therefore may be produced only if there is no dumping against private suppliers. Examples include cosmetic surgery in hospitals or consultancy provided by universities.

However, in the public sector this initial budget needs to get a formal approval from the legislative level. As mentioned before, the budget becomes a law or a bill or an ordinance with this supreme approval, usually from parliament or some other kind of oversight body. In some jurisdictions, this approval process may include changes to individual positions in all three or at least the first two perspectives (i.e. functional and by nature). In others, the budget needs to be rejected and changed by the government or the management and then reissued for approval. Both methods have their advantages. However, time constraints lead to the suggestion that changes should be possible without a full rejection of the budget. This should also increase the responsibility of the approving body, because it cannot simply reject a budget it dislikes without having any alternatives. The approved budget is sometimes also called the original budget.

After this, the budget goes into execution. Obviously it needs to be delegated to the various sub-entities and product owners. Therefore, it has to be disaggregated. Contrary to aggregation, this means bringing in formerly eliminated, mutual transactions and dividing it into its components. Usually, the budget may also be changed when doing so, as long as the approved budget is met. For instance, sub-entities may be given only quarterly or half-year budgets or there may be a withholding of, let us say, 10 per cent. The withholding is very tempting to superior levels; however, it is only feasible if the budgets include a discretionary part which is at least as big as the share that is subject to withholding. Therefore splitting the budget into shorter periods may be more feasible in most cases. This, of course, has to take seasonal fluctuations into consideration (e.g. a public outdoor swimming pool will use much of its budget during the summer months, thus spreading the annual budget equally among all months clearly would be inadequate and misleading for the management).

Like any other plans, budgets also may prove to be erroneous in some part. Assumptions made in respect of output levels may become invalid, unforeseen expenses may be incurred or changes in policy may take place, to name only a few of the reasons. In such cases, the budget needs to be adjusted. However, budget adjustments should not be envisaged deliberately, as they spoil the plan and control purpose of the budget. Most jurisdictions would therefore somehow limit the reasons for budget adjustments and require approval on the same level the original budget has been approved. No prior approval is usually needed if a natural disaster strikes or similar events, which clearly are out of control of the entity. In most jurisdictions there is also an option to compensate increases in one position with decreases in the other. All the budget adjustments will lead to the final budget. The legal authority of the final budget is the same as the one of the approved budget. However, large differences between the two explain the quality of planning, when examined more closely. On the other side, in many jurisdictions there is virtually no difference between the final budget and the actual amounts in the financial reporting. This is due to the authority of the budget, which makes it necessary to cover any position with a budgeted position.

3.4 Budget execution: appropriations and commitments

When the budget is approved as an original or final budget, in most jurisdictions this does not automatically authorise any transactions covered by the budget. This stage is often referred to as budget execution, for example in the PEFA PFM performance assessment framework discussed in Chapter 1. Expenses, revenues and investments generally require another formal decision, in addition to the approval of the budget. For instance, hiring of additional staff usually requires a formal decision, perhaps involving the human resources unit and the senior management. Or construction of a new school building needs an approved project and so does the replacement of a computer network. Such formal decisions to spend for expenses or investments are called appropriations or commitments. Similar requirements exist on the revenue side. Taxes or fines, for instance, are legally binding only once a formal invoice, including instructions on how this decision potentially may be challenged, is issued.

Which requirements have to be met is defined by the administrative laws, which may differ substantially from one jurisdiction to another. The concept of appropriations remains largely the same: an appropriation is a transaction or project-specific authorisation of expenses, investments or revenue generation. It requires an approved budget for the same transaction and project, but may occasionally cover one budget period. Thus, in the case of employees, the contract issued many years before may still be a valid appropriation or commitment together with a budget that is approved every year. And so does an appropriation or commitment for a project approved last year: there is no need for re-approval of the project, but the respective amount for each year has to be approved as a part of the annual budget. Obviously, there is not much space for changes of this budget item, but as it is a part of the total sum to be spent, it has to be included in the annual budget.

Often, appropriations or commitments require the involvement of non-financial units specialising in such transactions or projects. Thus most public sector entities legally would be required to involve the HR unit for a hiring decision or the facility management unit when it comes to construction. No formal appropriations or commitments are generally required for transactions only involving very small amounts, such as the payment of surcharges to couriers or minor travel expenses. These exemptions are usually limited by amounts at very low levels.

This topic is usually quite surprising for people with a private sector background. But at least larger corporations have similar policies or regulations in place. Lower level of management and employees are likely to be required to seek prior approval for hiring or larger expenditures, such as investment, even if they are part of the budget. Those policies and regulations are binding for their employees, although they are not formal laws. Despite the apparent differences in the legal setting, the way it works is very much the same.

Due to the large number of appropriations or commitments outstanding, there is need for a system to keep track of them, especially if they affect several years. Such systems are called commitment accounting systems.[10] Technically they are usually special features of management accounting systems, discussed in Section 3.6. However, the information requirements go beyond accounting information. Commitment accounting systems also need to record decisions made, phases cleared or completed, change requests and other more project-management-related features.

---

[10] Coombs, H.M., Jenkins, D.E. (2002) 127.

3.5 Performance budgets

Traditionally, the main perspective of public sector budgets was the one by institution, with further details classified by nature. This has directly reflected on budget preparation. However, this perspective clearly fell short of delivering any information about the achievement of political objectives, as well as the efficiency of the production and delivery of services, the third goal of public sector financial management. If a hospital is running on a budget of CU 100 million with a deficit of CU 10 million, this can be a very successful result or a pretty miserable one, if you have no information about the objectives and the services delivered for that amount of money. Even the comparison with previous years may be misleading, as an improvement from a very bad performance to a slightly less bad one looks exactly the same as the improvement from a very good to an excellent one. The perspectives by institution and nature do not provide any information about performance, just about results or – talking about budgets – planned results. In order to change this, instruments have been developed under the title of performance budgets, which technically are referred to as output- and outcome-based budgets.[11] The adopting of such budgets requires the identification of products.

Performance budgets are an important aspect of a broader development called 'new public management' (NPM). NPM, which is rather a mixture of reforms, is usually referred back to Hood (1991), although the mixture of various types of reforms makes it likely that there is more than one origin.[12] However, it is clear that financial management reforms, and herein budget reforms, are very significant components.[13] Especially in continental Europe there is a tendency to reduce NPM to a mere budget reform, introducing outcome-based budgets, with other characteristics of NPM such as competition, privatisation, decentralisation and incentives, to name only a few, being marginalised.[14]

3.5.1 Output- and outcome-based budgets

Output- and outcome-based budgets (OBB) essentially are part of the functional perspective. However, functional budgets tend to be highly aggregated, for instance using the COFOG classification, such as defence, health or education. Apparently such a classification represents rather large groups of products. These groups are too large for budget decisions on the government and management level, probably even on the level of the parliament. In every budget you will find products with increased allocations and others with smaller allocations in the very same group of products. Output- and outcome-based budgets try to focus on products that have the right size for budget decisions. As the identification of such products is firstly essential und secondly not trivial, the entire following section will address this issue.

But OBB are not only functional budgets with the right focus. They go beyond that by referring the financial information to output and outcome information. Outputs are the goods or – more likely – services delivered. Outcomes are the results that are expected from delivering these goods and services to the public. For example, the output of a

---

[11] Other names include programme budgeting.

[12] Hood, C. (1991).

[13] Guthrie, J., Olsen, O., Humphrey, C. (1999).

[14] A comprehensive overview of the characteristics of NPM can be found in Grüning, G. (2001).

school is teaching a number of children in a specific programme. The outcome is that they are able to read, write and solve mathematical problems. Actually one could even go beyond, and look at the impact, that they may find a job and contribute to society. Although examples of impact targets are sometimes found in budgets, the term impact-based budgets is not commonly used. They are usually called outcome-based budgets or performance (based) budgets.

Definition	
	Output Output is the amount of goods or services produced and delivered. It is measured in absolute numbers (e.g. students, meals, surgeries, investigations, sentences) or quantities (e.g. kg, doses). **Outcome** Outcome is the result from the delivery of goods or services to the public. It provides the rationale behind the supply of goods and services; e.g. children are able read, criminals are convicted, patients recover. It is measured by set objectives; e.g. 99.9 per cent of the children at grade 2 are able to read a text adequate to grade 2. However, it is often difficult to link the outcome directly to a specific output, e.g. children could also have learned to read elsewhere, at home or on the internet. **Impact** Impact is the long-term result from certain outcomes to the entire society. It provides the rationale behind the outcomes; e.g. employability, because people who can read are more employable. It is extremely difficult to link the impact directly with the outcome and the output, as it is very likely that other aspects influence the impact too.

Linking the output to the financial resources used for its production and delivery, in fact the input, leads to an important ratio: the efficiency.

Efficiency = output/input

For example, if 1 million currency units (CU) are used to educate 100 students the cost per student is 10,000 CU/student. This can easily be compared to other schools and used for the allocation of resources. However, care should be exercised, as what is included in the financial resources, as well as the services provided, may vary substantially. Sometimes, cost will include depreciation, sometimes not. Some students may enrol in full-time programmes, some in part-time courses and others have perhaps already dropped out. Thus efficiency consideration makes sense only if both the output and the input are measured in the same way.

Assessing the achievement in respect of outcome- and impact-based objectives leads to another important ratio: the effectiveness.

Effectiveness = % of achievement of outcome-based objective

Some authors would even distinguish between effectiveness, measuring the achieved outcome, and efficacy measuring the achieved impact.[15] Others would not make this

---

[15] Buschor, E. (1993).

distinction and would refer to both as effectiveness.[16] As impact objectives have not gained much importance, because of the predominant side effects, this is a rather academic discussion with not much practical relevance, although from a theoretical standpoint effectiveness and efficacy should be distinguished.

A third important comparative is economy. This compares revenue to cost, for example, how much of the cost is covered by fees paid by the beneficiaries, or by comparing two cost figures, for example, of the previous and the current year or of two entities.

All three, efficiency, effectiveness and economy, give substantial additional information in the budget process. That is the main advantage of OBB over the more traditional forms of budgets. However, the introduction of OBB generally goes hand in hand with further reforms of budgeting, including the following:

1 Budgeting of gross (or 'global') amounts: budgeting or perhaps rather budget authorisation does not go down to single line items, but approves total revenues, total expenses and total investments, or sometimes even only the total deficit. The management is allowed to shift between the line items freely, as long as it is within the gross amounts and reaches the targets in respect of efficiency, effectiveness and economy.
2 Allowing carry-over to next period: unused funds may be carried over to the next period, rather than spent in an inadvisable way during the last few weeks of the period.
3 Surpluses and deficits being carried over partly to the next period: surpluses may be used for discretionary spending or employee benefits; deficits have to be made up for in future periods.

Apparently, these reforms ease the budget rules substantially. This is the kind of trade-off that is provided in exchange for more detailed information on performance. If the management can be held more responsible for the entity's performance, it should also enjoy more freedom in the way in which it achieves its objectives. This freedom or flexibility is needed to manage the entity in response to its external environment and the internal capacities.

OBB may be seen as a different way of presenting budget information for authorisation. This is not wrong, because the budgets behind the scene are much more detailed than the budget presented to the legislative body authorising it. However, if the budget is really aggregated from the single product level, OBB should be considered as a different budget procedure. In fact, the process becomes similar to the one used in zero-based budgeting (ZBB) where all budget items are planned from scratch and then approved by priority. ZBB makes sense only if it based on activities, rather than line items by nature, as it would be impossible to determine their priorities. Activities obviously come dangerously close to products, although not exactly the same. Activities are still on a lower level than products. For example, launching a marketing campaign for blood donation is an activity that forms part of the product blood donation. That is why the ZBB process tends to be more elaborate than the OBB process. ZBB tends to be over-elaborate, as the number of activities that should be considered rapidly exceeds what can be handled on a regular basis.[17] It is therefore more suitable for a one-time effort, rather than for the usual annual budget cycle in public sector entities. OBB, on the other hand, tends to be feasible as a standard procedure, as many examples around the world show.

---

[16] Jones, R., Pendlebury, M. (2000) 10 ff.

[17] Jones, R., Pendlebury, M. (2000) 100 ff.

3.5.2 Identification of products

One of the main difficulties of introducing OBB is the definition of products. This is somewhat crucial, as they are at the core of the budgeting process and the basis for budget presentation and approval.

The first problem is to distinguish between products and activities. Processing payments is a common activity in any public sector entity. However, it is not a product. Products are only those goods and services that are within the mission of the entity and delivered to the outside world. Processing payments is an internal, auxiliary activity that takes place only in order to support the core activities, for example delivering courses or conducting surgeries. If it was only for processing payments, there would be no school and no hospital. There would not even be an accounting department inside a school or a hospital.

Definition	**Product**
	A product is goods or service that is produced and delivered by an entity to the outside world (i.e. customers, citizens, patients, students, enterprises). The entity does so, on purpose, as the production and delivery is part of its mission.

The second problem is to have a sensible list of products. Taking the hospital as an example, there are hundreds of different surgeries and other treatments delivered to patients. They all meet the definition of a product. However, if you add this lengthy list to the equally lengthy list of all other public sector entities and then present an OBB for each and every product, this will certainly exceed the capacity of the more senior management and government levels, not to mention the one of the legislative body approving the budget. There are examples of local governments' OBB well beyond one thousand pages. Therefore products need to be aggregated into groups of products. Obviously this should not go as far as the functional budgets go, with only a dozen functions remaining. Product groups should be adequate for the level of the decision maker. Thus at a ministry's level, there are perhaps more details needed than for the final approval in parliament. The latter should probably not be confronted with much more than one hundred products over all.

As will be seen in Section 3.6.2, there are attempts to have standardised product schedules at hand. While such schedules may assist tackling the first problem of distinguishing products and activities, it does not mitigate the task of defining appropriate levels of aggregation for the various levels of decision makers.

3.6 Management accounting

Although management accounting is in close proximity to budgeting in any private sector textbook, to raise it here may be somewhat strange for some of the readers. In fact, until recently, there has been no distinction made between financial and management accounting in most jurisdictions. However, the introduction of new public management (NPM), emphasising the product perspective as well as the introduction of competition to many previously sheltered public sector markets, has led to an increased interest in the concepts of management accounting by the public sector constituency. It is generally accepted, now, that public sector entities need both, management accounting to provide the information to the management and the government, as well as sound financial accounting and reporting to satisfy the information needs of the outside world, including lenders and citizens. The legislative bodies, i.e. parliaments and, to a lesser degree, also the citizens, are on the border of the two, as they generally refer to financial reporting for the overall appraisal and still get a limited set of management accounting information in the performance budgets and reports.

Obviously, one section in a textbook cannot make up for all management accounting. There are excellent textbooks that cover this issue comprehensively.[18] The aim of this section is, therefore, to show the implications of management to public sector entities and vice versa.

3.6.1 Product perspective, competition and size

Public sector entities have experienced an increased need to manage their products, i.e. the goods and services they produce and deliver, as the ideas of new public management (NPM) spread, usually rather slowly and gradually, but at least to some extent in most jurisdictions around the world. As we have seen in Section 3.5, NPM has introduced – among other concepts – the idea of performance budgets. Performance budgets look primarily at the products produced and delivered. But budgeting is obviously not the end of the story. Once budgets are executed, the proposed items, such as the cost of the product group, need to be accounted for and the actual items need to be compared to the budget. However, performance budgets are in a way only a surrogate for real competition. In fact, bringing competition to formerly monopolistic markets is another aspect of NPM. Although a full liberalisation of the markets has taken place only in very few cases, some elements of competition have often been introduced and many of the public sector markets are now regulated markets with a limited number of competitors. Examples of full liberalisation include, at least in some countries, telecommunication and domestic air transportation, while the postal services, education and health are more likely to have experienced the limited competition of a regulated market. Even limited competition in a regulated market requires a permanent calculation of product costs.

Many of those (semi-)market-oriented public sector entities have also reached a rather substantial size including several thousands of employees in hundreds of locations and organisational units. In addition to the product perspective and competition, such organisations clearly require a more detailed management accounting system, just to be managed properly. The information provided by financial accounting and reporting is clearly insufficient for this purpose. Hence the NPM-driven product perspective and competition, but quite often only the sheer size of the organisation, has led to the introduction of management accounting in public sector entities.

How does management accounting solve these problems? Basically three concepts have gained much importance in the public sector. These concepts are as follows:

1 The organisational concept of cost centres, profit centres and investment centres.
2 The concept of charging for internal services as well as for depreciation and capital employed.
3 Product costing.

---

[18] For example, Horngren, C., Foster, G., Datar, S. (2005).

Cost, profit and investment centres are organisational units that are held responsible for their financial performance. While the responsibility of cost centres extends only to its cost, i.e. accrued expenses, the responsibility of profit centres includes the revenue and thus the bottom line, i.e. the profit or the loss. In fact, many permanently loss-making, and therefore tax-financed, units have become profit centres, as they are held responsible for the amount of loss. Investment centres are less frequent, as many governments want to keep the responsibility for investments in their hands rather than delegating them to individual units.

Example Typical examples of cost, profit and investment centres

Cost centres (CC)	accounting units, human resource management units, staff of senior management, IT services, facility management, secretariat
Profit centres (PC)	clinics within a hospital, institutes/schools within a university, motor vehicle testing facilities, IT services also delivering to external customers
Investment centres (IC)	airports, hospitals, universities, mint

Apparently, investment centres tend to be larger and more independent units, while cost centres are internal support providers. However, even for those units, the concept of a cost centre includes increased responsibility, as they are held accountable for their cost. Technically speaking, this requires an accounting system, which not only provides for a chart of accounts, but at the same time also for a chart of organisational units; see, for example, Table 3.2. For example, a salary payment is no longer accounted for only in the line item 'salaries', but also in the cost centre 'IT services'. Obviously, total salaries of all units and total cost of each unit may also be calculated.

Table 3.2 Interaction of chart of accounts and chart of organisational units

Item	CC 1	PC 2	IC 3	Total all units
Salaries	1000	1200	900	3100
Repair/maintenance	100	50	120	270
...	...	...	...	...
Total cost	**1658**	**1790**	**1105**	**4352**
Fees	–	1650	1450	3100
...	–	...	...	...
Total revenues	–	**1705**	**1520**	
Surplus/(deficit)	–	**(85)**	**415**	
Investments	–	–	**350**	

The table shows only the responsibility of the three units, not the financial situation of the entitiy as a whole, i.e. including tax revenues or appropriation from higher levels of government.

As a logical consequence of holding individual units accountable for cost, profit or even investments, the second concept emerges. If they really should be accountable for all their activities and decisions, there must be charges for the internal delivery of goods and services. It would be a sound concept if, for example, one unit were charged for the rent of their offices, while another unit accommodated in government-owned property, does not incur any charges for its use of office space. To resolve this problem, every unit has to be charged for their respective use of office space, either by an external landlord or by the internal facility management unit. This, of course, immediately raises the question whether each unit may freely choose their supplier. Is it possible to return the expensive offices in a landmark government property and rent some cheap office space in the suburbs?

From a theoretical point of view, the freedom to select the supplier should be granted; at least if no capital investment has been involved. There is no economical reason why, for instance, office stationery should not be purchased from the cheapest supplier. If, however, capital has been invested, as in the example of the government property, a certain limitation of this freedom to select the supplier is economically sensible. In fact, renting another property in the suburbs while office space is available in government-owned buildings would increase total cost and thus is not feasible for the public sector entity, as a whole. However, in the medium to long term, market incentives should reach out to capital-prone supplies too. A minimum tenure of five or ten years may be an economically feasible compromise between the idea of protecting investments made as well as providing incentives to cost and profit centres. In larger entities IT systems are required to handle the numerous charges between the different units. The generated administrative cost is often criticised, as it might exceed the benefit from the incentive and enhanced management decisions. It is therefore recommended to charge only for material transactions. Material transactions generally include the permanent use of human resources, IT and property, but exclude short-term arrangements as well as the use of low-cost equipment such as overhead projectors.

The third concept is, quite obviously from the product perspective, product costing. Product costs are, in most cases, not identical with the cost accumulated in a cost, profit or investment centre. This would be the case only if one unit were the sole contributor to exactly one product and it did nothing else (one to one relationship). In most cases, several units contribute to several products (m to n relationship). For instance, the operating theatre in a hospital will be used for various kinds of surgery, but any surgery requires not only the operating theatre but also other units including aftercare, etc. Therefore costs incurred in each unit need to be charged to a product. The main cost incurred in many cases is personnel cost, i.e. staff working on an assignment to a product. Examples include medical doctors doing surgeries, teachers giving courses or police officers conducting investigations. The only, although not very popular, way to get this data requires the staff to report their hours to each assignment.

Obviously, this also needs to be done for other costs, although directly related or minor items are usually included in increased charge rates. For example, the hourly rate charged for a teacher typically would include employee benefits such as contribution to social security, paid leave, etc. It may also include minor items such as stationery used. The hourly rate in product costing is therefore higher than the salary. Usually, averages will be used anyway. However, major items such as the use of the property, e.g. classroom, are likely to be charged separately. Adding up all the charges of the product will lead to the total cost of the product. If the single product is rather small and delivered in large numbers, e.g. lessons, the total number of products will be charged, rather than a

| Table 3.3 | Illustrative example of product costing |

Cost	CU/qty	Product 1	Product 2
Work Unit A	90 CU/h	10 h = 900 CU	15 h = 1350 CU
Work Unit B	80 CU/h	20 h = 1600 CU	20 h = 1600 CU
Material used		250 CU	50 CU
...	...	...	...
Total cost		**2800 CU**	**3090 CU**
Number of units		1 project	35 lessons
Cost per unit		**2800 CU**	**88.29 CU**

single one. To get the cost of a single product, e.g. one lesson, the product cost will have to be divided by the number of units produced. But if products are large, e.g. construction projects, the cost may be charged specifically. This is shown in Table 3.3.

Apparently, there are two levels of charge involved in management accounting. A first charge is being made to cost, profit or investment centres; while these units make a second charge to products. Adding such a double charge system to the double entry bookkeeping system makes up quite a substantial IT system. In fact, this is the core of so-called enterprise resource planning (ERP) systems, although they usually include numerous additional features, e.g. human resource management, material management, consolidation, etc.

3.6.2 Standardised product schedules

The identification of products has been characterised as a main task introducing performance budgets and it is equally essential for product costing. While in the private sector it is clear that the identification and structuring of the products is the sole responsibility of the management, this is more controversial in the public sector. The limitations to competition cause a higher demand for comparisons between different entities.

While private sector corporations are compared on the market and inefficiencies are, in a perfect market, eliminated instantly, this is less the case for public sector entities. That is why oversight bodies such as parliaments or regulators, but also higher levels of management, frequently require cost comparisons between different units. For instance, they want to know the cost for a certain surgery in various public hospitals. As studies show, they are requesting this for good reason, as cost differences are often very substantial and far beyond what could be tolerated and endorsed.[19] For example, why should the average cost of a patient undergoing a standardised treatment be Sfr 9,413 instead of Sfr 6,627 in two different hospitals of the same type?[20] While such differences will be levelled out by the market if they are not justified by different service levels, there is no such market in a situation of public provision and the cost/price differences will persist if there is no intervention by the funding institution, e.g. the Ministry of Health. As this example shows, information from cost accounting is relevant for public sector decision makers.

---

[19] For example, *Gesundheitsdirektion Kanton Zürich* (2007).

[20] *Gesundheitsdirektion Kanton Zürich* (2007) 88.

In order to make such a comparison, it is necessary to compare the same kind of product. But if the management of each public sector entity, like its private sector counterparts, defines its products in a different way, such a comparison would be helplessly flawed. That is why standardised product schedules are proposed for public sector entities in an increasing number of jurisdictions.

Example	**Example of standardised product schedules, Germany**

> In 2005 the federal government of Germany decided to reduce the 'cost of bureaucracy'. In order to measure this cost, a standard-cost-model (in German: *Standard-Kosten-Modell* (SKM)) should be introduced. A national norm control council (in German: *Nationaler Normenkontrollrat*) with eight members is defining standardised product schedules for those services governed by federal legislation. By 2011 the cost should be measured nationwide and subsequently reduced by 25 per cent.[21]

Example	**Example DRG**

> In the healthcare system so-called diagnosis-related groups (DRGs) have been set up in order to define products of healthcare providers. First steps were taken in 1967 in the United States by Robert Fetter.[22] The DRGs had to be based on information gathered routinely and restricted to fewer than 1,000 groups, which had to cover all kinds of diagnosis at hospitals. Based on these early attemps the so-called AP-DRG (all patient DRG) were developed, which identified 641 DRGs within 25 major diagnostic categories (MDCs). While the idea of DRGs became increasingly popular in many countries around the world, the system was further developed. This development, however, led to different national systems such as the Australian Refined DRS (AR-DRG), the Scandinavian NordDRG, the German DRG (which is based on the Australian AR-DRG) or the Swiss Payment Groups (which is based on the American AP-DRG). The DRGs are used in order to define the relative cost that can then be used in order to allocate a budget that is adequate to the products provided by the hospital. Obviously other factors, such as age of the patient, also need to be considered. Due to the complexity of this system, the usual cost accounting systems are unable to handle the DRGs and the hospitals need to use specialised software products.

The recommendation of this book in respect of standardised product schedules is the introduction of such schedules in situations where competition cannot be achieved for whatever reason. However, public sector entities that are exposed to competition should not have to use such schedules, as it impedes their management. Standardised product schedules are part of a proxy for free market competition. This proxy is not needed if there is sufficient competition.

3.6.3 Full versus marginal costing

Management accounting systems may be characterised in various ways. One of the most common, and yet very relevant to the public sector, is the distinction between full and marginal cost systems.[23] Full cost approaches allocate all the cost elements to a

---

[21] Rohn, S. (2007) 13.

[22] Malk, R., Kampmann, T. (2006).

[23] 'Full cost' is sometimes also called 'total cost'.

product by charging the entire cost incurred by any cost or profit centres to the product. This includes all the cost related to the production and delivery of the product, but also all the cost of management, corporate level marketing, internal services or any other kind of overheads, even if they are not directly involved with the product. The rationale behind full cost systems is that any cost in fact needs to be covered by some revenue and thus allocated to some goods or services, in order to include them in the price calculation of the product. The excess of revenues over total cost is the profit margin.

Marginal cost systems, on the other hand, only charge cost directly caused by the production and the delivery of the product to the product. Any overhead costs would remain in the respective cost, profit or investment centre. It should be covered by so-called contribution margins from the sale of the products. Obviously contribution margins need to be larger than profit margins in the case of full cost systems, as contribution margins have to contribute to the overhead costs.

Definition

Full cost systems
Full cost systems are management accounting systems that charge the full costs incurred by the entity, including direct costs and overhead costs, to the products.

Marginal cost systems
Marginal cost systems are management accounting systems that charge only the direct cost associated with the production and delivery of goods and services to the products. Overhead costs are covered by contribution margins.

Contribution margin
The contribution margin is equal to the revenue of a product minus the direct cost of the product. Various levels of contribution margins may be distinguished if more or less directly related costs are charged to the product in several steps, as in the following example, possibly leading to the allocation of full costs:

Revenue	1,000
– direct production cost	200
– direct distribution cost	50
Contribution margin 1	**750**
– product management cost	150
Contribution margin 2	**600**
– product-related overhead	100
Contribution margin 3	**500**
– other business level overhead	200
Contribution margin 4	**300**
– corporate level overhead cost	100
Profit margin	**200**

Considering the economic situation of public sector entities, the argument in favour of full cost systems is rather weak, unless it is really a commercial enterprise rather coincidentally happening to be in the public sector. More typical for the public sector is the situation in which an entity needs to cover the cost of a limited range of its products, while others are financed through general tax revenue. Such examples frequently can be found in health organisations, which have to charge fees for some services but none for others. Often fees are to cover only part of the cost, for example in schools and universities where tuition fees are usually smaller than the full cost. Perhaps the fee charged even equals the marginal cost. Examples for this pattern can be found in the case of criminal investigation, where the marginal cost for the investigation of a crime may be reimbursed from a person found guilty. Such situations are well reflected and presented in marginal cost models.

Further advantages of marginal cost models apply equally to private and public sector entities. Marginal cost models better reflect the responsibilities in an organisation. A product manager is clearly responsible for the revenues, direct costs and the contribution margin of its product. However, he may not be held responsible for overhead costs, which are decided far away in central service units or on the senior management level. Marginal cost models better reflect the delegation of responsibilities within an organisation.

Altogether there is quite a strong a case for marginal cost models in most public sector entities. In fact, they are widely used in various parts of the public sector, both in central governments and service providers. Full cost models are recommended only for product pricing in situations where the entity is required to recover the full cost from external beneficiaries or customers through fees.

3.6.4 Benchmarking

Management accounting supports management decisions. They are usually based on the comparison with targets or previous periods, as well as ratios between various positions used as indicators, for instance contribution margin ratios.[24] However, all this is taking place just within the entity, based on the entity's data and previous decisions. It is a self-referencing system. If targets are inadequate, previous periods biased or actual performance questionable, this does not really help decision makers with their current and future decisions.

One solution is benchmarking. The main task within a benchmarking process is still comparing different data. But, unlike traditional management accounting, it includes – and this is really the point – external data from similar operations. When benchmarking was first developed, it was used in the competitive environment of the electronics industry.[25] For obvious reasons, the competitors in the private sector were not willing to provide management accounting information. Therefore the scope of the benchmarking had to be limited to a few processes, such as accounts receivable, which could then be compared with non-competitors from different industries. In respect of accounts receivable, companies in the manufacturing industry famously were comparing their results with the credit card industry which was, of course, much more proficient in handling accounts receivable. Apparently, the comparison included very detailed indicators about the process contemplated, such as average due period, due period until first reminder is sent out and so on.

---

[24] The contribution margin ratio is equal to the contribution margin as a percentage of the revenues.

[25] Bergmann, A. (2000) 50.

In the public sector the situation is markedly different. Often, public sector entities operate in designated areas with no immediate competition from other public sector entities, for example, school districts generally do not overlap or at least not extensively. Moreover, public sector entities in the same field are frequently funded by the same funding agency, i.e. all universities are funded by the higher education funding commission or the ministry of education. Such funding agencies have a legitimate interest in comparison with the various institutions funded. That is why public sector entities would often use very similar entities as benchmarking partners. This provides the great advantage of a much wider scope of issues and processes which can be covered at the same time. In fact, comprehensive benchmarking groups or circles have developed in the public sector over the last years, including typical service providers such as schools, hospitals or libraries. Such circles may be imposed by funding agencies, as part of their evaluation, or by the entities themselves. If individual entities are setting up benchmarking circles, their mission is to learn from each other and improve each entity's performance by comparing it with similar entities. That is the reason why benchmarking is usually seen as a method of organisational learning.

While the basic logic behind benchmarking is very straightforward, implementation turns out to be quite challenging. The main issue is definition, recognition and measurement. This is actually the reason why benchmarking is part of the management accounting section in this book. In order to compare information, the data must be collected and aggregated in the same way. If one school counts the students enrolled and the other the students by the end of term, the two figures will always be very different for a good reason and it is very dangerous to conclude anything based on such information.

While performance indicators can be adjusted by using the same definitions, financial information really requires the same measurement principles be observed by all benchmarking partners. For instance, if one partner recognises fees accrued during the period and the other fees paid during that period, the revenues, as well as all the indicators based on that, will not be comparable. If one depreciates its property over 30 years, the second the same kind of property over 50 years and a third is not charging depreciation at all, you should not be surprised to find very different cost levels and strongly biased indicators. This, of course, comes down to details of particular items, which may well be worth considering in a benchmarking process. The only way out of this difficulty is adopting the same definition, accounting policies and even structure of the management accounting system. As this can be a very challenging and costly task, it can be advisable to limit the scope of benchmarking, at least at the beginning, to a few main items highly relevant to the decision makers.

When implementing benchmarking these challenges perhaps raise the question as to whether top-down or bottom-up approaches are more feasible. Top-down approaches are prescribed from top-level management or funding agencies, while the bottom-up approach begins in individual entities that are looking for benchmarking partners and building up a benchmarking system. Practical evidence shows clear advantages in respect of the bottom-up approach regarding acceptance and actual use of its results by the management. The top-down approach, on the other hand, eases funding and adaptations to the systems, e.g. management accounting, if required. Thus there are valid arguments for both approaches; however, one should be aware of the potential advantages and disadvantages in order to take adequate measures in the management of such projects.

Example	**Benchmarking upper secondary schools**

The Conference of the State Ministers of Education in North-Western Switzerland decided in 2004 that schools at upper secondary level (i.e. years 9 to 12) should be benchmarked.[26] The goal of this ongoing benchmarking is to:

- support the schools in their quality development; and
- increase transparency between the schools, but also between the nine states (cantons) in the region.

The scope of the benchmarking was limited to the macro level, i.e. school systems and sub-systems, like grammar schools and vocational schools; and the micro level, i.e. individual schools. The so-called micro level, i.e. individual classrooms, teachers, etc., is out of scope.

There are three components of the benchmarking. These are as follows:

1 Financial and non-financial performance indicators.
2 Satisfaction surveys within the school, e.g. school finishers, teachers, headmasters.
3 Satisfaction surveys outside the school, e.g. graduates after two years out of school.

The performance indicators in component 1 are also collected by a survey; however, unlike components 2 and 3, the financial and non-financial performance indicators are collected on the institutional level.

The individual school gets its own results and the average results of the other schools. The other schools are not named and singled out because of concerns about competition. In Switzerland there is some competition on the upper secondary level as the school districts overlap considerably, offering a selection of different types of schools to the students and their parents. This includes grammar and vocational schools, but also different focus subjects in grammar schools and different professional fields in vocational schools. In the vocational type, there are also different levels of difficulty, for example, more challenging courses for the better students and more basic ones for the others. The schools do not compete throughout north-western Switzerland, as students are usually limited to the area in which they live. That is the reason why the schools opposed the idea of a full disclosure of the results of each and every school. Instead they opted for averages as a basis of comparison.

What the schools (and the ministries) do about the results lies in their own discretion. However, they are usually interested in following up on the results and realising improvements.

In the first stage of the project, between 2004 and 2007, each state selected a few schools that participated in some field-testing. In component 1, the field-testing revealed more substantial differences than expected in the financial and non-financial data collected by the schools and the ministries. Often, they use different accounting techniques, such as different depreciation rates. But also non-financial information, such as information about the school property, is not collected in a comparable manner. Therefore component 1 is more challenging and perhaps less rewarding than expected at this early stage. However, the lack of trustworthy information offers some evidence for a considerable improvement potential. The two other components, which do not include financial information, faced the usual difficulty posed by surveys, such as the data handling for very large numbers of participants.

During the second stage of the project, from 2007 to 2010, the tools and methods developed and improved based on the experience during the first stage will be rolled out on a larger scale. The larger number of schools included will also improve the comparability of information, as averages are less biased by individual results.

---

[26] http://www.ag.ch/nwedk/de/pub/projekt_benchmarking_sek_ii.php.

3.7   Accrual versus cash basis

Traditionally all public sector budgets and the corresponding management accounting, if there was any, were on a cash basis of accounting, i.e. transactions were recorded only once a cash transaction was involved. In fact, in many cases it was not double entry book-keeping but rather a single entry list of records that was added up and accounted for.

As we will see in Chapter 4, there are great efforts taking place worldwide to introduce an accrual basis of accounting, at least for the financial reporting purpose. This obviously leads to the question, is there such a thing as accrual budgeting? In fact, there is. Although important theoretical work is quite recent,[27] it is often forgotten that various countries, for instance Australia, New Zealand, Switzerland and Sweden, introduced accrual budgeting up to three decades ago, at least on the lower levels of government.[28] Obviously only accrual budgeting ensures that all the highly relevant information provided by accrual accounting is considered in the most important financial decisions of public sector entities, which are still made in the budget process. Many consider that accrual accounting can develop all its advantages only if budgeting also adopts the accrual principle.[29] Others, including France, are adopting an accrual basis of accounting, but remain on a cash basis of budgeting. Thus there seems to be a somewhat greater reluctance to adopt accrual budgeting rather than accrual accounting, although having the same basis would reduce the complexity of the system and in particular facilitate comparisons between actual and budget.

This main reason for staying on cash basis budgets even when introducing accrual accounting is the authorisation feature that is important to public sector budgets. The concept of authorisation goes well with expenditure, as they are transactions based on a decision. Other expenses, such as depreciation, are more difficult to relate to the concept of authorisation. For instance, depreciation charges should be made in accordance with the consumption of the value of the underlying asset, rather than based on political budget decisions. Practical evidence from those countries adopting an accrual basis for both accounting and budgeting suggests that politicians generally manage to distinguish between items they can decide on and others that are not feasible for budget debates and decisions. However, the advantage of having a sound and comprehensive system for budgeting and accounting is paid for by the disadvantage of adding complexity to political budget debates. This is perhaps the main reason why many are equally divided about the basis of budgeting, while accrual accounting is more widely accepted.[30] Accrual budgeting is one of the ongoing debates in public sector financial management. From the practical experience with both bases of budgeting, the author of this book recommends the adoption of the same basis for budgeting and accounting, as system consistency pays off in the long run and no jurisdiction has considered moving back, but he acknowledges the arguments of the opponents, as they are also based on sound practical evidence.

---

[27] Lüder, K. (1998), Hughes, J., *PSC* (2004).

[28] The larger innovative thrust in the field of public sector financial management experiences by lower levels of government is well documented by Lüder, K., Jones, R. (2003) 21. An example of this early move can be found in *Konferenz der Kantonalen Finanzdirektoren* (1977).

[29] FEE (2006) 6.

[30] FEE (2007) 21.

3.8 Budget reporting

In the private sector, financial reporting excludes budgets, as they are part of strategy deployment and any presentation to the public, including the competitors, would jeopardise the strategy as such. But as we have seen, this is quite different in the public sector. Budgets of public sector entities, at least of those not operating commercially, are a public matter. As we have seen in Section 3.3 this is the rationale behind budget approval by a legislative body. But this is also the reason why budgets should be presented to the public. Citizens, even though usually not involved by a referendum, have a legitimate interest to know what their taxes, fines and fees are used for. Publicity of budgets is a principle of democracy. But budget reporting should not stop at the presentation of the budget itself. It should also include a report on budget execution, comparing the budget with the actual, as well as any adjustment to the budget. In fact, this is the requirement that the International Public Sector Accounting Standards (IPSAS) impose on budgeting, leaving other issues discussed in this chapter, such as performance budgeting or accrual budgeting, at the discretion of the adopters.[31]

Currently there is no requirement by international standards to present interim reports on budget execution. But, in many jurisdictions, there is a requirement to present interim reports at least at mid-year. Some jurisdictions even require a quarterly report or forecasts for the whole period to be issued after three quarters. But, unlike quarterly financial reporting of listed private sector corporations, such budget execution reports generally do not include a full set of financial statements. Indeed, the measurement of assets and liabilities, i.e. adjustment to fair value where such an accounting policy has been adopted, usually is not undertaken for the purpose of interim reporting. The budget execution report is limited to items relevant for budget execution. This is different when shares of the reporting entity are traded on a stock exchange, but public sector entities, namely all governments, would rather issue bonds that have lesser requirements in respect of financial reporting.

3.9 Budget assurance

Another peculiarity of the public sector is the 'auditing' of budgets. In fact, in many jurisdictions the auditor general office (or whatever it is called) conducts an audit on the budget before it goes to parliament for approval. It proves if the budget includes all relevant positions, is calculated according to laws and regulations and represents a fair view of the planning of the entity. This audit is clearly less affirmative than the audit of financial statements, as there is a larger degree of uncertainty in budgets than in financial statements by their very nature. The auditor is also supposed to refrain from commenting on political decisions, for example, in which area more or less should be spent. But highly material misconceptions could also lead to a rejection.

As we have seen in Section 1.2.5, the term assurance might be more appropriate than the term auditing for the public sector. This clearly is the case in respect of budgets.

---

[31] This is due to the mandate of the IPSAS-Board, which is limited to financial reporting.

What has been described as an audit in the previous paragraph, does not meet the definition of audit used by the audit profession, but it perfectly matches the definition of assurance, as it is a measure to increase confidence of the users, namely the parliament, in the budget.

In respect of performance budgets discussed in Section 3.5 the International Organisation of Supreme Audit Institutions (INTOSAI) has issued guidelines for performance auditing that are based on their auditing standards (AS).[32] Performance auditing is 'concerned with the audit of economy, efficiency and effectiveness' (AS 10.38 and 10.40).

3.10 Bottom line

Chapter 3 has given an overview of what traditionally is the most important part of public sector financial management: budgeting. It has shown that budgets may have different time horizons and different perspectives. New public management has led to the introduction of performance budgets, which are focused on product groups. They provide more freedom to the management in budget execution, but take a closer look at the performance of the entity. Another recent development has brought budgeting closer to accounting by emphasising budget reporting and introducing accrual budgeting in some jurisdictions. The latter is perhaps the most controversial issue among academics and professionals alike.

Work assignments

1   Explain why public sector budgets are often assumed to be a special kind of law. What are the managerial consequences of this assumption?

2   Explain why a public sector budget almost always has two or three dimensions.

3   If you have to manage the development of such a three-dimensional budget, how would you proceed in order to have sufficient information on all three dimensions?

4   Explain the difference between a cost centre, a profit centre and an investment centre. Discuss why public sector entities have traditionally been cost centres rather than one of the other two forms.

5   What are the advantages and disadvantages of performance budgeting?

6   A country runs a passport office issuing passports to its citizens. The empty passport booklets are bought from a specialised manufacturer at the cost of 10 currency units (CU) per passport. The passport office itself has two units: the application unit, which operates the front desk and takes phone enquiries, but also verifies the personal information of the passport applicants; and the production unit, which prints the personal information into the passport and applies the necessary seals and stamps. The manager of the passport unit is supported by a few staff members who are responsible for managerial tasks.

---

[32] INTOSAI (2004).

The statement of financial performance of the passport office shows the following items:

Revenue	105 786 passports @ CU 50 each		CU 5 293 800
Cost	Passport booklets 120 000 @ CU 10 each		CU 1 200 000
	Payroll		CU 2 090 000
	thereof		
	Application unit	*16 full-time equivalent*	*CU 1 440 000*
	Production unit	*4 full-time equivalent*	*CU 320 000*
	Management	*3 full-time equivalent*	*CU 330 000*
	Rental of property (government internal)		CU 250 000
	Postage, office supplies, etc.		CU 607 900
	Depreciation of equipment		CU 200 000
	Total cost		CU 4 347 900

They used 106 500 passport booklets to produce the 105 786 passports, as there was some wastage. The remaining 13 500 booklets will be used in future periods. One full-time equivalent equals 2 000 working hours per year. Contribution margin 1 is defined as revenue minus the passport booklets minus the work of the application and production unit. Contribution margin 2 is after all costs except the government internal rental of property. Contribution margin 3 is after all costs.

(a) What was the full cost of each passport sold? What was the profit based on full cost?

(b) Prepare a schedule of all three levels of contribution margin, both for the entire operation (based on passports sold) as well as per passport sold.

(c) Imagine a new passport law leads to an increase in demand. The number of passports sold is expected to increase by 20 per cent. What is the impact on the cost for each passport based on the full cost model and based on the marginal cost model?

7 What is a contribution margin in the public sector context?

8 It is often discussed whether full or marginal cost models should be used. Take a position in this debate considering a situation in which the demand for the service provided is diminishing, staying about the same or increasing (for example, you expect fewer patients in a hospital, the same number or even more).

9 Why are some countries still on a cash basis for budgeting, but on an accrual basis for accounting?

10 What is commitment accounting? Discuss the relationship of commitment accounting and internal control.

11 Why are public sector budgets, unlike their private sector equivalents, usually being audited? Explain the difference between the terms audit and assurance using the budget as an example.

Interface to national concepts

1 Identify which budget system (e.g. cash/accrual, performance-based or not) is used in your country.

2 Find out whether budgets are presented, i.e. publicly available.

3 What are your experiences with more recent ideas like performance-based budgeting or other concepts under the title of new public management?

4 Are management accounting systems in place? If so, are there common product schedules?

4 Public sector financial accounting and reporting

Learning objectives

- Distinguish financial from management accounting.
- Describe the cash basis of accounting, including its limitations.
- Describe the advantage and potential disadvantages of the accrual basis of accounting.
- Adopt the main principles of accrual accounting to examples from the public sector practice.
- Show the difference between accounting models and standards.
- Describe the role assurance takes in public sector financial accounting.

- Analyse the most relevant balances and flow using the GFS Analytic Framework.
- Assess the implications of government financial statistics to public sector financial management.

Key terms

Accountability	Auditing	Independence of audit
Accounting models	Cash basis of accounting	Reasonable assurance
Accounting principles	Chart of accounts	Stewardship
Accounting standards	Government financial	
Accrual basis of accounting	statistics	

How can accounting possibly be any different from other sectors of the economy? Is accounting not following the same rules in every kind of economic entity? Is it not universal? These questions are often asked by people, even accountants, who are not familiar with the public sector. Public sector accounting is, perhaps still, different from private sector accounting, at least in most jurisdictions. There are very few significant exceptions, for instance New Zealand, where full convergence with private sector accounting has taken place towards the end of the last century, but the vast majority of countries still have a public sector accounting practice in place that differs more or less substantially from its private sector equivalent. Under title of accrual accounting there is a trend of convergence, but for some very good and some less valid reasons it hardly ever reaches the maximum magnitude. Actually, the introduction of accrual accounting is the main reason why public sector accounting is quite high on the agenda in many countries as well as in most international organisations and will stay there for a while. Substantial amounts of money, worldwide clearly totalling above $1 billion, are spent on these reforms. Therefore this textbook devotes quite a bit of attention and space to this issue, which is the most important innovation within the scope of this publication.

Before addressing the technical issues of financial accounting and reporting, the objectives of financial accounting and reporting should be considered. Financial accounting and reporting, in contrast to management accounting and management information systems, is focused on financial information used for financial decision making. In the private sector such decisions are mainly decisions by owners or investors who are investing their capital into a company. Such investment decisions also occur in the public sector, as most governments and numerous public sector entities are raising capital through loans, bonds and other financial instruments. Obviously investors buying such instruments need information similar to investors buying financial instruments issued by private firms. But for the public sector this is not the end of the story. Namely tax payers are playing quite a unique role in financing the public sector. Not only do they finance current operations through their taxes, but they also pay back loans. Their role is that of customer and investor. They hold some kind of equity, the net assets of the entity where they live, although there are no tradable instruments on this equity. They have a genuine interest in the financial status and performance of their public sector entity. The public sector entity, represented through its political leaders and senior management, is entrusted by the citizens as well as by the investors for the capital they get. This makes them accountable. Perhaps the English term stewardship best reflects their duty, although this term does not translate into most other languages and therefore admittedly has its shortcomings in an international textbook. While financial accounting is preparing the financial reports, the financial reports themselves have the following objectives:

1 Providing information about the source, allocation and use of financial resources.
2 Providing information that allows the readers to assess the current and future financial situation of the entity.

While the first objective is strictly objective, the second one is obviously more biased. It needs to take into account the information needs of the readers. It therefore takes a stance for the readers of financial statements – and sometimes against those preparing them.

4.1 Cash basis of accounting

The starting point for most entities in the majority of jurisdictions is, or has been, cash accounting. Very much like private households but unlike private sector enterprises, public sector entities under a cash basis of accounting record all their cash in- and out-flows. Cash should read cash or cash equivalents, as most transactions go through bank accounts or similar forms of cashless payment nowadays. Entities adopting a cash basis of accounting can typically classify and add up their transactions according to various criteria, but there is no double entry bookkeeping. There is no full balance sheet or statement of financial position, only a list of cash resources, i.e. a list of cash and bank accounts.[1] Obviously, this should not really be called statement of financial position, as it falls short of presenting something like a financial position. A more adequate name would be statement of cash and cash equivalents.

Cash-based accounting perhaps best compares with how most people account for their personal finances. They add up wages and other proceeds and then deduct large expenditures such as taxes, rent, insurance or holidays; and carry forward what's left to the next period in order to prepare for more substantial expenditures such as buying a house or a car.

The advantage of the cash basis of accounting is the really simplistic approach, which can be understood by everyone, without any knowledge of accounting. But it stays very simple only if the organisation itself is very simple. Its simplicity is no longer granted if various parts of the organisation account for various expenditure and easily comes to its limits in large entities. Just imagine you had to manage your personal finances together with several thousands of other people in hundreds of locations, who make transactions with the outside world as well as among each other. The compelling simplicity of adding up, what is really the core of the cash basis of accounting, immediately becomes a nightmare.

Only recently a standard for the cash basis of accounting has been issued by the IPSAS-Board. The standard prescribes the presentation of cash basis financial statements and suggests two levels of cash basis, the higher as a step on the way towards accrual accounting. The financial statements under a cash basis of accounting include only:

- the statement of cash receipts and payments; and
- accounting policies and explanatory notes.

Exhibit 4.1 shows the structure of a statement of cash receipts and payments of a government.

---

[1] The two terms 'statement of financial position' and 'balance sheet' are used synonymously.

Exhibit 4.1 Statement of cash receipts and payments

	Note	200X		200X-1	
RECEIPTS					
Taxation					
Income Tax	1	X		X	
VAT		X		X	
other	2	X		X	
			X		X
Grants	3		X		X
Borrowings	4		X		X
Disinvestments	5		X		X
Revenues	6	X		X	
Reimbursments		X		X	
			X		X
Other Receipts			X		X
TOTAL RECEIPTS			X		X
PAYMENTS					
Operations					
Salaries, employee benefits	7	(X)		(X)	
Supplies		(X)		(X)	
			(X)		(X)
Transfers					
Grants	8	(X)		(X)	
Other	9	(X)		(X)	
			(X)		(X)
Investments					
Purchase of Property, Plant and Equipment	10	(X)		(X)	
Purchase of Financial Instruments	11	(X)		(X)	
			(X)		(X)
Loans and Interest Repayments					
Repayment of Borrowings		(X)		(X)	
Interest Payments		(X)		(X)	
			(X)		(X)
Other Payments	12		(X)		(X)
TOTAL PAYMENTS			(X)		(X)
Cash at the beginning of the year			X		X
Increase/(Decrease) in Cash			(X)		X
Cash at the end of the year			X		X
RECEIPTS BY THIRD PARTIES					
International Agencies		Y		Y	
Others		Y		Y	
TOTAL RECEIPTS BY THIRD PARTIES			Y		Y
PAYMENTS BY THIRD PARTIES					
International Agencies		(Y)		(Y)	
Others		(Y)		(Y)	
TOTAL PAYMENTS BY THIRD PARTIES			(Y)		(Y)

Source: IFAC.

The cash basis of accounting is still used even by the largest and most affluent countries.[2] Surprisingly it is the lower levels of government rather than the public corporations that have adopted an accrual basis, with a notable number of national governments still on the cash basis. Also numerous international organisations still apply a cash basis of accounting. However, as things are changing rapidly, there is no list provided in this textbook. More up-to-date information can be found on the website of the International Federation of Accountants (IFAC).[3]

4.1.1 Traditional cameralistic approaches

In some countries, namely in Continental Europe, the increasing complexity of public sector entities was managed through a system called cameralism or cameralistic approaches. Cameralism is not a clear-cut concept, but a very general description of a system adopted in quite different ways from one jurisdiction to another.

As we have seen, the cash basis of accounting does not include a full balance sheet, but rather a list of cash or cash equivalents. Cameralism takes advantage of this very limited balance sheet by identifying the various types or classes of transactions or organisations not only once the cash flow occurs, but also by earmarking the funds designated for a certain kind of transaction. For instance, money dedicated for education is put into a separate account, which is to be used on purpose only. Technically these funds are usually not a whole array of real bank accounts at commercial banks, but rather current accounts at the treasury, which acts as a bank for the public sector entities under a cameralistic approach. There is also a possibility of overdrafts, if expenditure exceeds the money allocated to a fund. Whether negative funds are tolerable in the long run is less an issue of accounting, but more one of fiscal politics. Cameralistic accounting can cope with positive or negative funds. It can also re-allocate resources between the different funds if this is required by decisions on the political or management level.

Again, this compares very much with personal finance of private households. Many people earmark some parts of their wages for specific purposes, e.g. taxes or holidays, in order to ensure the money is available once the purpose arises. Only a few really will put the money into different bank accounts, but most will act like a cameralistic treasury and manage to maintain defined minimum amounts on their bank account to be ready once the expenditure takes place.

In fact, in cameralism, budgeting and accounting almost coincide. In the budgeting process money is set aside for various purposes and accounting merely records how this money is being used up. Budget compliance can be monitored easily by checking on the levels of the funds, at least if there is no so-called 'authorised borrowing' of the funds, which frequently can be observed for larger-scale projects. This raises the complexity dramatically and virtually destroys the close ties between budgeting and accounting, as the fund balance no longer tells anything about budget compliance.

Cameralism also brings close ties between the organisational structure and accounting. As all funds need to be managed, the structure of funds usually corresponds to the organisational structure. While this has some advantages in order to define responsibilities, it also imposes substantial limitations for both accounting and organising purposes.

---

[2] Lüder, K., Jones, R. (2003).

[3] www.ifac.org/PublicSector (case sensitive).

Any analysis that does not follow the structure of the funds is almost impossible to perform on a regular basis.

4.1.2 Simplified accrual approaches

Many public sector entities have improved their cash-based systems in order to take care of one or the other aspects of accrual accounting. Some entities have introduced accounts receivable and accounts payable, as they want to keep an eye on them. Others are making a distinction between investment expenditure and consumptive expenditure. Yet others account for debts. This all happens in the statement of financial position, which is limited to cash and cash equivalents under a strict cash basis of accounting. Taking up some elements of accrual accounting, like the ones mentioned above, adds more items to the statement of financial position. The more elements that are added, the more it deserves the name statement of financial position, although it should be used only in a full accrual context. Such simplified accrual approaches are sometimes called 'simplified accrual' or 'mixed approaches'.

Modified accrual approaches are certainly superior to pure cash approaches when it comes to assessing the financial situation of an entity. The degree of superiority depends on how many accrual elements are added. Modified accrual also allows an entity to introduce accrual accounting step-by-step, rather than all at once. Some would therefore suggest modified accrual to be a milestone, or perhaps a series of milestones in a project introducing accrual accounting. In fact this is what the IPSAS-Board proposes with its cash basis standard, especially for developing countries with limited capacities.

4.1.3 Disadvantages

The cash basis of accounting has substantial shortcomings in respect of the presentation of the financial position and performance. It does not – at least in its most basic form – distinguish between expenditure for consumption and investments. Neither does it present all assets, nor all liabilities. Revenues or expenses are presented only if they are cash payments or receipts. This may be in a different period, sometimes a long time before or after the relevant decisions are made. Moreover, within larger organisations, which are quite common in most countries as well as in international organisations, the number of funds will become a substantial problem. The potential advantage of a simple relationship between budgeting and accounting has been blurred in most cases by sophisticated budget rules which allow for provisions that may not be presented adequately by the accounting.

But even in modified accrual, the picture remains a partial one. It is unlikely that assets and debts can be associated in a way lenders would wish to asses their credit risk. Decision makers still have a limited picture. This could be acceptable if there was no concept or system at hand that relatively easily would overcome these limitations. But there is one: accrual accounting, as practised by millions of private sector enterprises and an increasing number of public sector ones.

4.2 Accrual basis of accounting

As the accrual basis of accounting seems to give opportunity for substantial improvements in public sector accounting, it should be contemplated more closely. Once again, as in the case of other terms, accrual accounting is not a sharp concept, but rather a captive for various concepts. This book uses the IPSAS-Board definition, which defines the accrual basis of accounting by a description of its features.

Definition	**Accrual basis of accounting**
	A basis of accounting under which transactions and other events are recognised when they occur (and not only when cash or its equivalent is received or paid). Therefore, the transactions and events are recorded in the accounting records and recognised in the financial statements of the periods to which they relate. The elements recognised under accrual accounting are assets, liabilities, net assets/equity, revenue and expenses.[4]

Apparently, timing is an important element of accrual accounting. However, it is noteworthy to emphasise it is not only about the timing of transactions, but also about the timing of events that are not undertaken actively by the entity. Thus accrual accounting is not limited to delimitations of invoices between two periods, as people sometimes assume, but includes aspects such as adequate depreciation or interest charges. It is a truly comprehensive concept.

The main advantages of accrual accounting in the public sector are in respect of the better information it provides to decision makers.[5] It provides a more realistic picture as it includes all economic flows rather than just cash transactions. It is supposed to provide a means to allow an accurate assessment of financial resilience. Comparison between different periods, but also between different service providers, is enhanced. This is very important in the context of privatisation and performance budgeting, where blurred comparatives almost inevitably cause false decisions. The advantages are altogether increasing the effectiveness of public sector financial management and even public policy. Further advantages include the assessment of economic viability.[6] Only accrual accounting allows the assessment of whether taxes or other revenues are sufficient to cover the costs. This holds true both in current periods and, at least to some extent, in an intergenerational perspective. Accrual accounting certainly distinguishes investments from consumptive spending and does account for future liabilities, at least if they reach threshold likelihood and can be estimated reliably.

4.2.1 Guiding principles

As a comprehensive concept, accrual accounting follows a set of guiding principles. Obviously the most central principle is completeness and faithfulness of the financial statements, as it directly refers to the timing issue. The financial statement should represent all transactions and events of a period, and do so in a faithful manner, i.e. in accordance with the substance of the transaction or event.

Thus accrual accounting has to provide the necessary information for financial statements that follow the principles. This focus on the financial statements, rather than the bookkeeping, represents a change of paradigm. The principles are no longer about accounting and accountants, but about their outcome. It somehow represents the performance-oriented perspective, which we have seen in Chapter 3. However, implications for the bookkeeping will be discussed in Section 4.2.4.

But the accrual-based principles include further qualitative characteristics, such as understandability, relevance and reliability. They clearly restrict the details that could be

---

[4] IPSAS-Board (2007) Glossary.

[5] FEE (2006) p. 1.

[6] Das, S. (2006) 9 ff.

onerous to prepare and yet not very meaningful in context. Thus accrual accounting, in contradiction to the understanding that the general public might have about accounting, is not so much about pea counting as about getting the general picture right. Some scrutiny, however, is necessary for the reliability of the information.

4.2.2 Main implications of accrual basis

Accrual accounting shifts the focus away from expenditure, which was the focus of the cash basis of accounting in the public sector, on to the statement of financial position. Assets, liabilities and the residual of the two, called net assets or equity, become a main issue. In the statement of financial performance it is expenses, rather than expenditure and revenues, that are the focus. But the emergence of the statement of financial position is clearly the main implication.

Public sector entities account for their assets and liabilities. They look after them and try to balance them in the long run. This is more than just an additional financial statement; it is another change of paradigm for public sector financial management. Managing public sector entities' finances is no longer limited to some reallocation of spending or deliberation about deficits and debts; it is about management of financial resources. Public sector entities traditionally did not consider their assets to be resources and their liabilities to be limitations to those resources. Sometimes, for example in some privatisations, such resources were given away for far less than their value or, for instance property, even destroyed by sheer negligence. Obviously, one could argue that accrual is not necessary for being careful with the resources, but it certainly helps if they are properly accounted for. This shift towards the statement of financial position obviously also shifts the indicators used in public sector financial management. Suddenly, relations between fixed assets and long-term liabilities or net assets as a percentage of total assets draw a lot of attention. For good reasons, as such indicators are valid representatives of financial sustainability.

The second most important implication is professional knowledge. While the cash basis of accounting did not have very much to do with professional accounting knowledge, this is different for accrual accounting. Good knowledge, and therefore education, are essential for the successful adoption of accrual accounting. This has been experienced by many countries moving from cash to accrual accounting, including South Africa and Slovakia, to name just two. Knowledge and education have been shown as critical in almost any project introducing accrual accounting.

Thirdly, consolidation becomes an issue. As completeness and faithfulness is required, other entities controlled by the reporting entity can no longer be omitted. Also in the public sector, such entities tend to be material and should thus be considered. Failure to do so may lead to very substantial errors, especially if mutual transactions are taking place. In fact, this has been a main reason for spectacular public sector defaults, when mutual lending and borrowing eventually came to an end.[7]

4.2.3 Financial reporting

As we have seen in Section 4.2.1, another change of paradigm is the one from book-keeping to financial reporting. As a matter of fact, under accrual accounting financial

[7] For example, the towns of Briançon (France) or Leukerbad (Switzerland).

reporting has become very much the mission of accounting. Financial reporting is the presentation of financial statements to the external world. Obviously, not every organisation is reporting to externals, such as shareholders, lenders or the general public. But public sector entities are highly likely to report externally, due to their public nature. Many are also borrowers. Thus the usual absence of shareholders should be no reason to underestimate the importance of financial reporting.

Financial reporting consists of the presentation of financial statements. Under accrual accounting this includes a statement of financial position as well as one of financial performance. Further statements, including a cash flow statement, a statement of changes in net assets, as well as one about accounting policies and notes, are required by IPSAS 1. At least the cash flow statement is warmly welcomed by first-time adopters of accrual accounting, as it provides information comparable to the one under a cash basis of accounting.

4.2.4 Accountancy

Although the main focus of accrual accounting is not on accountancy, there are implications. Accrual accounting requires double entry bookkeeping, as it needs to account for cash and non-cash transactions as well as transactions within and between the various financial statements. Surpluses or deficits need to be shown both in the net assets/equity and the statement of financial performance.

But it goes beyond double entry. Accounting for assets including depreciation over useful life requires quite an elaborate asset accounting. Consolidation is no easy issue, especially if it comes to the elimination of mutual transaction between consolidated entities. As in some public sector entities accounting operations take place in various decentralised units, internal guidelines need to be developed and implemented. Obviously, IT systems are different for accrual and cash-based accounting and are likely to be replaced when introducing accrual accounting. In fact, IT systems often make up for the largest fraction of project costs for the adoption of accrual accounting.

4.3 Accounting models and accounting standards

Accounting standards are well defined and recognised throughout the world. Private sector standards such as the International Financial Reporting Standards (IFRS), formerly known as International Accounting Standards (IAS) or the Financial Accounting Standards (FAS), at least outside the United States are better known as generally accepted accounting principles (US GAAP). While the concepts behind accounting standards are quite clear and increasingly convergent around the world, this cannot be said about accounting models. But they exist in many countries, especially in Continental Europe, and have some authority on public sector accounting in these jurisdictions.[8] International organisations have also been using accounting models, at least until many of them started adopting the International Public Sector Accounting Standards (IPSAS). Some people would argue that accounting models are perhaps something like accounting manuals, guiding the implementation of accounting standards within an entity. But as those jurisdictions using accounting models have no, or at least no substantial,

---

[8] For example, Italy and Switzerland.

experience with accounting standards, they are rather a substitute for accounting standards. Unlike accounting manuals set up for a specific entity, they – similar to standards – also are used by various entities without any modification.

4.3.1 Accounting models

Accounting models prescribe the financial accounting of the entities within their jurisdiction. Often, they address a particular kind of entity, e.g. local governments or international organisations, rather than being used across all parts of the public sector.

This makes it possible to tailor them to particular needs. Accounting models of local governments may or may not contain extensive guidelines in respect of tax revenues, depending on local governments' tax authority, which differs from jurisdiction to jurisdiction. Accounting models for international organisations usually include guidelines for project-specific donations, as many national governments earmark a substantial part of their contribution for projects. This high degree of accuracy in very specific issues is obviously an advantage over the much more universal concept of accounting standards. But, at the same time, it strongly limits its usability for other entities not specifically addressed.

An important aspect of accounting models is a defined chart of accounts (CoA). CoAs are lists of accounts that usually are based on a decimal classification. For example:

1	Assets
10	Current assets
100	Cash and cash equivalent
1 000	Cash
1 010	Bank accounts
...	...
2	Liabilities
...	....
3	Expenses
...	....

Accounting models prescribe at least the first two, perhaps even more, decimal positions. Further positions may be added at the discretion of the individual entity for internal purposes or just to take care of a large number of accounts. The decimal classification system makes is easy to add the accounts of the same group up to a total, which is comparable to the same line item of other entities, which perhaps have a different set of detailed accounts underneath. Obviously, mandating a CoA is quite rule-based, while most accounting standards in recent times have tried to adhere to principles, as we shall see in the following section.

Accounting models may also include guidelines in respect of recognition or measurement of certain positions or transactions. Such guidelines are usually quite detailed, for instance by stipulating periods of useful life for specific classes of assets. This, of course, is again the rule-based approach. Such strict rules are usually considered necessary, as the accounting models are often used as part of an allocation or redistribution system between poorer and more affluent entities. If such a system is based on financial performance, there is an obvious need for very detailed rules to avoid manipulation and scam.

However, it is recommended that such systems are not based on socioeconomic indicators rather than financial performance. This not only reduces the need for rules, but also creates more favourable incentives.

Like all rule-based systems, accounting models tend to be vulnerable for black spots or gaps.[9] Intended and unintended gaps are likely to be used in order to avoid unwanted results. Very prominent examples are Public Private Partnerships (PPP), a rather new phenomenon, which therefore is usually not covered by the rules in most accounting models. Many of these contracts include long-term liabilities of the public sector entities, as the private sector partner is making the investment upfront in exchange for a long-term stream of cash flows from the public sector entity. Examples include property, which is constructed by a private sector enterprise and then leased back to the public sector entity. Obviously, the public sector entity should recognise its long-term obligations. But as accounting models usually just remain quiet about PPPs and perhaps also leases, entities are in full compliance with the accounting model, without recognising such liabilities.

Accounting models are usually very close to bookkeeping. They include guidance for the accountants' work, their procedures, and not only for the result, but also the financial statements. Accounting models are usually designed to guarantee a certain level of convergence and conformity in a decentralised organisational setting. This perhaps is more typical for federal nations, but can be found in other situations as well.

Accounting models have their strength and advantage in the tailor-made and ready-to-use rules, which facilitate their implementation. But accounting models obviously also have their downside, which equally is due to their rule-based approach. In order to overcome this, they face the choice of either very frequent updates or a development towards a more principle-based form of guidelines. The latter, of course, moves them into close proximity with accounting standards.

4.3.2 Accounting standards

Accounting standards are codifications of high-level financial accounting principles. If they are followed in all parts without exception, and only then, the financial statements of an entity are supposed to present a true and fair view of the financial situation of the entity.[10] This may be certified by an external auditor.[11] Thus the focus of accounting standards is the presentation of a true and fair view. They are to enhance the quality and uniformity of financial reporting of a large range of entities. Accounting standards are not addressing issues relevant only for a few entities; nor do they deal with accounting processes and structures.

In order to fulfil this mission, the set of accounting standards needs to be comprehensive, but not complete. It should be comprehensive, as a true and fair view cannot be achieved if there are substantial parts missing. On the other hand, minor black spots and gaps are not critical, because today's accounting standards are principle-based. General principles, like the accrual principle, going concern, substance over form or relevancy, make sure that minor gaps cannot be filled in a way that contradicts the general principles. The general principles need to be observed, even if there is no specific standard in a certain area.

---

[9] Bergmann, A., Kälin, U. (2003) 747 ff.

[10] However, in some jurisdictions, for example the United Kingdom or Australia, the term 'true and fair' refers to the general concept of financial reporting while accounting standards may technically be 'not true and fair'. This of course should not be the case, given their mission.

[11] Here, the term auditor (and not assuror) is used, as it is clearly an audit that is undertaken.

Unlike many accounting models, accounting standards generally address issues such as consolidation of controlled entities as well as so-called constructive obligations. Both are included due to the substance over form principle, which requires financial statements to present the economic substance rather than the legal form of it. For the consolidation this means that ownership of shares is no prerequisite and for constructive obligations, there are not necessarily legal obligations in place. This economic view is clearly more challenging to the public sector than the private sector, as it is in most jurisdictions required to have a legal basis for each of its actions, while private sector entities may take the absence of regulation as an opportunity for unrestricted activities.

Definition	**Constructive obligation** A constructive obligation is an obligation that is based on valid expectations caused by the entity's past practices or current statements. Unlike a legal obligation it is not specified by legislation.

Accounting standards are – as their name implies – accounting standards. They do not follow any other purpose, such as fiscal policy or assurance. That is why accounting standards remain silent about many issues discussed in Chapter 2 under the title of public finance, as well as any aspects of budgeting not related to the presentation of financial statements. They are not financial management standards.

The only international accounting standards for public sector entities are the International Public Sector Accounting Standards (IPSAS). In various countries there are national standards for the public sector, for example the standards issued by the Government Accounting Standards Board (GASB) for United States local governments or the Financial Accounting Standards Board (FASAB) for the United States federal government, and the Public Sector Accounting Board (PSAB) in Canada. Other countries, like New Zealand, have only one set of national standards that applies to public and private sector entities. This raises the question whether there are sector-specific reasons in the public sector for accounting standards. There certainly are issues, for instance tax revenue, that are sector-specific and do not occur in a private sector environment. But are there reasons to treat transactions, which occur in both sectors, differently when they take place in the public sector?

Such differences would need to be differences in substance rather than in form. This leads back to the economics of the public sector. In fact there are three economic aspects in the public sector that are truly different. These are as follows:

1 **Assets are held for service potential instead of cash generation.** The rationale why a private sector corporation would hold assets is to generate cash flows. In many cases this does not hold true for public sector entities. They mainly hold assets in order to provide services to the public. Roads or schools are good examples of assets being held in order to provide services rather than cash generation.
2 **Importance of non-exchange transactions.** Most private sector transactions are exchange transactions, as there is an exchange of goods or services against payment or vice versa. Many public sector transactions are not on an exchange basis. Taxes are to be paid even if you have no children going to school or if you do not endorse some government policies.

3 **Democratic control.** In the private sector, assets and liabilities are generally controlled based on ownership. Although public sector entities may also own, and thus control, assets and liabilities, in a broader perspective the concept of ownership does not hold and is replaced by democratic control.

The existence of such fundamental economic differences does not require that all standards would be different in the two sectors. There are common areas, for example exchange transactions of public sector entities. Most public sector entities would involve such transactions and there is no public sector-specific reason to treat such a transaction any differently from a private sector one. But all the areas that accounting standards address need to be reconsidered under the public sector perspective. That is why separate standards are perhaps an easier strategy than common ones, which have to take into account the public sector-specific economics. This does not mean that the resulting bottom line, i.e. the quality of financial statements, of one or the other strategy is necessarily better.

4.4 Assurance of financial statements

There are three different categories of (external) audit:[12]

1 audit of financial statements;
2 compliance audit; and
3 operational audit.

All three play their role in assurance, although external users obviously are most interested in the audit of financial statements. However, in the public sector compliance audits have a somewhat greater importance, as in jurisdictions that follow a rule of law the compliance of the government and its entities with legal requirements is imperative. But all three categories of audit can be observed in the public sector.

Section 3.9, dealing with assurance, was perhaps a bit strange to those familiar with assurance in the private sector, as it was about budgets, which are subject to an external audit in the public sector. But this is nothing else than a compliance audit, as budgets are law-like instruments. In contrast, the assurance of financial statements of public sector entities is very much in line with its private sector counterpart. Financial statements are subject to an external audit, following the same principles as private sector external audit of financial statements. The external auditor gives an opinion on the financial statements, stating whether they are complete and presented in accordance with law and – if adopted – any accounting standards. A very generic audit process of financial statements would include the following steps:[13]

1 Planning of the audit, if necessary clarification of scope and mandate.
2 Evaluation of the internal control system of the reporting entity.
3 Collection of evidence on the fairness of the financial statements.
4 Proposal of necessary adjustments.
5 Follow-up on necessary changes.
6 Issue of auditor's report.

---

[12] Whittington, O.R., Pany, K. (2003) 10.

[13] Based on Whittington, O.R., Pany, K. (2003) 5, but adapted by the author.

However, given the different categories of audit as well as the different audit standards and, even more importantly the difference between limited and reasonable assurance, we will examine more closely, in Section 4.4.2, the process needs to be tailored to the specific audit. Step 3 especially also needs to be clarified in more detail.

4.4.1 Audit standards for independence

The most important sector-specific issue is the independence of the external auditor. While some jurisdictions would require a professional auditor from outside the entity, there are many jurisdictions with sector-specific audit institutions, e.g. an Auditor General's office or the Government Auditing Office (GAO). Although these audit institutions enjoy a certain statutory independence in most jurisdictions, they cannot be completely independent as they are part of the administration. Independence is in fact the core issue of the Lima declaration of the International Organisation of Supreme Audit Institutions (INTOSAI) back in 1977. The Lima declaration suggests that independence should be laid down in the constitution (section 5.3), that the officials and members of the audit institution should be granted (section 6) and the audit institution should enjoy financial independence, i.e. be able to request their budget directly from parliament (section 7).

Over the last 30 years or more, the statutory basis of many institutions has been changed in order to increase their independence. However, it is still controversial whether there are any statutory arrangements that are sufficient. The alternative at hand would be to contract professional service firms. However, independence is also an issue for them as many of them also provide consultancy services and therefore are likely to audit some information prepared on the basis of their previous advice. Furthermore, in many countries there is quite a limited number of professional service firms left that would be large enough to provide auditing services to entities of the size that public sector entities typically have. State audit institutions also point out that their operation is perhaps cheaper than the fees outside auditors would charge. However, in practice this debate is not as clear cut as it seems to be. Even in jurisdictions with statutory audit institutions, these institutions regularly contract some of their work out to professional service firms. This leads to a mixed system, taking advantage of both possibilities. This book endorses the need of a fully independent audit performed on the financial statements of public sector entities. It would not recommend relying entirely on state-owned audit institutions, but approves of the partial and full contracting options. This enhances independence and brings increased interaction with the profession, which certainly is beneficial.

Coming back to the audit process of financial statements, there are two major international standards that can be applied. These are as follows:

1 The International Auditing Standards (IAS) issued by the International Audit and Assurance Standards Board (IAASB) of the International Federation of Accountants (IFAC).
2 The Auditing Standards (AS) issued by INTOSAI.

While the IAS are not sector-specific, the AS apply only to the government sector, which of course is only one part of the public sector, as shown in Chapter 1. Thus both sets of standards are used throughout the public sector. Looking for differences, it can be said that the IAS are more, but still not exclusively, focused on the work of the professional auditor while the AS are more focused on typical audit institutions in the public sector, such as Auditor Generals offices. On the national level and for international organisations there is usually a law on auditing further specified in a handbook, which is actually used as a basis for the auditing work. However, they are adopting the international standards only to the national or organisational level.

4.4.2 Reasonable and limited assurance

As we have seen in Chapter 1, the term assurance refers to any measure increasing confidence of the user of the information provided. Especially when considering the audit of financial statements this is quite a risky position, as there may be different levels of confidence and if expectations about these levels do not coincide with the those using and those preparing assurance this may cause significant misperceptions. The International Audit Standards (IAS) therefore clearly distinguish in their conceptual framework between reasonable assurance on one side and limited assurance on the other.

Reasonable assurance aims at 'a reduction in assurance engagement risk to an acceptably low level in the circumstances of the engagement, as the basis of a positive form of expression of the practitioner's conclusion'.[14] The auditor will thus provide, if justified, a positive opinion such as the confirmation of compliance with the relevant standards or jurisdiction or the completeness of financial statements.

Limited assurance, on the other hand, aims at 'a reduction in assurance engagement risk that is acceptable in the circumstances of the engagement but where that risk is greater than for a reasonable assurance engagement, as a basis of a negative form of the expression of the practitioner's conclusion'.[15] The auditor's opinion is, therefore, just excluding some elements of risk, for example that in the process of consolidation no errors could be observed.

Apparently, both forms of assurance are justified under certain circumstances. Especially in larger organisations, which are quite common in the public sector, reasonable assurance is usually only possible based on several limited assurance engagements. The auditor general or whoever is responsible for the assurance of the financial reporting, needs previous reports prepared by other auditors to obtain a comprehensive picture of the entire financial reporting. Limited assurance is also often used when auditing of specific systems, e.g. payroll systems, takes place. Obviously, the professional fees for limited assurance engagements are smaller than the ones for reasonable assurance engagements.

To the user it is very important to understand the difference between the two types of assurance and to distinguish it when reading a report. Clearly it would be misleading to take a limited assurance opinion as a proxy for a reasonable assurance opinion, as the assurance work for limited assurance deliberately excludes some aspects that would be relevant for reasonable assurance.

However, reasonable assurance does not mean absolute assurance. Main sources of risk include the use of sampling rather than full testing and the persuasive nature of much evidence used. Increasingly, the assurance of financial statement relies on the reliability of internal control systems. These systems are, of course, evaluated during the audit process. But collusion may not always be detected during the audit process. Obviously, in an ideal world, assurance would overcome such shortcomings. But in the not so ideal world, they could be defeated only at excessive cost and enormous time

---

[14] IAASB (2007) *International Assurance Framework* paragraph 11.

[15] IAASB (2007) *International Assurance Framework* paragraph 11.

requirements. Therefore the responsibility of the preparation and presentation of financial statements always remains with the management of the preparing entity. Finally, it should be kept in mind that even reasonable assurance is assuring only the financial statements covered by the assurance, which may be only a subset of all the information presented.

4.5 Government financial statistics

One of the peculiarities of public sector financial management is the existence of a comprehensive statistical framework. Government financial statistics (GFS) are prepared in most countries around the world and in some instances even more prominently used in decision making than the information provided by financial and management accounting. Their appearance with the strongest perception in the media and the general public probably is the use as convergence criteria in the Treaty of Maastricht, which determine a country's eligibility for the euro zone. Among other criteria, each country has to meet targets in respect of public sector debt and deficit, which are both determined by GFS.

4.5.1 GFSM2001

Government financial statistics (GFS) are, very much like financial accounting, following various international and national standards. This is particularly important, as GFS are widely accepted as a basis for economical comparisons between different countries. Therefore GFS has a longer tradition of harmonisation on a global scale than financial accounting. The International Monetary Fund (IMF) has developed and issued standards with a global range in its Government Financial Statistics Manual (GFSM). The latest version of this manual has been issued in the year 2001 and is therefore generally referred to as GFSM2001. The other set of international financial statistics standards with a greater importance are standards issued by the European Commission under the names European System of Accounts (ESA; latest version dating from 1995 and therefore referred to as ESA95) and European Manual on Government Deficit and Debt (EMGDD). All those public sector-specific standards are brought together with the other sectors of the economy in the System of National Accounts (SNA; latest version dating from 1993 and referred to as SNA93), which is used for the measurement of macroeconomic aggregates such as the gross domestic product (GDP).

As the differences between the standards are rather subtle, the following considerations are based on the globally accepted GFSM2001. This manual – unlike earlier versions – is adopting the accrual principle that is well known from financial accounting (cf. Section 4.2). It is in fact based on the concept of value creation. As the GFS Analytic Framework shows (Exhibit 4.2) the government financial statistics, exactly like accrual accounting, are based on the assumption that the opening balance sheet plus or minus flows during the year lead to the closing balance sheet.

The balance sheet looks similar to the balance sheet from financial accounting, with the exception of the item 'net financial worth' which is specific for GFS. It is defined as the total of financial assets minus the total of liabilities.[16] However, the flows during

---

[16] IMF (2001) paragraph 4.53, p. 44.

Exhibit 4.2 **GFS Analytic Framework**

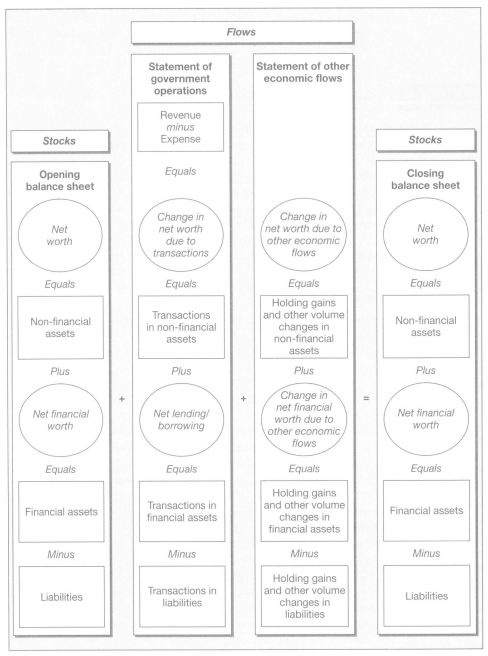

Source: *Government Finance Statistics Manual 2001* http://www.imf.org/external/pubs/ft/gfs/manual/pdf/all.pdf, Statistics Department, IMF, 2001

the year are classified under GFS in quite a different way to the one we know from financial statements. GFSM2001 requires two separate statements, one presenting 'government operations' and the other showing 'other economic flows'. Other economic flows are characterised as 'holding gains' and 'volume changes', i.e. unrealised gains or losses due to differences in the measurement of assets or liabilities. In government operations, GFSM2001 requires a differentiation between financial and non-financial transactions, as well as transactions of liabilities. By requiring two different statements GFSM2001 differentiates between realised actual transactions and unrealised gains and losses.

The practical implication of this difference between financial accounting and financial statistics is the need for an additional classification when recording transactions, if the records should also be used for the preparation of government financial statistics.[17] This classification should distinguish between operational transactions and the various types of 'other economic flows'. As there are not more than nine different types of transaction, this classification could be made by adding one digit to the numbering in the chart of accounts.

Government financial statistics are prepared for entities of the government sector. The other important determinant of government financial statistics is therefore the definition of the government sector. Following SNA93 the GFSM2001 uses the concept of the general government sector (GGS), see Exhibit 4.3.

The general government sector (S13) includes all levels of government, i.e. central, state and local, as well as social security funds on those three levels of government. It also includes non-market entities controlled and mainly financed by governments. However, it does not include public financial and non-financial corporations, i.e. commercial operations controlled by the government. They are part of the non-financial

Exhibit 4.3   Sector model

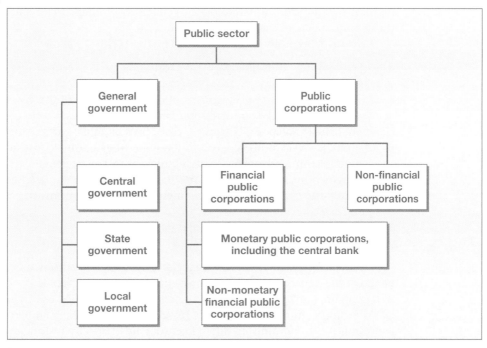

Source: *Government Finance Statistics Manual 2001* http://www.imf.org/external/pubs/ft/gfs/manual/pdf/all.pdf, Statistics Department, IMF, 2001

---
[17] Bergmann, A. *et al.* (2006).

sector (S11) or the financial sector (S12), regardless of their public sector ownership. The distinction between the GGS and public corporations is based on the source of their revenues. Entities are considered to be public corporations rather than GGS entities if they sell 'all or almost all' of the goods and services they produce at market prices.[18] In practice, the line is usually drawn at 50 per cent of the revenues. If more than 50 per cent of the revenues are generated by market transactions, an entity is considered to be a public corporation rather than an entity of the GGS. International organisations are a separate sector (S222) which is part of the foreign economy from the perspective of the System of National Accounts (SNA), which takes – as its name suggests – a national point of view.[19]

4.5.2 Upgrade under development

An updated version of GFSM2001 is due to be issued in 2008. A few aspects of this update have already emerged and are worth reflection in this section. The information provided, as it treats work in progress, is not comprehensive and may be subject to changes.

Certainly one of the main issues to be addressed by this update is the harmonisation between government financial accounting and government financial statistics. In 2003 a task force on the harmonisation of public sector accounting (TFHPSA) led by the International Monetary Fund (IMF) and including among others representatives from the Organisation for Economic Cooperation and Development (OECD), the European Union and the International Public Sector Accounting Standards (IPSAS) Board, has been formed. The task force rapidly identified the similarities and differences between the various standards and collected them in a matrix. This matrix was a basis for the IPSAS on the disclosure of information on the general government sector. But it is also used for the current update of the GFSM.

The main areas of difference identified by the TFHPSA included:[20]

- scope of entities consolidated, i.e. sectorisation versus control; including ownership relations;
- recognition as an asset versus recognition as an expense for a few kinds of transactions (research & development, intangible assets, computer software, mineral exploration, defence weapons, borrowing costs, private-public-partnerships);
- recognition versus non-recognition for some transactions (constructive obligations, decommissioning/restoration costs, employee stock options);
- measurement of a few kind of assets/liabilities (impairment, transaction costs, non-performing loans, low interest or interest-free loans, inventories, biological assets, subsoil assets);
- time series issues (i.e. in respect of taxes); and
- terminology and definitions.

Very generally speaking, in the financial statistics transactions are expensed in the period of the transaction rather than accrued as an asset or liability.

It is highly unlikely that all the differences will be levelled out by the update of the GFSM or future improvements to the IPSAS. However, all the members of the task force are committed to minimising differences that are caused by historic coincidence rather

---

[18] IMF (2001) 10.

[19] Schwaller, A. (2005).

[20] Summarised by the author, based on the matrix issued by TFHPSA.

than difference in mission. On the other hand, both financial statistics and financial accounting will adhere to its mission, which provide macroeconomic aggregates on one side and provide general purpose financial statements of a reporting entity on the other. This will help to facilitate the preparation of financial statistics as well as financial accounting. In many cases it will be helpful if guidance for the bridging of the gap has been provided already, as it has been done for the scope issue by the IPSAS on the disclosure of information on the general government sector. These developments on the international level will enable preparers on the national or sub-national level to bring their operations in respect of financial statistics and accounting closer together.

4.6 | Bottom line

In this chapter we have seen that public sector accounting is distinctively different from private sector accounting in that many countries are still adopting a cash basis of accounting. This approach is strongly related to the cash-based budgeting allocation of financial resources in cameralistic manner to the various purposes or entities. Almost literally, money is set aside in dedicated accounts, earmarked and thus spent out of these accounts. Adopting an accrual basis of accounting is perhaps the most important reform currently undertaken in the field of public sector financial management. This improves the information available for decision makers substantially, as this approach reflects the economic substance of both transactions undertaken during the reporting period and the financial position at reporting date. Further enhancements depend on the accounting system or accounting standards applied. While accounting systems tend to reflect the entities' situation more accurately, as they are often tailored to the situation, accounting standards are more universal and due to their principle-based approach less vulnerable for gaps. The current trend obviously rather goes towards accounting standards.

Public sector accounting is also strongly influenced by government financial statistics (GFS) which are to be prepared in a uniform way based on guidelines issued by the International Monetary Fund (IMF). These guidelines require a definition of the public sector and its sub-sectors based on the importance of market transactions of the respective entities. GFS also distinguish between government operations and other economic flows. The latter represent changes due to changes of price levels or volumes. These distinctions need to be reflected in public sector accounting, namely the chart of accounts. Adjustments are more substantial for those entities still adopting a cash basis of accounting, as the GFS are following an accrual model.

Work assignments

1 The terms accountability and stewardship best represent the obligation of the person preparing financial statements towards their readers. Please explain what these terms imply.

2 What is the rationale behind the use of a cash basis of accounting in many countries over many years? Or the other way around: why is accrual accounting moving into public sector accounting at a much slower pace than in the private sector? Discuss.

3 A local government gives a $10 million loan to a private health care supplier operating in the area, in order to allow for improvement of the facilities of the supplier. What happens to this loan, the interest on the loan as well as the improved facilities if the health care supplier is to be consolidated into the local government?

4 Taking the example from work assignment 2, what could be arguments in favour of a consolidation, and what could be arguments against it? Why is it perhaps less clear cut than in private sector corporate groups?

5 Take the chart of accounts (CoA) of an institution in your country and link the accounts or group of accounts to aggregates required by GFSM2001. It is possible that you will not manage to identify all aggregates, as the CoA in many countries still falls short of the GFSM2001 requirements. If this is the case, what should be changed in the respective CoA?

6 Outline an audit process for the audit of the financial statements of a government agency.

7 GFSM2001 makes a distinction between operations and other economic flows. What is the rationale behind this distinction? Make a real world example for both operations and other economic flows.

8 One of the more substantial differences between accounting standards and GFS is in the field of constructive obligations, which are usually recognised according to accounting standards, but not according to GFS. What is the practical consequence of this difference? Discuss.

Interface to national concepts

1 Check whether your country's governments are on a cash or accrual basis of accounting. Be careful, there may be differences between the various entities and/or levels of government even within one country.

2 Draw a comprehensive list of all models, standards and other regulations in the field of public sector financial management in your country. You may base this on preliminary findings when working on Chapter 1.

3 Check the adoption of GFS in your country. Look at the comprehensiveness of the framework as well as the definition of the general government sector, which should include social security schemes, versus public corporations.

5 Full accrual financial reporting under IPSAS

Learning objectives

- Identify the elements of standards-based accrual financial reporting and differentiate them against mixed forms.
- Read and interpret accounting standards.
- Evaluate the various forms of implementation and adoption of accounting standards.

Key terms

Disclosure

Face of the financial
    statements

Government Business
    Enterprise

Judgement

Measurement

Net assets/equity

Notes

Recognition

Statement of financial
    performance

Statement of financial
    position

Statement of cash flows

As the introduction of accrual accounting has been portrayed in the previous chapter as the most important current reform in public sector financial management, it is considered more in depth in this chapter. This is done by examining the International Public Sector Accounting Standards (IPSAS), which provide the momentum for this reform in many countries and international organisations, including the United Nations and the Commission of the European Union. This is also another opportunity to look at the concept of accounting standards, which is also a more recent one for the public sector than for the private sector.

Devoting a separate chapter to specific standards is perhaps a privilege the author enjoys if he is a member of the standard setter. However, unlike in the private sector for many years, there is no competition between various standards on the global level. Thus it is no partisanship for one of several options, but rather a portrait of the only internationally available option right now.

Countries with a tradition in accrual-based accounting and their own national standards particularly may be more focused on the enhancement of their own set of standards. However, the rationale behind the national standards and the international ones remains the same. Even in those countries the IPSAS are followed closely and eventually taken as a basis of conclusion when updating or enhancing the national set of standards.

5.1 Presentation of financial statements

As we have seen in Chapter 4 accounting standards are focused on financial reporting, which is the output of accounting, rather than bookkeeping techniques or other more process-related matters. Therefore the presentation of financial statements is the core issue, other issues clearly depending on it. There are no other issues addressed unless they are relevant for the presentation of financial statements. This certainly holds true for the International Financial Reporting Standards (IFRS) and the International Public Sector Accounting Standards (IPSAS), which are based on IFRS. But it would be difficult to find any recent national standard that is different from this.

At this stage it should be noted that the IPSAS should be used by public sector entities other than government business enterprises (GBEs). GBEs are entities that are controlled by public sector entities but are in commercial activities and do not rely on ongoing government funding. In some instances GBEs would be either public financial corporations (PFCs) or public non-financial corporations (PNFCs) in the sector model introduced in Chapter 1, although technically the definition is not the same and the delimitations may therefore be different. The sector model uses a 50 per cent threshold of revenues, while the GBE definition taken by IPSAS may be more rigorous, as it requires independency from government funding, which on some occasions may be reached only if market revenues account for much more than 50 per cent, perhaps close to 100 per cent. Thus some of the PFCs and PNFCs will not qualify as GBEs and should therefore adopt IPSAS, while GBEs are to apply IFRS. Examples of PNFCs not qualifying as GBEs often can be found in public transportation in urban areas. Public subways, trams and buses tend to generate revenue from ticket sales which often may exceed the 50 per cent line, but still rely on subsidies in order to successfully compete with individual transportation such as cars. They are PNFCs but not GBEs.

5.1.1 General purpose financial statements

Although it is clear that accounting standards focus on the presentation of financial statements, this does not automatically answer the purpose of financial statements. What are they there for? Who should read and eventually base their decision on them? Is it for the investors and financial analysts? The parliament? Perhaps the media? The citizens? The employees?

The answer in the case of the IPSAS is basically all of them.[1] The financial statements of public sector entities should give any reader a true and fair view of the financial situation of the entity. However, it does not address specific issues, which are relevant only for certain parts of the constituency. It is not focused on budget preparation and authorisation, as this would be a special purpose, but relevant only for those involved. Neither does it focus on specific requirements of the government financial statistics or issues raised only by investors. The target group of such general purpose financial statements is thus a very broad one. This is an advantage if it comes to a cost-benefit analysis and it also prevents the statements from being biased in one direction or the other or obstructing the view by giving too much space to relatively marginal issues. The disadvantage is that it rarely satisfies all the information needs of the more influential and powerful parts of the constituency, namely the parliament and its finance committees. Performance-related information, such as performance budgets and reports, are very likely to be requested. However, for a general picture of the financial situation, general purpose financial statements are indispensable. And, unlike parliaments and finance committees, large parts of the constituency are not in a position to ask for additional information. Particularly in the public sector, entities are accountable to a wide range of individuals, groups and organisations. This range is indisputedly wider than for private sector corporations, whose accountability is bound primarily to the shareholders.

> **Definition**
>
> **General purpose financial statements**
> Financial statements to provide a wide range of users with information useful for decision making and to demonstrate accountability of the entity for resources entrusted to it.

Contemplating the set of IPSAS that have been issued, the definition of general purpose financial statements raises the question, why do standards such as IPSAS 10 Financial Reporting in Hyperinflationary Economies, IPSAS 22 Disclosure of Information about the General Government Sector or IPSAS 24 Presentation of Budget Information in Financial Statements exist? The main reason is that those issues are considered to be relevant for general purpose financial statements, at least under certain circumstances. This circumstantial relevancy obviously can be observed in basically any standard, perhaps

---
[1] IPSAS 1.2.

with the exception of IPSAS 1 and 2 on the Presentation of Financial Statements and Cash Flow Statements respectively. But there are certainly public sector entities that have no foreign currency transactions or no investment property or no inventories, just to name a few examples. But nobody would doubt that these standards are there for good reason, as there are, of course, entities whose circumstances make the standards relevant. If there is hyperinflation, all reporting entities will be affected. All the public sector reporting entities around the world should ask themselves how they should manage the different scopes of consolidation under GFS and accrual financial reporting, as well as the comparison between actual and budget. The latter two are, as a matter of fact, public sector-specific issues. But the existence of such issues is perhaps the strongest argument for public sector-specific standards. GFS and budgets are a vital part of the public sector reality and make it substantially different from the private sector reality.

General purpose financial statements prepared and presented under IPSAS have to observe distinctive qualitative characteristics. The main principles can be found in IPSAS 1, which assigns responsibility to the reporting entity, which is to formulate and impose accounting policies that ensure that financial statements meet those characteristics (IPSAS 1.37). Appendix 2 of IPSAS 1 provides a summary of the qualitative characteristics, which are listed below:

1 understandability;
2 relevance;
   (a) materiality;
3 reliability;
   (a) faithful presentation;
   (b) substance over form;
   (c) neutrality;
   (d) prudence; and
   (e) completeness;
4 constraints;
   (a) timeliness; and
   (b) balance between benefit and cost.

While the first three groups represent positive characteristics that will improve financial reporting when observed, the fourth group, constraints, is imposing limits on the first three groups, in the sense that perhaps more and deeper investigation could improve completeness or faithful representation, but would take so much time or be so costly it would harm the quality of the financial reporting. The accounting policies must observe further principles prescribed in IPSAS 1, 3 and 14, which are:

1 going concern (IPSAS 1.38 ff.);
2 consistency of presentation (IPSAS 1.42 ff.);
3 materiality and aggregation (IPSAS 1.45 ff.);
4 prohibition of offsetting in most instances (IPSAS 1.48 ff.);
5 comparative information (IPSAS 1.53 ff.);
6 prospective adoption and disclosure of effects of changes in estimates (IPSAS 3.37 ff.);
7 retrospective correction of errors (IPSAS 3.46 ff.); and
8 recognition of adjusting events after reporting date and disclosure of non-adjusting events after the reporting date (IPSAS 14).

These two lists of principles and qualitative characteristics may look abundant and perhaps also a bit disorganised at first glimpse, but they are the core of accrual-based accounting according to IPSAS. In the absence of a conceptual framework, something other standards like IFRS have issued, the IPSAS-Board has included and enumerated the necessary principles and characteristics in IPSAS 1, 3 and 14. This may change once the work on the conceptual framework, which was started in 2006, is completed, tentatively by 2012. This situation does, however, not infringe the suitability of the principles and qualitative characteristics which are generally accepted throughout the profession and the academic world.

5.1.2 Statement of financial performance

From the users' perspective the most prominent financial statement is perhaps the statement of financial performance. At least in the public sector, where statement of financial position has only recently attracted attention, the statement of financial performance will probably be looked at first. Other names for the statement of financial performance are profit and loss (P&L) statement or statement of revenues and expenses or operating statement. While the term P&L refers to a for-profit situation not typical for the public sector, other names may be familiar in some jurisdictions but may be a source of confusion in others. It is therefore suggested to use the term statement of financial performance, at least for public sector entities.

The statement of financial performance shows the revenues, the expenses and – bottom line – the surplus or the deficit. IPSAS 1.102 and 1.103 require a minimum of the following line items to be presented, respectively:

1 revenue from operating activities;
2 finance costs;
3 share of net surpluses or deficits of associates and joint ventures accounted for using the equity method; and
4 surplus or deficit.

    (a) surplus or deficit attributable to minority interest; and
    (b) surplus or deficit attributable to owners of the controlling entity.

Further items are needed if this is required by another IPSAS or is necessary to present fairly the entity's financial performance. This is good example of a principle-based accounting standard, as it gives rationale behind it and thus does not allow reporting entities to provide insufficient information just because it was named in the list.

IPSAS requires a two-tier statement of financial performance, making a distinction between operating and finance activities. But compared to what is traditionally presented by public sector entities, this list is relatively brief. IPSAS 1.45 requires those preparing financial statements to aggregate immaterial amounts. This, of course, holds true not only for the statement of financial performance but equally for all the other financial statements and the notes. Financial reporting is not just printing out what is in the computer systems; it requires a reflection of the information presented before it is presented. In fact, many traditional, not standard-based financial statements are abundant in immaterial information, e.g. about expenses for newspaper subscriptions, but have critical black spots in highly material areas, such as pension schemes.

An example of a statement of financial performance under IPSAS, using both the functional classification and the classification by nature, is supplied in Exhibit 5.1.

The example in Exhibit 5.1 shows a one-tier statement of financial performance. However, IPSAS also allows the presentation of two- or three-tier statements of financial performance, distinguishing between operational, financial and extraordinary activities. Under IPSAS extraordinary items are still allowed, although not encouraged, because the public sector rather than private enterprise is confronted with natural disasters that are truly extraordinary, such as a tsunami. The downside of these items is that they do not follow the same classification of line items, as the ordinary ones, and are more vulnerable for excessive use. In fact, the IFRS no longer allow for extraordinary items and also in

Exhibit 5.1   Sample statement of financial performance (by function)

	Note	200X	200X-1
Revenue			
Taxes	1	X	X
Transfers	2	X	X
Fees	3	X	X
Other		X	X
Total Revenue		X	X
Expenses			
General public service	10	(X)	(X)
Defense		(X)	(X)
Public order & safety		(X)	(X)
Education	11	(X)	(X)
Health	12	(X)	(X)
Social protection		(X)	(X)
Housing		(X)	(X)
Culture		(X)	(X)
Economic affairs		(X)	(X)
Environment		(X)	(X)
Other		(X)	(X)
Finance cost	13	(X)	(X)
Total Expenses		X	X
Share of surplus (deficit) of associates		X	(X)
Surplus/(deficit) of the period		X	X
Minority interest		X	X

▶

Exhibit 5.1 *(Continued)* **Sample statement of financial performance (by nature)**

	Note	200X	200X-1
Revenue			
Taxes	1	X	X
Transfers	2	X	X
Fees	3	X	X
Other		X	X
Total Revenue		X	X
Expenses			
Salaries, employee benefits	4	(X)	(X)
Transfers	5	(X)	(X)
Supplies	6	(X)	(X)
Depreciation	7	(X)	(X)
Impairment losses	8	(X)	(X)
Other		(X)	(X)
Finance cost	9	(X)	(X)
Total Expenses		X	X
Share of surplus (deficit) of associates		X	(X)
Surplus/(deficit) of the period		X	X
Minority interest		X	X

the IPSAS the official option has been suppressed, although it still allows the presentation of such items.[2]

5.1.3 Statement of financial position

The statement of financial position is sometimes also called balance sheet. It shows the assets and liabilities of the reporting entity. Bottom line is an item called net assets/equity. This is what is called equity in the private sector. If assets exceed liabilities, net assets/equity is positive. However, many public sector entities experience a negative net

---

[2] 1 January 2007, effective 1 January 2008.

assets/equity position. In the private sector this would lead to the immediate default of the entity, but public sector entities are usually protected from default. This is certainly the case for governments, but often includes other entities such as public agencies and international organisations. That is why negative net assets/equity may prevail over a longer period of time than in the private sector. But despite the different legal circumstances, it should be clear that negative net assets/equity describes a situation that economically is not feasible in the long run, certainly not for public sector agencies, but not even for governments or international organisations. It says no less than that the assets would not cover the liabilities. Obviously liquidation or not a going concern is less likely in the public sector and may be ruled out in the short run, but if the situation persists, in the long run it means that the borrowings are never backed by any assets. This is, even under an eternal going-concern assumption, not feasible.

This is, however, exactly why there is an increased interest in the financial position of public sector entities and the emergence of this sort of statement. The statement of financial position is required by IPSAS 1.88 to include the following items:

1 property, plant and equipment;
2 investment property;
3 intangible assets;
4 financial assets (excluding amounts shown under 4, 6 and 8);
5 investments accounted for using the equity method;
6 inventories;
7 recoverables from non-exchange transactions (taxes and transfers);
8 receivables from exchange transactions;
9 cash and cash equivalents;
10 taxes and transfers payable;
11 payables under exchange transactions;
12 provisions;
13 financial liabilities;
14 minority interest; and
15 net assets/equity.

IPSAS requires a distinction between current and non-current assets and liabilities. The term current refers to assets and liabilities that are due to be settled within one business cycle or 12 months; or what is cash or cash equivalents (IPSAS 1.76 and 1.80). Other classifications, e.g. the one used in many Continental European countries distinguishing between administrative and non-administrative assets, may be used, but only as a secondary classification in full compliance with the current and non-current classification.[3] Exhibit 5.2 features an example of a statement of financial position.

5.1.4 Statement of cash flows

The statement of cash flows obviously is closest to the former cash basis of accounting. It is therefore used to bridge the gap between cash and accrual basis by many first-time adopters of accrual accounting. But it has a purpose on its own and therefore should be maintained even after the conversion. This purpose is to present the way cash and cash equivalents are generated and used.

---

[3] Administrative assets are the ones used for administrative purposes, i.e. the production and delivery of goods and services by the public administration. Non-administrative assets are held for investment purposes.

Exhibit 5.2 Sample statement of financial position

	Note	200X	200X-1
ASSETS			
Current Assets			
Cash/Cash Equivalent	1	X	X
Receivables	2	X	X
Inventories	3	X	X
Other current assets		X	X
Total Current Assets		X	X
Non-Current Assets			
Investments in associates	4	X	X
Other financial assets		X	X
Infrastructure, property, plant & equipment	5	X	X
Land and buildings	6	X	X
Intangibles	7	X	X
Other non-financial assets		X	X
Total Non-Current Assets		X	X
TOTAL ASSETS		X	X
LIABILITIES			
Current Liabilities			
Payables		X	X
Short-term borrowings		X	X
Short-term provisions	8	X	X
Short-term employee benefits	9	X	X
Other	10	X	X
Total Current Liabilities		X	X
Non-Current Liabilities			
Long-term borrowings	11	X	X
Long-term provisions	12	X	X
Long-term employee benefits	13	X	X
Total Non-Current Liabilities		X	X
TOTAL LIABILITIES		X	X
NET ASSETS/EQUITY			
Capital contributed		X	X
Revaluation reserves	14	X	X
Reserves		X	X
Accumulated surpluses/deficits	15	X	X
Minority interest		X	X
TOTAL NET ASSETS/EQUITY		X	X

IPSAS 2.9 requires the cash flow statement to be based on cash and cash equivalents. This deliberately excludes positions like receivables and payables, which of course may not be used to make payments. IPSAS 2.18 requires the distinction between operating, investing and financing activities. It is thus not permissible under IPSAS to use the T-account type of cash flow statement distinguishing only between cash inflows and outflows. The cash flow from operating activities may be determined by either the direct or indirect method, although the direct method is given priority. The indirect method is easier to adopt, while the direct method in practice requires IT systems to be configured that way. Exhibit 5.3 features an example of the direct method and Exhibit 5.4 one of the indirect method.

Exhibit 5.3 Sample cash flow statement (direct method)

	Note	200X	200X-1
CASH FLOWS FROM OPERATING ACTIVITIES			
Receipts			
Tax Receipts	1	X	X
Sales of Goods and Services		X	X
Grants	2	X	X
Other	3	X	X
Payments			
Employee cost		(X)	(X)
Suppliers		(X)	(X)
Other	4	(X)	(X)
NET CASH FLOW FROM OPERATING ACTIVITIES		X	X
CASH FLOWS FROM INVESTING ACTIVITIES			
Purchase of Property, Plant & Equipment	5	(X)	(X)
Purchase of Financial Instruments		(X)	(X)
Proceeds from Sale of Financial Instruments		X	X
NET CASH FLOW FROM INVESTING ACTIVITIES		(X)	(X)
CASH FLOWS FROM FINANCING ACTIVITIES			
Proceeds from Borrowings		X	X
Repayment of Borrowings		(X)	(X)
NET CASH FLOW FROM FINANCING ACTIVITIES		X	X
Net Increase/(Decrease) in Cash Equivalents		X	(X)
Cash and Cash Equivalents at beginning of period		X	X
Cash and Cash Equivalents at end of period		X	X

Exhibit 5.4 Sample cash flow statement (indirect method)

	Note	200X	200X-1
CASH FLOWS FROM OPERATING ACTIVITIES			
Surplus/(deficit)		X	(X)
Non-Cash Movements			
Depreciation	1	X	X
Increase in Provision	2	X	X
Increase in Payables		X	X
Increase in Receivables		(X)	(X)
(Gains)/Losses from sale of Property		(X)	(X)
NET CASH FLOW FROM OPERATING ACTIVITIES		X	X
CASH FLOWS FROM INVESTING ACTIVITIES			
Purchase of Property, Plant & Equipment	5	(X)	(X)
Purchase of Financial Instruments		(X)	(X)
Proceeds from Sale of Financial Instruments		X	X
NET CASH FLOW FROM INVESTING ACTIVITIES		(X)	(X)
CASH FLOWS FROM FINANCING ACTIVITIES			
Proceeds from Borrowings		X	X
Repayment of Borrowings		(X)	(X)
NET CASH FLOW FROM FINANCING ACTIVITIES		X	X
Net Increase/(Decrease) in Cash Equivalents		X	(X)
Cash and Cash Equivalents at beginning of period		X	X
Cash and Cash Equivalents at end of period		X	X

There is, as for the statements of financial performance and position, a list of minimum line items (IPSAS 2.22, 2.25 and 2.26) that are required.

5.1.5 Changes of net assets/equity

Changes of net assets/equity can occur basically because of two reasons. First, the entity reports a surplus or deficit. Under double entry accounting this result is shown in the statement of financial performance and at the same time in the statement of financial position. A surplus leads to a situation in which the assets exceed the liabilities plus the previous net asset/equity; a deficit will have the opposite effect. The surplus or the deficit are then allocated to the net asset/equity or – more likely in private sector corporations – paid out as a dividend. These transactions are handled through net assets/equity and shown in this statement.

The second reason for transactions is less normal and in most cases raises serious concerns. The entity books transactions directly to net assets/equity, rather than through the statement of financial performance. There are valid reasons for such a booking, e.g. contributions from owners such as share capital. Other valid examples include the optional treatment of actuarial gains and losses of pension plans according to IPSAS 25.105. But it can be tempting, for example, to write off losses directly like this, avoiding their presentation in the statement of financial performance. In most cases this is illicit and against accounting standards. Thus this statement of changes in net assets/equity should illustrate that there have been no such transactions. In good, positive examples it will indeed show very little information, perhaps only the surplus or deficit and its allocation (see Exhibit 5.5).

The statement of changes in net assets/equity is required by IPSAS 1.118 and 1.119 to include the following positions:

1 surplus or deficit for the period;
2 each item of revenue and expense, which, as required by other standards, is recognised directly in net assets/equity, and the total of these items;
3 total revenue and expense for the period, showing separately the total amounts attributable to owners of the controlling entity and to minority interest; and
4 for each component of net assets/equity separately disclosed, the effects of changes in accounting policies and corrections of errors.

The slim character of the statement of changes in net assets/equity often leads to its integration into the statement of financial performance. This is understandable, but not in accordance with the rules-based formulation of paragraph 118 requiring a separate component.

5.1.6 Notes

While the requirements discussed and the examples featured in Sections 5.1.2 to 5.1.5 apply the so-called face of the financial statements, there is substantially more information required behind that face, as part of the so-called notes. The notes are required by IPSAS 1.127 to present the following:

1 information about the basis of preparation of the financial statements and the specific accounting policies selected and applied for significant transactions and other events;
2 information required by International Public Sector Accounting Standards that is not presented elsewhere in the financial statements; and
3 additional information that is not presented on the face of the financial statements but that is necessary for a fair presentation.

Point 1 is often more briefly referred to as 'accounting policies'; points 2 and 3 as 'disclosures'. Point 2 includes two types of requirements. These are as follows:

1 Information required to be presented either on the face of the financial statement or in the notes.
2 Information required to be presented in the notes only.

Sub-classifications obviously can be presented either on the face or in the notes, while supplementary information such as related party disclosures (IPSAS 20) are to be presented in the notes only. The face of the financial statements should not be cluttered with excessive information.

Exhibit 5.5 Sample statement of changes in net assets/equity

	Attributable to owners of the controlling entity						Minority Interest	Total net asset/equity
	Contributed Capital	Revaluation Reserves	Other Reserves	Translation Reserves	Accumulated Surpluses/(Deficit)	Total		
Balance at 31 December 20X0	X		X	(X)	X	X	X	X
Changes in Accounting Policies					(X)	(X)		(X)
Restated Balance	X		X	(X)	X	X	X	X
Changes in Net Assets/Equity for the Year 20X1								
Revaluation Gains on Property, Plant and Equipment		X				X	X	X
Loss on revaluation		(X)				(X)	(X)	(X)
Exchange rate differences on translating foreign operations				(X)		(X)	(X)	(X)
Actuarial gains/(losses) on Post-Employment Benefits		X				X	X	X
Transactions recognized directly in Net Assets/Equity		X		(X)		X	X	X
Surplus/(Deficit) for the Period					X	X	X	X
Total recognized changes to Net Assets/Equity	X	X		(X)	X	X	X	X
Balance at 31 December 20X1	X		X	(X)	X	X	X	X
Changes in Net Assets/Equity for the Year 20X2								
Revaluation Gains on Property, Plant and Equipment		X				X	X	X
Losses on revaluation		(X)				(X)	(X)	(X)
Exchange rate differences on translating foreign operations				X		X	X	X
Actuarial gains/(losses) on Post-Employment Benefits		X				X	X	X
Transactions recognized directly in Net Assets/Equity		X		(X)		X	X	X
Surplus/(Deficit) for the Period					X	X	X	X
Total recognized changes to Net Assets/Equity	X	X		(X)	X	X	X	X
Balance at 31 December 20X2	X		X	(X)	X	X	X	X

5.2 Functionality of accounting standards

There is large number of IPSAS. So far 26 accrual-based standards have been issued. Beside IPSAS 1 on the Presentation of Financial Statements, IPSAS 2 on Cash Flow Statements, IPSAS 3 on Accounting Policies, Changes in Accounting Estimates and Errors and IPSAS 14 on Events after the Reporting Date, each IPSAS addresses a particular kind of item. They are portrayed in Section 5.3.

But all the IPSAS follow a common functionality, which is taken from the IFRS. This functionality includes three main issues, recognition, measurement and disclosure, which are addressed by all standards, although they may be more or less important in a particular area. If this functionality is fully understood, it is relatively easy to read and understand each IPSAS, even if no further information is available. Furthermore, the most recent standards include practical examples in the so-called 'IG' (implementation guidance) and rationale behind the standard in the 'BC' (basis of conclusion) at the end of each standard. This also helps the understanding of the standards.

5.2.1 Recognition

Recognition is whether an item or a transaction is booked into a double entry accounting system and presented on the face of the financial statements. The answer is obviously yes in many instances, but may be no in some. Let us consider an easy example: a truck. Everybody would instantly agree that a truck needs to be booked into the statement of financial position under property, plant and equipment. Thus it should be recognised. But what about a truck that has been presented to us as a donation? Even if it has been purchased: what about booking it as an expense, as it has been done under the cash basis of accounting for many years? This relatively easy example shows that some thoughts and guidance about recognition is well worth it. Certainly more controversial are examples of pension plans or provisions for environmental damages.

That is why all the IPSAS are addressing recognition. In many cases they are requiring recognition if certain criteria are met; in a few other cases, such as contingent liabilities, they deny recognition.

5.2.2 Measurement

If recognition is required, but also only if disclosure is required, the IPSAS are providing guidance in respect of measurement. This could also be called valuation. If the truck from the example in the previous section is recognised, what is its value? What is the value of pension plans or environmental damages? Usually there are several options in respect of measurement, certainly for the standard setter, but in some instances also for the preparer as IPSAS allows for different options. The main methods of measurement for assets and liabilities are listed below.

1 **Fair value method**
The amount for which an asset could be exchanged, or a liability settled, between knowledgeable, willing parties in an arm's length transaction.[4] This may be either a price traded on a market or a best estimate, usually based on the discounted cash flow method.

---

[4] IPSAS-Board (2007) Glossary.

2 **Cost method**
The amount that has been paid upon acquisition minus the depreciation over useful life.

3 **Lowering of cost or net realisable value**
The amount that has been paid upon acquisition or one that could be realised when selling it, whichever is lower.

4 **Nominal value**
The face value of a financial asset or liability.

IPSAS 16 Investment Property, for example, requires measurement based on the fair value method, while IPSAS 17 Property, Plant and Equipment offers both the cost method or the fair value method under the revaluation model. IPSAS 12 Inventories is an example for the lower of cost or net realisable value and IPSAS 15 Financial Instruments allows nominal values, although with important exceptions. Thus, saying IPSAS brings fair value to the public sector may be right for those jurisdictions that previously have been under a cash basis of accounting, immediately expensing everything. But compared to other accounting standards, such as IFRS or FRS, IPSAS is clearly less focused on the concept of fair values. IPSAS takes into account that situations with an absence of a market are typical for the public sector. Even best estimates based on future cash flows are not feasible for the public sector in many circumstances, as the value of an asset is not so much dependent on future cash flows but on future service potential. For instance, a bridge may rarely attract any cash flows but still be very valuable to the community. A more cautious position on fair values is one of the characteristics of IPSAS.

But regardless of the method applied, measurement in almost any case requires some degree of judgement by the preparer. Even the very straightforward cost method requires a judgement about the classes of assets and the respective period of useful life for each class of assets. Conceding that judgement is necessary is sometimes difficult to accept for accountants. But accounting standards, such as the IPSAS, are helping them by providing generally accepted guidance for their professional judgement. Although judgement is also part of the recognition and disclosure functions, it is most important in respect of measurement.

5.2.3 Disclosures

The last, but certainly not the least, functionality of accounting standards is disclosure requirements. In order to keep the face of the financial statements clean, but also to report information that cannot be presented adequately in a financial statement, such as risks, the IPSAS require disclosures. In a few cases, e.g. for contingent liabilities, IPSAS has taken a deliberate decision not to recognise them, but to disclose them instead (IPSAS 19.35). Disclosures are, as described in Section 5.1.6, part of the notes. Obviously they may take different forms of presentation. Some information is best presented in tables or exhibits, other in plain text. If there is a preferential form of presentation, IPSAS will include this guidance. In many cases, however, it leaves this decision on the layout to the person preparing the financial statements.

For many public sector entities, disclosures are a rather new phenomenon. Its effects should not be underestimated. Very much like any information on the face of the financial statements, the information needs to be gathered during the reporting period, consolidated and presented in a timely manner. Unless the entity is really very small, systems for data collection and storage are likely to be necessary.

5.3 Issue- or item-related IPSAS

While IPSAS 1, 2, 3 and 14, which are portrayed in the previous two sections, are general standards, applying across all items that are presented in the financial reports, all the other IPSAS are related to specific issues or items. This can be either a specific issue like consolidation or a specific line item like property, plant and equipment. These standards obviously are applicable only if this issue or item arises in the reporting entity. For instance, many local governments and their entities will not have any positions or transactions in foreign currencies. They do not have to worry about this – not because of their size or level, but because the issue or item is absent. If they decide to make transactions in foreign currencies, no matter how small or local the entity is, it has to comply with the respective standard. There may be local governments, for instance in border regions, that constantly experience substantial transactions and clearly need such a standard. That is why IPSAS does not scope out certain issues for certain entities. It is the entities that have to find out whether it is relevant or not.

If these standards are to be classified into groups with common characteristics, there is no way of avoiding double counts. Many standards address both the statement of financial performance and the statement of financial position or even both the active and the passive side of the balance sheet. This is, of course, a result of double entry bookkeeping. An attempt of such a grouping is made in Table 5.1, but it is by no means exhaustive.

Obviously, all standards are following the same principles, which have been outlined in the previous sections. However, they require quite specific treatments of the positions

Table 5.1   Non-exhaustive classification of IPSAS

Presentation and general principles	IPSAS 1 Presentation of Financial Statements
	IPSAS 2 Cash Flow Statements
	IPSAS 3 Accounting Policies, Changes in Accounting Estimates and Errors
	IPSAS 10 Financial Reporting in Hyperinflationary Economies
	IPSAS 14 Events after the Reporting Date
	IPSAS 22 Disclosure of Information about the General Government Sector
	IPSAS 24 Presentation of Budget Information in Financial Statements
Non-financial assets	IPSAS 11 Construction Contracts
	IPSAS 12 Inventories
	IPSAS 13 Leases
	IPSAS 16 Investment Property
	IPSAS 17 Property, Plant and Equipment
	IPSAS 21 Impairment of Non-Cash Generating Assets
	IPSAS 26 Impairment of Cash Generating Assets

Table 5.1 *(Continued)*

Financial assets and liabilities	IPSAS 5 Borrowing Cost
	IPSAS 7 Investments in Associates
	IPSAS 8 Interest in Joint ventures
	IPSAS 13 Leases
	IPSAS 15 Financial Instruments: Disclosure and Presentation
	IPSAS 21 Impairment of Non-Cash Generating Assets
	IPSAS 25 Employee Benefits
	IPSAS 26 Impairment of Cash Generating Assets
Other assets and liabilities	IPSAS 19 Provision, Contingent Assets and Contingent Liabilities
	IPSAS 25 Employee Benefits
Consolidation	IPSAS 6 Consolidated and Separate Financial Statements
	IPSAS 7 Investments in Associates
	IPSAS 8 Interest in Joint Ventures
	IPSAS 15 Financial Instruments
	IPSAS 22 Disclosure of Information about the General Government Sector
Expenses	IPSAS 4 The Effects of Changes in Foreign Exchange Rates
	IPSAS 5 Borrowing Cost
	IPSAS 12 Inventories
	IPSAS 13 Leases
	IPSAS 16 Investment Property
	IPSAS 17 Property, Plant and Equipment
	IPSAS 21 Impairment of Non-Cash Generating Assets
	IPSAS 25 Employee Benefits
	IPSAS 26 Impairment of Cash Generating Assets
Revenues	IPSAS 9 Revenues from Exchange Transactions
	IPSAS 23 Revenue from Non-Exchange Transactions
Additional ways of presentation	IPSAS 18 Segment Reporting
	IPSAS 22 Disclosure of Information about the General Government Sector
	IPSAS 24 Presentation of Budget Information in Financial Statements
Governance-related information	IPSAS 20 Related Party Disclosures

and transactions they address and bar other possible treatments, although they might offer different options in some instances.

It is noteworthy that the entire set of IPSAS is on consolidated financial statements. Consolidation is essential for a true and fair presentation of the financial situation of an economic entity that comprises various legal entities. If there is no consolidation, transactions between the various entities are likely to inflate revenues and expenses, as well as financial assets and liabilities. This inflation of the items presented is not necessarily caused by illicit activities. It is quite normal that entities of the same group lend and borrow among each other. They are also likely to prefer goods and services provided by other group members, either because of loyalty or because of discounts and rebates offered. But these internal deals are not adding any value to the group as a whole; it is just a shifting of resources between the entities. This is eliminated when consolidating the entities, rather than just adding up the items.

5.4 Adoption of IPSAS

For the adoption of IPSAS there are basically two options. The first option is to implement IPSAS directly, the second to adopt IPSAS through national standards. While the two options differ substantially on the top level, they converge further down in the implementation process, as it comes to drafting and implementing the accounting manual. This can be seen in Exhibit 5.6.

Exhibit 5.6 Adoption of IPSAS directly or through national standards

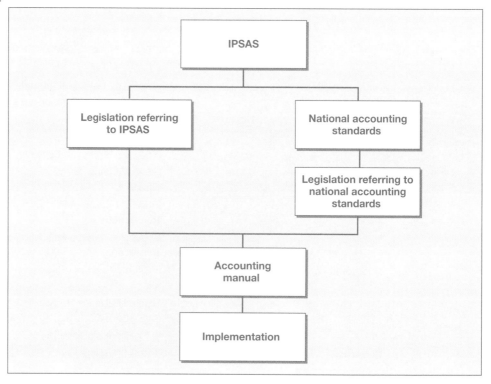

5.4.1 Implementation

The obvious option of a full set of accounting standards for public sector entities is to implement them in such entities. This would resemble very much the pattern observed when International Financial Reporting Standards (IFRS), then called International Accounting Standards (IAS), and Financial Reporting Standards (FRS-US GAAP) emerged late in the last century and listed companies, certainly the so-called blue chips, were required by stock exchange regulation to report under compliance with either IFRS or FRS, depending on the location of the stock exchange. This is sometimes referred to as soft legislation, because stock exchanges have no legislative power to impose such standards on the general public, but may set up rules to be observed by listed companies. They did so by straightforwardly implementing the respective standard. Only at a later stage of this development, in various countries and the European Union, the accounting standards (outside the United States usually the IFRS) become mandatory through legislation. Thus the same process might happen again for the International Public Sector Accounting Standards (IPSAS).

But as public sector entities generally are subject to administrative legislation, in most jurisdictions they are required to follow formal legislation for all parts of their activities, including financial reporting. This is contrary to private sector entities which generally are free to do what they want as long as it is within the boundaries of the law. Therefore the implementation of IPSAS usually will require the change of an existing law, e.g. a law on public sector financial management. This revised law will endorse the IPSAS and thus provide a legal basis for their implementation. However, implementation is compulsory for all entities under this law. Similar decisions can be observed in international organisations. Theoretically a partial endorsement of selected IPSAS is possible; however, this is not encouraged by the IPSAS-Board and financial reports under partial compliance with IPSAS may no longer be certified as true and fair in accordance with IPSAS. However, in practice partial endorsement takes place very much like partial endorsement of IFRS has taken place. Perhaps the most prominent example is Switzerland, which is implementing IPSAS on the federal level as well as in some states with a very small number of exceptions which are defined by law.

Example   City of Kloten – one of the first adopters of IPSAS back to status quo ante

> As part of a research project evaluating both the potential and the risks of an adoption of IPSAS in the accrual accounting system of Swiss local governments, in 2002 and 2003 the City of Kloten participated as a sample city. With 17,000 inhabitants the city is home to Zürich's international airport and faced an economic downturn after major setbacks to the aviation industry in the aftermath of 9/11 and SARS (severe acute respiratory syndrome), including the bankruptcy of the former flag carrier. It was therefore eager obtain a true and fair view of its financial situation and volunteered for the research project, which included the preparation of financial statements.
>
> In fact the study showed that IPSAS improves the financial reporting significantly, revealing substantial differences in about half a dozen positions as well as the overall presentation format, even when starting off from an accrual accounting model. The implementation proved to be challenging but manageable, mainly in terms of human resources. The results were well received by the city's authorities.[5]

---

[5] Bergmann, A., Gamper, A. (2004) Bergmann, A. (2006b).

> However, the State of Zürich legislation required the City of Kloten to present financial statements under the old accounting guidance in addition to the voluntary IPSAS-based reporting. This coexistence of old and new standards for many more years to come was simply too resource intensive for a relatively small city. The City Council therefore decided to go back to the minimum legal requirements and abandon the adopted IPSAS.

After a sufficient legal basis is provided, the entity needs to prepare for the implementation. The core document in this process is the accounting manual, which defines the way IPSAS is implemented in the reporting entity. It is obviously binding for all parts of the entity, as well as consolidated entities in respect of the information they provide to the reporting entity. The accounting manual decides on options IPSAS still provides. It also provides technical guidance for implementation, such as a chart of accounts or detailed definitions of classes of assets and liabilities, including the assumption on their useful life. The units of the reporting entity are actually implementing the accounting manual, rather than the IPSAS.

5.4.2 Adoption through national standards

There are many countries, especially the larger ones, noting the development of the IPSAS with interest, without directly implementing the standards in the various reporting entities. The IPSAS are rather taken as a basis for national standards, which may differ from the IPSAS, although they are following them more or less closely. This gives each jurisdiction the opportunity to make certain adaptations without having to draft their standards from scratch. The national standards are based on the same principles and adaptations may include country-specific terms and definitions, an opinion taken in respect of options IPSAS offers or additional guidelines for relevant areas. There are two main approaches to adopting IPSAS through national standards. These are as follows:

1 **Sector-specific approach**
   There is a separate set of national standards for the public sector.
2 **Sector-neutral approach**
   There is only one set of national standards that are applicable to private and the public sector, taking the differences of the two sectors into consideration and providing different guidelines where necessary. This approach is sometimes also called transaction neutral, as the same transaction is treated in the same way, regardless of within which sector it occurs.

While there are more countries, including particularly large ones like the United States, Canada or South Africa, that are taking the sector-specific approach, others such as Australia and New Zealand are taking a sector-neutral approach. The main advantages of a sector-neutral approach are enhanced comparability and understandability of financial information, mobility of the workforce involved, efficiency in standard setting and possibly better quality of standards.[6] The downside is in the higher complexity of standard setting and potential negligence of non-financial aspects.[7] As both approaches

---

[6] Simpkins, K. (2006) 64.
[7] Simpkins, K. (2006) 65.

exist in practice and show their strengths and weaknesses, we are likely to see both on an ongoing basis.

However, all the countries named as examples, except South Africa, traditionally have taken the International Financial Reporting Standards (IFRS) rather than IPSAS as a basis. While this is unlikely to change for the sector-neutral approach, unless for issues where there is no IFRS, this might well be different once a full set of IPSAS is available for those countries following a sector-specific approach. As a matter of fact South Africa is basing its public sector standards primarily on IPSAS and so is the Slovak Republic. Other countries monitor the IPSAS closely and use them in order to update their standards in public sector-specific areas. Thus there may well be an increasing number of countries issuing national standards for the public sector that are based directly on IPSAS. But those countries also acknowledge country-specific issues when issuing national standards.

Obviously, taking the approach to adopt IPSAS through national standards will lead to direct implementation of the national standards by the reporting entities. Thus one step further down, the reporting entities are confronted with very much the same situation as described in the previous section. They need a legal basis to implement the national standards and they need to set up an accounting manual and implement this.

5.5 Cash basis standard as a stepping stone

Beside the twenty something accrual basis of IPSAS, there is one cash basis standard. The IPSAS-Board clearly follows the mission to introduce and enhance the accrual basis of accounting in the public sector; it has provided this single cash basis standard as a stepping stone for those countries on the way to an accrual basis. It includes among its sections, a first section with the mandatory requirements, and a second one with additional non-mandatory encouragements. Developing countries especially are offered stepping stones like this on the way to accrual.

The first section and a part of the second section is indeed adopted by a few developing countries such as Vietnam, Mongolia and Mozambique, to name but some of them. This has clearly led to an improvement of the presentation of their cash basis financial statements as well as a first contact with the world of international accounting standards. They are now presenting a consolidated statement of cash receipts and payments as well as accounting policies and notes in accordance with the cash basis standards. Consolidation is clearly the most challenging requirement of this cash basis standard and perhaps the most substantial improvement considering the quality of financial statements.

However, for many countries and entities the cash basis standard is no feasible stepping stone, as they are already on a modified accrual basis of accounting. They have a statement of financial position, financial performance and a cash flow statement in place. They account for their assets and liabilities. The IT systems in place are fully fledged enterprise resource planning (ERP) systems. However, they may experience shortcomings in the field of consolidation or other areas such as provisions or employee benefits. Why should such countries or entities first be sent back to a cash basis on the way to full accrual? This may be considered as not only patronising, but also quite inefficient. This issue is often captured by the term sequencing. In such cases it is suggested to adopt full accrual accounting directly, in a project with a step-by-step approach. Examples of countries on this track include India, China, Azerbaijan and many Latin American countries.

5.6 Bottom line

The main objective of this chapter was to draw attention to accounting standards, in particular IPSAS, and how they work. Accounting standards, much more than any other aspect of public sector financial management, are highlighting the presentation of financial reports. The rationale behind accounting standards is one that is typical for an information society; they aim to provide all decision makers with the relevant information they need, without having to rely on further, perhaps restricted sources of information. The adoption of accounting standards is supposed to ensure this, at least in respect of information about the financial situation of the reporting entity.

While there are a few very broad standards about the presentation of financial statements, most of the accounting standards address specific issues and/or items. That is why it is difficult to give a comprehensive overview. However, most have implications on the statement of financial position as well as on the statement of financial performance. They all address recognition, measurement and disclosure, which are the three basic functionalities of accounting standards. These commonalities make it easier for the first-time user to understand a standard they have never seen before. But they also answer the basic questions that need to be answered in accounting.

The adoption of IPSAS takes two different ways around the world. While some countries, as well as most international organisations adopting IPSAS, have decided in their legislation to implement them directly, more countries are adopting the IPSAS through national standards, which are then implemented, instead of the IPSAS. While the indirect option obviously requires additional steps in order to develop the national standards in the first place, it provides the opportunity to make adaptations to each jurisdiction's needs. This may, after all, facilitate the implementation, although technically the same steps are required as for an implementation of an international standard. A certificate confirming compliance with either a national or the international standard may be obtained only if the respective standard is adopted in full.

For lesser developed countries the IPSAS offer a cash basis standard which is supposed to be used as a stepping stone towards full accrual. While this is certainly the way to go for those countries still on cash accounting, it is rather doubtful whether countries that already have significant elements of accrual accounting in place would bother going back to that. They would rather select a step-by-step strategy, gradually improving their accruals towards full compliance with IPSAS.

Work assignments

1 All the financial statements under IPSAS give a rather condensed, highly aggregated view. This is sometimes seen as a lack of accuracy. Take a view about this issue.

2 Under IPSAS the statement of financial position gains a prominent role. Please illustrate the benefit of this statement.

3 The IPSAS all refer to a common set of accounting principles. Name these principles and show how they work in connection with the detailed provisions in the standards.

4 Decide whether the following issues are referring to recognition, measurement or disclosure. Give a reason for your answer.

(a) Minor purchases of stationery.

(b) Asbestosis class action by the users of an affected building.

(c) Renovation and improvement of a property.

(d) Potential financial risk of the upcoming sports championships for the local council (e.g. security costs).

(e) Difficulties finding new tenants for a vacant investment property.

(f) Downsizing of defence forces resulting in redundant property.

5 The IPSAS can be adopted either directly or through national standards. What are the advantages and disadvantages of each way? Propose which kind of institution/country should use which way by using characteristics such as size of the country, languages used, tradition in standard setting, private sector standards in place, legal system and perhaps others.

6 Evaluate the use that cash-basis IPSAS can have in promoting the adoption of full accrual accounting.

Interface to national concepts

1 Check if the IPSAS are adopted by some/all public sector entities in your country/international organisation. If so, is it the cash or accrual basis of IPSAS?

2 Are there national accounting standards making reference to IPSAS?

3 Are there any plans in respect of change in the situation in the near future?

6 | Internal control

Learning objectives

- Understand the rationale of internal control and appraise its relevancy.

- Discuss internal control in the context of the other tasks of public sector financial management.

- Position the two schools of internal control, the Napoleonic and the Nordic school.

- Describe the implications of the Sarbanes-Oxley Act from an international public sector perspective.

- Describe the COSO model as one of the options to comply with section 404 of the Sarbanes-Oxley Act.

- Appraise the COSO model without the implications of the Sarbanes-Oxley Act.

- Locate the additional implication the PIfC initiative has.

- Discuss the concepts of Sarbanes-Oxley, COSO and PIfC from the perspective of the two schools.

- Argue for or against various types of Central Harmonisation Units.

- Devise a simple internal control system for a public sector entity.

Key terms

Central Harmonisation Unit (CHU)	Financial control	PIfC
CHU	Information asymmetry	Public Internal financial Control (PIfC) initiative
COSO	Internal audit	Sarbanes-Oxley Act
COSO model	Internal control	

In the previous chapters we have looked at various tasks of public sector financial management, especially financial planning and budgeting, as well as financial accounting and reporting. This has included a discussion of auditing or rather, as we have seen, assurance, in both the planning and the reporting tasks. However, even the most sophisticated concepts of planning and reporting cannot prevent misconduct by directors, managers and staff. Such misconduct may result in strong biases to public sector financial management, possibly overshadowing its positive effects. In some instances, such misbehaviour even qualifies as a crime. That is where internal control takes the floor.

> **Definition**
>
> **Internal control**
> Internal control means any systems, measures or processes in order to ensure that public sector financial management operates in an efficient and effective manner, as well as in full compliance with any standards or laws.

Internal control is supposed to ensure proper, unbiased working conditions for the other tasks of public sector financial management, as well as to prevent and uncover criminal behaviour of the actors. As this book is about public sector financial management, rather than criminal law, its focus is on the proper and unbiased working conditions.

6.1 Role of internal control

6.1.1 Systems against information asymmetry

The fundamental problem that internal control is trying to resolve is not the misconduct itself, but rather the information asymmetry that potentially results in misconduct. Now what is information asymmetry? Information asymmetry means that actors in a specific process have information superior to that of other actors in the same process. Let us consider the example of the preparation, auditing and presentation of a financial report. Staff and management involved in the preparation obviously have the largest amount of information.[1] They have full access to the IT systems running the financial accounting, as well as other processes including sales, payroll and others. Of course, their perception may be obstructed by the sheer volume of information, but if they have a strong interest in a

---

[1] It is unclear, but also irrelevant, whether staff or management has more information. The management clearly takes the ultimate responsibility. There are information asymmetries between the two, which may obviously cause the same difficulties as any information asymmetry.

specific matter they may find out. Getting the information is, however, not the most critical process; delivering or withholding the information is obviously more risky. Staff and management normally have the very human tendency to overstate positive information and withhold the not so good bits and pieces. This may, of course, be just the opposite in the first few weeks a new management takes over. They are perhaps overstating the negative aspects, in order to attribute them to their predecessors and not be held accountable.

Coming back to the process of preparing, auditing and presenting the financial reports, a biased preparation is quite difficult for auditors to uncover. Auditors generally have access to all information, but compared to the staff and management only limited time and resources. For them it is simply impossible to check all the transactions and review all the judgements the management has to make when preparing the reports. The auditors' opinion is already potentially biased by information only the management is aware of. Further down the process the financial reports are presented to the general public. The readers of these reports obviously have an extremely limited amount of information available, usually not much more than what is written in the report. Staff, management and even the auditors have a strong information advantage over the general public.

Internal control has the role of:

1 limiting the information advantage of staff and management in critical areas; and
2 ensuring that the remaining information advantage is not used for their own interest, which contradicts with the interest of other stakeholders.

Internal control should give special attention to those abuses of the information advantage that are criminal acts defined as such by criminal law. But it should also address adverse behaviour below that level, as such behaviour may also bias the information provided to decision makers and is often considered to be an early stage of what perhaps later develops into a criminal act. In an international context it is important to understand that the thresholds of a criminal act, as well as its appraisal by the legal system, vary strongly among different countries due to cultural differences. Although crimes like corporate fraud are crimes in most countries, they are defined in different ways and attract substantially different sentencing. But in many countries the criminal laws have recently become more rigorous in the aftermath of corporate scandals.

Information asymmetry as well as internal control as a remedy against information asymmetry have been taken more seriously in the public sector than in the private sector. In fact, the so-called Bureaucracy Model developed by Max Weber in the early twentieth century, which is one of the classic organisational theories and was perhaps most rigorously implemented by public sector entities, is focusing on a legal and logical way to exercise power within organisations. Many elements of Max Weber's Bureaucracy Model have been unearthed by the much more recent developments in the field of governance and internal control, unfortunately often without making proper reference. However, these more recent developments have taken place instead in the private sector, as a reaction to the corporate scandals.

6.1.2 The two schools of internal control

Information asymmetry is the undisputed rationale behind internal control systems. However, the public sector has a long tradition of two entirely different schools of how such systems should approach and resolve the task, the Napoleonic (or Latin) school and the Nordic (or Anglo-Saxon) school. As a matter of fact, the two schools are not limited to the issue of internal control; they are instead more general concepts of public administration. But the differences between the two schools are rarely as clearly visible as in the field of internal control.

The Napoleonic school could long be observed in countries like France, Italy, Belgium, Spain, Portugal and Greece, as well as in their former colonies in Africa, Latin America and South-East Asia. But in recent years the Nordic approach, which has long been used in Anglo-Saxon countries and Scandinavia, has gained ground, namely by the European Commission endorsing this approach during its reform in 2000.[2]

The Napoleonic school addresses the information asymmetries by a centralised and often very detailed transaction approval process. While line ministries, departments or agencies have some responsibility for the matter of the transaction, they first need to gain formal approval from financial controllers, which are usually part of the budget ministry or department, rather than line entity. Thus every transaction, on both the expenditure and the revenue side, basically needs to be approved by both the line entity and a financial controlling entity (and often a third entity responsible for the cash transaction itself). This shared responsibility obviously reduces information asymmetry in favour of the line entity, as the financial controlling entity may require full disclosure of any relevant information before the approval. As both entities are clearly set apart, their structural independency is probably improving compliance and making any form of misconduct more difficult and thus less likely. The downside is the relatively complicated, uneconomic and time-consuming process and, perhaps more relevant, the risk of unclear responsibilities in case of misconduct, as both (or all three) parties involved may hide behind formalities and blame the other for not paying enough attention.

The Nordic approach, on the other hand, follows the concept of managerial accountability and responsibility. The manager of the line unit is held accountable for each and every decision, transaction and the results thereof. In larger entities, the manager obviously needs to delegate some of the decisions; however, they remain responsible for the design and implementation of an internal control system. Internal audit will assist the manager in assessing and improving the control system. In contrast to the Napoleonic approach, the responsibility remains united and processes may be kept slim. But there is a need for internal control and audit systems to be in place.

Especially in countries on the historical borderline between the Latin and the Nordic culture, such as Canada or Switzerland, the systems used may differ between different parts of the country or include elements from both schools. However, the combination of the two approaches is not trivial, as it may easily lead to an overdose of control, paralysing the system, or insufficient control leaving the organisation exposed to substantial risks. These risks usually are not apparent, as they are due to information asymmetry and therefore emerge only when damage has already been done.

6.2 Private sector developments with implications for the public sector

Although the public sector has a long history of internal control, important developments have taken place in the private sector over the last few years, mainly in the aftermath of corporate scandals such as Enron or WorldCom. They are increasingly influencing the public sector. Two main private sector developments are discussed hereafter.

---

[2] De Koning, R. (2007) 38.

6.2.1 Sarbanes-Oxley Act

Some may find it difficult to understand why a textbook with a deliberately international scope is devoting an entire section to a United States law. As a matter of fact, the so-called Sarbanes-Oxley Act (briefly referred to as SOX here, otherwise also SarbOx or SOA) is a federal law of the United States of America (Pub. L. No. 107–204, 116 Stat. 745). Its official name is Public Company Accounting Reform and Investor Protection Act. But within its relatively brief existence, it was first introduced in 2002, it has gained an unparalleled influence on internal control well beyond the corporate sector and in countries around the world. And, even more importantly, there is no international equivalent, such as an international standard. Critics would add that this is for good reason, as the Act tends to be very bureaucratic and causes much inefficiency, but there is no real alternative in the field of internal control.[3] Although the official name Public Company Accounting Reform and Investor Protection Act might suggest that SOX is applicable only to listed commercial corporations, most of it has become applicable to the non-profit and public sectors in the United States, especially through tax and banking legislation, if not through specific laws on such entities.[4] That is why the pronouncement of this piece of national legislation in respect of internal control is addressed in this section.

SOX is divided into civilian law (sections 101 through to 501) and criminal law (sections 601 through to 1107), thus it also reflects the two tiers referred to in Section 6.1 of this book. Exhibit 6.1 provides an overview of the sections within SOX.

SOX apparently addresses various issues, including the overseeing of public accounting and auditing firms, independence of auditors, financial reporting, corporate governance, management responsibilities and, as mentioned before, corporate crimes. Internal control is addressed specifically in section 404 (SOX 404), which will be examined more closely hereafter.

Section 404, as presented in its full length in Exhibit 6.2, looks rather tame at the first glimpse. Basically it requires the management of an entity to report regularly on the internal control structures and procedures, including an assessment on their effectiveness. This assessment requires auditing and attesting by a registered public accounting firm. In fact, this leads to the requirement of three audit opinions on the following:[5]

1 Financial statements.
2 Management assessment of the internal control.
3 Auditor's own opinion about the internal control.

The requirement of such a report about internal control structures and procedures, together with the requirements of section 302, implicates that such structures and procedures are effectively implemented and documented. Recommendations specify features of such an internal control system. One of the models endorsed is the COSO framework, which is discussed in the next section of this book.[6]

Thus SOX itself does not give any precise guidance on how internal control should work, but it does require entities to develop, introduce and periodically assess an internal control system covering all structures and processes that are relevant to financial

---

[3] *Economist* (2007) 12.

[4] Jackson, P., Fogarty, T. (2006) 21 ff.

[5] Auditing Standard Number 2 issued by the US Public Company Accounting Oversight Board (PCAOB).

[6] Jackson, P., Fogarty, T. (2006) 176 ff.

Exhibit 6.1   Overview of the 2002 Sarbanes-Oxley Act

TITLE I – PUBLIC COMPANY ACCOUNTING OVERSIGHT BOARD

Sec. 101. Establishment; administrative provisions.

Sec. 102. Registration with the Board.

Sec. 103. Auditing, quality control, and independence standards and rules.

Sec. 104. Inspections of registered public accounting firms.

Sec. 105. Investigations and disciplinary proceedings.

Sec. 106. Foreign public accounting firms.

Sec. 107. Commission oversight of the Board.

Sec. 108. Accounting standards.

Sec. 109. Funding.

TITLE II – AUDITOR INDEPENDENCE

Sec. 201. Services outside the scope of practice of auditors.

Sec. 202. Preapproval requirements.

Sec. 203. Audit partner rotation.

Sec. 204. Auditor reports to audit committees.

Sec. 205. Conforming amendments.

Sec. 206. Conflicts of interest.

Sec. 207. Study of mandatory rotation of registered public accounting firms.

Sec. 208. Commission authority.

Sec. 209. Considerations by appropriate State regulatory authorities.

TITLE III – CORPORATE RESPONSIBILITY

Sec. 301. Public company audit committees.

Sec. 302. Corporate responsibility for financial reports.

Sec. 303. Improper influence on conduct of audits.

Sec. 304. Forfeiture of certain bonuses and profits.

Sec. 305. Officer and director bars and penalties.

Sec. 306. Insider trades during pension fund blackout periods.

Sec. 307. Rules of professional responsibility for attorneys.

Sec. 308. Fair funds for investors.

TITLE IV – ENHANCED FINANCIAL DISCLOSURES

Sec. 401. Disclosures in periodic reports.

Sec. 402. Enhanced conflict of interest provisions.

Sec. 403. Disclosures of transactions involving management and principal stockholders.

Sec. 404. Management assessment of internal controls.

Sec. 405. Exemption.

Sec. 406. Code of ethics for senior financial officers.

Sec. 407. Disclosure of audit committee financial expert.

Sec. 408. Enhanced review of periodic disclosures by issuers.

Sec. 409. Real-time issuer disclosures.

TITLE V – ANALYST CONFLICTS OF INTEREST

Sec. 501. Treatment of securities analysts by registered securities associations and national securities exchanges.

Exhibit 6.1 *(Continued)*

TITLE VI – COMMISSION RESOURCES AND AUTHORITY
Sec. 601. Authorisation of appropriations.
Sec. 602. Appearance and practice before the Commission.
Sec. 603. Federal court authority to impose penny stock bars.
Sec. 604. Qualifications of associated persons of brokers and dealers.

TITLE VII – STUDIES AND REPORTS
Sec. 701. GAO study and report regarding consolidation of public accounting firms.
Sec. 702. Commission study and report regarding credit rating agencies.
Sec. 703. Study and report on violators and violations.
Sec. 704. Study of enforcement actions.
Sec. 705. Study of investment banks.

TITLE VIII – CORPORATE AND CRIMINAL FRAUD ACCOUNTABILITY
Sec. 801. Short title.
Sec. 802. Criminal penalties for altering documents.
Sec. 803. Debts nondischargeable if incurred in violation of securities fraud laws.
Sec. 804. Statute of limitations for securities fraud.
Sec. 805. Review of Federal Sentencing Guidelines for obstruction of justice and extensive criminal fraud.
Sec. 806. Protection for employees of publicly traded companies that provide evidence of fraud.
Sec. 807. Criminal penalties for defrauding shareholders of publicly traded companies.

TITLE IX – WHITE-COLLAR CRIME PENALTY ENHANCEMENTS
Sec. 901. Short title.
Sec. 902. Attempts and conspiracies to commit criminal fraud offences.
Sec. 903. Criminal penalties for mail and wire fraud.
Sec. 904. Criminal penalties for violations of the Employee Retirement Income Security Act of 1974.
Sec. 905. Amendment to sentencing guidelines relating to certain white-collar offences.
Sec. 906. Corporate responsibility for financial reports.

TITLE X – CORPORATE TAX RETURNS
Sec. 1001. Sense of the Senate regarding the signing of corporate tax returns by chief executive officers.

TITLE XI – CORPORATE FRAUD AND ACCOUNTABILITY
Sec. 1101. Short title.
Sec. 1102. Tampering with a record or otherwise impeding an official proceeding.
Sec. 1103. Temporary freeze authority for the Securities and Exchange Commission.
Sec. 1104. Amendment to the Federal Sentencing Guidelines.
Sec. 1105. Authority of the Commission to prohibit persons from serving as officers or directors.
Sec. 1106. Increased criminal penalties under Securities Exchange Act of 1934.
Sec. 1107. Retaliation against informants.

Exhibit 6.2 Section 404 of Sarbanes-Oxley Act

SEC. 404. MANAGEMENT ASSESSMENT OF INTERNAL CONTROLS.

a RULES REQUIRED – The Commission shall prescribe rules requiring each annual report required by section 13(a) or 15(d) of the Securities Exchange Act of 1934 (15 U.S.C. 78m or 78o(d)) to contain an internal control report, which shall:

  1 state the responsibility of management for establishing and maintaining an adequate internal control structure and procedures for financial reporting; and

  2 contain an assessment, as of the end of the most recent fiscal year of the issuer, of the effectiveness of the internal control structure and procedures of the issuer for financial reporting.

b INTERNAL CONTROL EVALUATION AND REPORTING – With respect to the internal control assessment required by subsection (a), each registered public accounting firm that prepares or issues the audit report for the issuer shall attest to, and report on, the assessment made by the management of the issuer. An attestation made under this subsection shall be made in accordance with standards for attestation engagements issued or adopted by the Board. Any such attestation shall not be the subject of a separate engagement.

reporting. This is very much in accordance with the rationale behind internal control discussed in Section 6.1 of this book. This does not mean that this book endorses all the practical consequences. In fact, there is much valid criticism about the way the originally sound idea of section 404 is implemented in practice.[7] There is clearly no justification for a 'foolish, heavy-handed state interference', if this is its effect.[8]

In the author's view, the concept of materiality is applicable to internal control, like any other part of public sector financial management. Materiality levels may be quite low for some procedures, such as payments, but may be substantially higher for others. The practical implications of section 404, which are experienced by many corporations and an increasing number of public sector entities, in many instances could be avoided by adopting the principle of materiality. Obviously this concept currently is not being followed when applying SOX in the corporate world. In fact, this view has not yet gained many supporters within corporations that are obliged to comply with section 404. But as the public sector, and even more so the public sector outside the United States, may not be required to adopt section 404 legally, the principle of materiality should be taken into consideration. Only if SOX and the concept of materiality can be brought together may the outcome of the former be beneficial bottom line.

6.2.2 The COSO framework

Only with the emergence of SOX and similar legislation in other countries have entities been obliged to actually introduce an internal control system. But such systems have been in place well before, one of the more famous ones remarkably for non-profit institutions in close proximity to the public sector: the COSO Internal Control – Integrated Framework. COSO stands for Committee of Sponsoring Organisations of

---

[7] A comprehensive discussion about the various elements of the implementation guidance on SOX section 404 is provided in: FEE (2005).

[8] *Economist* (2007) 12.

the Treadway Commission. This framework for internal control in not-for-profit organisations, especially charities, has been there well before SOX, being first issued in 1992. But with SOX it has attracted attention well into the for-profit sector, as it has been endorsed as one of the possible frameworks to be used in order to comply with section 404 of SOX.

| Exhibit 6.3 | Policies and procedures for internal control |

List of policies and procedures to be defined and implemented in a public sector entity[9]

Budgeting
    i.e. budget preparation, budget authorisation, budget adjustment.

Appropriation/commitment
    i.e. authorisation, adjustment, record keeping.

Accounts receivable
    i.e. system requirement for invoice processing, payment deadlines, action to be taken to enforce payment, credit card procedures, cash storage and transportation, handling of errors.

Accounts payable
    i.e. record in system, check for appropriateness, check for errors, authorisation of payment, execution of payment, handling of errors.

Accounting
    i.e. recognition/inventory procedures, measurement/valuation procedures, general ledger procedures, consolidation procedures.

Human resources
    i.e. hiring procedures, dismissal procedures, new employee orientation, anti-discrimination and harassment policy, use of IT policy, continuous education policy, compensation policy.

Sales
    i.e. pricing guidelines, discount policy and procedures, refund policy and procedures, anti-corruption policy.

Expenses
    i.e. authorisation, travel policy, ticketing procedures, corporate credit cards policy.

IT/communications
    i.e. encryption procedures, privacy policy, illicit or inappropriate usage policy.

Facilities
    i.e. energy saving policy, building access procedures, dangerous goods procedures.

Public relations/media
    i.e. authorisation procedures, information policy.

Corporate governance
    i.e. committees, nomination procedures.

COSO defines internal control as 'a process, effected by an entity's board of directors, management and other personnel, designed to provide reasonable assurance regarding

---

[9] Based on Jackson, P.M., Fogarty, T.E. (2006) 180, but extended by the author.

the achievement of objectives in the following categories:

- effectiveness and efficiency of operations;
- reliability of financial reporting; and
- compliance with applicable laws and regulations'.[10]

This definition reflects the strong ties between internal control and financial reporting in compliance with any authoritative, binding guidance. This is similar to the definition used in this book. However, it goes beyond that, by including effectiveness and efficiency not only of public sector financial management, but of operations in general. This is not necessarily in contradiction to the author's view; it rather indicates a potential impact of internal control well beyond the scope of this textbook, which obviously is limited to public sector financial management. Taking this into account, the framework's implications on operations in the field of financial management, especially in respect of financial reporting, shall be examined more closely. But the definition also brings internal control in direct relation with the concept of assurance, which has been discussed in various earlier chapters. Thus internal control is an additional, further measure taken to ensure confidence in financial information. This reflects how much at risk the reliability of this information is. However, internal control takes care of the issue from within the organisation, emphasising the responsibility of the board, the management and the staff. In the public sector, however, as we have seen in Chapter 1, the delimitations between internal and external assurance are often blurred by delegating internal as well as external functions to the same organisation, such as the auditor general's office.

The COSO framework consists of five components, which are supposed to be viewed as an integrated process. They are integrated in the sense that there are strong relations and even dependencies between them that permanently need to be addressed by the management.

0 Starting point are the financial reporting objectives that need to be defined by the entity itself, as they vary from one entity to another. In particular, public sector entities follow financial reporting objectives that are different from those in other sectors, as they include aspects such as budgeting or financial statistics, but also follow slightly different principles, which put a lesser emphasis on future cash flows, as we have seen in Chapters 4 and 5.

1 The first component, but in fact the second stage of the process, is a risk assessment, which is related to the defined financial reporting objectives. This risk assessment refers to potential, material flaws in the financial reporting. It includes the definition of management action taken to mitigate these risks. Taking a broader perspective than just financial reporting, the risk assessment should include other operational risks, including criminal misbehaviour such as fraud.

2 The management needs to define the control environment. Perhaps the term environment is misleading for some readers, as it often refers to aspects outside the entity. However, in the COSO framework it refers to the so-called soft factors such as ethics and philosophy within the organisation.

3 Control activities are to be defined and implemented. Such activities include policies, for instance in the field of compensation, procedures, for instance for the approval of contracts, or IT-related measures, such as passwords or encryption.

---

[10] www.coso.org, 18 January 2007.

4 The fourth component is referred to as information and communication. It includes the capturing and processing of information used for the financial reporting, but also information needed for internal control itself.

5 The last component is devoted to monitoring. This includes an ongoing, independent evaluation of internal control as well as the reporting about internal control in order to take timely action if necessary.

The COSO framework does, of course, provide detailed guidelines as well as examples for each of the five components, as well as for the management of their interrelations.

Implementing COSO in a public sector entity, or in fact in any entity, means that policies and procedures need to be defined and implemented. Policies are general guidelines for the management and staff of the entity on how to handle certain issues, for instance staff compensation, travel expenses, the use of IT systems and others. They usually read like a list of activities that are encouraged, allowed but not encouraged, discouraged and forbidden. Procedures, on the other hand, are detailed workflows that describe what should be done and who is responsible for it. Procedures may be attached to policies, for instance travel approval procedures to the travel policy. However, the procedures will not provide any guideline for the decision maker, just state who is making which kind of decision. The guideline for the decision makers is part of the policy. Exhibit 6.3 lists the policies and procedures required in a public sector entity.

6.3 The PIfC – Public Internal financial Control initiative

In order to improve public sector internal financial control in the EU member states, namely the new accession states in Central and Eastern Europe, the European Commission has launched a Public Internal financial Control (PIfC) initiative. Beyond transparency and accountability this initiative aims at an eradication of corruption, which gives it a somewhat broader mission, well beyond those otherwise interested in public sector financial management or even public management.[11]

PIfC is clearly based on the Nordic school (see Section 6.1.2), which follows the concept of managerial accountability. It therefore requires:

1 a financial management and control (FMC) system including (among other things such as budgeting or accounting) internal control; and
2 an internal audit (IA).

These are to be introduced by public sector entities. As public sector entities usually consist of a rather large number of decentralised units, such as ministries and agencies, PIfC further requires a Central Harmonisation Unit (CHU) governing both FMC and IA or two separate CHUs governing FMC and IA respectively.

Thus the PIfC requires present and future EU member countries to implement a formal structure taking responsibility for internal control and internal audit. This structure is defined in a way to suffice with the needs of independency and managerial accountability. The countries are also required to provide an independent, centralised unit providing the necessary guidance for the decentralised internal control and internal audit units. PIfC further outlines the processes these institutions need to perform in order to achieve their goals. It also provides examples of legislation that should be enacted.

---

[11] De Koning, R. (2007) 11 ff.

In the following sections each of the three elements of PIfC, i.e. financial management and control, internal auditing and the Central Harmonisation Unit are further characterised and discussed.

6.3.1 Financial management and control

Financial management and control is perhaps the most pre-conditional element of the three. There need to be sound and comprehensive accounting systems, which provide clear and unbiased information about any position or transaction and compare it against the budget.[12] But this is not sufficient, as mere compliance is not enough to guarantee value for money. The system therefore needs to integrate performance information.

If systems are mentioned, this usually includes IT systems, but also human systems, i.e. organisational processes and structures. Financial management and control requires organisational provision to ensure managerial accountability. The public sector usually distinguishes between authorising officers and financial controllers. While the authorising officers are senior staff of the line entities (e.g. ministries or agencies), the financial controller used to be part of the centralised financial control unit. Apparently, spending decisions required ex-ante approval from both, as any ex-post approval would most likely fail to be effective if third parties in good faith were involved.

During new public management style reforms, financial controllers were, in some cases, decentralised. While decentralisation certainly improves the flow of information and speeds up decision making, it has a substantial downside. The financial controller is no longer independent from the authorising officer; the latter is usually the boss of the financial controller. Therefore independent control fails if no overruling rights are given to the financial controller or some sort of centralised financial control is still maintained. Both models can be observed in practice. However, any kind of financial control needs to be ex-ante, as otherwise it fails to prevent illicit transactions. Despite the preventive control mechanisms, the responsibility remains with management.

Therefore, management usually also requires some sort of ex-post financial control. In the public sector this ex-post control element is called inspectorate, but there is no conceptual reason why this task needs to be separated from financial control.[13] While this element may no longer prevent errors it should detect them and allow the management to take corrective action, if possible in respect of the transaction detected, if not at least for any future transactions. Thus both ex-ante and ex-post elements are necessary for an effective financial control system.

Financial control systems, however, tend to be onerous for management and staff. In order to keep the impact limited, they need to reflect the results of a risk analysis. The financial control measures taken need to reflect the risk and potential damage and balance them against the cost of the measure. It is not feasible to require the same sort of approval for small and standardised transactions as for large and unsystematic ones. If financial control can be addressed on the systems level, it is usually more efficient than on a case-by-case basis. Risk analysis and management provide the necessary information to tailor both effective and efficient financial control systems. One possible approach for the risk analysis and management is the COSO framework (see Section 6.2.2).

---

[12] De Koning, R. (2007) 52 ff.

[13] De Koning, R. (2007) 65.

6.3.2 Internal auditing

The second element, internal auditing, is relatively new to the public sector. It goes hand in hand with managerial responsibility.[14] If there is no managerial responsibility, there is also no need for internal auditing. In a system of managerial responsibility, internal audit has the role of assessing financial management and control, as well as proposing improvements to the management. It supports the management in operating a sound financial management and control system and therefore reports to the management and – unlike external audit – not to external stakeholders.

Internal audit should be functionally and operationally independent from the day-to-day operations. This is also the reason why it may not be included in the financial control, which is strongly involved in day-to-day operations. It obviously also needs to be independent from the management. There is an agreement between the manager and the internal auditor, called Internal Audit Charter. The internal auditor, similar to the external one, needs to follow a Code of Ethics and, of course, the law. In the public sector, the establishment of internal audit requires in most jurisdictions a separate law that guarantees the auditor's independence. The independence of the internal auditor is also the main distinction of the financial inspectors, which are part of the financial management and control system.

The work of the internal auditor should follow a multi-year plan, which needs to be endorsed but not otherwise influenced by the management. As internal audit is supporting the management, it becomes clear that there are several internal audit units within very large operations such as national or sub-national governments. Their multi-year plans may therefore become quite different, perhaps too different to be effective. That is where the Central Harmonisation Unit steps in.

6.3.3 Central Harmonisation Unit

In the two previous sections we have seen various elements of financial management and control, as well as of internal auditing. We have also seen that financial management and control, as well as internal auditing, are substantially decentralised, i.e. relevant units exist in all the line ministries and many other entities such as agencies. In order to improve the efficiency and effectiveness, however, some harmonisation is needed. That is where the central harmonisation usually steps in.

There are models of one or two Central Harmonisation Units.[15] In the two-unit model there are separate units for the harmonisation of financial management and control, and for internal auditing. This is the only feasible option if the Centralised Harmonisation Units are actively involved in the respective tasks, e.g. if the financial control and internal audit units of the Ministry of Finance act as Centralised Harmonisation Units and at the same time as the operational units within the ministry. The separation of control and internal audit then leads to the requirement of two separate units. There may, however, also be one overarching Central Harmonisation Unit, if this unit is not involved in any control or audit operation.

---

[14] De Koning, R. (2007) 61.

[15] De Koning, R. (2007) 71.

6.4 Bottom line

Internal control is perhaps one of the uglier but nonetheless necessary aspects of public sector financial management. It is ugly in the sense that it imposes sizeable restrictions on the members of an organisation, which are led by a certain amount of suspicion and distrust. If everybody was just perfect, there would be no need for internal control. But human insufficiencies unfortunately exist and need to be addressed if damage to the organisational entity, other members of it or, most importantly, the outside world including providers of capital or – specifically in the public sector – taxpayers is to be prevented from happening.

We have seen in this chapter that the so-called Sarbanes-Oxley Act (SOX) has added a legal imperative to this, certainly in the United States of America but, through similar legislation, it will follow in other jurisdictions in many countries around the world. In the public sector of EU member countries and candidates, it is rather PIfC that plays the music. This follows basically the same mission, however, and puts more emphasis on structural requirements, which typically have been missing in the public sector context. The COSO framework provides a potential system for internal control in compliance with the requirements in SOX section 404, but also under PIfC. Although the COSO framework takes internal control well beyond this, its starting point is financial reporting and the management of risks associated with financial reporting.

SOX and COSO, which both have their roots in the private sector, put a stronger emphasis on financial reporting. This is, as we have seen in the previous chapters, a relatively new aspect of public sector financial management or at least one that has been underestimated constantly until recently. PIfC leaves this aspect open to some extent, although making some reference to the IPSAS. Thus the increased prominence of internal control and financial reporting should be seen in a close relationship. Both are measures to ensure (or perhaps regain) the confidence of the public, especially providers of capital and taxpayers. There is no obvious reason why the public sector should be exempt in any way from this. On the contrary, democracy is a very strong argument that adds even more importance to accountability and transparency in the public sector than in private enterprises.

Work assignments

1 Describe the relevancy of SOX for public sector entities within the United States of America and elsewhere.

2 What is the requirement of SOX section 404? What is the rest of SOX all about?

3 How do SOX and COSO interact with each other?

4 COSO is a risk-sensitive framework. Describe in which sense it is making reference to risks. What are the consequences for public sector entities adopting COSO?

5 What is the relationship between financial reporting and the often very detailed policies and procedures developed and implemented by internal control systems?

6 Draft sample procedures and policies from the list in Exhibit 6.3. What is the potential downside of such documents?

7 Why is internal auditing necessary under the managerial responsibility approach?

8 The PIfC includes both centralised and decentralised elements. Explain why.

Interface to national concepts

1 Identify the national and, if applicable, sub-national jurisdiction in the field of public sector financial management. Federal republics or unions of independent states are likely to have at least two, perhaps even more levels of jurisdiction.

2 Check whether SOX has been partly or fully adopted by your organisation/jurisdiction. If the adoption was a partial one, is section 404 part of it?

3 Check whether COSO has been adopted. If so, what are the results?

4 Check whether PIfC has been adopted. If so, what are the experiences?

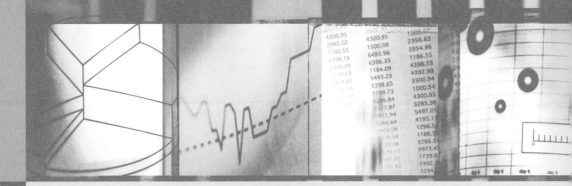

7 Current and future developments

Learning objectives

- Understand the challenges sustainability poses in the field of public sector financial management.
- Prescribe accurate treatment of emission certificates.
- Describe generational balances and their implications.
- Describe XBRL and its advantages, as well as its downsides.
- Define Public Private Partnerships (PPP) and service concessions.
- Identify up- and downward risks of PPPs in practical examples.
- Discuss the options for adequate treatment of PPPs in accounting.

Key terms

Emission certificates	Generational balances	Service concessions
Environmental reports	Public Private Partnerships	XBRL

Although the previous chapters have given an in-depth treatment of the main issues for public sector financial management, including the current challenges such as accrual accounting or government financial statistics, they did not provide an outlook beyond the current agenda. This outlook is provided in this chapter before the case studies in Chapter 8. Public sector financial management has in many countries remained unchanged for quite substantial periods, sometimes half a century or more. Stability has undisputed advantages, namely in finance-related fields, where accountability and transparency are core issues. But the economic and social environments are changing at a high rate and public sector financial management needs to cope with those changes in the environment. And there are no indications of a slower pace in the near future. A textbook should therefore not stand still at the current stage of practice, but give indications of future developments. Such developments are, for obvious reasons, tentative only, but reflect discussions that are currently in their initial stages.

7.1 Sustainability

Sustainability has emerged as a major issue over the last few decades. Mainly driven by ecological or environmental concerns at first, it is a much wider concept now. Widely accepted, at least in academia, is the inclusion of social issues, e.g. child labour, staff accidents. However, at least for the public sector, the concept is even wider than this.[1] It also includes fiscal matters, as it becomes clearer that some public sector schemes result in inter-generational shifts and other unwanted outcomes. Sustainability is, in a way, the going concern for society as whole or specific entities when exposed to more fundamental developments such as global warming or demographic changes. Looking at the public sector, it is even more likely that it will be affected by such developments as it is closer to what is called society and is almost certainly playing a vital role in the management of these issues.

Fiscal sustainability has been an issue in various countries, including the United States, Canada and the United Kingdom, for a while. While some specific issues, such as the influence of programmes like Medicare in the United States or the tax gap discussion, which addresses tax compliance, have first come to the agenda, after 2000 some more comprehensive studies were published.[2] Perhaps the most well-known one is the 2004 Fiscal Sustainability Report by the United Kingdom Treasury.[3] But also organisations like the International Monetary Fund directed more attention to the issue, appraising the situation in all G7 countries.[4]

---

[1] Schaltegger, S., Bennett, M., Burritt, R. (2006) 7 ff.

[2] For example, Walker, D. (1999) http://www.gao.gov/archive/1999/he99294t.pdf; http://www.gao.gov/new.items/d05527t.pdf.

[3] HM Treasury (2004).

[4] Hauner, D., Leigh, D., Skaarup, M. (2007).

| Exhibit 7.1 | Sustainability square |

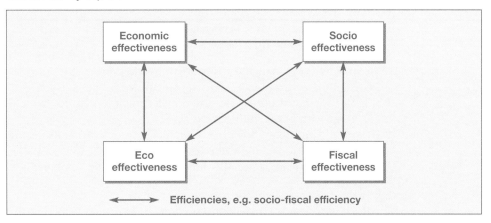

What is well known as the sustainability triangle should thus be extended to a sustainability square, including the concept of fiscal sustainability (see Exhibit 7.1).[5] Some people might argue that the fiscal component is included in the economic component. However, the economic effectiveness is usually used in a very commercial way, e.g. referring to profits and losses. Fiscal sustainability is, in contrast, using a much longer time horizon. It is also, by definition, strongly influenced by the political system and not the exclusive responsibility of the management.

In this sustainability square the boxes denote the effectiveness, i.e. achievement in respect of the particular targets. Examples for eco effectiveness may be reductions in emissions, for fiscal effectiveness a reduction of public sector debt. The arrows between the boxes denote efficiencies, i.e. relations between the two areas. For example, eco-fiscal efficiency could mean by how much the debt needs to be increased to achieve a (one unit) reduction in emission. Apparently there are relations between all the boxes, which results in six different efficiencies.

More narrowly, in the field of public sector financial management, sustainability is bringing up three concepts. The first one is very close to the microeconomics behind many of these problems, especially in the field of ecology, the so-called externalities. Externalities are costs that are not borne by those persons or entities actually causing them, but by somebody else or the entire society. Public sector entities are likely to play an important role in measures taken to internalise these costs, i.e. shift them to those causing them. This includes recently emerged phenomena such as carbon dioxide certificates. The second concept is the one of sustainability reporting. This includes ecological or generational balances. Such reports are produced to inform the public how much or how little is done in certain areas or how much of the burden is shifted to future generations. The third concept is really about public finance as such. Public finances may or may not be sustainable. This largely refers back to deficit and debt which have been discussed in Chapter 2.

[5] Schaltegger, S., Bennett, M., Burritt, R. (2006) 8.

7.1.1 Internalising externalities

As shown in Chapter 2, taxes and transfers raised by governments are issues that fall into the scope of public finance. Taxes usually are attributed three different functions or any combination of them. These are as follows:

1 **Fiscal function.** Financing government operation.
2 **Redistributive function.** Collecting wealth from one group, e.g. the more affluent, those with more children, etc. and transferring it to another group, e.g. the less affluent, those with fewer children, etc.
3 **Incentive function.** Providing a financial incentive or disincentive for a defined behaviour, e.g. increasing the price of petrol in order to curb the use of gas guzzlers and the emission of carbon dioxide or a property gains tax to reduce speculation with property.

The third function, the incentive function, is used increasingly in order to internalise externalities. Externalities are costs or revenues that are not experienced by those who make the economic decisions, but by somebody else. Environmental damages often cause external costs, as the damage is not incurred by the polluter, but by local government which has to take remedial action or by the individuals who suffer from financial or non-financial damages. In some instances moral persuasion may be sufficient to stop the environmental damage and thus the creation of external costs. If the environmental damage can be attributed clearly to one polluter, legal compensation will usually resolve the problem of external costs. However, if the external cost is caused by a very large group of individuals, e.g. car drivers, this way of compensation will not be effective, and therefore taxation may step in.

Such taxes are known as Pigou taxes, named after the English economist Arthur Cecil Pigou (1877–1959). The Pigou tax taxes each unit of the unwanted emission that causes external costs. The level of the tax should reflect the level of internal costs and therefore shift those external costs to the polluter. Through the Pigou tax external costs become internal costs and will then be considered by the polluter's decisions. From the government's point of view, the Pigou tax creates the revenues required to pay for remedial action. Sometimes Pigou taxes, especially if they are not immediately required for remedial action, are also redistributed to the general public through the income tax system. By doing so the government is prevented from increasing its share of the GDP.

Another way to internalise external costs is through emission certificates. The Kyoto protocol is taking a stance for the introduction of such certificates for greenhouse gas emissions, e.g. especially carbon dioxide. In this case the polluter is not required to pay a Pigou tax, but has to buy emission certificates giving them an emission allowance. Such certificates are issued by the government to individuals or corporations that are involved in favourable activities. They may then sell the certificates to those involved in unfavourable activities and create a financial profit. Those who have to buy the certificate to obtain the allowance for pollution will, on the other hand, incur an additional cost. Thus the external cost of pollution is also internalised.

Unlike the Pigou tax the certificates have the advantage of being traded on a market. Their price automatically adjusts to demand and supply, while the Pigou tax, like any other tax, is adjustable only through legislative procedures. The number of emission certificates issued by the government will calibrate the total level of emission. For example, in the case of carbon dioxide, one certificate corresponds to one metric tonne of emission. In 2006 the European Union issued certificates for 1865 million tonnes, which was slightly more than the market accepted, causing the price for one tonne to fall from €30.00 in April 2006 to only €0.80 in April 2007.[6] The market is likely to remain volatile and strongly influenced by the decisions of the issuer. The price for emission certificates is a market rate and therefore likely to be more volatile than any tax rate in any country. While some flexibility is generally considered to be welcome, it is unclear whether such tremendous levels of volatility will adversely affect the incentive function of the scheme.

Thus there are various ways of reducing and internalising externalities. These are as follows:

1 Moral persuasion.
2 Financial compensation.
3 Pigou tax.
4 Emission certificates.

While moral persuasion and fiscal compensation are likely to involve the government or judicial system, they are not really public sector financial management issues. The Pigou tax and tradable emission certificates, in contrast, are issues of public sector financial management. While in most countries there is a substantial level of theoretical knowledge and practical experience with Pigou taxes, emission certificates are still rather new. While their economic rationale is sound and generally accepted, the practical experience is still on a rather low level and in need of further improvement.

7.1.2 Sustainability reporting

Like any other aspect of sustainability, the reporting perspective has also been addressed first from an ecological or environmental point of view.[7] Private sector firms that were accused by stakeholders of damaging nature, e.g. oil producers, airlines, power plants, to name only a few, found it increasingly necessary to limit the environmental damage they cause and report on their success in doing so. From a financial point of view they usually include some additional information directly related to the ecological issues addressed, e.g. investment spending for ecological improvement of facilities. These reports are correctly called environmental reports, sometimes – as it perhaps sounds a bit more fashionable – also sustainability reports. Surprisingly, relatively few public sector entities followed this trend. To some extent this may be explained by the fact that many of them are not damaging nature greatly, e.g. primary schools or courts; or they are even cleaning it up and protecting it, e.g. waste water treatment facilities or national parks. But the more environmentally damaging ones, e.g. publicly operated airports, power plants or extractive industries, are moving in the same direction as their private sector siblings. Environmental reports may look quite different from one another, as usually they focus on the most important environmental issues of the reporting entity. An environmental report of an airport will address noise prominently, but radioactive substances not at all – that of a nuclear facility is quite the opposite. Thus environmental reports are non-standardised regular reports on important ecological issues of the reporting entity.

Later on, often also due to pressure from stakeholders or the general public, such reports started to include other dimensions, especially the social behaviour of the reporting firm. This may include issues such as stopping child labour, providing equal

---

[6] http://www.learn-line.nrw.de/angebote/agenda21/daten/treibhausgase.htm.
[7] Schaltegger, S., Bennett, M., Burritt, R. (2006) 3 ff.

opportunities to employees of any race and gender or other aspects of the social behaviour of the firm. The inclusion of more than one dimension obviously better justifies the use of the term sustainability report. Further dimensions could include economic sustainability, e.g. the protection of capital employed. Defining the scope of sustainability as wide as this brings the issue of sustainability reporting very close to financial reporting, as discussed in Chapters 4 and 5. A widely scoped sustainability report is therefore moving more closely to public sector financial management, as it is no longer restricted to rather coincidental financial information that can be found in environmental reports.

However, there is neither a generally accepted definition of sustainability reporting, nor a rigorous concept behind it.[8] It is a pragmatic approach to control and structure the discussion between the reporting entity and its stakeholders. Depending on the situation of the reporting entity the amount of financial information included in a sustainability report varies substantially. A (public) insurance company may issue a sustainability report that is very much financially focused, while an airport or a nuclear facility will – for obvious reasons – put more emphasis on non-financial information. But even in such cases there usually will be some limited financial information related to non-financial issues, e.g. about investments into improved facilities, cost of protection measures or the proceeds from the trade of emission certificates.

On the scientific side it remains to be seen whether a more rigorous conceptual approach will be developed and how it will be implemented in the public sector-specific context. As the public sector is somewhat closer to civil society than any individual or private sector corporation, the issues are slightly different from the more individualistic perspective of the private sector.

7.1.3 Fiscal sustainability

Public finances may be a subject of sustainability as well. As we have seen in Chapter 2 government deficits and even more so government debts may jeopardise sustainability, as they are likely to infringe the government's political options dealing with other issues, and they may lead to a crowding out of private investments and, after all, they may be shifting the burden to future generations.

The discussion about targets in Section 2.3.3 reflects those concerns. The message can be summarised as follows:

1 Deficits should be a temporary phenomenon balancing out the economic cycle.
2 Consequently, debt should remain stable over the economic cycle.
3 Except if the debt is backed by an asset of at least equal value as a collateral.

If these three conditions, which collectively are often referred to as the 'golden rule', are met, there is no debt which cannot be serviced or needs to be passed over to future generations, infringing their opportunities.[9]

While the concept of fiscal sustainability is an economic concept, the decisions are not necessarily economic decisions. It is more likely that fiscal decisions are political decisions, made by governments or – through the budget process – parliaments. Therefore such decisions do not necessarily follow the economic rationale as discussed above. However, it is a task of public sector financial management to provide the basis of conclusion for such decisions and show their implementation and impact.

---

[8] Schaltegger, S., Burritt, R. (2006).
[9] HM Treasury (2004) 4.

Even comprehensive studies see the demographic changes as the main challenge to fiscal sustainability.[10] They reveal that even moderate reforms over the last couple of years have improved fiscal sustainability only gradually, as the impact of demographic change is very strong. However, they also show that early adjustment in public finance has significant advantages over later moves.[11]

While there are many pieces of evidence from fiscal sustainability discussions in various areas, there is, however, no integrated concept. This is very similar to the situation in respect of environmental and social sustainability described above. Even macroeconomists have shown that there is very little recent literature about fiscal sustainability, and that available focuses on past deficits and debt. In their macroeconomic model they define fiscal sustainability as the situation in which the ratio of the primary government deficit to GDP remains finite.[12] This is a more formal but less comprehensive concept than fiscal targets discussed in Section 2.3.3 and reproduced above.

Thus fiscal sustainability also needs substantially more research as well as a further development of consensus among public sector financial management practitioners.

7.2 XBRL

Only in rather rare cases are acronyms better known than the full text version of them. XBRL certainly belongs to this species. It stands for eXtensible Business Reporting Language and essentially is a computer language belonging to the group of eXtensible Markup Languages (XML), which are standards for the exchange of data. So far so good, but what does this have to do with public sector financial management? With the public sector variation of financial management, not very much, for the time being. But XBRL has rapidly gained importance in the private sector, where it is used as a standard for the exchange of financial information, i.e. the reporting between business units or on the corporate level for the filing of financial information with stock exchanges. It can also be used on the internet when distributing financial information to professional parts of the constituency, such as financial analysts. In fact, large information providers such as Reuters are increasingly providing information about financial reports in the XBRL format.[13] In the public sector, so far it has not attracted very much attention for the public sector financial management perspective, but is used by some tax authorities for the tax returns of private sector corporations as well as for the gathering of statistical information about the private sector by statistics offices.[14] Given the increasing importance in the private sector, the question if and to what extent it is applicable to the public sector should be discussed in this section.

Definition

> **XBRL**
> XBRL stands for eXtensible Business Reporting Language and is computer language used as a standard for the exchange of financial data.

---

[10] HM Treasury (2004); Hauner, D., Leigh, D., Skaarup, M. (2007).

[11] Hauner, D., Leigh, D., Skaarup, M. (2007) 22.

[12] Polito, V., Wickens, M. (2005) 6.

[13] Starr, J. (2007).

[14] Domingo, L. (2004).

XBRL is organised in so-called jurisdictions. Jurisdictions are organised groups that take care of so-called taxonomies. Most jurisdictions are national associations, representing those that prepare financial reports, financial market organisations and perhaps standard setters or regulators. The taxonomy is something like a dictionary translating the national terminology, standards or regulation into the XBRL format. There is also a jurisdiction and taxonomy for the International Financial Reporting Standards (IFRS) which obviously is not driven by one nation. On the international level, the XBRL International Organisation, which is a not-for-profit consortium, accredits and coordinates the jurisdictions. It is also involved in the further development of XBRL as well as oversight and training.

7.2.1 Functionality of XBRL

However, before discussing the potential use of XBRL in the public sector, its functionality should be looked at more closely. XBRL has, broadly, three main functionalities. These are as follows:

1 **Unique identifying tags.** Such tags are applied to specific items of financial data, e.g. current assets, in order to identify them clearly. This is obviously very import when exchanging information between various entities, to make sure a specific item has the same meaning throughout the exchange process. This unique information tag is also used to translate the item's name from one (human) language to another.
2 **Information relating the items to one another.** XBRL also contains information necessary for conducting calculations, such as sums or percentages.
3 **Extensible information.** Special information required by individual enterprises or organisations.

The technical definition of how XBRL works is called specification, while the dictionaries used for defining the unique tags and relating information in various jurisdictions are called taxonomies. There are two types of taxonomies:

● financial reporting (FR); and
● internal reporting (GL).

Currently there are more than 20 drafted and final FR-taxonomies and one GL-taxonomy in place with more FR-taxonomies to come. In some countries, e.g. Ireland or New Zealand, there is just one taxonomy which makes reference to its local accounting standard. In others, e.g. the United States or Thailand, there are different taxonomies for different kinds of sectors of the economy, such as banks, or different reporting issues, such as for pensions in the USA. These national taxonomies obviously bias the potential advantage from making data comparable.[15] However, in many jurisdictions there is no national taxonomy, as yet. An international taxonomy for the International Financial Reporting Standards (IFRS), however, is – unlike some of the national taxonomies – only acknowledged and not approved by both XBRL International and the International Accounting Standards Board (IASB).

Taking the example of the IFRS-FR-taxonomy the various parts of such taxonomy should be looked at more closely. There is a so-called link base file, which is an XML-type file, for the following groups of items:

● balance sheet, classified;
● balance sheet, order of liquidity;

---

[15] Domingo, L. 'XBRL debate', *Accountancy Age* 13 October 2004.

- balance sheet, net assets;
- income statement, by function;
- income statement, by nature;
- cash flow, direct method;
- cash flow, indirect method;
- statement of changes in equity, general purpose;
- accounting policies, general purpose;
- disclosures, general purpose;
- disclosures, first time adoption of IFRS;
- classes, general purpose; and
- other, general purpose.

For each of these items there a separate link base file for the presentation and the calculations. There is also a code list file. Most of the files are provided in an adapted version for financial institutions, such as banks; all of them are also available as printouts.[16]

The first type of taxonomy, the reference to accounting standards as well as the structure of the IFRS-FR-taxonomy, make it very clear that XBRL is very much about the presentation of financial statements. However, technically it is not limited to this, as it may be used internally, for management accounting purposes, as well. That is why it is called extensible. But certainly the financial reporting side currently is higher on the agenda, as entities in both sectors are trying to keep things together internally by using the same kind of enterprise resource planning system (ERP) as widely as possible for the internal flow of data.

Despite the very straight and convincing concept of XBRL, it has attracted some scepticism, besides the dominance of corporate interest[17] and the burden or cost introducing it, namely from the perspective of principle-based accounting standards.[18] Remember: accounting standards should be principle based in order to cover all potential varieties of the issue rather than adhering to a narrow rule which may produce awkward outcomes in certain jurisdictions or even reporting entities. Now, defining XBRL taxonomy obviously requires the definition of rules that computers are able to apply, for instance calculations are to be defined by mathematical operators. There is no room for a principle-based judgement, at least not on a case-by-case basis. Therefore XBRL is said to put the advantages of principle-based accounting principles at risk. However, as XBRL is operating on a much aggregated level of information, this protects it from the most immediate risk of exposure. In fact, the main line items of financial reporting are generally well accepted. More critical is whether a potential transaction is included or excluded and XBRL is not interfering on the single transaction level.

7.2.2 Potential role in the public sector

While the initial use of XBRL has been in the private sector and there even more specifically by listed companies which have to file financial reports, it is a fair matter to assess the potential use of XBRL in the public sector. Public sector entities may participate in financial markets, however, by issuing bonds. Bond markets are somewhat less dependent on financial information, especially in the case of governments or government-guaranteed entities,

---

[16] The entire IFRS-FR-taxonomy including all parts is available for download at http://xbrl.iasb.org/.

[17] Starr, J. (2007).

[18] Domingo, L. (2004).

because they are often protected against default by sector-specific legislation. Thus, because the financial information is less crucial for the investors, the pressure to use XBRL is less significant than in the private sector and so is to potential advantage of a voluntary adoption of XBRL by individual entities.

Obviously public sector entities could benefit from XBRL in their internal information exchange, as the IT environment is often rather heterogeneous in the public sector. Usually different ministries or agencies, but sometimes even smaller entities, are using different IT infrastructure which makes the exchange of information, even if it is only for consolidation purposes, a difficult and exhausting operation. XBRL is a very obvious option to overcome this without having to replace the entire systems, which would be not only costly, but also generally attract strong opposition because the entities are reluctant to hand in some of their independency. XBRL may be less susceptible to this kind of opposition than a full-scale centralisation project and still provide some of the efficiency gains.

The downside, for both the commercial interest and the more principle-based view, however, needs to be taken into account too. Perhaps the public sector is even more vulnerable than the private sector to rules-based views, because the administrative legislation is traditionally rules-based and there is an even weaker tradition of principles-based accounting standards. Thus at least some extra care should be exercised by bringing XBRL to the public sector. Perhaps an XBRL FR-taxonomy based on IPSAS could be beneficial; at least once a conceptual framework is in place. A conceptual framework could limit the risk of moving into a more rules-based view by providing an XBRL taxonomy.

7.3 Public Private Partnerships and service concessions

Public Private Partnerships (PPPs) bear different names in different places and under different circumstances. For instance, in the United Kingdom some call them public (sector) financial initiatives (PFI).[19] But the term Public Private Partnership perhaps captures best what is behind the concept. Public sector entities are engaging in a usually long-term partnership with private sector corporations in order to provide a certain infrastructure and, in many cases, also some of the services based on this infrastructure, e.g. maintenance, security or, in some cases, even operation. If not just the provision of infrastructure but also services provision using this infrastructure are involved, perhaps the term service concession is equally adequate. However, for both PPPs and service concessions there is no generally accepted definition.[20] If this section attempts to define them, it is following an international mainstream rather than particular definitions in various countries, which may vary substantially.

Definition

Public Private Partnership (PPP)
Partnership between public and private sector entities to deliver a public sector asset (normally infrastructure or a public facility) and/or service. The partnership includes multiple exchange relationships, typically over a longer, defined period of time. The risks involved are usually allocated between the public and private sector partners.

---

[19] Coombs, H.M., Jenkins, D.E. (2002) 192.

[20] Bolz, U. (2005) 13.

> **Service concession**
> Service concessions are Public Private Partnerships (PPPs) in which the public sector entity conveys the right to provide services to the public through the use of infrastructure or a public facility to the private sector entity. They may or may not include the delivery of the asset involved.

As PPPs and service concessions are usually long-term relationships which comprise an often larger investment as well as expenses and revenues, but generally some sort of risk transfer, they are clearly issues that need to be addressed by public sector financial management. The combination of various elements or transactions, which is characteristic, leads to a great variety of forms and makes them rather complex. In fact, complexity is an element of the definition, because otherwise any kind of regular procurement activities, with the public sector buying from private sector suppliers, such as buying a car, stationery or contracting a consultant, could be classified misleadingly as a PPP. This would overstate the issue of such a transaction.

7.3.1 Generic classification of Public Private Partnerships

In order to assess PPPs, a generic classification of the typical elements is needed. Each PPP may combine the various elements and thus end up in quite a different manner. Quite widely accepted are the classifications shown in Exhibit 7.2, although they differs slightly between various sources.

The rather narrow definition of PPPs that is used by this textbook covers only steps 4 to 9 in Exhibit 7.2. Steps 1 to 3 are simple exchange transactions with very limited transfer

Exhibit 7.2   Classifications of PPP

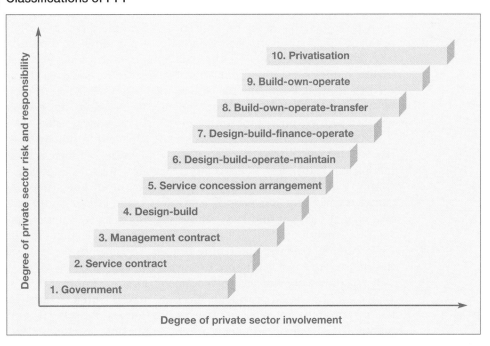

of risks, if any. They have been used for ages as traditional procurement options. Step 10 defined as privatisation is, in contrast, the idea of PPP as a definitive solution, separating entire entities from the government, ending any substantial ongoing partnership.

Steps 4 to 9 are multiple exchange, multi-period, risk-allocating partnerships between public and private sector entities, usually involving some kind of asset or infrastructure. But unlike simple construction or procurement contracts, they involve additional features such as operation, maintenance or financing of the asset or infrastructure. In some rarer cases no asset or infrastructure is involved, only the provision of a public service, such as garbage collections or public transportation. But even in this case, it is a PPP only if more than just the provision of the service is involved, e.g. the private operator takes some commercial risk (e.g. number of passengers or tonnes of garbage).

7.3.2 Implications for public sector financial management

The generic classifications basically suggest separating at a first stage the various transactions from each other and putting them in a time frame. Thus a PPP may end up being a combination of loans, leases, sales and others. All these transactions represent cash flows, both in and out of the public sector entity. In such a situation, the discounted cash flow method (DCF) is the most feasible economic concept for an assessment of the issue, as it considers that the cash flows happen at different moments in time and should not just be added up without taking the time value of the money into consideration. Thus PPPs should be assessed using the same method that is also suggested for the appraisal of investments. In fact, investments are an important part of many PPPs; however, not necessarily of all of them. Pure service concessions especially may exclude investments. But even they are usually subject to deferred payments, which make the DCF method a feasible instrument.

A proposed PPP thus should be analysed by public sector financial management, in most cases using the DCF method, in order to compare it with an alternative proposal. Such alternative proposals are often the more traditional kind of procurement transactions, for instance investing the entities' own funds into property, plant and equipment or taking up a loan to pay for investments or providing the services with the entities' own or contracted employees. The traditional transaction obviously also includes cash in- and outflows in various moments of time; thus it should also be analysed by using the DCF method. Essentially the DCF method will provide the net present values of the PPP proposal, as well as any other proposals. The economic advice would be to select the proposal with the highest (or the least negative) net present value.

As the example in Table 7.1 shows, the DCF method is strongly biased by the interest rate adopted and by long-term so-called residual values, if there is no specified contractual period. It therefore leads to more accurate results if the period of an underlying contract can be used and if this period is not excessively long. Unfortunately, many PPP contracts cover very long periods, e.g. 30 years, and even include some options that go beyond that time horizon. The example suggests there is an upfront payment and then some lease return thereafter. Obviously, PPP contracts sometimes use different scenarios, e.g. no upfront payment and rent to be paid. This changes the table substantially, even the prefixes are different, but not the method used.

But public sector financial management does not finish with this cash-flow-based analysis. It also should provide the decision makers with a comprehensive overview of the impact on the statement of financial position and the statement of financial performance. The statement of financial position or balance sheet especially may be strongly

Table 7.1 Valuation of an asset using the DCF method

Discounted cash flow valuation of a PPP asset

Discount and capitalisation rate: 5.00%

Year	2005	2006	2007	2008	2009	2010	2011	2012	2013	2014	residual period
Initial investment on 1 Jan 2005	−1 800 000										
Revenue from lease	115 000	115 000	115 000	115 000	115 000	115 000	115 000	115 000	115 000	115 000	115 000
– administration cost	−4 600	−4 600	−4 600	−4 600	−4 600	−4 600	−4 600	−4 600	−4 600	−4 600	−4 600
– expenses non-reimbursable from tenant	−288	−288	−288	−288	−288	−288	−288	−288	−288	−288	−288
– repair/maintenance								−50 000	−155 000		−15 000
– forgone leases									−60 000	−40 000	
Total cost	−4 888	−4 888	−4 888	−4 888	−4 888	−4 888	−4 888	−54 888	−219 888	−44 888	−19 888
Net cash flow	−1 689 888	110 112	110 112	110 112	110 112	110 112	110 112	60 112	−104 888	70 112	95 112
Capitalised value of the asset at 1 Jan 2015											1 902 240
Present value of the net cash flows at 1 Jan 2005	−1 609 417	99 875	95 119	90 589	86 276	82 167	78 255	40 686	−67 612	43 043	1 167 810
DCF value of a PPP asset	**106 791**										

141

affected by PPP transactions, as well as the alternative proposals. Future obligations that arise out of PPPs are likely to be liabilities and the corresponding assets may or may not be recognised. Thus we are back in the field of public sector accounting, as PPPs should be treated in accordance with the accounting principles and standards. In the field of accounting standards there are no International Public Sector Accounting Standards (IPSAS) available, as yet. But it is clear that assets should be recognised only if they meet the definition of assets, i.e. future economic benefit or service potential is generated. On the other side, liabilities should be recognised if a future outflow of resources is probable and may be estimated reliably. Thus it is very likely that PPPs affect the balance sheet of the public sector entity, as well as the one of its private sector partner. For the private sector counterpart's accounting treatment there is an interpretation of International Financial Reporting Standards (IFRS) available.[21]

But even the balance sheet is not the end of the story for public sector financial management. PPPs tend to have an operational component, consisting of the production and delivery of certain goods or services. There may be increases or decreases in efficiency in real terms, for instance due to special expertise or economies of scale provided by private sector partners. For example, the construction of the same property may be undertaken in a more or less efficient way, resulting in a different price of the property. The same applies for ongoing services, such as maintenance or security. The public sector entity may be very proficient and efficient in their core activity, such as education, health care or policing. But they may be less efficient in non-core activities such as facility management, IT, etc. Thus despite the future cash outflows and liability on the balance sheet, the entity may be better off by engaging in a PPP. As research shows, such real-term efficiency gains are often the strongest or even the only economic argument for a PPP. Thus an assessment on such real efficiency effects is also to be undertaken by public sector financial management, prior to engaging in PPPs. It is likely that this analysis involves experts from other areas such as facility management or engineering, because only they may provide a reliable estimate of these effects. But it is part of the public sector financial management's tasks to bring this analysis into the context of the DCF analysis as well as the assessment of the influence on the financial position. Decision makers should have all kinds of assessments or analysis presented in a comprehensive manner when making the decision. There may be increases or decreases in efficiency in real terms, for instance due to special expertise or economies of scale provided by private sector partners, as shown in Exhibit 7.3.

7.3.3 Future developments

Future developments in this area include more research about economic analysis of PPPs, including the full picture with financial and real effects. The example in the previous section is very stylised, because there is no good practice for more complex PPPs available, as yet. The second important development includes the drafting and issuing of an IPSAS in this area of growing importance.

Perhaps the other implication is not related directly to PPPs but rather a result of their emergence. Public sector entities traditionally have not paid too much attention to the time value of money. Investment decisions were often made without conducting a prior assessment using the DCF method. This was feasible in a very simple situation where

---

[21] International Financial Reporting Interpretation Committee (IFRIC) Interpretation 12.

| Exhibit 7.3 | Efficiency gains through PPP |

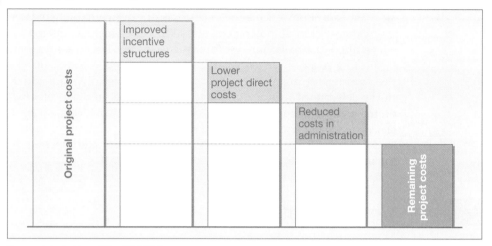

Source: Adapted from Alfen, W. (2006).

there was only one cash flow right at the beginning of the investment which determined the loan to be taken up and paid off afterwards. Thus the size of the initial investment was the only variable; a larger investment meant that future payments (interest, amortisation of the principle of the loan) were also larger. Thus two options of the project could be assessed solely on the basis of the initial investment. More recently, the introduction of PPPs changed this simple model as cash flows were no longer the same under the different options. Perhaps one option had smaller initial cash flows, but larger ones in the end and vice versa. In such a situation, the DCF method is the only method for assessing the different options. Thus public sector entities should be very wary about not using the DCF method, as many real-world proposals nowadays include deferred payments.

7.4 Convergence of financial reporting and financial statistics

This book has explained in various sections the commonalities, differences and implications of financial reporting and financial statistics. There is a gap between the two, although it is perhaps smaller than expected. Especially recently the development of government financial statistics (GFS) towards a full accrual concept very much coincides with a similar move on the financial accounting and reporting side.

Basically, both financial reporting and financial statistics follow the same (high-level) objective: they should provide the public with the relevant information for financial decisions. It is obvious that GFS are aggregated on a macroeconomic level and used towards macroeconomic decisions, while financial reports generally are more on a microeconomic (i.e. entity) level. Apparently, this is not going to change. Perhaps some entities are going to present reconciliation between statistical and accounting information, following the guidance of IPSAS 22, but the vast majority of countries will not be presenting statistical information on the same level as financial reports.

More feasible and likely is a convergence on a transaction level. Most transactions are already accounted for in the same way by statisticians and accountants. However, there are a few exceptions, such as defence assets or external training of government employees. Other technical differences and difficulties include international transactions, which are of particular interest for statisticians but less so for accountants. This is not meant to give a comprehensive overview of all the differences, but it shows that a further convergence might make life easier for both the statisticians and the accountants. If the so-determined relevant information is gathered automatically by the accountants, on the level of each transaction, this would not only reduce the cost of preparing financial statistics, but also enhance their quality.

If this potential for simplification is realised, this would also lead to a clarification of the role of accounting offices, as discussed in Section 1.3.

Work assignments

1 Explain which kind of sustainability should be considered in an analysis of a pension fund for government employees.

2 A public sector entity wants to present its financial reports using XBRL. Show what the prerequisites are. Is it possible for an individual entity, e.g. a public hospital, to implement XBRL?

3 A public sector entity is due to invest CU 10 million into new facilities with a useful life of an estimated 20 years. There are two options. The first option is that it could finance this investment with a loan from a commercial bank. The interest rate is 4 per cent and the full amount has to be paid back in equal instalments within the 20 years. Both interest and the instalments are due by the end of each year. Some maintenance is necessary after 5, 10 and 15 years, each costing CU 0.5 million and to be paid as current expenses. The second option would be a PPP with the contractor that is constructing the new facility. The contractor would charge a fixed amount of CU 1.6 million at the end of each year and transfer the facility by the end of the 20 years to the public sector entity at no charge. This lump sum includes the same sort of maintenance that is undertaken by the three projects after five years each. Please advise the entity on whether to take the proposal of the contractor or the loan from the bank.

4 Discuss the influence that interest rates have on the decision in work assignment number 3.

5 Are there situations in which there is no need to use the DCF method to appraise a public sector investment project?

6 Calculate a DCF value for the following PPP project. A public hospital wants to set up a diagnostic centre. As the hospital does not have sufficient funds to purchase the necessary equipment, it enters a PPP agreement with a supplier of such equipment. It is more than just a lease, as the supplier will take care of the technical operation of the equipment. The hospital has to pay an annual fee of CU 500,000 over the next 10 years. It will generate annual revenue of CU 550,000 by charging the use of the diagnostic facilities to the patients. It may purchase the whole equipment for CU 2,000,000 at the end of year 10 and then operate it at an annual cost of CU 200,000 for another 5 years. The revenues will be the same during this second period. The discount rate is 5 per cent.

7 What happens if the option of buying the equipment at the end of year 10 is not exercised, the equipment is returned to the supplier and thus the operational forecast for the years 11 to 15 does not materialise in work assignment 6?

8 What happens if the discount rate is changed from 5 to 10 per cent in work assignment 6? Why?

Interface to national concepts

1 Check on national initiatives in the field of sustainability.

2 Which XBRL taxonomies are available in your environment?

3 Are there any PPPs in your country/international organisation? If so, which methods were used to assess the proposals before signing the contract? How are they accounted for by the public sector entity? Is there any regulation on PPPs? Is there any generally accepted definition?

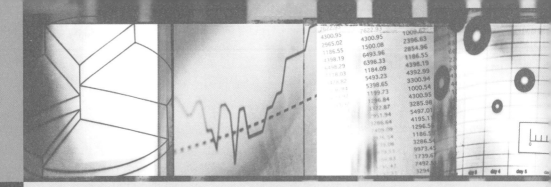

8 Case studies

Learning objectives

- Adopt the concepts learned in real-world examples.
- Reduce the complexity of real-world examples to the categories used in this textbook.
- Propose different ways to move forward; evaluate them and take a decision.

Case studies are just work assignments used for the rehearsal. They are comprehensive, real-world examples that obviously include some elements discussed in this textbook, but go well beyond that. They should be discussed in groups or in the classroom. In most case studies there are no assignment questions and there is no right or wrong answer. As in the real world, there are different ways forward, although not all of them are feasible.

8.1 NEAT – financing a multi-billion infrastructure

Public sector financial management is not a dire topic with little real-world influence. The construction and financing of the so-called NEAT (German: *Neue Eisenbahn Alpen Transversale*; English: New Railway through the Alps) is a good example of the real-world connectivity of public sector financial management.

8.1.1 The project

Although railway lines across the Alps have been operational for well over one hundred years, Switzerland decided to construct two more lines back in the 1990s. These lines, unlike the previous railway lines and also unlike the motorways across the Alps, cross the Alps through a tunnel that is almost at the same altitude as the flat lands in the north and the south. Previous crossings first climbed roughly 1,000 metres before entering shorter tunnels. This was not only inefficient, but also slowed traffic down and caused congestion. Increasing capacity and decreasing travel times was virtually impossible with the existing network. The decision to build a railway tunnel rather than a road tunnel was not only a technical one (railway tunnels are much safer than road tunnels), but also an ecological one (environmentally friendly railways should gain a competitive advantage over roads).

In Switzerland it was decided to construct two tunnels rather than one. The longer tunnel, in fact the longest railway tunnel in the world at the time of construction, was to cross underneath the Gottardo Pass from Erstfeld in the north to Bodio in the south,

| Exhibit 8.1 | Map of the NEAT project |

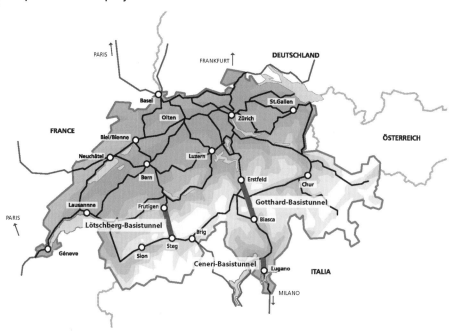

Source: Swiss Federal Office of Transport.

with a main tunnel stretching over 57 kilometres and including new access lines with several smaller tunnels both in the north and the south (see Exhibit 8.1).

The second line, more to the west, includes a 35 kilometre main tunnel under the Lötschberg and some access lines. This tunnel was constructed mainly as a concession to the users in Western Europe and also due to its much smaller construction time. In fact the new Lötschberg tunnel was opened for traffic in 2007, while the new Gottardo line will only enter into service in 2019.

Trains can travel inside the tunnels at a speed of 200 to 250 km/h. Both tunnels save more than one hour in travel time compared to the existing lines higher up in the Alps, with the gains on the Gottardo line being more substantial.

8.1.2 The expenditure

The official, initial estimate of the investment expenditure by the Swiss Government was at Sfr 15.6 billion. In 2007 the cost estimate was revised to Sfr 19.8 billion. The longer and technically more challenging Gottardo line accounts for about two-thirds and the Lötschberg line for one-third of the total cost, although not every single cost component may be attributed to either one of the lines.

Obviously such an amount needs to be financed. A special challenge is the long construction period of more than 20 years during which expenditure is accumulated but no revenues are generated. But even after that, the payback period was considered much too long for a private sector investor. Equally the Swiss Federal Railways, a state-owned enterprise with an annual revenue of about Sfr 6 billion (2006) and a cash flow from operations of about Sfr 1 billion – which is entirely needed for the replacement of current assets, especially trains – was unable to finance such an endeavour. It was therefore decided that the project needed to be financed by the Swiss Federal Government. The Swiss electorate agreed with the proposed financial concept in a referendum in 1998 and therewith endorsed the financial involvement of the Federal Government. However, the technical construction was contracted to two separate legal entities, the Alptransit Gottardo AG and the BLS Alptransit AG.

8.1.3 The financial concept

The financial concept approved in the referendum in 1998 includes at its core a special purpose entity, the so-called FinÖV Fund. This fund was created to finance not only the two new lines across the Alps but also other improvements of the railway infrastructure, namely other high-speed lines and improved noise protection along existing and new lines. The fund is managed by the Swiss Federal Government through the Federal Office of Transport (FOT).

The fund receives its financial means from four sources. These are as follows:

1 A special toll charge for heavy vehicles (German acronym: LSVA), which goes entirely to the FinÖV fund.
2 One per thousand of value added tax (VAT), while most of the VAT is considered general tax revenue.
3 Petrol tax; however, limited to a maximum of 25 per cent of the fund's revenue.
4 The rest through 'advances' from the Swiss Government.[1]

The FinÖV Fund's statement of financial performance can be seen in Exhibit 8.2. From 1998 to 2006 the first three sources, which are revenues with no repayment obligation, accounted for Sfr 7.8 billion, while the advances were accumulated to Sfr 6.7 billion. Before the fund was created in 1998, a further Sfr 2.2 billion was paid through the general budget of the Federal Government. The advances are expected to increase further up to Sfr 10 billion in 2013. From 2014 onwards the revenues (sources 1, 2 and 3) will exceed the expenditure and the advances will be paid back to the Federal Government. However, the payback becomes substantial only once construction is completed in 2019. Based on this timing the advances will be paid back in full by 2027, about 30 years after the fund was created.[2]

Thus over a time period of more than 30 years, the new tunnel infrastructure will be paid by taxes and special levies dedicated to this purpose. As it is allowed to borrow only from the Federal Government, it does not add to the debt as presented by the Federal

Exhibit 8.2 Statement of financial performance of the FinÖV Fund

Statement of financial performance of the FinÖV Fund	
Investment grants (and loans)	Revenues from heavy vehicles toll charge, VAT and petrol tax
	Net loss: covered by advances
Interest on advances	

[1] Nicollerat, A. (2007).
[2] Nicollerat, A. (2007) 10.

Government. The fund and hence also the project enjoy the same conditions on the capital market as the Federal Government, as there are no separate, earmarked loans for this matter. The borrowing goes hand in hand with general treasury activities.

8.1.4 A fund of debts

At first glance the term fund may be difficult to understand, taking into consideration that the FinÖV Fund is clearly a concept of debt, rather than one of assets. In fact, the newly constructed infrastructure is, beside a few expenditures in the form of loans, not on the balance sheet. The fund does not hold any property, plant or equipment. These are held and managed by the two construction companies Alptransit Gottardo AG and BLS Alptransit AG during the construction period and by the two railway companies Swiss Federal Railways and BLS Railways after completion. So why is there a fund?

The main purpose of the fund is to make the financing of those massive projects transparent. It should make clear how much each of the earmarked taxes and levies has contributed and how much borrowing was needed from the Federal Government. It also accumulates the interest on these borrowings, thus also showing the cost of capital. The relatively few different transactions make it easier to understand – if such a special purpose entity is easy to understand at all. The form of a separate legal entity has the advantage of a clear identification of all transactions. However, there is also a downside, as the fund is no longer part of the separate financial statements of the Federal Government. It will be consolidated, as soon as consolidated financial statements are prepared. But at least for the first 10 years of its operation, it was not consolidated and therefore not included in an overview of the financial situation of the Federal Government. The special purpose transparency was lost at the expense of the general purpose transparency.

8.2 Temasek Singapore – a sovereign wealth fund makes business

As governments are no longer inevitably in a debt situation, the management of positive balances becomes an issue, but perhaps even more so an opportunity. In such situations governments tend to create sovereign wealth funds or even investment corporations. The Singaporean Temasek Holdings is perhaps a government-owned investment corporation more than a wealth fund, as it describes itself as:

> 'an Asian investment house, headquartered in Singapore, focused on creating and maximising long-term shareholder value as an active investor and shareholder of successful enterprises'.[3]

This self-description includes much information about the holding's mission. At least in 2007 it considers itself an 'Asian' institution that is 'headquartered in Singapore'. This was not always the case. When Temasek Holdings was founded in 1974 it had a more national focus on the economic development of the Republic of Singapore, which had gained independency a decade earlier. Although return on investment was part of the concept from the beginning, the 'building of institutions and infrastructure'[4] and better management of the various entities controlled by the Ministry of Finance[5] were equally

---

[3] Temasek Holdings (2007).

[4] Temasek Holdings (2007b) 16.

[5] Temasek Holdings (2007b) 34.

important in the early years. The second relevant piece of information is the notion of 'long-term shareholder value'. Temasek is not dedicated and has never been dedicated to short-term treasury activities. Its investments are of a long-term nature, with a clear intention to increase their value. In fact, the annual rate of return since inception was around 18 per cent.

8.2.1 Investing

Still controlled by the Singapore Government, Temasek Holdings is selecting its investments both by themes and by economic sectors as shown in Table 8.1.[6]

Both the themes and the sectors not only include generic investment targets, such as technology or transforming economies, but also more political ones, such as the commitment to the middle class or the energy and resources. However, the value no longer needs to be created entirely within Singapore, but may equally come from different countries, as long as it creates value to the Singaporean shareholder.[7] Over the last few years, Temasek has decreased its shareholdings in Singapore and increased the ones in other parts of Asia, keeping other OECD countries at the same level.[8] The increase in other parts of Asia was focused on Northern Asia, namely China, Taiwan and Korea.

Perusing its mission, Temasek Holdings follows three functions.[9] These are:

1 Evaluating potential investments.
2 Managing existing portfolios.
3 Creating and maximising long-term shareholder value.

Table 8.1   **Temasek Holding's investment focuses**

Themes
Transforming economies
Thriving middle-class
Deepening comparative advantages
Emerging champions
Sectors
Financial services
Telecommunications & media
Transportation & logistics
Infrastructure, industrial and engineering
Technology
Energy & resources
Real estate
Consumer & lifestyle

---

[6] Temasek Holdings (2007).
[7] Temasek Holdings (2007b) 7.
[8] Temasek Holdings (2007b) 10.
[9] Temasek Holdings (2007b) 37.

In all three functions the so-called value test, i.e. the proof of positive wealth added in excess of a capital charge, is core. Obviously risk management is part of this, as risk and return go hand in hand. While the evaluation is focused on portfolio decisions, the management of the existing portfolio includes issues such as leadership and human capital but also operational excellence and competitive strategy. Temasek is therefore clearly more than a mere portfolio manager; it gets involved in the management of its subsidiaries. In order to create and maximise long-term shareholder value, Temasek may not only buy and sell, but also restructure its shareholdings.

8.2.2 Governance

Legally, Temasek Holdings is a private company, as its shares are not traded on the stock exchange. However, as it is fully owned by the Ministry of Finance, it is still accountable to the public, although it denies any legal responsibility in this respect, e.g. it presents its financial statements on a voluntary basis. But good governance is one of its stakes. As with any other sovereign wealth fund, the connection between the government's and the fund's or company's governance is most critical. Temasek describes the division of responsibilities as follows:

> 'This represents a policy commitment for these investments to be managed by Temasek on a sound commercial basis, as distinct from the government's public interest role of policy-making and market regulations. This frees the government to act in the larger interests of the overall economy.'[10]

While this makes it clear that Temasek is no regulatory body whatsoever, it does not resolve the conflict of interest between the commercial goals of Temasek and possible government intervention in favour of these goals, although both Temasek and the government clearly deny any such intervention.

The company Temasek Holdings operates under the direction of a Board of Directors. The Board is appointed by the elected President of the Republic of Singapore. The Chairman and the CEO report to the President not only in respect of the overall achievements, but also in respect of any transactions – although the Board is free in its investment decisions.

The Board of Directors itself works with three committees, an Executive Committee, an Audit Committee and a Leadership Development and Compensation Committee (LDCC). While the Executive Committee and the LDCC are chaired by the Chairman of the Board, the Audit Committee is chaired by an independent Board Member. Neither the Chairman of the Board nor the CEO is a member of the Audit Committee.

8.2.3 Major investments

In order to get a better idea of how Temasek is working, it may be beneficial to look at a few selected major investments.

1 Singapore Airlines

Singapore Airlines is one of Temasek's traditional investments; it has been held almost since the inception of Temasek. Today Temasek holds 55 per cent of Singapore Airlines. In the 1970s it was part of infrastructure and institution building, but nowadays Singapore Airlines has to meet the value creation targets like any other

---

[10] Temasek Holdings (2007b) 58.

investment. However, as one of the leading airlines of the world, it has outperformed the Singapore stock market in recent years.

2 **Bank of China and China Construction Bank**

Only back in 2005 would the Chinese Government allow foreign direct investments into commercial banks on the mainland. Temasek took the chance and acquired a 5 respectively 6 per cent share through its subsidiary Fullerton Financial Holdings (FFH), which holds virtually all its investments in the financial industry. This investment is in line with the strategy to increase investments in China.

3 **Chartered Semiconductor Manufacturing**

Chartered has been an investment since 1987, when the semiconductor industry was not at its very beginning, but still far from a mature industry. Chartered manufactures in Singapore and is still one of Temasek's Singapore-focused investments. However, today Chartered is equally benchmarked based on the value criterion.

4 **Shin Corporation**

Shin Corporation is perhaps the most controversial of Temasek's investments. Shin is a holding itself, investing, among others, in wireless communication and satellite broadcasting. It is controversial because Shin was owned previously by the former Prime Minister of Thailand, Mr Thaksin Sinawathra, who sold Shin in 2006 to Aspen Holdings, which is controlled by Temasek. The potential conflict lies in the fact that a Thai Prime Minister sells his private assets to a Singapore Government-owned company. From Temasek's point of view, the investment is in line with its goals, but the political implications, namely in Thailand, are perhaps more doubtful. However, Shin Corporation is one of the few investments that currently is not meeting the commercial targets. This, of course, fuels speculation about political side effects.

Essentially, it is obvious that Temasek is investing the sovereign wealth of the Republic of Singapore in a profitable way. In fact it has not only helped the development of highly commended companies such as Singapore Airlines, but also strengthened Singapore's economic position in the world. In contrast to many other countries, which had to subsidise what they call core industries over decades, Singapore has enjoyed a substantial financial return on its investments. Even if the concept attracts scepticism now and then, it was certainly beneficial to the citizens of Singapore.

8.3 Performance budgeting for high schools

In 1996 a new Minister of Education took office in the State of Zürich, Switzerland. Ernst Buschor was previously Professor of Public Management at St Gallen University and therefore familiar with the concepts of new public management from the very beginning, back in the 1980s when he was a senior government official in the State of Zürich. He became Minister of Health about two years earlier but moved on to the Ministry of Education. Based on his experience both in the academic world and in the political as well as administrative systems he not only started reforms in the field of education, but also an entire reform programme for the entire State of Zürich Government. This programme was titled '*Wirkungsorientierte Führung der Verwaltung*' (English: outcome-oriented management for public administration; in short, WiF). Obviously, the Ministry of Education was spearheading the reforms, which rapidly involved all ministries. Within the Ministry of Education the high schools were selected to take the lead, as they were fully state owned and operated and had some management structure, with principles for each of the 20 schools, in place. With an annual budget of slightly more than Sfr 300 million ($280 million) they were also of reasonable, but not excessive, size.

8.3.1 Budget reforms as the core

The core of the WiF reforms was the development and implementation of performance budgeting. Apparently this is a more narrow focus than new public management takes if various jurisdictions are being considered. However, other reform elements, such as human resource management or organisational reforms, were also included, but with less emphasis than the budgeting. In this area traditional line item budgets should be replaced by product budgets allocating a lump sum to each of the products and controlling the institutions through performance indicators rather than individual line items.

The downside of the traditional budget was seen in a lack of political relevance and unwanted administrative behaviour such as using up budget resources for insensible expenditures rather managing them properly. In fact big spending peaks were observed towards the end of every year, much of it in rather discretionary positions, such as office equipment or media. Political discussion often focused on easy to understand but immaterial items such as travel expenses or paper, in the case of education, while the more material things, such as school size or electives, were not touched, as they were hidden in the salaries. In fact, the discussion about the salaries was often restricted to very broad issues such as inflation adjustment, leaving the overall number of staff aside.

The indicators under the WiF reform should focus on outcomes, as they were deemed to be most relevant for the political discussion. Outputs, such as number of students, should be used especially in order to calculate per capita indicators such as cost per student. The financial part of the budget would in most cases be reduced to two line items per product, the net expenditure and the net investments. As the State of Zürich has been on accrual accounting and budgeting for more than 10 years this distinction was not new, only the elimination of individual line items was a novelty.

This budget reform was to be supported by organisational reforms bringing more managerial choice but also more responsibility to the level of individual schools. Previously the schools were very much operative arms of the ministry in respect of any non-pedagogical decisions. Pedagogical decisions, including such on the curricula, were taken by a special Education Council on the state level and permanent appointment of high school principles and teachers was even the responsibility of the State Council, the cabinet of ministers. School principles' decisions were limited to electives, temporary appointments, school events and minor expenditures. In order to become effective, performance budgets therefore required a much greater degree of managerial freedom.

8.3.2 What is a product?

Moving to performance budgets made it necessary to identify individual products. The concept of product was equally new to the public administration and to the schools. The latter had difficulties accepting that they were producing something and pursuing more visionary tasks. But the other challenge was to get the concept of product at the right level. What should a product be? Is it the individual lesson? Or even each handout in the classroom? Or perhaps each student? Each class or each school? It rapidly became clear to Professor Buschor and his team that products should not be defined too narrowly. If a narrow definition applies, there are dozens of products within the high school system and hundreds or thousands within the entire state. While getting rid of strongly itemised budgets, there would be myriad products that equally are immaterial from an overall perspective.

In the case of the high schools, the different programmes offered were defined as products and grouped in a product group high school. This was certainly feasible from an overall point of view. However, it raised the question of what the role of each of the twenty schools was supposed to be. If they were no longer visible on the budget level, how should they or their principles influence the outcome and output? It became clear that a management and budget structure on the lower level, between the ministry and the schools, was needed. Performance contracts, of course in the context of the overall high school performance budget, should control each of the 20 schools. These contracts should be negotiated between the ministry and the schools on an annual basis, similar to the budget. They should reflect the school's share of the overall 'production' and its contribution to the performance indicators.

While this is quite straightforward in theory, practice proved to be difficult as the 20 schools, which were assumed to be quite homogeneous as they were previously governed by the Education Council and the Ministry of Education, turned out to be substantially different.

8.3.3 Different service levels

The first surprise was the huge difference in cost per student. This figure had never been calculated before. Therefore the project team had to harmonise financial statements before calculating this efficiency indicator. What came out was shocking for many: the variation between the most and the least expensive schools was more than 30 per cent, i.e. the most expensive one a third more expensive than the cheapest one. The results can be seen in Table 8.2.

This was really surprising for both the Education Council and the Ministry of Education, both of which previously thought they were treating the schools on equal terms. A first explanation found was the different age, and therefore wage structure, of the teachers. However, this explained barely 20 per cent of the difference. After further research, supported by the principles, the project team discovered that the main explanatory factor was the number of lessons per student. Apparently, there was a large variation between the schools. How could this happen, bearing in mind that schools were not really autonomous and almost any decision required prior approval by the ministry?

Over the years some of the schools had undertaken different pedagogical reforms, including the introduction of electives, team-teaching, conversation groups for foreign languages, etc. These reforms were very different between the schools and led to huge differences in their cost level. They were all approved by the ministry, but not part of a broader reform agenda. Despite the approval by central authority, different service levels were introduced. The number of lessons per student became quite different between the different schools, as many reforms were about student choice introducing electives and other special forms of provision. In fact the service level was the main explanation for the cost of provision. Exhibit 8.3 shows the cost and number of lessons per student.

Together with the teacher population, the service level, i.e. the lessons per student, could explain almost the entire variation. The main cost drivers were identified.

Table 8.2 Cost per student

School	Cost per student (Sfr)	Index (100 for cheapest school in sample)
1	15 834	123
2	15 934	124
3	16 729	130
4	15 285	119
5	14 336	112
6	15 358	120
7	15 084	118
8	14 518	113
9	15 902	124
10	15 351	120
11	14 729	115
12	13 634	106
13	15 449	120
14	16 412	128
15	15 597	122
16	15 219	119
17	14 499	113
18	16 761	131
19	12 834	100
20	15 749	123

Exhibit 8.3 Cost and lessons per student

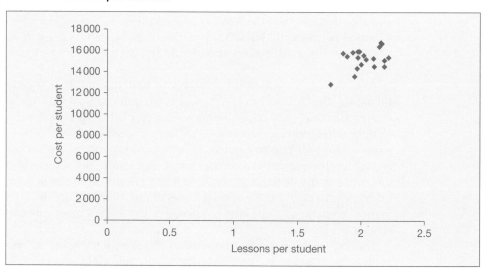

8.3.4 Finding performance indicators

As performance indicators are a main feature of performance budgets, the selection of such indicators was crucial. As the WiF reform was to focus on outcome indicators such indicators also needed to be defined for the high school system when they introduced performance budgets. Obviously this was different from the service levels discussed in the previous section. Unlike in many other countries, this typically Swiss type of high school was dedicated to the preparation for university studies. Therefore one of the principal ideas was to measure the success rate of high school graduates at university level. In fact, the university register system allows the tracking of high school graduates. But it became rapidly clear that the main determinant of success at university level was the university programme selected. Other factors of influence included gender and the type of high school. The Swiss high school system has about five different types, i.e. classical languages, science, economics, modern languages, arts. This was the only statistically significant influence from the high school system on the success rate at university. Other factors such as the school itself were not significant.[11]

This led to some frustration. While the success rate at university level would be a theoretically very sound outcome indicator, it is obviously not of much use if the high schools have so little influence on it. This was, of course, the destiny of many outcome indicators. Their distance to the system itself makes them vulnerable to many other influences. This frustration led to a shift of focus from outcomes to outputs which were much easier to measure and to influence. The remaining outcome indicators were survey results about the perceived quality of the high school two years after graduation.

8.3.5 Organisational and programme reforms

While the budget reforms were the most important, organisational reforms were undertaken at the same time. The entire curricula was reviewed and then reformed. During this reform, the schools were given substantial autonomy in pedagogical terms, but a more standardised financial framework. The schools were encouraged to introduce innovative programmes, such as programmes in English or special programmes for athletes. But all these reforms were subject to the financial guidelines that were narrowing the gaps in respect of service levels.

On the system level, school choice was introduced. Future students or their parents could decide on which school they wanted to attend. A new law, approved in a referendum in 1999, even introduced a school voucher scheme, which was supposed to extend school choice to non-government schools. This scheme, however, never became effective; it would have increased the total cost for the government, at least during a transitional period. This was unacceptable during the recession in the early 2000s and the scheme was therefore abandoned.

8.4 Whole of government accounting in New Zealand

Whole of government accounting is a rather recent concept, as accounting was following the statistical treatment in many countries. The scope of entities included was then limited to the general government sector, however, usually excluding other

---

[11] Bergmann, A. (2000).

levels of government, such as states or local governments. New Zealand was one of the first countries to adopt a different approach back in 1989, when it was enacting a new Public Finance Act. The reporting entity is specified as the economic entity that includes all entities controlled by the government. Beside the Ministries and Departments this includes the Offices of Parliament, the two superannuation funds, the Reserve Bank of New Zealand as well as the state-owned enterprises (SOE) and Crown entities. SOEs include the Electricity Corporation, the Post and – we will later examine more closely – Air New Zealand. Crown entities are typical agencies, such as Radio New Zealand, the Museum of New Zealand or the Pharmaceutical Management Agency.

This scope apparently is much wider than the concept of the general government sector, as namely the SOEs as well as some of the Crown entities generate more than half of their funds on the market, as revenues in exchange for goods and services. In fact the scope follows the same concepts that the scope of financial reporting of a private sector group follows. According to the Public Finance Act all entities included in the reporting entity need to be fully consolidated. Full consolidation means line-by-line consolidation of the separate financial reports, which have to be prepared according to the same accounting principles, eliminating transactions between the sub-entities.

8.4.1 High-level anchorage

One of the issues to be resolved when determining the scope of consolidation is at which level the control criterion should be established. In the case of New Zealand, the lawmakers established a list of entities to be consolidated within the Public Finance Act, as determined in Part 3 Section 27:

27 Annual financial statements of Government

1 The Treasury must, as soon as practicable after the end of each financial year, prepare annual consolidated financial statements for the Government reporting entity for that financial year.
2 The annual financial statements of the Government must:
   (a) be prepared in accordance with generally accepted accounting practice; and
   (b) include the forecast financial statements prepared under section 26Q, for comparison with the actual financial statements; and
   (c) include, in addition to those financial statements required by generally accepted accounting practice:
      (i)   a statement of borrowings that reflects the borrowing activities for that year, including budgeted figures for that year and comparative actual figures for the previous financial year;
      (ii) a statement of unappropriated expenses and capital expenditure;
      (iii) a statement of emergency expenses and capital expenditure incurred under section 25;
      (iv) a statement of trust money administered by departments and Offices of Parliament; and
      (v)   any additional information and explanations needed to fairly reflect the consolidated financial operations of the Government reporting entity for the financial year and its consolidated financial position at the end of that year.

3 The annual financial statements of the Government must include the Government reporting entity's interests in:

(a) all Crown entities named or described in the Crown Entities Act 2004;

(b) all organisations named or described in Schedule 4;

(c) all State enterprises named in the Schedule 1 of the State-Owned Enterprises Act 1986;

(d) all Offices of Parliament;

(e) the Reserve Bank of New Zealand;

(f) any other entity whose financial statements must be consolidated into the financial statements of the Government reporting entity to comply with generally accepted accounting practice.

This high-level decision on the scope of consolidation saved the Government from establishing the control criteria, which is referred to in Section 27, 3 (f), in every single case. It also resolves a few, perhaps more doubtful, cases such as the Offices of Parliament and the Reserve Bank of New Zealand. In respect of the Offices of Parliament it could be argued that they are under control of the legislative power, the Parliament, and therefore not controlled by the Government. However, in the case of New Zealand the legislative power itself has decided to include the Offices of Parliament. In fact, in New Zealand the Government is defined in a way that includes all three 'branches', the legislative, the executive and the judicial.[12] The reporting entity therefore is established on the level of the sovereign power of New Zealand. This also resolves the case of the Reserve Bank of New Zealand. The Reserve Bank is the central bank, i.e. the monetary authority of New Zealand. Monetary authorities should be independent from the Government when determining the monetary policy of a country. However, they are obviously part of the sovereign power of a country and should therefore be consolidated if the reporting entity is defined on this level.

Thus the high-level anchorage comprises two features: firstly, the definition of the requirement of consolidation and of the scope of consolidated entities in a formal law; secondly – and this perhaps is more unique in the case of New Zealand – the definition of the scope on the level of the sovereign power of the nation.

8.4.2 The issue of tertiary education institutions

Although the Public Finance Act appears to be quite clear, there is one exception to the rule: the tertiary education institutions, i.e. universities and similar institutions. These institutions, although being Crown entities, are not consolidated but accounted for using the equity method.[13] The issue is the statutory autonomy and independence of these institutions.

New Zealand has so-called sector or transactions-neutral Financial Reporting Standards (FRS), which are based on the International Financial Reporting Standards (IFRS). Consolidation is treated in FRS 37, while so-called associates are the subject of FRS 38. FRS 37 establishes control based on the two elements of power and benefit. However, it does not address the public sector-specific issue of statutory autonomy and independence. This lack of public sector-specific guidance has led to a controversy between the

---

[12] The treasury of New Zealand (2005) 45.

[13] Government of New Zealand (2006) 43.

| Table 8.3 | Tertiary education institutions |

Tertiary education institutions as at 30 June 2006 (NZ$ millions)	Equity accounting (current treatment)	As if full line-by-line combination was adopted
Operating result		
Revenues	–	1 843
Expenses	–	1 789
Net surplus of tertiary education institutions	54	–
Operating balance	**54**	**54**
Assets and liabilities		
Assets		
Financial assets	–	867
Property, plant and equipment	–	5 684
Other assets	–	248
Net investments in tertiary education institutions	5 475	(5 475)
Total assets	**5 475**	**1 325**
Liabilities		
Gross debt	–	226
Other liabilities	–	1 099
Total liabilities	**–**	**1 325**
Net worth	5 475	–

Source: Government of New Zealand, Financial Statements 2006, Note 13.

Treasury and the tertiary education institutions. Therefore, the Government's Financial Statements currently account only for the tertiary education institutions using the equity method. However, the notes show the effect that full consolidation would have.[14]

As Table 8.3 shows, the different accounting treatment leads to different results in the statement of financial position, while the statement of financial performance is unaffected, at least bottom line.

8.4.3 Inclusion of commercial businesses

The scope of consolidation does, however, not only include Crown entities, but also state-owned-enterprises (SOEs). These enterprises undertake, to a large degree, commercial activities. They sell the goods and – more often – services to their customers. This includes entities like the Post, but – although not legally an SOE – also the airline Air New Zealand. New Zealand very closely follows the accounting principles that come, as

---

[14] Government of New Zealand (2006) 62.

we have seen before, from the private sector, and makes no exception for commercial activities. Other countries, for instance Canada, exclude government business enterprises (GBEs) from the scope of consolidation, as they would not like to 'co-mingle' commercial and government activities.[15]

The case of Air New Zealand shows both pros and cons of the consolidation approach. The former flag carrier Air New Zealand was privatised as part of the market-oriented reforms in New Zealand in the 1980s. Therefore it was not included in the schedule of the State-Owned-Enterprises Act 1986, which is also the relevant source for the definition of the scope of consolidation in the Public Finance Act 1989. However, in 2001 the privatised airline got into financial difficulties due mainly to earlier investments abroad, which became very severe after the events of 9/11 and the subsequent downturn of air traffic.

Due to its remote location, air transportation is crucial for the New Zealand economy. That is why in October 2001 the government eventually decided to step in and avoid the bankruptcy of Air New Zealand. The carrier was renationalised and supported with a fresh capital stock. The government plans, however, to reprivatise Air New Zealand. In respect of financial reporting and consolidation any such transaction leads to a change in the scope of consolidation. As a private enterprise, Air New Zealand was not consolidated until 2001 and will also drop out of consolidation if the government sells a majority of the interest in the company later on. Apparently the financial statements look different with or without a major airline being integrated. Comparability is perhaps the downside of the integration of more volatile commercial activities. On the other hand, it cannot be denied that such a rescue mission has some impact on the financial situation of a country. Therefore it is fair to include this entity if it is controlled by the government. The term 'whole of government' comes to life if such examples are considered.

8.4.4 Consolidation is an issue of governance

New Zealand is often referred to as a role model for public sector accounting. In fact, also in the field of consolidation, the Treasury of New Zealand is very close to the principles of generally accepted accounting practice. But even in New Zealand there is no shortage of controversial issues. The two examples, tertiary education institutions and Air New Zealand, are similar because they became issues as clarification is needed about effective control. If the government is not clear about its plans and how it intends to interact with the entity, the definition of the scope of consolidation becomes a difficult, if not hopeless, task. Thus bottom-line consolidation problems show only where there is an issue in the field of governance.

8.5 Consolidated financial reporting in Switzerland

Author: Christoph Benz/translated by Andreas Bergmann

8.5.1 Introduction

In April 2006 the Swiss Federal Council, the Cabinet of Ministers in Switzerland, enacted the new Government Financial Management Law (German: *Finanzhaushaltgesetz*) which

---

[15] Public Sector Accounting Board (2006) 21–25.

was approved almost unanimously by both chambers of Parliament a few months earlier. Although the new Act enjoys great support from all political parties, the Federal Council excluded article 55 on consolidation from immediate legal effect for an undefined period of time. This prompted a parliamentary proposal in the House of Representatives demanding immediate effect for article 55.

Article 55 of the Government Financial Management Law requires the government to:

1 present a consolidated financial statement at the same time it presents the separate financial statements for the government and the ministries;
2 fully consolidate – beside those entities already included in the separate financial statements – those entities and special purpose funds that report to parliament but are not included in the government's financial statements, as well as those government agencies presenting separate financial reports;
3 exclude entities from the scope of consolidation at the discretion of the Federal Council; and
4 include further entities (e.g. state-owned enterprises) if they fulfil public duties or have strong financial ties with the government.

The Federal Council may require the consolidated entities to observe defined accounting principles in order to make sure consolidated financial statements provide accurate information or in order to simplify consolidation procedures.

The rationale behind the idea of consolidated financial statements is the close and intense economic relationship between the entities within the scope of consolidation. In fact, those entities should be considered as one economic entity. Transactions between the entities make it almost impossible to understand the financial situation and performance if only the information from the separate financial statements is available. Some of those consolidated entities are large enough to change the overall picture from what is often referred to as a 'whole-of-government' perspective. Smaller entities may be less relevant from the overall perspective but should be included if they meet the same criteria. However, the consolidated financial statements clearly are focusing on material information, which is required for an educated reader to get a true and fair view. This information should be given both to the decision makers in parliament and to the general public.

Consolidation is not all about the scope. Equally important are consolidation methods. Article 55 requires full consolidation, i.e. a line-by-line consolidation of all financial statements eliminating mutual transactions and balances. Article 55 does not mention entities under significant influence but no control, however, as article 47 and 48 require fair presentation adopting internationally accepted standards, i.e. the International Public Sector Accounting Standards (IPSAS). Therefore it is clear that associates and financial instruments will be treated accordingly.

However, the controversial issue in article 55 and also further down the road during implementation is not consolidation methods or techniques, but the scope of consolidation. Although there is an IPSAS on consolidation, the control criteria taken from the private sector accounting standards proves to be controversial and also article 55 is in contradiction with IPSAS 6. Control – defined by the two elements of benefit and power – is difficult in the public sector, because power does not always go hand in hand with ownership or capital invested. The government may exercise regulatory power on entities controlled by someone else or surrender power to independent bodies for the sake of political opportunity or professional competence. The latter case is not captured by IPSAS 6. As this does not mean that the close financial ties are cut off, quite often the benefit element is still in place, even if there is no power, and financial risk of the government may be very substantial. Therefore the Ministry of Finance decided to revisit the scope of consolidation and discuss it with the relevant parliament committees.

The following aspects should be considered:

1 requirements and current developments of the IPSAS;
2 international experience;
3 political relevance of the consolidated information.

Table 8.4 presents a non-exclusive list of important entities that should be considered.

8.5.2 Determining the scope of consolidation

In order to determine the scope of consolidation for the Swiss Federal Government, it is crucial to understand which objectives are pursued with the presentation of consolidated financial statements and which information shall be disclosed.

Private sector standards such as IFRS and IPSAS apply the control principle in order to determine the scope of consolidation. This principle requires the presence of both power and benefit. While this control principle is easily applicable to entities where there is no

Table 8.4 **List of entities to be considered**

	Federal Government's share
Public transportation fund (FinÖV Fund)	100%
Public infrastructure fund	100%
Publica (legally independent superannuation scheme for civil servants)	100%
Federal Institute of Technology	100%
Social Welfare schemes (AHV/IV/EO)	100%
Unemployment scheme (ALV)	100%
Federal Alcohol Administration (independent tax collector for taxes on spirits, wine and beer)	100%
Swissmedic (drug administration)	100%
Institute of Intellectual Property (intellectual property administration)	100%
Federal Post	100%
Federal Railways	100%
RUAG (state-owned defence and space techology company)	100%
Skyguide (air traffic control)	99.9%
Swisscom (state-owned telecommunications company)	62.4%
Swiss National Bank (central bank owned by the federal states and private investors)	0%

control, especially international organisations, examples with more control are also more critical. Many institutions have been split apart from the Federal Government or its ministries in order to limit power or share benefit and risks. Examples include the social welfare funds – which are predominantly funded by contributions from employees and employers and are therefore managed by representatives of these groups rather than the government. However, the government is far more than a regulator, as it is still closely involved and bears a substantial, but not exactly defined part of the risk. There are different perspectives that could be taken into consideration when determining the scope of consolidation, such as:

- economical;
- budgetary;
- organisational and legal;
- statistical; and
- risk.

These perspectives will be examined in the following sections. However, it is also unclear who should be representing the controlling entity. While it is clear that private sector corporations are controlled through boards, in the public sector control could be exercised potentially by any one of the following powers:

- electorate;
- legislative (i.e. parliament);
- executive (i.e. government); and
- administration.

While it is quite obvious that the scope of consolidation should not be defined based on electoral power, even for a direct democracy with a long tradition, such as Switzerland, both parliament and government are feasible candidates. Perhaps the government is most similar to a private sector board, although it is still quite different in respect of decision making or mission. Administration, on the other hand, is controlled by the government and therefore not really a feasible alternative. The legislative power, the parliament, decides on important issues such as the main organisational features and, more importantly, on the budget. But it is not usually exercising power over the management of controlled entities. Despite a few difficulties, the Swiss Federal Government decided it should in fact be the government, which is considered as the controlling element when determining the scope of consolidation.

8.5.3 Economical perspective

The economical perspective is taken by both IFRS and IPSAS. Their idea is to present consolidated financial statements for economic entities. As mentioned before, this requires control, i.e. the presence of both power and benefit. The controlling entity has to have the necessary power to control the controlled entity. It also has to enjoy the benefit (or loss) from the controlled entity's economic activity.

The application of an economical perspective leads to a relatively large scope of consolidation, if the government is supposed to be the controlling element and it is supposed that the government is willing to exercise its power. Obviously the power criterion should not be extended to operational elements – for private sector firms this is also not part of this criterion.

Consolidated financial statements for such a scope of consolidation would allow an overview of all the economic activities of the 'group' Swiss Government. This information is obviously relevant for the strategic management of this group, but clearly less so for the more short-term budgetary discussion. Important information would include:

- debt of the entire economic entity; and the
- economic result.

On the other side, the budgetary organisations are likely to become a relatively small part of the economic entity, as there are some very large commercial corporations such as the Federal Railways or Post to be taken into account; but the likes of Swisscom would also be consolidated.

8.5.4 Budgetary perspective

The budgetary perspective takes – as its name suggests – a budgetary view. Entities should be consolidated if they are relevant for the budget or budgetary decisions are influential or even critical for them. The budgetary perspective includes the control principle, but is adopting it in a more rigorous way as it requires budgetary influence. Therefore the scope of consolidation is smaller and excludes entities that are neither receiving funds from the government budget nor contributing to it. This is the case for entities that have to charge fees that recover the full cost of provision.

The application of a budgetary perspective is obviously providing information that is highly relevant for the budgetary decisions. On the other hand it is dependent on the definition of budgetary influence. Thresholds need to be defined and they may strongly influence the outcome. These thresholds should also account for the difference in size between the entire federal budget and the budget of a potentially small entity.

Consolidated financial statements would take into account the financial situation of important recipients of budgetary means. It also provides some information on debt and economic result. However, not for the entire economic entity. But on the other hand it relates back to the budget.

8.5.5 Organisational and legal perspective

It is quite straightforward to follow an organisational structure that is defined by legislation. This governance is legally binding and therefore highly relevant. It is also relatively easy to impose common accounting principles if there is a clear legal situation.

Unfortunately this straightforward idea is not quite as straightforward when it comes to its adoption. In the case of the Swiss Government there is no coherent, overriding governance. Organisational decisions are made in individual pieces of legislation and are therefore by definition not really comprehensive. Depending on which law is being considered, the outcome may vary greatly.

If there were a coherent organisational legislation, the consolidated financial statements obviously would reflect this and could be useful to present the financial situation and outcome. But with the non-coherent definitions there is a substantial risk of presenting non-coherent financial information.

8.5.6 Statistical perspective

Government financial statistics (GFS) present a somewhat consolidated view, as they look at the so-called general government sector (GGS). The delimitations of the GGS are defined by the share of market revenues. Entities with more than 50 per cent market revenues are excluded from the GGS; entities with less are included in the GGS. However, GFS are part of the System of National Accounts (SNA) and aim at the presentation of macroeconomic information on the various sectors of the economy. Control is no prerequisite; the GGS includes all level of governments, even in a federal setting where states are clearly not controlled by the national government.

For the Swiss Federal Government the presentation of consolidated financial statements for the GGS would firstly pose severe difficulties because it does not control many entities from within the GGS, namely all state and local-level entities. Secondly, it would not provide any additional information not yet provided by the GFS. The only difference would come from the slightly different accounting principles for the GFS and consolidated financial statements, e.g. the former not recognising weapon systems as assets.

Even if the practical problems could be resolved, GGS-scoped consolidated financial statements would not provide a great deal of information not yet provided by the GFS. And the limited additional information would not be really relevant from either a political or a managerial perspective.

8.5.7 Risk perspective

Adopting a risk perspective would lead to a scope of consolidation comprising all entities that cause financial risks for the Swiss Federal Government. This would be a very large group of entities, at least as large as in the economic perspective. Potentially the scope could even be larger, as very large private sector corporations could also be risky for the government, even if they are not government owned, as governments often have to step in if such corporations are in trouble ('too big to fail').

However, it would have to be examined which risk model should be applied. Eurostat applies one model in order to determine the convergence criterion in the Treaty of Maastricht, but Switzerland is not part of this treaty and therefore a one-to-one adoption of these risk criteria is not mandatory. In many cases the Federal Government does not control the entities and would find it difficult imposing common accounting principles.

Obviously such consolidated financial statements would reveal highly relevant information about the risks of the government. But it is unlikely to achieve the desired goals. Perhaps it is easier and more appropriate to disclose such risk information in the notes about contingent liabilities, rather than in consolidated financial statements.

8.5.8 Application of the five perspectives to selected entities

In order to illustrate the effects of the five different perspectives, the important entities listed in Section 8.5.1 were examined with the results shown in Table 8.5. This table shows the great variation of the outcome depending on the perspective taken.

In Table 8.5 the letter X denotes that the entity would be consolidated if this perspective was taken. In order to better understand the decisions, a few remarks on each perspective are necessary. These are as follows:

● **Economical perspective.** All entities are consolidated except for Publica, which is by definition a joint venture of both the employees and the employer, and the Swiss National Bank, which is owned by the states and constitutionally independent in its monetary policy. However, the Federal Government nominates 6 of the 11 non-executive and all 3 executive directors, including the president. That is why even the economical perspective leads to an ambiguous result.

Table 8.5 Effects of the five perspectives on selected entities

Perspective...	Economical	Budgetary	Organisational and legal		Statistical	Risk
X = to be consolidated			(1)	(2)	GGS	
Public transportation fund (FinÖV Fund)	X	X	–	–	X	X
Public infrastructure fund	X	X	–	–	X	X
Publica	–	–	–	X	X	X
Federal Institute of Technology	X	X	–	X	X	X
Social welfare schemes (AHV/IV/EO)	X	X	–	–	X	X
Unemployement scheme (ALV)	X	X	–	–	X	X
Federal Alcohol Administration	X	–	–	X	X	X
Swissmedic	X	X	–	X	–	X
Institute of Intellectual Property	X	–	–	X	–	X
Federal Post	X	X	–	–	–	X
Federal Railways	X	X	–	–	–	X
RUAG	X	–	–	–	–	X
Skyguide	X	–	–	–	–	X
Swisscom	X	–	–	–	–	X
Swiss National Bank	(X)	–	–	–	–	X

(1) central federal administration units
(2) decentral federal administration units

- **Budgetary perspective.** The budgetary perspective eliminates those entities from the scope of consolidation that are neither relying on budgetary funding nor contributing to the federal budget on a regular basis.
- **Organisational and legal perspective.** The only feasible legal definition is the decentralised federal administration. This would lead to the consolidation of the very large Federal Institute of Technology, but also some very small entities such as the Institute of Intellectual Property.
- **Statistical perspective.** As mentioned before, the statistical perspective would lead to the inclusion of many more non-controlled entities. The entities listed in Table 8.5 are only those from Table 8.4 that are covered by the statistical perspective, but there are other entities, which are not at all controlled by the Federal Government, such as

167

states or entities controlled by the states, but which are part of the general government sector.

- **Risk perspective.** This is the most comprehensive perspective as it neglects the power criterion and (over)emphasises the risk/benefit criterion.

8.6 PPP or joint venture: the new convention centre for Zürich

Author: Daniel Bietenhader

8.6.1 Introduction

This case study presents experiences from the Public Private Partnership (PPP) project 'New Convention Centre Zürich'.[16] In this project the city of Zürich is planning a complex of buildings which includes a new convention centre, a business hotel, several restaurants, bars, shops and car park as well as new premises for a concert hall. The goal of this infrastructure project is to position Zürich as a well-known international congress destination and to design a magnificent example of architecture for the city.

The case study describes various aspects of the PPP project, such as the financing model, economic benefit, project difficulties, efficiency potentials of PPPs and legal problems.

8.6.2 Project planning

For the development of the new convention centre the City Council of Zürich decided to found a limited corporation. The holders of this Public Private Partnership corporation are the city of Zürich, various private companies as well as a foundation for the convention centre. The capitalisation of the corporation is Sfr 7 million which is equivalent to the costs for the development of the project. The municipal government has a share of 21 per cent and two private companies each have 21 per cent. The remaining three shareholders hold smaller amounts. The corporation was founded to simplify the collaboration between the public administration and the private partners and with the intention to realise the project in much less time than it would require without a PPP.

The project development corporation launched an international architectural competition for the design of the complex. The winning design of the Spanish star architect Moneo (see Exhibit 8.4) will be refined and afterwards sold to a new, joint PPP corporation which is responsible for the construction and operation of the convention centre. The City Council plans to release the land for the whole project to this joint PPP which in return has to realise the project and give financial support to it. The government is responsible for the supervision of the project and retains step-in rights.

An overview of the project schedule can be seen in Table 8.6.

---

[16] In this case study, the term Public Private Partnership is defined as a long-term partnership between the public administration and private partners for a mutual benefit.

| Exhibit 8.4 | Architectural model of the new convention centre |

Source: © Raumgleiter GmbH, Zürich

| Table 8.6 | Project schedule overview |

2002/2003	Analysis of the demand situation for a new convention centre
2003	Public invitation for investors and operators of the new convention centre
2004	Selection of a partner for the Public Private Partnership (PPP)
2005	Formation of a project development corporation
2005/2006	International architectural competition: selection of the well-known Spanish architect Moneo
2007/2008	Project planning Public invitation for the operation of the new convention centre
2009	Final decision about the whole project made by the citizens of Zürich, conversion of the project development corporation into a new PPP corporation which is responsible for the construction and operation of the convention centre
2010–13	Planning and construction period
2013	Opening of the new convention centre

8.6.3 Approach for financing and risk management

The new convention centre is estimated to cost around Sfr 380 million. It is planned that the city of Zürich invests approximately Sfr 120 million in the joint PPP corporation. This financial contribution should allow a minimum return on investment of 6.2 per cent gross, respectively 5 per cent net for investors. The remaining share capital of Sfr 260 million is financed by private companies.

169

The investment risk is born by the PPP corporation. The city of Zürich will not offset any losses made by the corporation and is liable only for a possible financial loss according to the relevant ownership percentage. In this way, the risk is easier for the government to calculate.[17]

8.6.4 Economic benefit

The economic benefit is significant for the city of Zürich through its positioning as an international congress destination. According to a survey it is estimated that the convention centre creates a direct added value of approximately Sfr 111 million and around Sfr 164 million indirectly per year.[18] With an estimated 60 000 additional overnight stays, Zürich also benefits as a tourist destination. Further, the convention centre supports the image of the city as an education and knowledge centre.[19] This enhances the attractiveness of the city to foreign investors and companies.

8.6.5 Why a PPP for a convention centre?

Due to different reasons the City Council decided to launch the project as a PPP. The main reason is to optimise the risk allocation between the public and the private partners. In the partnership the city bears only the risk of the invested capital in the PPP corporation and has no obligation to finance a deficit. A further intention of the public administration is to gain explicit know-how and to receive support from the private partner for managing such complex projects. Without the partnership the city would have to invest a larger sum for hiring people with this specific know-how. In addition, the PPP releases a large amount of capital that could be spent on other essential public services and infrastructures.[20]

8.6.6 Obstacles and set-backs

The realisation of the convention centre through a PPP has caused some difficulties and initiated a controversial discussion about the benefits of it. A number of politicians criticise the financial model, i.e. the cooperation with investors in a PPP. Their opinion is that the public administration should realise and finance the project itself and also bear the risks as they receive funds at more favourable terms than private companies. Further, they are convinced that a convention centre is a payable investment; hence the administration should undertake the project on its own. Besides that, the City Council, which is the initiator of the project, is faced with strong opposition in parliament. The reason for this is that several members of parliament feel bypassed by the City Council concerning aspects such as the chosen location or the financial contributions made to the project development corporation and they therefore criticise the project. In their opinion the City Council was obligated to obtain approval from parliament. Due to all these facts it is not yet clear whether the project can be realised on schedule. A final decision will be made by the citizens of Zürich who decide in a referendum about the entire project.

---

[17] City Council minutes, Zürich (2007).

[18] Institute for Public Services and Tourism, University of St. Gallen.

[19] www.zuerichforum.ch.

[20] City Council minutes, Zürich (2007).

8.6.7 Efficiency gains through PPP

There are several incentives to realise a project in the form of a PPP. Some of them have already been described. This section illustrates in detail the aspect of efficiency in a PPP. If a PPP is carefully thought out it is possible to realise significant efficiency potentials in various project phases, which are also relevant for the project 'New Convention Centre Zürich'. The different efficiency potentials can be split into three main types. These types are as follows:

1 Improved incentive structures.
2 Lower project direct costs.
3 Reduced costs in the administration.

Exhibit 8.5 shows schematically the three types of efficiency potential in a PPP and their possible effect on the original project costs.
The different efficiency potentials are given and explained in Tables 8.7 to 8.9.

8.6.8 Legal aspects

Up to now no specific legislation on PPPs exists in Switzerland. As a result certain legal aspects are unclear in the convention centre project and have evoked some problems. One of the problems is that it is unsure under the current legislation whether the PPP project is in or excluded from government procurement. If this PPP is included it might be possible that the general contractor, which made significant contributions in the design phase and participates in the project development corporation, is not allowed to bid in the following phases. Furthermore, it is uncertain if the public invitation has to be published regionally, nationally or internationally.

Exhibit 8.5 **Efficiency gains through PPP**

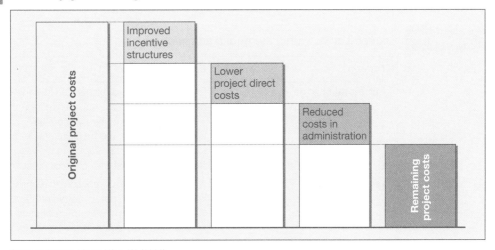

Source: Adapted from Alfen, W. (2006).

Table 8.7 Improved incentive structures

Criteria	Explanations
Transparent risk management	Risk analysis and management is a key issue in a Public Private Partnership. If a PPP is the preferred approach for a project and a contract is entered into, then risk management plays an important role in the life cycle of the contract. In a PPP the risks are allocated to the party that is best able to manage it. An advantage of the risk allocation is that the private partner that bears certain risks in the project shows a strong interest for an efficient realisation of the project.
Output specification / performance-based reward	In a PPP contract it is possible for the government to specify outputs for the whole life cycle of the project such as quality or quantity. These specifications can be linked to performance-based rewards which improve the incentives for the PPP.

Table 8.8 Reduced project costs

Criteria	Explanations
Price advantages for the whole PPP project	PPPs are commonly used for large-scale projects with one general contractor. Such projects normally contain various components. In a PPP these different components can be bought in a package which allows certain price advantages. But this is possible only as long as the PPP is not linked to government procurement.

Table 8.9 Reduced costs within the public administration

Criteria	Explanations
Structural change	Provided that the public administration does not have certain professional competences for tasks, as for instance the management of complex projects or coordination, it would be more efficient if the private partner completes or supports these tasks. This allows the public administration to reduce costs.
Learning effects	If a project of high complexity is realised in a PPP it is possible for the public administration to acquire knowledge in the management of such projects. This enables the public administration to increase its efficiency and consequently to reduce administration costs.

8.7 Fiscal sustainability of Medicare

Sustainability has much to do with long-term developments and their equilibrium. Environmental sustainability is about long-term effects of human activities on nature and fiscal sustainability is about long-term developments relevant for public finances. Equally, disequilibrium is a risky situation for both nature and public finances, which asks for remedies.

One of the first long-term effects identified as a threat to fiscal sustainability was demographic change and its effects on social benefit schemes. One of the largest social benefit schemes in the world is Medicare.[21] Medicare is, as its name suggests, a health care scheme. Beneficiaries of Medicare are all United States citizens and residents over the age of 65. The programme was first introduced in 1965 and today comprises four types of benefit, called parts. These are:

- Part A. Hospital insurance covering hospital stays of more than three days.
- Part B. Medical insurance covering physician and nursing services but also diagnostic tests, certain therapies and medical equipment such as wheelchairs.
- Part C. Medicare Advantage plans, which were introduced only in the late 1990s; as we will see, also in response to fiscal issues.[22]
- Part D. Prescription drug plans, which is a non-standardised plan, introduced only in 2006, also to some extent due to fiscal issues.

Part A is free for those beneficiaries who have paid Federal Insurance Contributions Act taxes over more than 40 quarters, i.e. 10 years. If the contributions exceed the benefits, the excess amount goes into a fund called Hospital Insurance Fund. Part B requires the payment of an insurance premium which is income based since 2007. Parts C and D differ between the various private providers, also in respect of their premiums. All parts have certain out-of-pocket costs which are not covered and have to be paid by the beneficiary or the insurance coverage the beneficiary has purchased.

8.7.1 Demographic change

The initial Medicare Parts A and B, introduced in the mid 1960s, were designed under the impression of large economic growth rates and the so-called baby boom generation. Both effects made it easy to pay for the health care cost of a relatively small population of beneficiaries. While the economy has seen both booms and recessions in the years thereafter, the demography has constantly changed in the same direction. Although net reproduction rates (daughters per woman) of the United States are still relatively large compared to other developed nations, they also fell dramatically in real terms and even the slight recovery after 1985 never brought reproduction back to the levels experienced in the 1950s and early 1960s, in fact not even to 1.0, as Table 8.10 shows.[23]

However, the large baby boomer generation born in the late 1940s, the 1950s and early 1960s will reach the age of 65 over the next few years. They will become eligible for Medicare while generations entering the workforce are much smaller. This leads to smaller revenues from contributions, while the expenses for benefits will increase. Obviously

---

[21] This case study is about the US Medicare programme. However, there are programmes using the same name in other countries such as Canada or Australia.

[22] Initially called Medicare+Choice when first introduced in 1997.

[23] The average of the group of more developed countries was at 0.75 in the 2000 to 2005 period.

| Table 8.10 | United States net reproduction rate |

Period	Net reproduction rate
1950–55	1.60
1955–60	1.74
1960–65	1.56
1965–70	1.20
1970–75	0.96
1975–80	0.86
1980–85	0.87
1985–90	0.92
1990–2000	0.96
2000–2005	0.98

Source: UN Population Division Database (2006 revision).[24]

| Exhibit 8.6 | Financial outlook: Hospital Insurance Fund |

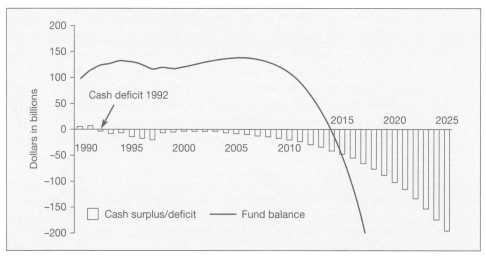

Source: Walker, D. (1999) 8.

this effect is strongest on Medicare Part A and the Hospital Insurance Fund, which is financed mainly through contributions of the workforce and is free for most beneficiaries.

Until about 2010 the cash deficits to be incurred by the Hospital Insurance Fund are relatively small, although increasing. However, after 2010 they become very substantial and may use up the funds balance within a few years. Exhibit 8.6 shows that the fund will be used up entirely by 2015, although other, more recent projections show a slightly later scenario. But the original 1999 exhibit, submitted as part of David Walker's testimony before the Subcommittee of Health of the House of Representatives, is seen

---

[24] http://esa.un.org/unpp/p2k0data.asp.

| Table 8.11 | United States life expectancy at birth |

Period	Life expectancy at birth (both sexes)
1975–80	73.3
1980–85	74.1
1985–90	74.7
1990–95	75.3
1995–2000	76.5
2000–05	77.4
2005–10	78.2
2010–15	78.9
2015–20	79.5
2020–25	80.1

Source: UN Population Division Database (2006 revision).[25]

as a milestone in the discussion. After 2015 the deficits will also exceed $50 billion per year, reaching almost $200 billion in 2025. The increase of life expectancy (Table 8.11) makes the whole development even more dramatic.

8.7.2 Fiscal sustainability is a long-run issue

The Walker testimony was obviously not the first acknowledgement of demographic change and its impact on Medicare. In fact changes to the Medicare programme introducing Part C, which increased private funding, were already in place in 1999. These reforms were part of the 1997 Balanced Budget Act and were therefore also closely related to public finance issues. In 1999, when Walker gave his testimony, the United States indeed enjoyed surpluses, whether due to the specific measures taken in earlier years or due to the favourable economic development is debatable. What is important is that David Walker, Comptroller General of the United States, raised the issue in a period of fiscal surpluses and after the successful adoption of reforms to Medicare. Both the general fiscal and the specific programme situation were favourable in 1999.

But Walker raised the issue nevertheless, as he was certain about the long-run imbalances due to demographic change. Demographic change, especially when considering old-age-related programmes, has relatively high predictability over several decades, as future beneficiaries are born more than six decades before they first claim their benefits and even contributors are born about two decades before they first start contributing. At least the next 20 years can be predicted very precisely as almost everybody involved is already born.[26] The forecast of a deteriorating situation after 2010 was therefore not at all esoteric, but based on highly reliable data about the current population. But he was quite brave addressing such an issue in a surplus situation.

---

[25] http://esa.un.org/unpp/p2k0data.asp.

[26] One element that may change at shorter notice is migration.

| Exhibit 8.7 | Federal Government expenditure in relation to GDP (fiscal discipline assumption) |

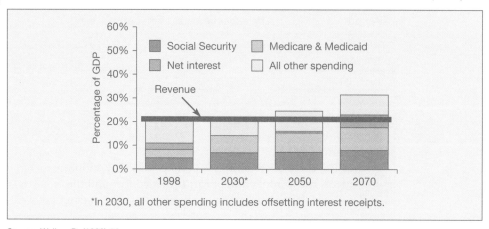

Source: Walker, D. (1999) 11.

Perhaps less robust, but equally threatening, is the danger from the increase of the expenditure per beneficiary. It is expected that not only the number of beneficiaries will rise, but also the expenditure per capita will increase 1 per cent above GDP growth.[27]

8.7.3 Overall fiscal sustainability

The other important element of the Walker testimony was its reference to the general fiscal situation, rather than the programme's specific situation alone. The Hospital Insurance Fund's outlook was only the starting point; the arguments then addressed the general fiscal situation. Walker showed that the deficits from Medicare and other demographically influenced programmes such as Social Security will drive the federal budget into certain deficits of a substantial size even if all the other surpluses and spending caps are maintained (Exhibit 8.7), and even more dramatically if there is less fiscal discipline.

Interestingly, Walker did not compare the demographics-based spending forecast with a macroeconomical forecast of government revenues. Such forecasts are, of course, produced. But they are strongly biased by the assumed growth rate of the economy, i.e. GDP growth. By calculating both expenditure and revenue as fractions of GDP, the growth rate of GDP is cancelled out. This, however, implies another assumption. The comparison is valid only if GDP growth affects government revenues and expenses in the same way. This is not necessarily the case, as the revenue from payroll taxes, which is the main source of financing for Part A, is expected to grow more slowly than the economy.[28] This would, of course, make things even worse. The Walker report also showed that early action makes a substantial difference compared to a later reaction, regardless of which scenario is most likely. This is due to intergeneration effects, which are quite obvious in this case: if the generation of today finances its current expenditure level, the future

[28] Board of Trustees of the Federal Hospital Insurance and Federal Supplementary Medical Insurance Trust Funds (2006) 12.

[27] Board of Trustees of the Federal Hospital Insurance and Federal Supplementary Medical Insurance Trust Funds (2006) 7.

generation – at least – will not have to finance this part of the burden plus the interest accrued. This is quite a common phenomenon of fiscal sustainability: the earlier issues are addressed, the less is carried forward and the smaller are longer-term effects.

8.7.4 Fiscal sustainability leads to incremental measures

The Walker testimony thus also shows that even in the very robust world of demographic developments fiscal sustainability always includes forecasting. And if forecasting is involved, the data is not certain but at its best probable. Introducing the concept of fiscal sustainability therefore includes the introduction of probabilities and thus accepts some uncertainty.

Addressing these uncertainties is perhaps easier by adopting incremental policy decisions. Indeed, the introduction of Part D of Medicare and the move to income-based premiums for Part B are such incremental measures. The apparent downside is that Part A, which is the most challenging one, remains largely untouched and therefore the overall fiscal sustainability is still at risk. But this is perhaps the way politics works if there is a system with probabilities rather than full certainty. Why should politicians impose a burden on today's voters, if it is uncertain about the extent of the future burden?

However, it needs to be acknowledged that both a good economic situation and the incremental measures taken have postponed the adverse effects for a couple of years. The Hospital Insurance Fund is now expected to drop into cash deficits by 2010[29] and become exhausted by 2018,[30] only about three to five years later than expected in the Walker Testimonial in 1999. But the adverse situation is getting closer, although at a slower pace than expected and, of course, at least to some extent due to the measures taken in the meantime.

The concept of fiscal sustainability has thus proven some effectiveness even in an imperfect world.

---

[29] Board of Trustees of the Federal Hospital Insurance and Federal Supplementary Medical Insurance Trust Funds (2006) 12.

[30] Board of Trustees of the Federal Hospital Insurance and Federal Supplementary Medical Insurance Trust Funds (2006) 18.

References

Alfen, W. (2006) 'Efficiency potentials of PPP', Working Group Paper, Zurich.

Bergmann, A. (2000) 'Steuerung von Institutionen im Bildungswesen', St. Gallen/Bamberg: Difo.

Bergmann, A., Kälin, U. (2003) 'Das öffentliche Rechnungswesen im Umbruch: Materielle Harmonisierung durch Rechnungslegungsstandards notwendig', in: *Der Schweizer Treuhänder*, Zürich, 77, 747.

Bergmann, A., Gamper, A. (2004) 'Rechnungslegungsstandards für Kantone und Gemeinden: im Rahmen von IPSAS', Zürich: kdmz.

Bergmann, A. *et al.* (2006) *Anforderungen der Finanzstatistik an den Kontenplan des HRM2*, Winterthur/Bern.

Bergmann, A. (2006b) 'Do Accounting Standards Matter If The Reporting Entity Already Applies Accrual Accounting? Lessons From The City Of Kloten Case', *Public Fund Digest*, ICGFM (Hrsg.) 1/VI, 47–62.

Board of Trustees of the Federal Hospital Insurance and Federal Supplementary Medical Insurance Trust Funds (2006) Annual Report, Washington DC.

Bolz, U. (2005) *Public Private Partnership in der Schweiz*, Zürich: Schulthess.

Buschor, E. (1993) *Wirkungsorientierte Verwaltungsführung*, Zürich: ZHK.

Caperchione, E., FEE-PSC (2006) *The New Public Management – a perspective for finance practitioners*, Brussels: FEE.

Chaitrong, W. 'Economists back proposal – invest US dollars to generate income', *The Nation*, 31 July 2007.

Collett, J. 'Future Fund to be a force', *The Western Australian*, 28 January 2007, 38.

Coombs, H.M., Jenkins, D.E. (2002) *Public sector financial management*, 3rd edition, London: Thomson.

Das, S. (2006) *Rethinking Public Accounting*, New Delhi: Oxford University Press.

De Koning, R. (2007) *PIfC Public Internal financial Control*, Brussels.

Domingo, L. 'XBRL debate', *Accountancy Age*, 13 October 2004.

Economist 'Regulating Business – Smelly old SOX', *The Economist*, Vol. 384, Nr. 8539, 2007, 12.

Economist 'The invasion of the sovereign-wealth funds', *The Economist*, Vol. 386, Nr. 8563, 2008, 11.

Eurostat (1996) *Europäisches System Volkswirtschaftlicher Gesamtrechnungen – ESVG 1995*, Luxembourg.

FEE-PSC (Fédération des Experts Comptables Européenes' Public Sector Committee) (2005) 'Risk management and control in the EU', a discussion paper.

FEE-PSC (Fédération des Experts Comptables Européenes' Public Sector Committee) (2006) *Accrual accounting for more effective public policy*, Brussels.

FEE-PSC (Fédération des Experts Comptables Européenes' Public Sector Committee) (2007) *Accrual accounting in the public sector*, Brussels.

Gesundheitsdirektion Kanton Zürich (2007) *Somatische Akutversorgung*, Kenndaten 2006, Zürich.

Government of New Zealand (2006) Financial Statement for the Year Ended 30 June 2006.

Grüning, G. (2001) 'Origin and theoretical basis of New Public Management', *International Public Management Journal,* Vol. 4, Number 1.

Guthrie, J., Olsen, O., Humphrey, C. (1999) 'Debating developments in New Public Financial Management: the limits of global theorising and some new ways forward', *Financial Accountability and Management,* Number 3–4, 209–228.

Hauner, D., Leigh, D., Skaarup, M. (2007) 'Ensuring Fiscal Sustaninability in G7 Countries', IMF Working Paper WP07/187, Washington.

Hayes, R., Dassen, R., Schilder, A., Wallage, P. (2005) *Principles of Auditing,* 2nd edition, FT Prentice Hall.

HM Treasury (2004) 'Long-term public finance report – an analysis of fiscal sustainability', London.

Hood, C. (1991) 'A public management for all seasons?' *Public Administration,* number 69.

Horngren, C., Foster, G., Datar, S. (2005) *Cost Accounting – a Managerial Emphasis,* 12th edition, Upper Sadle River: Prentice Hall.

Hughes, J. (2004) *PSC:* 'Budget Reporting – Research Report', New York: IFAC.

Institute of Public Services and Tourism (2003) *Bedarfsanalyse Kongresshaus,* Zürich: St. Gallen.

International Monetary Fund (2001) *Government Financial Statistics Manual 2001 Handbook,* 2nd edition, Washington DC.

INTOSAI (1977) 'Lima declaration of guidelines on auditing percepts', Lima.

INTOSAI (2004) 'Implementation Guidelines for Performance Auditing'.

IPSAS-Board (2007) 'International Public Sector Accounting Standards Pronouncements'.

Jackson, P., Fogarty, T. (2006) *Sarbanes-Oxley and non-profit management,* New York: Wiley.

Jones, R., Pendlebury, M. (2000) *Public Sector Accounting,* 5th edition, Harlow: Financial Times Prentice Hall.

Konferenz der Kantonalen Finanzdirektoren *Handbuch öffentliches Rechnungswesen,* 1. Ausgabe, Luzern, 1977, 2. Ausgabe, Luzern, 1981 (2 Bände).

Lüder, K. (1998) 'Konzeptionelle Grundlagen des Neuen Kommunalen Haushaltswesens', *Staatsanzeiger für Baden-Württemberg,* Stuttgart.

Lüder, K., Jones, R. (2003) *Reforming governmental accounting and budgeting in Europe,* Frankfurt: Fachverlag Moderne Wirtschaft.

Malk, R., Kampmann, T. 'DRGs (Diagnosis Related Groups) – Grundlagen', in Malk, R., Kampmann, T., Indra, P. (2006) *DRG-Handbuch Schweiz,* Berne: Huber.

McCaffery, E., Slemrod, J. (2006) 'Toward and Agenda for Behavioural Public Finance', *Behavioural Public Finance* (eds.), New York: Russel/Sage.

Musgrave, R., Musgrave, P. (1989) *Public Finance in Theory and Practice,* 5th edition, MacGraw Hill.

Nicollerat, A. 'Fonds für Eisenbahngrossprojekte', *Eisenbahn Revue,* 28 November 2007.

PEFA Secretariate (2005) *Public Financial Management – Performance Measurement Framework,* Washington DC.

Polito, V., Wickens, M. 'Measuring fiscal sustainability', CDMA conference papers 2005, 1–56.

Public Sector Accounting Board (2006) *About the Government Reporting Entity – 20 Questions,* Toronto.

Rohn, S. 'Bürokratiekosten als Standortfaktor', *Euro,* 18 November 2007, 13.

Rosen, H. (2002) *Public Finance,* 6th edition, New York: McGraw Hill.

Schaltegger, S., Bennett, M., Burritt, R. (2006) *Sustainability accounting and reporting,* Dordrecht: Springer.

Schedler, K., Proeller, I. (2002) *New Public Management,* 2nd edition, UTB.

Schwaller, A. (2005) *Finanzstatistik auf der Grundlage des GFSM 2001,* Bern: EFV.

Simpkins, K. (2006) *A review of the policy of sector-neutral accounting standard-setting in Australia.*

Smith, A. (2003) *The Wealth of Nations,* originally published 1776, New York: Bantam Classics.

Starr, J. 'Information politics: The story of an emerging metadata standard', http://www.firstmonday.org/issues/issue8_7/starr/index.html#s5, 23 January 2007.

Stiglitz, J. (2000) *Economics of the Public Sector*, 3rd edition, Norton.

Temasek Holdings, 2007 Facts Sheet, www.temasek.com.sg, 26 December 2007.

Temasek Holdings 'Creating Value', *Temasek Review*, 2007 (b).

The Boards of Trustees, '2006 Annual Report of the Boards of Trustees of Federal Hospital Insurance and Federal Supplementary Medical Insurance Trust Funds', Washington DC, 2006.

The Treasury of New Zealand (2005) *A Guide to the Public Finance Act*, Wellington.

Walker, D. (1999) *Medicare Reform – Ensuring Fiscal Sustainability While Modernizing the Program Will Be Challenging.* Washington: GAO.

Whittington, O.R., Pany, K. (2003) *Principles of Auditing and other Assurance Services*, 14th edition, New York: McGraw Hill.

World Bank (1998) *Public Expenditure Management Handbook*, Washington DC.

Index